MW00806946

*Praise for IPPY Award winning novelist*

# Darden North

"North's visually acute, action-packed style … is likely headed for the silver screen."

~George Halas
*New York Journal of Books*

"A rollercoaster ride of murder, intrigue, and plot twists. *Wiggle Room* keeps you turning the pages to the final, climactic finish."
~Robert Dugoni, *New York Times* best-selling author
*The Jury Master*

"*Wiggle Room* [is] a cleverly plotted, strongly written medical thriller [that] will pull you into a story world filled with danger, excitement, and conflict at every turn."

~D.P. Lyle, Macavity Award winner
*Run to Ground*

"Darden North is one of those writers who pays meticulous attention to getting the detail right in the course of his riveting thrillers and *Wiggle Room* is no exception."

~*Mason's Bookshelf*
*MBR Bookwatch*

"*Wiggle Room* is a suspense-chocked, mature, medical/military mystery with smarts to boot. The end was a surprising—but exceptionally satisfying—conclusion to a shivering ride of deception and murder."

~*BookFetish*

# PARTY FAVORS

# Also by Darden North

*House Call*
*Points of Origin*
*Fresh Frozen*
*Wiggle Room*
*The 5 Manners of Death*

# PARTY FAVORS

a novel

## DARDEN NORTH

WordCrafts Press

**Party Favors**
Copyright © 2022
Darden North, MD

ISBN: 978-1-957344-49-2

Cover concept and design by David Warren.

Published by WordCrafts Press
Cody, Wyoming 82414
www.wordcrafts.net

*"I believe most people are good."*
*~Luke Bryan*

*"A successful life is problems well handled."*
*~Robert St. John*

*"Don't sweat the small stuff."*
*~Robert Murphree*

# Chapter 1

Dr. Scott Mack set his cell phone in the center console and backed out of his driveway. He decided that a face-to-face confrontation with Jessica Kile, his secretary and quasi-office manager, would be better than over the phone. He could just see her squirm. The two drug dealers who approached him in the alley late Friday afternoon claimed that Jessica had sent them. How do you explain that?

In less than a half hour and after a weekend of emergency call duty, Scott was due back at Biloxi Memorial Hospital to pre-op his only surgical patient of the day. His sparse office clinic schedule would follow, if a mere two orthopedic patients on the books could be considered a schedule—and no-shows were common.

From the intersection of Scott's street and the road leading to Highway 90, he could see heavy morning traffic and chose to take the less-traveled, alternate route to the hospital. Despite the meandering route through neighboring streets, much pricier real estate than his, he would still save time.

"You're going to do awesome practicing surgery here on the Mississippi Gulf Coast, Dr. Mack," the realtor had said when she presented his house keys. Her perfectly aligned, smiling white teeth were encased in bright red lipstick. "Not too long from now, I can see you living over in Waterview, Dr. Paul Caston's neighborhood. Dr. Caston fixed my knee after I fell skiing in Deer Valley. His residence is spectacular and not all that far from your cozy new home. Just give me a call whenever you're ready to move up."

Scott remembered juggling the keys to his cozy house and

1

worrying about his fresh signature on the documents of the twenty-year mortgage. The ink had not dried.

He pushed his phone aside for a package of breath mints and took the route through the tree-lined boulevards of Waterview. Blooming shrubs, thick ferns, pampas grass, and more trees filled the wide medians between the opposite stretches of curbed asphalt, all untouched by the tidal surge of Hurricane Katrina nearly twenty years earlier or by any major storm since. The drive led him directly past Caston's place, a two-story brick mansion with slate roof and floor to ceiling windows also surrounded by lush landscaping. The estate covered a full block of the upscale neighborhood.

Dr. Caston's residence included a six-car garage, expanded from three when he added a guest house, Olympic-sized pool, and additional spacious bedrooms to total seven. During a previous drive by one Saturday, Scott spotted an overweight woman in an ill-fitting, floral design dress, walking a dog along the front sidewalk. He guessed her a housekeeper and the leashed dog a labradoodle. Several cars waited parked against the curb and inside the gate, crowding the driveway and motor court. Brick pillars to the right and left defined the entrance to the property, and a row of multi-colored, helium-filled balloons tied with streamers waved in the breeze from the top of the iron fence along the sidewalk.

This morning, however, the mansion and grounds seemed quiet. Scott shook his head. The cozy house he was likely to lose soon in foreclosure would fit inside Caston's garage.

He made the next corner and pulled behind a white suburban stopped at the intersection. A dark green, compact sedan waited in front of the suburban with a third vehicle ahead at the stop sign. A young, blonde woman dressed in a relaxed T-shirt, blue jeans, and tennis shoes jumped from the suburban, leaving the driver's door open. She waved her arms frantically behind her and ran toward Scott—her screams muffled. Scott lowered his driver's window to hear.

"There's a man in that Mercedes at the stop sign," she panted in broken speech. "The car in front of me and I both blew our horns, but the man won't move his car."

Scott opened his door and nudged the woman out of the way.

"I'm trying to get my kids to pre-K, and I'm already late," the young woman said. "I thought about just driving around him."

"Is the man okay?" Scott asked and stepped from his vehicle.

"I don't think so," she answered. "I ran up to his car and knocked on the window. He's all slumped over the steering wheel and not moving."

Another woman appeared behind her, the driver of the green sedan between the Suburban and the stalled vehicle at the stop sign. The panic in her voice was more desperate, her breathing even heavier than the younger women with the kids. She had brunette hair cut in bangs with the rest pulled into a short ponytail and wore T-shirt, blue jeans, and white tennis shoes—the apparent uniform of the day.

This second woman seemed to notice Scott's white lab jacket, the front pocket embroidered with his name and that of his orthopedic surgical practice. "Oh, my God. You're a doctor. Maybe you can help that man."

Scott stepped quickly around both women and broke into a run toward the Mercedes. The women followed. He spotted a couple of screaming children, one a toddler and the other maybe two years older, strapped inside car seats in the rear of the suburban. The green car was empty. He noticed a faint exhaust plume rising from the rear of the Mercedes. The vehicle seemed to be just inside the intersection, past the stop sign. There was no other traffic.

A siren approached from the distance.

"I called 911," the woman with the ponytail said.

The siren grew louder. Another one followed.

Scott found the driver motionless and alone in the vehicle, the rear of his head tilted toward the left shoulder with face turned away and torso leaning into the door. The man's blue hospital scrubs matched Scott's, although Scott's were wrinkled. He touched the side of the car to the soft vibration of a running engine and tried the door handle several times with no luck—the same for the backseat.

A screaming police cruiser pulled nose-to-nose against the Mercedes. A male police officer popped out and silenced the noise but left the revolving blue lights. "Hey, Doc. You put in the call?"

"No, sir," Scott answered and stepped out of the officer's way. His right shoe slid in a thin pocket of gravel on the asphalt pavement. "One of those two ladies over there did."

The officer checked all four doors. None of them would budge. A back-up squad car arrived, its siren extinguished as the vehicle pulled to a stop, flashing blue lights again left to drape the area. A female officer bolted from the second cruiser for the passenger side of the Mercedes, also finding both doors locked. She inspected the front and rear seats through the windows.

"Hey, Roger. There's a pistol on the floorboard," she said, "I can see it from over here. Just below the guy's right hand."

"What?" Scott asked. He scrambled ahead of the first officer on the scene and scattered the gravel to beat Roger to the passenger side of the Mercedes. The pistol was obvious from that angle. A trickle of dark blood ran from behind and just above the driver's right ear. "Good God. That's Dr. Caston." Paul Caston's vacant eyes stared at him almost at peace, his lips slightly parted. More dried blood ran from the nostrils.

"Hey, Jeremy," the female officer called back to her partner. "Get the bat out of the trunk."

"One step ahead of you, Nicole." Jeremy appeared behind Scott with the bat. "Sorry, Doc, but please step aside," he said.

An ambulance pulled up beside the first patrol car and halted the scarce traffic at the intersection. Two EMTs produced a stretcher from the rear. "Sure, officer, glad to move out of the way," Scott said, "but from what I see inside this car, there's not much anybody can do for him."

Scott stepped back a few feet into an adjacent driveway and shielded his face with his right forearm and the back of his hand.

The police officer shattered the passenger door with a single swing of the bat and tossed the bat to the ground. He produced gloves from inside his jacket and reached over the jagged glass to unlock the door, then shifted the transmission into PARK before turning off the engine. "Guy's foot isn't near the brake, so I guess the vehicle just rolled to a stop," he said. "And that's a .38 on the floorboard."

"Forensics will want photos before that revolver is secured," the female officer said and snapped photos with her cell phone.

One of the EMTs opened the driver's door and checked for a carotid pulse. He shook his head.

Scott gestured to his surgical scrub suit and the white jacket worn over it. "I guess you already figured out that I'm a physician, but I think we can all agree this fella's gone."

The EMT initially ignored Scott and double checked the carotid pulse before nodding in agreement. Scott saluted him with a flick of the forefinger against his right eyebrow. A photographer with a police badge suspended by a cord around the neck pushed through. Scott again backed away while the camera clicked repeatedly to record the scene. The EMT motioned to his counterpart who swung a gurney near the Mercedes. Scott noticed another vehicle, absent flashing lights, pull up behind the police cruisers.

As the EMTs lifted the body from the vehicle and onto the gurney, the female police officer pried a wallet from the back pocket of the driver's scrub suit pants. She flipped through it. "Caston, Paul Caston," Scott heard her say.

The policer officer with the bat retrieved the revolver from the floorboard and lowered it carefully into a brown paper bag.

"Jeremy, bag the guy's hands too. ME will want to check for residue."

# Chapter 2

*Three months earlier*

Immaculate Davis dropped the cooler under the receptionist's nose, sending a loud thud throughout the front area of the medical clinic. Glad to be free of the twenty pounds of fresh shrimp packed in ice, he flexed his biceps and smiled several shades of yellow and brown nubby teeth. "Trish, you got a cup I can use?" he asked.

"You nearly split my counter with that heavy thing," the receptionist said. "After all, it's nothing but Formica. You'd think Dr. Caston could afford better." Trish grimaced and handed Immaculate a small, white paper cup from the water cooler.

He spat tobacco juice and tossed the used cup into the waiting room trash receptacle as a well-dressed Caucasian man brushed past him for the exit. The man paused a moment at the front door of the Caston Center for Orthopedic Surgery and shook his head at the spectacle. Immaculate stepped to the window and watched the man pull away in a red Jaguar.

"Nice wheels," he said. Using his tongue, Immaculate wedged the wet dip of tobacco between his lower teeth and inside lip. "I got Gulf shrimp caught this mornin', not more 'n five miles out from downtown." He spit into a fresh cup, again provided by the receptionist. "Iced 'em down special for Dr. Caston—big chunks of clean ice. He'll like these beauties."

From the computer desk a foot or so below the counter, Trish frowned once more at Immaculate while speaking into the microphone of a metal headset wrapped across her head. The chrome band cut a thin trench into her teased dishwater blonde hair.

"I'm sorry, Mrs. Thompson, but Dr. Caston must personally see you for a consult and physical on your next visit to the clinic. You can't just talk with his nurse or come by my desk. Sorry, it's the rule." Trish forced a wide smile, her teeth full, smooth, and white in contrast to Immaculate's grin. "Like I've explained before, you've got to see the doctor before he's gonna give you any more pain meds," she said, shaking her head. "And, no, he can't see you today. Dr. Caston is with his last appointment and then he's out the door. Bye-bye—now."

She tapped the button on the headset with the pad of her right forefinger and ended the call. A miniature butterfly painted on the long fingernail seemed to fly between the strands of hair. The telephone smile vanished. "And, Mr. Davis, I've told you more than once: Cash only to satisfy your account—no bartering. Besides, you've probably scratched the counter with that ice chest, and I should charge you for damages."

The walls of the surgical clinic were thin, so Immaculate assumed Dr. Caston had heard the commotion. He strained for a look down the hall from where the man with the Jaguar had appeared and spotted the doctor. *Bingo!* Immaculate smiled. *I've got a chance.*

Paul Caston, M.D., stood with his back to Immaculate. His long, white medical lab coat pulled at his stooped, rounded, but broad shoulders. Immaculate remembered that the doctor's name was monogrammed in black above the left breast pocket. Dr. Caston handed an envelope to a stern-faced, white woman about Caston's age, somewhere near early sixties. The two spoke in hushed tones, and Immaculate took a few steps closer to try to hear.

The woman with Caston wore no make-up, her grey hair woven into a tight bun and the skin above her lip a shadow. *Probably shaves a mustache,* Immaculate decided. *And Doc always gives me my stuff inside one of those rooms, not out in the hall.*

When she seemed to notice Immaculate's stares and frown in

annoyance at Dr. Caston, the woman turned to disappear through a rear exit. Dr. Caston followed her.

"That door must lead to the parking lot out back," Immaculate muttered.

"Never you mind what's going on down there, Immaculate," Trish said. "You heard me on the phone. Dr. Caston was finishing up with his last patient. Everything between doctor and patient is strictly confidential." She pushed her chair back and stood for a peek into the cooler. "Now, let's see what you got in here."

Careful not to mar her new manicure, Trish popped the top to the faint smell of seawater and unpeeled, translucent gray shrimp packed in ice. She used the tip of a long fingernail to pick at a few of the firm, glossy shells. "You're right. These babies are fantastic—so fresh and no black spots. But headless is better."

"Dr. Caston likes him some good shrimp, no matter what," Immaculate said and returned to lean onto the counter. "He told me so … the last time he gave me my 'scription."

A stocky woman in a dingy white uniform pushed through the levered doors into the reception area and lobby and nearly knocked Immaculate to the floor. The tips of the lapel and sleeves of her medical jacket were tinged yellow. "Okay, Immaculate," the clinic nurse said. "Settle down out here. I could hear you all the way in the back. Dr. Caston is very annoyed."

Immaculate recoiled. Nurse Betty towered over him and was twice as wide, but he needed to remain focused.

"No, I'd say he is extremely pissed, and that's not good for you. He had to talk over the noise just to give that patient her instructions," Nurse Betty said.

Immaculate swallowed hard at his best effort to stand tall and straight. "Doc will forget all about that when he gets an eyeful of these—the finest shrimp I ever seen from the Gulf of Mexico. Just what he asked for." He put his hand to his lower stomach. Sweat dripped down the side of his face onto his neck and to the top of his T-shirt. His breathing became rapid. His true fear of Nurse

Betty helped him play his part. "My belly's been cramping me all morning. Doc's gotta help me and help me quick."

"Trish is correct, Immaculate," Betty gestured toward the receptionist. "Dr. Caston's services are cash only. And anyway, you're supposed to be physically disabled. Dr. Caston signed your Social Security papers over three months ago. What if someone out in the parking lot saw you lifting that heavy ice chest?"

"Dr. Caston will take care of me. Always has."

"We'll let you get by this time with shrimp instead of cash. But don't try it again, fella. All of us gotta get paid around here. The doc's checks got to clear the bank."

"I'll do better next time, Nurse Betty," he said. "I promise. You can count on me."

Trish shook her head at the conversation and took another call.

Condensation pooled around the base of the cooler. "Move that messy thing off the counter, Immaculate, before the ice starts to melt and those fish stink up the place," she said.

"I told you. That ain't no trout in there. It's the best Gulf shrimp money can buy." Immaculate picked up the ice chest with a grunt. "Stuff's heavy, and like you just said, I'm disabled. Can't you give me a hand?"

"Shut up. Stop complaining. We'll see what Dr. Caston has to say about this tomorrow."

Betty shoved Immaculate toward the doors to the hall that led to Dr. Caston's office. He strained under the weight of the ice chest but followed on the nurse's heels. Trish wiped the reception counter clean behind them.

"Why you being so rough on me, nurse? Me and you always got along so good."

Betty halted midway in the hall. Her back stiffened, and Immaculate nearly ploughed into her rear. She turned around to hover over him again. He feared that a slap in the face was next and ducked his head.

"I've got a husband at home who just lost his job and two

couch-potato kids who do nothing but play video games." Betty pointed back toward the lobby. "Trish out there has three kids and no husband," she said. "He disappeared right after he got her pregnant the last time."

"I get it. I get it. You ain't interested in no shrimp. You want cash," Immaculate said.

"So … you ain't as dumb as you look," Betty said. "We got to be paid: me, Trish, and the janitor at night that cleans up after scum like you. Doc can't pay us unless there's green in that drawer up front."

"I get it. Got to keep Doc on my side. The pills help the pain and the jitters. Bricklayers can't lay brick if they got a sorry back."

"Cash only, Davis. Understand? Bartering around here doesn't work."

"But Doc gave his okay. Said he wanted to make jambalaya and shrimp gumbo."

"I'll let your shenanigans go this time. Follow me."

"Yes, ma'am," Immaculate said. He took a few steps back and tried to brace the weight with a raised knee. The ice and shrimp slid inside the cooler.

Betty slammed the folder of medical records against the wall. "I've run this place for Dr. Caston for over ten years," she said. "He couldn't have pulled off any of this without me. I'm the one who makes the rules around here, and I won't stand for any more of this kind of crap."

"So, what do you want me to do? I send Doc a lot of business, lots of customers." Immaculate shifted the weight to the opposite knee.

"The next time you bring in this kind of stuff, leave it out back at the receiving entrance. No one will see you there. And those other customers you're talking about—make sure they know they gotta pay in cash too."

"Yes, ma'am," Immaculate repeated. His grip began to weaken. His fingers felt numb like they were buried deep in the ice with the shrimp. "You want me to go ahead and set this chest out back at receiving?"

10

"No, just put it down in that corner." She pointed. "That's good enough for this time. No one else is coming through here tonight, and the janitor won't bother it." She raised her eyebrows. "He better not."

Immaculate lowered the cooler to the floor in the designated corner of the hall, immediately outside the entrance to Dr. Caston's personal office. He tipped his sweat-stained baseball cap and turned to leave. "But what about my stuff? The catch in there is worth over a hundred bucks, and I'll need to get the ice chest back—but I'll come back with cash next time. I promise."

Nurse Betty shook her head and frowned in disgust.

"I gotta have a fix today. I took my last Roxi last night." His hands and head quivered. The watering eyes surprised him. "It's gonna be bad if I don't get my pills."

"Hold on a sec'," Betty said. She grabbed the key dangling on a chain from her coat pocket and unlocked a wall cabinet mounted at eye level in the adjacent hall. One brown envelope remained inside. The nurse popped it open, counted the contents, and resealed it. She stepped back around the corner and handed it to Immaculate.

"Remember, no charity next time. Trish will take care of making your next appointment."

Immaculate took the envelope in his right hand and nervously rubbed his lower back with the left. Dr. Caston's nurse would assume his bad disc had flared up, but the tape that secured the wire stung and nagged at his sweaty skin. He ramped up the drama, drew on his best acting skills, and breathed faster.

Immaculate knew rapid respiratory rate as a symptom of opioid withdrawal, although the reaction came easy around Nurse Betty. She stood taller and wider than most of his recent cellmates, especially the ones who roughed up little guys like him. He needed a free pass or else that detective would throw him back inside.

He reached once more for his lower back and let out a soft groan. The nurse would never suspect the wire located there, not from a sleaze bucket like Immaculate Davis. But if she figured out

11

the deception, a whipping from her would be worse than another trip to jail.

*I gotta pull this thing off,* he resolved. *It's a free pass.*

Immaculate jerked his hand away from behind his back to run his fingers back and forth across the envelope with the pills. The beads of sweat on his forehead and sweaty underarms were not an act. "Thank you, nurse." He turned for the reception area. "Instead of shrimp, I'll bring some dead presidents with me next time."

# Chapter 3

"Here's a reminder of your next visit." Trish handed Immaculate an appointment card. He wanted to run to the men's room, lose the extra-large sized T-shirt and the remote transmission equipment, and tell Detective Reed Spearman to find some other snitch. Then he thought again about the smelly cell with three other drug dealers and remembered the other questions he was supposed to ask today in Dr. Caston's clinic.

Immaculate studied the appointment card. "Don't the doc need to check me over next time? Uhhh … ask me some medical questions or somethin'? Or will Dr. Caston just write the script for pain meds like usual?"

"Just keep your appointment, Mr. Davis. Pay us, and we'll take care of you," Trish said.

Nurse Betty stepped up behind Immaculate. "Davis? You still here?"

Immaculate froze and did not answer.

"Trish, I need to take care of some things in my office before we close up for the day."

"If you can call that cramped closet with an electric outlet and no air vent an office," Trish said.

"Don't remind me," Betty said. She stepped away from the front reception area, then twisted her head over her shoulder to Immaculate. "Don't you worry, Davis. Dr. Caston will be adding another two days in the clinic since his surgery case load is down and things are tight. There'll be plenty of time for patients and their medical needs."

"But is there any way I can see the doc today? I got some other problems that can't wait until next week." He spoke a little louder: "I gotta see Doc now."

She stepped back toward him. "Get outta here, Davis. I've already done you a huge favor, and you've taken up a lot of my time ... not to mention distracted Trish from her work in the front office. I've got charting to do and exam rooms to straighten up. Get lost."

Immaculate tried to remember the detailed list of prepared questions. Spearman told him to talk directly to Dr. Caston. If he didn't, his deal was screwed. "Only just a second with the doc. It's personal problems. You know, guy stuff."

Betty pushed closer to Immaculate and nearly pinned him against the counter. The leftover smell of garlic from lunch or maybe supper from the night before lingered on her breath. "I already told you. Doctor Caston left after he finished the scheduled patients. His time is valuable. He keeps a strict schedule."

She put her hand on his shoulder, her long, thick arm slipping around to his mid back. He pulled away a little and to the side; her fingers barely missed the wire. "How's that scoliosis been treating you?" she asked.

"It's mostly my slipped disc that bothers me," Immaculate said. "Working that shrimp boat on the weekends after doing construction all week was tough, ma'am. Pulling in those nets felt like an electric knife rippin' open my back." He stretched further away with his hand to his hip, careful not to disturb the wire. "Ooh, wee. When will this suffering stop!"

"I'm sure your pain is real ... just like everybody else."

Immaculate imagined a glimmer of compassion in her voice, then shook the silly notion away.

"Dr. Caston will update your neuro exam at your next visit," she said. "Now, why don't you let us get back to work. I gave you what you needed."

"This back pain, it shoots down my leg, makes my toes go numb.

I even got headaches now, killer headaches, like my head's gonna explode. Sometimes the pain, it …"

"Thank you for the shrimp, Immaculate. I'll text Dr. Caston to circle back around to the clinic and pick it up. Maybe he'll share some with Trish and me."

Betty forced a smile.

Immaculate saw fangs.

Betty hurried him to the front exit. "See you at your appointment next week," she said. "Remember, there's a fifty dollar fee for no-shows. Now, go."

Immaculate backed out of the door into the street, his eyes locked on Nurse Betty until he was safe outside. He feared she would come after him and touch his back again, rip loose the wire, and string him up with it.

Just as Detective Spearman had promised, a white van waited on the other side of the parking lot of the strip mall with GULFSIDE PLUMBING SERVICE painted across the side. The detective would be inside the van with the surveillance equipment, disgusted that his new informant, Immaculate Davis, had not done a better job. Immaculate figured that policemen cursed like everyone else and that Spearman would hurl his best at him.

Once out of Caston's office, Immaculate's instructions were to ignore the van, get in his own truck, and leave the area. Instead, he looked back at the front of Dr. Paul Caston's clinic building, noted that the lights inside had been turned off, and ran across the parking lot to the disguised police van. He pounded on the rear door.

"Hey, let me in."

When the doors to the van popped open, Immaculate shivered at Detective Reed Spearman's tall, muscular frame and angry expression that seemed to fill the space. The detective jerked him inside the van, narrowly missing the technician positioned at the rear with headphones. The technician helped Immaculate into the adjacent seat, then peeled away the listening equipment from underneath his shirt.

"What are you doing, man? We had an arrangement," Reed said.

"You were supposed to leave the clinic and get in your truck and drive away, not call attention to the surveillance van. You blow this covert operation, and the judge sends you right back inside. You understand?"

"I know. I know, Detective Spearman." Immaculate pointed frantically toward the clinic. "But that nurse in there … that woman is super creepy. I thought she was gonna eat me alive. I think she's on to me and knows about the wire."

"Settle down," Reed said. He tapped on the front partition to signal the driver to leave the premises, and the engine started.

"Check around and see if we've got a fresh T-shirt or something to give him," Reed said to the technician. "The one he's got is drenched … smells like a dead skunk."

The technician tossed Immaculate a souvenir football jersey from the University of Southern Mississippi, emblazoned across the front with the team's golden eagle insignia. "I tried my best, detective," Immaculate said, removing his T-shirt and pushing his arms through the openings in the jersey. "Don't need no more prison. Might not make it out next time."

Reed put on headphones and replayed some of the afternoon's interaction inside Dr. Caston's clinic. "This is some good stuff," he said and scribbled a few notes on a pad. "At least it's a start." The driver jerked the van into gear and exited the parking area.

"I told you I'd put a good word in for you with the judge if you helped us bust that slime ball doctor. It's good that Detective Brisdell spotted you outside Caston's Clinic a while back when she was working undercover."

"You mean that we still got a deal?" Immaculate settled into the seat and smoothed the wrinkles in the jersey. He decided it was a good fit. Maybe the detective would let him keep it.

"How'd they like that shrimp I packed up for you," Reed said. "Nice prop. You agree?" He realized he spoke too loudly and removed the headphones. "Let's see where this stint goes. Sometimes the medical types try to cover up for each other."

16

The van pulled further into the street, and Immaculate tried to relax. He let his head fall back against his seat.

Reed noticed the fast, shallow breaths and that Immaculate's fingers trembled. "Hey, man. You weren't faking it in there," Reed said and replaced the headphones. "You do need a fix." Reed slid a tiny envelope from inside his jacket, pressed it open to double-check the contents, and passed it to Immaculate.

"Here take one of these and save the other three for later," Reed said. "You deserve it."

The surveillance technician handed Immaculate a bottle of water from the small cooler near the door and returned his attention to the electronic equipment.

"We'll get you back in there again with a wire," Reed said with a thumbs up to Immaculate. "This was just a trial run."

A seldom-used public park and recreation area abutted the far side of the rear parking lot of Dr. Paul Caston's one-story, brick clinic building—an area out of view of the police surveillance van across the street. With Immaculate Davis still inside the building, Caston had followed the woman with the tight hair bun and dark upper lip through the rear exit. His Mercedes occupied the single reserved parking space located beside the door.

The area was deserted except for a young father with earbuds in place who pushed a double stroller, his face focused forward and tilted downward at the serenity of two sleeping infants. A fat squirrel bounded out of one of the oak trees to land on the stone path in front of the stroller. The animal narrowly escaped the front wheels.

Standing between the doctor and his vehicle, the woman seemed to sense the movement in the park behind her. She turned in that direction and hesitated for a few seconds. When the man continued along the path with the stroller and without concern for her or Caston, she said, "I ain't got all day, Doc. I've sent everyone I

17

know to see you and volume is good. But since they built that new truck stop up the highway, my dinky store and gas station just don't get the foot traffic it used to. And that makes it tougher to push product. Guess I need to advertise," she chuckled.

Caston shot a glance around the area. Satisfied they were not being watched, he answered. "Keep your voice down, Mrs. Kile. I get the feeling they're on to me, the police or maybe the DEA. I can't put my finger on it, but I've been around a long time, seen lots and lots of patients. I know how to make a chart look good, but over the last couple of years it's started to get sticky."

"You're a smart fellow, Dr. Caston. You can keep pulling this off. The junkies will keep coming."

Caston shook his head and stared out into the park. "My surgery numbers are down, and cash is tight. I'm just too old and tired to patrol the emergency rooms for car wrecks and athletic injuries like I used to." Caston's eyes followed the father and the stroller. "I ... I don't know how I've let myself get so deep into this. How did I sink so low?"

"It's just business," Mrs. Kile said. "Supply and demand."

"I've written more than my share of narcotics and anti-anxiety meds over the years—most of them indicated, or at least I tell myself so. Now there's a requirement to report any controlled scripts you write to the state pharmacy board—have to log into a computer to do that. But I blow it off half the time."

"You're a smart man. You make your records read good and clean. You just said so yourself."

The stroller had reached the far side of the path. Several more squirrels scampered under the trees. "If the watchdogs at the pharmacy board and the DEA, not to mention the state licensure board, take a good look at me, I'm busted. They'll see all the orthopedic fakes and frequent flyers who flock into my clinic these days. Most have no true medical problems."

"Come on, Doc. It's those phonies that keep us in business," Mrs. Kile said. "It's easy, and it's working. I send the patients to you.

18

They show up with a good story, and you write a script. There's even room to expand the business."

"You're missing the point, Mrs. Kile. Most orthopods like me should be writing fewer pain meds, not more. The newer, less-invasive orthopedic procedures don't require long-term opioid prescriptions." Dr. Caston gauged the area again, then took a few steps back toward the rear door. "Betty is going to wonder where I am."

"Who's Betty. I ain't sent nobody named Betty in to see you."

"Betty's not one of your drug seekers; she's my office nurse. She'll want me to close out the day's patient charts."

"Can this chick be trusted?"

"Absolutely. She knows how to deal and has worked for me long before you came along. However, if somebody outside of this clinic ever did a serious audit of my patients' charts … God knows what would happen to me." He turned away from Kile, stepped to the door, and took a deep breath. "I've got to start taking care of people, patients with actual problems. Get my surgery volume back up to where it was. Update my office furnishings—paint the place." Another deep breath. "There're new doctors out there … always trying to take over, Mrs. Kile."

She moved nearer. "Mrs. Kile was my sorry mother-in-law. I've told you, call me Momma Kile. And face it, Doc. We got a good thing going here. You write for the meds. My people fill the pre-scriptions at their favorite pharmacy. They turn the stuff into me. I sell the product, and you get a commission. You don't need to worry about working harder."

Caston considered this. "Definitely enjoy the extra cash. In fact, I depend on it, but the longer this goes on the more uneasy I feel. I actually feel a little guilty," Caston said, "a little slimy." He wiped perspiration from his forehead with the back of his right hand. "We physicians, we surgeons, are supposed to help people and get paid if we work hard and do a good job. I didn't spend over twelve years in medical school and surgical training and all these years in practice to be a drug dealer."

19

"No need to worry, Doc. You deserve a bonanza after all those late hours, your nose in a book and stuck in an operating room. My people know just how to do it, know just the right thing to say for a prescription."

Caston stared blankly ahead. Gone from view were the father and baby stroller, likely on the section of track behind the tall row of shrubs at the opposite end of the park. An older couple now occupied the central area of the park, cozy on a bench with sandwiches and large paper drinking cups complete with straws. The man wore an old baseball cap, the woman a thin, purple sweater. Caston believed he had seen them before. *Maybe they're patients?*

"I'm not sure I could face the other hospital physicians, much less my friends, if this ever came out—about what I've been doing." His voice broke a bit. "There's this one patient. He's a shrimper. In the clinic all the time, makes lots of noise and seems agitated. Name is … Davis. He one of yours?"

Momma Kile ran her hand across the top of her head and gently squeezed the hair bun, then darted her eyes away. "Don't know a Davis, but I tell my people not to use their actual names or birthdates."

"The fella always asks me to skip the medical questions and the physical exam and go straight to writing a narcotic prescription for him. But it seems that his back pain is genuine. He's not a total phony."

"If he's not one of mine, then maybe I need to sign him up," Momma said.

"The first time in the office he asked for zannies or planks, even before he told me his symptoms. At first, I didn't know what he meant, so I slipped away and Googled on my computer. I figured out those were street names for Xanax, so are footballs and school bus."

"You write him a script?"

Caston took another deep breath and wipe of the forehead. "Surgery wasn't indicated. All he needed was a muscle relaxer, so I did give him the Xanax," Caston said. "He keeps coming back for more."

# Chapter 4

Immaculate settled into his seat on the witness stand, happy to be on display in front of the courtroom and free of the defense table. He turned his head away from the judge, a woman he recognized from a hearing a year or two before, or maybe it was longer than that. He beat that marijuana rap, even with a lousy court-appointed attorney. Immaculate forced an erect posture despite his sore back and looked over and up to the judge. This time he managed a weak smile. The stern face in the heavy, black robe seemed to burn right through him.

At the thought of being prosecuted again and a possible return stint in jail, sweat dripped from his scalp to run down the side of his face, despite the air-conditioning. The nape of his neck and his underarms were wet and sticky. Immaculate ran his hand behind his head and wiped the sweat on the front of his right pant leg. He remembered his instructions from Detective Reed Spearman.

"Immaculate, just tell them what happened in that doctor's office," the detective had said. Spearman reassured him that the female prosecutor from the D.A.'s office would be patient and sympathetic to his medical plight. The D.A. was after the doctor, not him. "After all, you're on the right side of the law this time. You were in a lot of pain and a patient in need of help. But you began to feel that Dr. Caston was overprescribing, that he might hurt others, and you wanted to put a stop to it."

"They just gonna think I'm doing this for money—for some kinda reward," Immaculate told him.

"You are doing your civic duty. You reported Caston's clinic to the police and offered to help us. You even agreed to wear a wire," Reed said.

Immaculate spotted the detective on the third row behind the prosecution bench and smiled at him. Reed managed a slight shake of the head, *No*, then Immaculate remembered he was not to make eye contact for fear the court would think Detective Spearman had coached him.

*I guess I've already screwed this up. That detective's gonna throw me back in the hole*, Immaculate decided.

At least he came across as respectable to the judge and jury—or thought he did. Immaculate pulled at the collar of his white shirt and at the sleeves of his suit. The scratchy, light wool fabric felt smoother in the dusty dressing room of the resale shop than it did now. The suit was a light shade of brown, not his favorite color, but the only one near his size that did not reek of moth balls. Plus, it still had the price tag from a men's store in Jackson that had gone out of business several years ago. He pulled again at the sleeves and then at the lapel of the suit and to his surprise got a whiff of moth balls.

The polyester-cotton blend dress shirt stuck to his lower back. Complete with laundry tags and a metal hanger branded with the dry cleaner's logo, the shirt had—unlike the suit—been worn before but was a pass once he trimmed away a stray thread from one of the cuffs. Immaculate also scrubbed away a brown, dime-sized stain from the front of the shirt with an old toothbrush and soap.

Since Immaculate had forgotten to pick up a tie in the resale shop to finish out the ensemble, Reed loaned him a conservative design: navy-blue background with thin yellow and white stripes. "This one will look good to a jury," Reed had said.

Immaculate hoped the detective would let him keep the tie.

Dress shoes, like the tie, had been an afterthought. With no offer from Reed to buy or loan him footwear, Immaculate selected the better of his two pair of tennis shoes and the cleanest pair of dark socks he could find in the bedroom drawer of his trailer.

The judge removed her reading glasses, cleared her throat, and stared at Immaculate. "Mr. Davis, are you going to answer District Attorney Ramsey's questions, or do I have to hold you in contempt?"

Sarah Ramsey stood five-two in heels with straight posture, her black hair pulled tight behind her head into a ponytail that draped the top of her shoulder. She wore dark-rimmed glasses and stared over them when questioning the witness or gazing off into the distance as though in thought. In chronological order she played excerpts of the recorded conversations between Immaculate and Dr. Caston's nurse, identified as Betty Thibodeaux. The date and time of each recorded encounter was noted in bold, black ink on a poster board displayed on an easel at the front of the courtroom.

Immaculate's testimony lasted forty-five minutes. His instructions from Reed were to ignore the jury, remain focused on the person asking the questions, and be straight with them. Immaculate failed the first directive. He could not resist and stole glances at the panel of twelve people—numbered about even between blacks and whites, men and women—sensing the burning gaze of each person. Of particular interest was the older white man on the front row with short, cropped gray hair who took notes on a pad from his front shirt pocket and the scrawny, well-dressed black lady two over who shook her head and lowered her eyes whenever Immaculate spoke. Most members of the jury leaned forward as though to catch every word.

He thought he caught a worried expression from one or two others, a tear from one woman, and the look of shock from several others. Another black lady who resembled his Aunt Dollie smiled and nodded at him several times.

"Ignore the jury." Immaculate jerked his head forward at the memory of Reed's voice, felt embarrassed, then checked for the detective. Reed Spearman stared back at him and shrugged his shoulders. He had seen all of it.

"It's okay," Reed mouthed, "You're doing good."

"Your Honor, I'd like to play for the court this final recording and ask Mr. Davis for his comments," the D.A. said. "It's the last interaction between Mr. Davis and Dr. Caston."

The court reporter again tapped on a keyboard and the voice of Immaculate Davis filled the courtroom. "Okay, Doc. Thanks for the script. Thirty Percs, that's good—awesome in fact."

The sound of an opened door followed, and an authoritative female voice said, "Dr. Caston, are you finished with Mr. Davis?"

"Yes, Betty. Give him an appointment for next week."

"Got it right here. Here's your appointment card, Immaculate. And don't be late. Dr. Caston's time is valuable."

"Yes, ma'am," Immaculate said.

The recording ended, and Immaculate grinned. Detective Spearman had nailed this. The polite lady from the district attorney's office had been nice to him. Her smile after each question soothed his bad nerves under the ugly nose of the judge.

However, when the ugly nose judge called up Dr. Caston's defense lawyer, Immaculate sensed a 180-degree turn.

In defense attorney William Runnels, Esquire, Immaculate saw a privileged, all-American white guy—tall and trim with smooth, white teeth—dressed in an expensive-looking suit with stylish haircut to match.

Runnels hurled one question after another at him, all angry and to the point. Immaculate assumed that to this lawyer he was nothing more than a sleazy liar for the prosecution. The judge allowed Runnels to ask Immaculate if he was an opportunist and with Immaculate's brief hesitation to answer defined the word for him. Immaculate denied that he sought only to ruin the name of a productive citizen, a good doctor—a person totally different from someone like Immaculate Davis.

Immaculate put his hand to his lower back and let out a soft moan now and then after Attorney Runnels's questions—even winced a time or two, a trick he remembered from Detective Spearman. The nice lady who resembled Aunt Dollie noticed and smiled with encouragement. The lady sitting next to her in the jury box winked at him.

Runnels finally sat down.

"I have no redirect, Your Honor," Sarah Ramsey said.

Immaculate grinned at her.

"You may step down, Mr. Davis," the judge said. "The attorneys have no further questions for you. You may go."

Immaculate slid out of the witness box and held back from a sprint for the rear of the courtroom. He slid his hand over the side of his face in an attempt to shield the judge's scowl. Again he wondered if she recognized him from that case a few years before. The past forty-five minutes had felt like four hours, every eye and ear in the courtroom directed toward him and sucking in every word he spoke.

From the courtroom gallery, the detective had seemed pleased. But Immaculate's current goal was to navigate a straight line toward the double doors into the hall of the courthouse and all without a stumble between the defense and prosecution tables. He kept his eyes down and away from Dr. Caston's piercing glare of disdain and betrayal.

*Screw Dr. Caston.* The sympathy he felt towards the end of his testimony from the Aunt Dollie look-alike and her friend boosted Immaculate's self-worth and opinion of his court performance. He wished, however, for a thumbs-up from Detective Spearman as he passed the detective in his third-row seat but figured the judge would disapprove.

Immaculate dropped into a bench in the hallway outside the courtroom doors. He noticed another grey-haired, even older man drag a portable oxygen tank behind him as he crept up the hall with the aid of a cane. The young woman dressed in a business suit and seated earlier beside Defense Attorney Runnels stepped from a tight group of people and greeted the old man.

"Mr. Simpson. You okay?" Immaculate heard her say.

The man released his weak, trembling hold on the handle of the cart, and the oxygen tank it supported fell to the floor in a loud clang. An echo filled the hall. The woman grabbed the man and his cane to prevent a fall.

Immaculate heard the elderly man say, "Thank you for what you're trying to do to help the doc. Yes, Dr. Caston is a good doctor. A lot of people like me love him … and need him."

The man with the oxygen tank and cane seemed nice, but at the same time seemed so sad. He was good folk, like his Aunt Dollie.

Immaculate wished he could talk to Detective Spearman. He needed reassurance, but he knew what the detective would say: "Yep, Immaculate, you did the right thing, helping to bust that bad doctor." But it was an easy decision for Immaculate Davis to help the police. He didn't have a choice.

# Chapter 5

M r. Hardy Simpson tugged at the plastic prongs pinching his nostrils and struggled to respond to the judge. The portable oxygen tank and cart were on the floor by his chair, the dull silver valve at the top of the green tank just visible to the jury. He rested his boney fingers on the mahogany railing of the witness box.

"Mr. Simpson, please do your best to answer counsel's question," the judge said. Her stern demeanor and facial expression unchanged despite the man's obvious illness.

"Yes, ma'am." Simpson's spinal osteoporosis and the associated stooped shoulders and stiff neck prevented him from turning to address the judge. "I'll do my best, Your Honor." A tall man when young, Simpson now stood no more than five-eight when he wobbled into the courtroom a few minutes prior and dragged the portable oxygen tank behind him. He coughed and sputtered and adjusted the oxygen prongs.

"Maybe you should repeat the question, Mr. Runnels," the judge said.

"I'll be happy to, Your Honor," the lead defense attorney said. "You're one of Dr. Caston's patients. Is that right, Mr. Simpson?"

"Yes, sir. I've been seeing Doc for a couple of months, almost three."

"And how did you become Dr. Caston's patient? See an ad, call the hospital, or something like that?"

"No, sir. A friend told me that Dr. Caston had helped him—fixed him right up—so I thought I'd give the doc a try. You see, sir, no one could stop the pain." Simpson answered with a hand rub to his lower back and bent forward a little more. "I was hurting all over."

"Then you made an appointment?" Runnels added. His eyes did not leave the witness.

"Objection." Sarah Ramsey stood. "Everyone in this room likely understands the process of scheduling a doctor's appointment. Besides, counsel's manner of questioning is on the fringes of leading the witness."

"Sustained," the judge said. "Mr. Runnels, move things along in questioning your witness."

"Yes, Your Honor," Runnels said. His eyes still glued to Simpson. "Mr. Simpson, please tell the court what happened next."

"You see, once any nurse or doctor caught a glimpse of me, a stooped-over old man with an oxygen tank, they walked—said I was too much of a risk to take on as patient. Hell, they practically ran away from me instead of treating me." His voice grew stronger. "Damn, I was in bad shape."

"Mr. Simpson, just answer the questions," the judge interjected.

A pale-faced, tortured Simpson again leaned forward and struggled to turn his head in the direction of the judge, seeming suddenly weaker and even more frail. With a pull at the plastic tubing, he said, "Sorry, ma'am, but I couldn't get a follow up appointment with any of those other bone surgeons at Biloxi Memorial. I had to do something. The pain … it was more than any human being could stand."

Each member of the jury appeared empathetic.

"The pain … it shot down my right leg every time I put weight on it. One nurse—a nice one—told me to rate the pain from one to ten. I told her a ten-plus."

Runnels paced in front of the witness box. He glared at the three-member prosecution table and dared an objection. "So, Mr. Simpson, you were not able to establish, I believe the term is, continuity of care with any doctor at any time until you learned of Dr. Caston?"

Sarah Ramsey objected.

The judge ignored her and said, "Go ahead and answer the question, Mr. Simpson."

Simpson remained in character. "I hurt so bad I couldn't work at all. Like I said, no doctor would touch my case … said I was too much of a risk for surgery. And I didn't want nobody sticking no more needles in my back and shooting me up with steroids like those pain specialists." He scanned the jury. "My whole body would shake when those doctors or nurses would get near me with needles. I just knew in my soul that the next injection was gonna paralyze me."

"Your Honor, please. The witness has answered the question," Ramsey said. "We don't need a speech, a monologue, with the same information repeated over and over."

"Good point, Miss Ramsey. Objection sustained. However, I will decide what we need or don't need in this courtroom. You may sit down," the judge said. "Mr. Runnels, ask your next question of this witness."

"You established care as a patient with Dr. Caston—is that correct, Mr. Simpson?" Runnels followed.

"Yes, that nice young lady in Dr. Caston's office, the one with the sweet, kind voice who works up front, made me an appointment. And I only had to wait a week to see the doctor. He was extra nice. He treated me like an actual person."

"I have no other questions for this witness, Your Honor."

Sarah Ramsey made few points in the prosecution's cross examination of Mr. Simpson. After the final question, Simpson added, "Like I said, I just couldn't take no more needles. Nobody else would help me, but I needed some relief somehow. I couldn't take it no more." Simpson gasped for breath and grabbed the oxygen tubing.

"You may step down, Mr. Simpson. Thank you," the judge said.

Except for the woman on the far right of the second row, the members of the jury dropped their eyes as Simpson worked his way from the witness box and stumbled off the last step. The bailiff grabbed him and the oxygen tank to prevent a fall and led Simpson slowly from the courtroom.

The woman on the second row kept her eyes on the witness until he disappeared through the large wooden, double doors into the hall, then blotted her right eye with a tissue. Runnels noted that the man next to her looked up for a few seconds and wiped an eye with a finger. Several others took notes on a paper pad. One woman chewed on the tip of her pen.

Attorney Runnels called his second witness for the defense, another one of Dr. Caston's patients, a woman in her mid-forties named Brenda Hicks, whose face and posture screamed more than a decade older.

"Nobody took me seriously," Hicks said in sharp, quick cadence as the court reporter tapped furiously in sync on her machine. The woman's wide eyes darted from one side of the room to the other. Her fingers trembled and she wedged her hands under her thighs and hips to hide them.

"Before Dr. Caston took me on," she said, "I was in and out of the emergency room every few days with burning leg and foot pain … and numbness. One morning I woke up and thought I was paralyzed."

The court reporter paused for a breath, then resumed typing.

"All my doctors fired me as a patient. First my neurologist, then two different orthopedists—even the foot specialist—and the foot specialist could have done something for me. I wasn't a quack. I used to teach college algebra, for God's sake. But they all said they couldn't help me, that I should just pick up a copy of my medical records at the front desk and take a hike." Brenda Hicks shrugged her shoulders and grinned. "Take a hike, sure. I could barely walk."

Quiet laughter drifted throughout the courtroom, and the judge pounded her gavel. "Quiet. Quiet. That's enough of that," she said. "Simply answer the questions, Miss Hicks."

"Yes, ma'am. But even my psychiatrist told me he wouldn't see me anymore. He couldn't talk me out of feeling my pain." The

30

woman paused and rocked from side to side in the witness chair. Her hands remained under her.

Runnels asked, "And what happened next?"

"I did a Google search and found Dr. Caston's name in the list of area doctors. I called, and his secretary saved me. She got me right in for an appointment. Dr. Caston took time to listen to me."

On cross examination Attorney Ramsey addressed Hicks's two arrests for narcotic trafficking in another state fifteen years prior and her early departure from rehab against medical advice.

Runnels objected.

The witness smiled. "I was acquitted of those narcotics charges, and I had no choice but to leave that expensive rehab facility. I ran out of money, and they didn't do charity. But I'm a regular at my local Narcotics Anonymous chapter, and they ..."

"Thank you for answering my question," Ramsey interrupted.

Runnels objected. "But, judge, the witness should be allowed to complete her answer."

"Sustained," the judge said. "You opened this window, Miss Ramsey. Would the witness please complete the answer?"

"I'm clean now, and my NA sponsor told me that it's okay to take narcotics if you have a legitimate medical indication. I'm not a fake. My pain never lets up ... and Dr. Caston knows it." The woman snapped her hands free and raised them above her head with palms open and fingers raised toward the ceiling. "Praise God that He led me to my Dr. Caston."

Ramsey clinched her fists and spun nearly 180 degrees on her heels to face the prosecution table, her back to the judge. She exhaled deeply. "I have nothing further, Your Honor."

The witness stepped down and moaned with each movement.

William Runnels called his third witness for the defense.

A thin woman with stringy, long grey hair and faded blonde tips appeared on crutches in the opened doors of the courtroom. Her shoulders were rounded, similar to Simpson's, but not quite as severe. Her fingers and joints were gnarled and swollen.

She worked her way down the aisle with the crutches, moving side-to-side and halting several times to brace against the support. This enabled her to hold her hands in front of her face—as though on display. Her thick-soled, orthopedic shoes knocked with a loud thump against the wooden sides of the row seating in the spectator area. The sound echoed with each step.

A bailiff walked slowly beside the crippled woman to support her at the shoulder and arm until she reached the witness stand. Several indifferent-appearing female jurors suddenly seemed distressed at this struggle. One blotted an eye with a handkerchief and even a couple of male jurors fidgeted in their seats. Ramsey feared that one particularly concerned gentleman was set to jump over the railing to help the woman, but she finally reached the front of the courtroom.

The bailiff remained at the foot of the two short steps to assist the struggling witness into her seat at the judge's left hand. All this action brought more pained expressions from the jury. One of the witness's crutches slid to the floor. The bailiff retrieved it and propped it at the opening into the witness box.

The woman answered Runnels's first question: "I suffer from incurable arthritis, just like my momma and her momma."

Runnels nodded in approval.

"Dr. Caston came to my rescue. He helped me endure the pain."

The second crutch slid toward the floor. Runnels caught it and positioned it next to the other.

"Thank you. Thank you so much," the woman said, her voice weak.

"Now, please hold up your hands so that the court can see your condition and share with us, if you can, or just describe, the treatment you received from Dr. Caston," William Runnels said.

The woman leaned forward toward the attorney. Wincing, she placed each crippled finger, one-by-one, at the top of the railing to steady herself and slowly turned to focus attention on the group of jurors. Her voice more strained, raspy. "What I need to share, Mr. Runnels, is that Dr. Caston ain't runnin' no pill mill for profit; he's a fine …"

"Your Honor!" The district attorney jumped to her feet. "I object. This is improper. The witness is speculating."

"Sustained," the judge said. "The jury will disregard the witness's comment." The judge turned from the jury to the witness. "You will only answer the attorney's questions."

"I've been to lots of specialists all over the state, even saw an arthritis doctor, a rheumatologist, in New Orleans," the woman said. "None of the fancy arthritis medicines or know-it-all doctors helped me—that is, when I could afford to get my prescriptions filled or pay the doctor fees. The health insurance through my job wouldn't cover half the expense." She lifted her hands off the railing and pushed her forearms forward. "Just look at my fingers," she cried. "I can't use them unless the pain stops."

Runnels expected an objection but after a second or two pushed forward with a follow-up question. "You were in a lot of pain," he said. "And you could find no one in the medical field to help you?"

"Objection, Your Honor," the D.A. said, rising from her seat. "Leading the witness."

Runnels grinned in expectation.

The judge shook her head and said, "Overruled. The witness has a medical condition. That is obvious. She has testified that she was unsuccessful in obtaining medical care. Mr. Runnels merely summarized."

She motioned to the witness. "Please go ahead. You may explain in detail."

The woman's eyes remained focused on the jury while she lowered her hands to her lap. She glanced toward the defense attorney and immediately returned her hands to the wooden railing. "Dr. Caston examined me every four weeks, sometimes every two weeks, or at least his nurse did."

"Ma'am, you stated that no one could … or would … help you." Runnels stepped to the side to make individual eye contact with each juror, then turned back midway toward the witness. "You found help in Dr. Caston. Didn't you say that?"

"Yes, sir. I did."

"What was Dr. Caston trying to do for you?"

"Dr. Caston helped me get through the day. He eased my pain." She put her right hand to her lower back and rubbed it. "There was no room for me to complain, no way a woman could be caught slacking at work. I had to push through the pain. My kids—my children—would have starved if I hadn't pulled a full shift every day."

"How long were you a patient—there at Dr. Caston's clinic?"

"About two years, and I sure would like to go back. I hope those nice folks over there in that jury box will see to that." She turned to the jurors and smiled. Her front teeth were nubs.

"Objection, Your Honor." The district attorney stood exacerbated, almost stomping her right foot. "How much more of this, Your Honor!"

"Sustained. Jurors, disregard the last sentence from the witness. Just answer the questions, please," the judge said.

"I'll be glad to," the witness said. "At first, I only took the pain pills at home, until they stopped making me sleepy—so they wouldn't affect my work at the factory. And I took them only as Dr. Caston prescribed. Then I tried taking them on the job, not too many at first and when nobody was watching. I work the conveyor belt controls with foot pedals, and my meds let me work through the pain."

She wiped a tear from the corner of her eye and looked over and up to the judge. "Your Honor, I had to work and still need to. I need money to pay the rent, money for my kids—for food, for school clothes. I'm desperate. There ain't no one else in my family to help. Dr. Caston saved my family."

# Chapter 6

By 2:00 PM the lobby of the orthopedic clinic had cleared of patients—no one left to check in or out. The soft hum of the air conditioning unit timed off, and the air around her went still. Even the telephone was silent.

The calm deafened Jessica. The receptionist and secretary stood from her desk at the front of the medical office and walked through the lobby toward the employee restroom, hoping to break the stagnation and boredom of a slow day. She wondered how much longer Dr. Scott Mack would spend with that lady in the last exam room down the hall. Her knee problem had already consumed a half hour of her boss's time.

The *tap-tap* of the patient's single support crutch broke the silence as she worked her way up the hall to the checkout area. "You're not over at your desk to check me out," the woman grunted. "I guess you don't want me to pay anything?"

"Oh … no, ma'am," Jessica said. The door to the ladies' room snapped shut behind her. "Just taking a quick break. Do you have your checkout ticket, the slip of paper the nurse gave you?" Jessica crossed behind the patient to return to her desk.

The woman balanced the crutch between her left elbow and hip and rummaged through the purse over her opposite shoulder. She produced a yellow sheet of paper from deep inside the bag. "Here you go, young lady. And by the way, I returned the orthopedic scooter y'all loaned me from a few weeks ago," the woman said. "Remember? So, I don't owe anything for that."

"Yes, ma'am," Jessica said. "I already credited your account for the equipment rental deposit of your scooter, but there is the rental fee for the time you used it." Jessica tapped a few keys on the computer keyboard. "And I need to collect your insurance co-pay for today's office visit before you leave. I'll print out the total balance due."

Still managing the crutch, the woman pulled a lipstick, a couple of pens, and a hairbrush from her purse, then dropped them back in place. She scanned the room including the glass front doors. "Seems I left my wallet at home. And, oh, my goodness. I won't have my driver's license for the drive home."

"But the clinic policy is to collect on day of service. Cash, check, credit card …"

"Sorry. No wallet, no money. Besides, my health insurance is supposed to pay first. Tell Dr. Mack that I'll pay him the rest when I get my short-term disability check at the end of the month."

"Ma'am, the clinic payment policy is …"

"Just send in the paperwork to my insurance; fax or email it—or whatever you do these days. We'll see what happens. Then bill me the rest." The woman hobbled to the front exit with the crutch. "Oh, and, Miss Policy-Know-It-All, just add the cost of this damn thing to my bill." The woman popped the door open with the end of the crutch and stood in the doorway. "Just so you know, by now Dr. Mack should have me walking without this damn thing. I might have to leave a bad review of him on Facebook." The woman disappeared through the clinic exit, and the door shut behind her.

From the exterior window inside the reception area, Jessica had full view of the street in front of Mack and Associates Orthopedic Clinic. The disgruntled female patient stood at the curb with the single crutch and tapped it against the concrete as though impatient. Within seconds, a shiny blue Lexus pulled up next to her. The woman waved in recognition, opened the rear door, and tossed the orthopedic appliance onto the backseat. Standing securely on two feet, she opened the front passenger door and slid in. The Lexus disappeared.

"That woman is disgusting. What an act, all to keep from paying what she owes Dr. Mack," Jessica muttered. "I should have shot a video with my phone."

The AC unit kicked back on. Jessica shut the cash drawer and sank into her chair, sick at the sight of the empty lobby beyond her desk. Early to mid-afternoon in a doctor's office should be swarming with patients. When she snapped her legs crossed at the ankle, the tip of her right shoe heel struck the inside of the desk unit. The hard sound reverberated through the thin wall and echoed throughout the vacant lobby. Jessica checked the shoes for scuff marks, a favorite pair bought at an outlet mall in Foley, Alabama.

"Dr. Mack's not gonna be happy with how it went down with that woman." She popped open the cash drawer for another look inside and pushed it closed again. "Nope, not gonna be happy at all. We sure could have used that thirty-five-dollar copay." She thought about her own wallet and checkbook. "I hope he can make payroll this week."

Jessica flipped through the desk calendar. She traced the day's date with a long fingernail covered in chipped purple polish—although the tiny, pearl-white star at the tip remained perfect. *I need a payday ... and a manicure. Too bad those Vietnamese women at the nail shop don't work for free like I do for Dr. Mack*, she decided.

She popped a black Sharpie from the ceramic pencil holder on her desk and yanked away the plastic tip cover with her teeth. Jessica then skipped over a few spaces on the calendar to draw a thick X marking the next payday. "No way I'm gonna work for free," she quipped.

For the past sixteen months, Jessica Kile had punched the clock at Mack and Associates Orthopedic Clinic—she and the part-time nurse were the associates—never late, never a complainer, at least not to Dr. Mack, and never one to skip out early. Her receptionist pay scale had morphed laterally into scheduling patient appointments, sending out appointment reminders by phone or email, wrestling with poorly written electronic medical records software, ordering office supplies, paying bills, and balancing the books at the end of the day.

She drew on her C grade from junior college business courses and handled all of it, very well she supposed, and without complaint from Dr. Mack. After all, nowadays there was not much business to handle or reconcile. Jessica had even filled in for the office nurse, who often called in sick or was a no-show.

Jessica believed she nailed the nurse look. The white medical jacket left behind in the breakroom closet by a previous tenant looked awesome, even a bit sexy when pinned up to shorten the length and flatter her hips. She also decided she played the nurse part just as well—taking an occasional blood pressure or temperature or changing a bandage now and then—particularly after she learned the lingo and other professional mannerisms from TV.

However, the actress duties stopped there. She declined Dr. Mack's offer of another dollar-an-hour raise for the title of Office Single-Person Cleaning Crew, despite the light janitorial duties. Dr. Mack did not seem mad—or surprised—when she said no.

Using a tissue, Jessica took a swipe at the layer of dust on her desk and stared at the wilting house plant in the lobby. The tips of the large, narrow leaves nearly touched the floor. One of the leaves lay shriveled on the dingy carpet, victim to the abrasive, deadbeat patient who knocked it free with her crutch and nearly crushed it with her foot.

"Dr. Mack ought to tip that night lady who comes in and cleans to keep that thing watered. I'm not taking care of the plants around here either—not until I get at least a two-dollar an hour raise." Another dead leaf fell to the floor. "And no vacuuming the floor either," Jessica said.

She shook her head and thought about the lightweight vacuum cleaner in the front office closet. "No, no, I'm not gonna vacuum that up. No. Not gonna do it."

"You say something, Jessica?" Dr. Mack pushed through the door from the hall into Jessica's work area and smiled straight, white teeth framed by high cheek bones, tight fair skin, and a square jaw. She jumped to busy herself and thumbed through a short stack of papers at the side of her computer monitor.

Even with the low hourly pay and financial condition of Dr. Mack's orthopedic practice uncertain, he was easy to work for—professional, yet friendly. She almost slipped once and called him Scott. Sometimes Scott wore fitted scrubs to work, no long white doctor's coat, as though his six-two, trim physique were on display. She wished her husband had the same flat stomach and broad shoulders.

"No sir, Dr. Mack. I didn't say anything—just thinking about a new country song I heard on the car radio this morning."

He smiled again and opened the closet with the vacuum cleaner inside, then removed a box from the upper shelf.

"Been lookin' for this—a free sample of that new knee brace a surgical sales rep dropped off for me to try out. Might work for that patient I just saw—super nice lady. Hate it that she twisted her knee walking her dog."

"Need me to help you with anything?" Jessica asked.

"No, I got it." Dr. Mack shut the closet door and moved closer, the orthopedic appliance held in both hands. "I dread the answer, but any way you'll find us in the black for the month when you settle the books today?" he asked.

"I'm sorry, Dr. Mack, but if that 'nice lady' you're talking about had just paid her bill when she left, we might have had a chance," she answered. "Doubt it will take long to tally up today's work." She caught herself staring at his waist and the dangling front ties of his scrubs and twisted her chair back to face the computer.

"That patient thinks she needs more work done to her knee, but from what you say, I guess we'll never see her again," Scott said, "much less get the money she owes me for her surgery or even get back the crutch I loaned her."

Jessica took a deep breath and walked to the coffee maker behind her, a less expensive drip model than the machine from the coffee delivery service that required individual pods. She filled her

Styrofoam cup and selected a packet of artificial sweetener and a wooden stirrer out of a box.

Scott said as she stirred, "The lady asked me for more pain pills today, but there's no way I could justify another prescription. I pulled her up on my office computer and checked the prescription monitoring site. She's gotten too many opioids already over the last few months—even a script for oxycodone from her family doctor. Those meds aren't party favors."

"Can I make you a cup too, Dr. Mack? I made it right after lunch. And there're some leftover doughnuts from yesterday, chocolate and sprinkles. The Stryker rep brought them."

"Too much caffeine today already, and I need to watch the calories." He stepped into the hall, then turned back. "Thanks for your help this week, Jessica. I can always count on you. Wanna take off a few minutes early today? And it's on me."

Scott Anderson Mack, M.D., was a graduate of the Alaska State University Medical Center Orthopedic Surgery program, a passage representing the completion of thirteen consecutive years of education beyond high school. He finished medical school in the upper lower third of his class and landed a spot in its orthopedics residency program when ASU came up short. Scott filled the program's vacancy in the National Residency Matching Program.

Jessica Kile knew none of that. The impressive diplomas and certificates embossed in fancy print and gold medallions hung on the wall of Scott's office at the end of the hall, with copies in each exam room. However, for the first time Jessica noted bags under Dr. Mack's eyes and early crow's feet. She knew his exact age from the birthdate on his driver's license, a copy required for her to complete some of the clinic's paperwork.

"Sure, I could use an hour or two to run errands on the way home," she answered. Jessica returned to her desk and set her cup of coffee next to the computer. "Biloxi has better shopping than the stores around my house." She slid a few last paper forms from the counter into a drawer, yanked free another moist towelette from the nearby plastic dispenser, and worked around the coffee to wipe the counter surface clean.

Jessica turned back toward her boss. "Dr. Mack, if you don't mind me saying, you look tired to me. You seem worried too."

Scott rested the orthopedic knee brace on the clean counter and pulled the extra office chair toward him, straddling it. "Yeah, I guess I do look a little rough, not getting much sleep these days," he said. "I hope the patients haven't noticed."

Jessica tore open her packet of artificial sweetener, tapped the contents into the cup, and stirred. "I forgot that you were on hospital call last night. Maybe it's good that the afternoon clinic ended early today." She stirred some more and again peeked out into the empty lobby, this time with a slight grimace. "Are you worried about the clinic, Dr. Mack? The patients all seem to like you."

"The few patients we have, that is," Scott said.

Jessica's incessant stirring of the coffee created a tiny, brown whirlpool in the cup. "I hope you think I'm doing a good job around here. I do like working for you."

Scott jumped from the chair. It rolled backwards toward the hall entrance into the room. "I've changed my mind. I think I will have that cup of coffee and maybe one of those stale doughnuts."

"I'll get it for you," Jessica said.

"No, no. You do enough around here already," Scott said. He poured the coffee, took a long sip, and reached into the flat box for one of the sprinkled doughnuts. "Jessica, you're great. No, you're awesome. I definitely appreciate your work ... more than you know." He took a bite of the doughnut, swallowed it with a sip of coffee, and tossed the remainder in the trash. "But I don't know why you haven't quit already, with what little I pay you."

"Like I said, I like working here. In fact, I love working here, Dr. Mack. And I'm sorry about turning down that extra janitor stuff. I'm good at just being a secretary ... and a receptionist. But I do like working here ... for sure." She took a long drag on the coffee.

Scott chuckled. "I was only half kidding about you adding janitor to your CV… just fishing to see how far I could stretch you. A dollar-an-hour raise wasn't much bait." He smiled the straight, white teeth, and they both laughed softly.

"I've been emptying some of the trash cans myself," Scott said, "but I think I've worked out something with the landlord going forward that won't break the bank."

"Dr. Mack, I hope it's okay if I ask you this since I'm sort of in charge of the office … except for the housecleaning." She grinned and hesitated a few seconds before pushing ahead. "I try to do my job without snooping around, but I do open the mail."

Scott sipped his coffee. "You can ask me anything. Go ahead," he said.

"I remember when I was hired you told me that some of my salary would be supplemented by Biloxi Memorial. You said you had a financial arrangement with the hospital," Jessica said. "At first, you got a check from them every month. I would put the envelope on your office desk. But that stopped a couple of months ago."

Scott took another sip of coffee, a long one. "You're right. Biloxi Memorial recruited me down here to bring the medical community 'some fresh blood.' At least, that's what they said. The hospital administrator even promised financial support of my new practice."

"That sounds like a good deal." Jessica forced a smile.

"Because of my contract with the hospital marketing program, I treated more new orthopedics patients in the first ninety days of my practice than I have since. You remember how busy it was when the clinic doors first opened, especially during the first three or four months," Scott said.

Jessica nodded. "There were tons of ads on TV … and radio too."

"And those goofy billboards on the highway."

"You looked good in a suit in those big pictures, Dr. Mack."

"But all that eventually went away," Scott said. "The hospital administrator told me that I was just too much overhead expense. Next thing I knew, they stopped supporting the practice expenditures, like utilities and your salary." He took another sip of coffee and then a hard swallow to finish the serving. "It seems I didn't read the fine print of the agreement."

Scott stood for another cup. "The guaranteed cash flow stipend to support everything around here dried up January first—six months earlier than promised. That's when the checks totally stopped coming."

"Why?" Jessica asked.

"Because practice revenue did not meet some money pusher's expectations. I met several times with the hospital accountants and with the same hospital administrator who made all the promises to try to get them to change their minds," Scott said. "But no luck. I've been on my own financially ever since."

Jessica thought about the shrinking number of patients and sparse cash flow. "So that's why you started signing my check after Christmas. It used to come from the hospital." She considered dumping her coffee. It was getting cold.

"I've tried to keep my head above water. I've even offered to take extra nights of hospital duty for drop-ins or what they call "unreferred" patients. But it's still a struggle. I suspect that the ER routes the patients with good insurance or the ones more likely to pay to doctors who've been around here longer." Scott poured his second cup of coffee. "Particularly if the cases seem easy and less uncomplicated."

"That doesn't seem fair, Dr. Mack."

"There's no way to get past the established ortho guys who grew up around here and have been in practice for so long," Scott said. "The old-guard docs like Paul Caston scarf up everything they can. I think they pay the ER docs not to send me stuff."

"Is that legal?"

"I don't mean money under the table but probably invitations to go deep sea fishing or play golf at their fancy clubs," Scott said. "I wouldn't put it past 'em."

Scott took a sip of the coffee and grimaced slightly as though it was too hot. He glanced over at the expensive orthopedic appliance laid on the counter a few minutes ago and stood to walk back to his office. "Whether fair or not, it's the way it is. Or the way I see it."

Jessica signed in online to route the after-hours calls to the answering service. "Oh, Dr. Mack, I almost forgot. That Mrs. Roberts, the post-op shoulder surgery patient from just before lunch, she left this in the exam room."

Jessica removed a prescription bottle from a top drawer and handed it to Scott. He unsnapped the lid of the plastic container and peered inside, then checked the label. "Yep, this is Percocet. Call Mrs. Roberts and ask her to come back and pick this up."

"I already did. She said that she took less than half after her surgery and didn't know what to do with the rest. Oxycodone usually makes her nauseated, and she doesn't like to keep it around. From the Walgreens label on the bottle, you prescribed forty of 'em for her."

Scott jiggled the container. The pills swirled against the plastic sides. He again examined the contents, counting. "Yep, that's what I usually prescribe, ten milligram oxycodone mixed with acetaminophen and that quantity of pills. Why didn't she just flush this?"

"I suggested that, but she kept going on and on about not spoiling the environment. I told her that the pharmacy had drop-off points for leftover meds, but she wouldn't hear of it."

A text from her mother-in-law lit up the display of her cell phone. Jessica ignored it.

"I'm not worried about sedating a few fish with some dissolved oxycodone," Scott said. "I'll flush it for her. Even if we toss these into the clinic biohazard trash, they could fall into the wrong hands."

He returned the bottle of pills to the counter next to Jessica's keyboard. "Try her again about this. I'm calling it a day. See ya tomorrow." Scott stood and pushed away from the chair. "Oh, and by the way. Geraldine told me that this was her last day. She was a good nurse but said she can make more at a walk-in clinic across town. We'll figure something out."

Jessica watched him leave the front office and once out of hearing range grumbled, "If I'm gonna be the permanent nurse around here too, I'll need a spare white jacket—if the clinic can afford it. I'm sure not paying for it."

She considered another cup of coffee for the ride home, then remembered her recent problems with sleeping and decided against it. She picked up Mrs. Roberts's unused Percocet and remembered something else: a radio news cast from the car ride home a few days ago. The Coast Guard had arrested the small crew of a sailing boat suspected of smuggling off-label narcotic tablets into the Port of Gulfport. The officers confiscated multiple large packets of oxycodone and hydrocodone. The newscaster said the street value was a least a dollar per milligram.

*When Dr. Mack prescribes thirty Percocet 10s, that's three hundred dollars worth of medicine,* she figured. *A person with medical insurance would pay less than thirty or forty for the whole prescription at a regular pharmacy, someone without insurance—almost that much a pill.*

Jessica stepped into the hall and called out: "Dr. Mack, it might be a better idea if you held those pills in your office until I reach Mrs. Roberts. Why don't you lock them up in your desk?"

"You're right," he answered. He returned to Jessica's reception area, unsnapped the top of the plastic bottle, again checked the medication inside, then closed the container and dropped it into the front pocket of his surgical scrub shirt.

Jessica stood with her bag over her shoulder and walked toward the front exit of the clinic. "Those pills are generic brand. Aren't they, Dr. Mack? Might not have cost that woman much at the pharmacy with her insurance, but worth a good bit to others." She smiled. "Worth a lot, in fact."

"Hey, wait a minute, Jessica. I'll talk to the hospital administrator. Maybe even threaten a lawsuit for breach of contract. I'll get Biloxi Memorial to float my practice overhead for a couple of months more. That way, I can cover your paycheck at the end of the week, pay the janitor and the light bill, and hire a new nurse. I should know by next Monday afternoon, if you can wait that long. Please don't quit on me. Let me get this straightened out."

Jessica turned the corner into the empty patient lobby and leaned her head back through the opening over her desk. "Dr. Mack, you're a smart guy. You'll manage somehow. By the way, there are over twenty of those oxycodone pills in Mrs. Roberts's bottle. Do the math. Oh, and you're kinda cute. That counts for something ... at least with your patients."

Scott followed Jessica into the lobby and stood at the glass door entrance. He admired her as she walked to her car—his secretary and office manager and now substitute nurse. Scott knew she felt uncomfortable with parking in the deserted alley out back of the strip mall and preferred the more open area in the front of the building generally reserved for patients. A few feet from her vehicle, Jessica turned and waved. She took out her cell phone and seemed to make a call.

Catching his stare at the young secretary, Scott stepped back a bit from the door before he returned the wave. She was too young for him ... or maybe she wasn't, at least he assumed so when the hospital personnel director hired her.

Scott had requested someone under fifty who would work cheap, and Jessica Kile fit that bill, though under twenty-five. She was of medium build, blonde, and with a complexion attractive enough to skip much makeup. Her chatty, perky, and agreeable personality worked well with patients—the few that remained in his practice.

He watched Jessica's car disappear down the street and secured the door lock. Unlike his secretary, the quiet of the parking spaces in the alley did not bother him. In fact, he preferred the anonymity of the area. The area out back felt safe.

Still standing inside the front door he said, "Hope my entire practice doesn't disappear like those TV ads and the billboards, but I wouldn't be surprised. Jessica wants to be paid just like I do. Maybe I can call a temp service if she doesn't come back after the weekend."

He went to his private office, signed into the computer, and pulled up the office schedule for the following week. Monday had several names scattered throughout the time slots. Tuesday showed a little better. Wednesday had only four patients, Thursday two, and next Friday morning was wide open. "Schedule is so light next week that I can get by without a receptionist, but I'll need a nurse."

Scott shut down the computer and checked his backpack. Inside was his spare shaving and toiletry kit, along with his keys and wallet. He threw the backpack over his shoulder and walked to the rear of the clinic for the exit into the alley.

# Chapter 7

Scott entered the exit code into the keypad of the security alarm system. A series of beeps meant he now had forty-five seconds to make the corner to the rear alley door and out to the parking lot. His car was two spaces from the garbage pick-up bin. Several fifty-gallon, black plastic trash bags lay strewn haphazardly along the side of the dumpster.

A teenage male, about fourteen—maybe fifteen—and dressed in a leather jacket with faded jeans ripped horizontally across the thighs, leaned against the front passenger door of Scott's car. He wore a baseball cap pushed down tight over his scalp with the bill pointed to the back and seemed to be scrolling through his phone. "Hey, man. I thought doctors drove Ferraris or Jaguars or maybe a Porsche," he said. "The name's Jamal."

Scott remembered the handgun kept in the front center console of his car. His back stiffened and his knuckles whitened in a fist as he took a half-step forward. With the fob on his keychain, he could unlock the driver's door remotely and land behind the wheel of his Camry in seconds.

*Damn, my keys are in my backpack.*

"Okay, Jamal. What's up?"

"You Dr. Mack?" Jamal slid the phone into his right rear pocket. "Got a call a few minutes ago from Miss Jessica. I used to be a stock boy for her momma-in-law."

"You talking about my secretary, Jessica Kile?"

"Yeah. She not give you a heads-up about me?"

"No, and I don't see the connection here. Clinic is over for the day. If you need an appointment, you'll need to call ahead and bring an adult with you. Jessica probably explained that to you."

"What she explained is that I can do you a favor, and you can do me a favor," Jamal said. "We both win."

"If you need an appointment, call the office on Monday and Jessica will get you in, same day if you like."

"Doc, I don't need no appointment witchu. Miss Jessica's my friend. She called and said you might want to talk business."

"Look, kid. I don't know you, and my secretary never mentioned anybody by the name of Jamal. I can't see my secretary having anything to do with you or …"

"You not gonna get all uppity with me, are ya, Doc? Like racist or sumthin'?" Jamal's sudden movement to grab his phone from his pocket and resume scrolling startled Scott, and he stepped back a foot or so toward the rear of the building.

"I'm just a poor, young black guy tryin' to make a living," Jamal said.

Darting back into the clinic through the rear door to call the police instead of pushing past this guy to his car was also a problem, since the exit had locked behind him and the key to the building was with his car keys and wallet in the backpack.

On the bright side, this Jamal guy was smaller than he. "Talk straight. What is it that you want here with me?" Scott asked.

"Don't act so uptight. My usual stiffed me. Said he had some Percs but sold 'em to somebody else."

"Percs?" Scott put his hands to his breast and the plastic prescription bottle in his front pocket. He had planned to lock the pills in his desk drawer before he left. "What's going on here?"

Scott reassessed a possible run to the driver's door of his car.

Jamal said, "You got some extra Percs floating around in that office in there. Number 10s, Jessica said. Maybe you still got 'em on you."

Scott jerked his hand away from his shirt and pulled his cell out of his jacket. "I'm gonna call the police right now if you don't get the …"

"Hold on a second, Doc. It's very simple. I'm one of those young

49

businessmen, a street vendor of sorts. You might even call me an entrepreneur. I buy wholesale and sell retail. Some of my buyers get product cheap enough from me to resell for themselves. You'd be surprised what some dudes'll pay for a Perc."

"I still don't know why you're talking to me. I've got to get to the hospital and check on my patients." Scott took a deep breath and moved toward his car. "Get away from my vehicle."

"Hey, man. Miss Jessica said you were a little short on cash right now, somethin' about patient load kinda slim? Said you'd wanna deal with me and unload the Percs. And I need some Xannies, too, if you got 'em."

Scott popped his hand to his chest, cupping the leftover Percocet. "Listen, fella. I'm tellin' you to get outta here."

Jamal pushed away from Scott's car and blocked his path to the vehicle. Jamal stood straight, about a half-foot shorter than Scott. "You got those pills in that pocket right there?"

Scott jerked his hand away and stepped around Jamal. Jamal blocked him again.

"Wait a second, Doc. This ain't no shakedown. Those pills will cover Miss Jessica's salary, easy, and I know you're worried about that," Jamal said. "Jessica says that you're a decent guy, and I can see that. No time to run this through Momma. I got ready cash on me to cover the sale."

Scott checked up and down the alley—no movement, no sound. "I can't sell these meds to you." He lowered his voice to a hush just in case and took another look around. Everything remained quiet. "That's unethical ... as well as illegal."

"Miss Jessica said there's no way that lady will be back for those Percs. She says you need the money, but it's your choice. You gonna make the deal?"

"The patient will remember she left her prescription bottle and be back for them."

"Miss Jessica said that if the lady called back, she would handle it. She would 'splain that she could trade them in."

50

"Trade them in?"

"Doc, you don't understand who you're talkin' to. I'm a big thinker. If the lady shows back up, just tell her she can exchange those leftover meds for your doctor services … or whatever," Jamal said, then grinned. "Or tell her you can forgive her bill in exchange for them pills. Miss Jessica gave the plan a thumbs up."

"I'm not going along with any of this, and you're likely to cause Jessica Kile to lose her job, if not send her to jail."

"Get real, Doc. Jessica Kile's a smart girl. I see a lot of her mom-in-law in her." Jamal produced a roll of twenty-dollar bills. "If those Percs ain't been fixed and can still be melted into I.V., then they can bring up to fifty bucks each. 'Course, pure Roxies would be extra nice."

Scott listened. He knew the street value of what was in his pocket, at least a thousand dollars, more than enough to cover the two-week salary of an overworked secretary in a one-man medical clinic. *Won't need a salary if she's locked up in Parchman,* he decided. *Neither will I.*

Two bars of rap blurted from Jamal's cell phone. He answered, listened for a few seconds, mumbled something, then returned the phone to his back pocket. The weight of the phone tugged at his lax jeans. Bright red boxers rose above the waistband.

"You want to do business, Doc? Seems that time's almost up," Jamal said. "My partner's got a client down at the beach. And my partner ain't patient, neither is the dude that wants to buy."

Scott knew that the margin between red and black for Mack and Associates narrowed every day, and if he did not come up with money soon, there wouldn't be a clinic. Plus, in another two weeks payment on the Camry was due, so was the mortgage payment on his house and one of his med school loans. *Thank God I passed on that BMW convertible.*

"Doc? You listening? If you can't help me move product, then I'm screwed. My partner will be pissed, and that beach dude will walk away."

The sight of the toppling pile of personal and business bills stacked in the tray on his desk dropped in front of Scott like the closing curtain on a play. He slipped his fingers into his pocket and rolled the bottle of pills between them. He remembered another patient from last month who handed him unused pain medication, stating that there were about thirty Xanax tablets left. He immediately returned the pills and instructed her to dispose of them at the pharmacy.

"No telling how much thirty Xannies would bring," Scott mumbled as the curtain suddenly vanished leaving Scott with Jamal.

"You say something, Doc?" Jamal asked. "So, what's it gonna be?"

Scott's brow sweat, and his arm pits felt sticky. A stack of overdue bills waited at home on the kitchen table. For the third time, he checked the alley and parking lot. The hospital had not provided security cameras in his office lease.

His pulse quickened. "How much we talking about? I mean, if we deal right now, how much can you give me, and I never hear from you again."

"Dat's more like it, Doc. This buyer that my partner's got dangling, the guy's very, very impatient—an attorney or something, wants delivery like yesterday. So ... for *right now* I'll give you an extra hundred." Jamal pulled a roll of bills from his jeans pocket and peeled away multiple twenty-dollar bills, then pulled a thick brown paper envelope from inside his jacket and slid the cash inside. He smiled as he gestured to the envelope. "See? Very professional transaction."

Even in the dim light of early evening, Scott noticed the guy's gold-capped front incisor.

"I'm gonna lay this envelope with the cash on the curb here, about halfway between you and me, Doc," Jamal said and stepped forward.

Scott took a half-step back.

Jamal smiled again and dropped the envelope, the gold tooth beaming. "I trusted Miss Jessica when she said you would want to deal. If you trust the nice lady like I do, then you can trust me,

Doc. No need to touch. Gently toss me the bottle of pills and take the envelope in payment."

Scott tossed the pills to Jamal. He expected Jamal to catch the bottle, retrieve the envelope, and run—a better scenario for maintaining his medical license.

Instead, Jamal said, "Doc, you kinda hurt my feelings a second ago. You told me you never wanted to see me again. We gotta trust each other. Take the envelope. I ain't leaving until you pick up your money."

The alley remained still. Scott quickly grabbed the envelope and jammed it into his backpack, finding his car keys. "Now, get outta here," he said.

"Not so fast, Doc." Another young black male appeared from behind one of the heavy plastic waste cans arranged alongside the large metal garbage bin. Dressed in jeans and a baseball cap similar to Jamal, he wore a football jersey with an eagle on the front instead of a T-shirt. He punched a few keys on his cell phone and held it up for Scott to see. Scott could hear his recent exchange with Jamal.

"Hey, what's going on here?" Scott said. He thought again about the gun in the car.

"Relax, Doc. I stretched the facts a bit when I said my business partner was down at the beach. That was my mom on the phone a second ago. Wanted to know what I want for supper." He motioned to the other guy. "This is him, my partner, Immaculate. Friends call him 'Maculate."

"Get lost." Scott pushed Jamal away and unlocked the driver's door.

"You sold pills to Jamal, and it's all on my phone, Dr. Mack," Immaculate said. "Crystal clear video. See, me and Jamal are legit businessmen. We like to keep records."

"You guys forced me, threatened me. My lawyer will …"

"Nobody forced nobody, Doc," Jamal said. "I don't see no weapons 'round here. No knives, no guns—not unless you got one in that backpack or inside that cheap car."

Immaculate increased the volume on the video. To Scott the

sound seemed to echo throughout the alley. "This clip will play sharp on YouTube. I can see it now: lots of thumbs up," he said. "You continue to do business with us, Dr. Mack, and my channel goes dark."

Scott stared at both of them. Sooner or later, there would be some traffic through the alley. He tossed the backpack to the front seat. "Come on, guys," he tried to laugh, spreading his arms out and shrugging his shoulders. "What do you want from me? You want this money back? Here!"

Scott tossed the envelope back to Jamal and slid into the front seat. He started the engine and reached to pull the driver's door shut.

Immaculate jumped forward and blocked the door. "Keep the product coming, or I post this video. I got it set up so there's no way it can be traced to me, but all your patients will drop you and maybe you go to jail, Doc."

Scott's shoulders collapsed. He would try to reason with them—put them off until he could figure this out. Jamal motioned for Immaculate to step aside.

"Man, let me converse with Doc for a sec," Jamal said. He tossed the envelope to the front seat next to Scott and slid a small, white plastic bowl and thin wooden coffee stirrer from inside the other side of his jacket. He held the bowl in one hand and emptied the contents of Scott's pill bottle into the bowl with the other. He pushed each narcotic tablet along the surface with the stirrer, counting and studying. "Very, very nice," Jamal said. "None of those damn marks. We scored big with this shit, 'Maculate."

"Lemme see." Immaculate pushed in to examine closer.

"Hey, careful. Don't spill!" Jamal said. "These will make easy injectables. 'Xactly what our customers want, 'specially those who like I.V. morphine."

Scott glanced around again and lowered his voice. "You're talking about tablets or capsules manufactured so that they stay potent and can't be melted down," Scott said. "They're labeled that way.

54

How do kids like you two know something like that? I learned all that in med school."

Immaculate took the stirrer from Jamal. "Those letters OROS REMS would have been printed tiny, right here." He pointed to one of the blank tablets. "But no letters, so no problem."

"Knowledge is king, Doc," Jamal said. "Essential to the trade."

Scott watched as Jamal poured the Percocet, like jewels, into a clean plastic sack, then sealed it at the top. He tossed the empty prescription bottle toward Scott. Surprised, Scott caught it in mid-air.

"Doc, fill that back up before our next meeting and forget what you learned in med school. Street smarts … what 'Maculate and I can teach you … that's what you need from here on out." He slid the sealed bag with the narcotics into his jacket pocket. "You got your cash, now put it away before some narc walks up on us."

As both Jamal and Immaculate watched, Scott ripped opened the envelope and stuffed the wad of bills into the back pocket of his scrubs.

"There's a good boy," Immaculate said. "We're in for a very productive business relationship."

Scott frowned. He wanted to shoot them the bird, or even spit at them, but only pushed them away from his vehicle. "I don't plan to ever see you two assholes again. And if you come back around here, I'll …"

"You'll do what, Doc?" both Immaculate and Jamal said nearly in unison, each with a wide grin.

Immaculate said, "Like we've been trying to explain to you, Doc. You just sold a narcotic dealer drugs, drugs you stole from a patient, some poor little ol' lady who trusted you. And I got it on video. I may have a rap sheet, but the cops want me on their side. They think I make a badass witness in court."

Scott reached into his pocket and pulled out the money. He crumpled it in his fist.

"Relax," Jamal said. "Hang on to that. You already in this too deep, way too deep. Besides, Miss Jessica done you a big favor. All you need to do is change your prescribing habits. Ramp up your dosage."

"Ramp up my dosage?" There was still no alley traffic, no sight or sound of approaching vehicles or pedestrians. Most of the neighboring businesses were either closed for the day or had gone out of business. Scott spotted a single light burning in the dentist office three doors up toward the main street. He almost wished for a patrol car to end this misery. "What are you talking about?" Scott managed.

"It's simple, Doc. You ramp it up to Percocet 10, instead of five or seven-and-a-half. For example, ninety tablets of Percocet 10 cost some little ol' lady only about ten bucks at her drug store if she has insurance," Jamal said. "But that shit brings me nine hundred on the street. Do the math, and get rid of the weaker stuff."

Immaculate disappeared around the corner and returned in a mid-80s, black Lincoln Town Car with tinted windows and elevated on 28-inch Bentchi wheel rims, the chrome finish highlighted with a circular, gold stripe. "We'll be in touch soon, Doc," Jamal said, walking to the vehicle. "Better yet, get me some straight oxycodone. Get rid of that Tylenol shit, and we'll be the heavy weights around here."

"But I never prescribe OxyContin," Scott said, almost shouting across the alley.

"Wise up, man. You got the power of the pen," Jamal shouted back. "You need to find more patients who need what you can give."

Scott watched the Town Car pass in front of him with front windows lowered. He squeezed the cash in his right hand and pulled the money up to his face, flipping through the bills and counting—until he felt dizzy—more than enough to cover Jessica's two-week secretarial salary and maybe half of the water bill.

Then there was the problem with the other guy's cell phone video, the guy who looked slightly older. Jamal called him 'Maculate. Jamal popped up to sit on the frame of the open window and waved goodbye over the hood.

"Hey, kid. How do I get in touch with you?" Scott stood with one leg out of the car, surprised at himself, tossing the cash on the car seat. This time he had yelled louder.

The car slowed and Jamal smiled. A gold tooth beamed at Scott. "Every Friday, noon sharp," Jamal said. "All you gotta do is supply the stuff behind the scenes. Either you or Miss Jessica meet me with the goods."

Scott trotted after them. "I don't know about this. I'm not a drug dealer. I …"

Immaculate stopped the Town Car. He swung open the door and jumped outside. He stood in the opened door with the motor running. "Don't let me and Jamal down, Doc. Or Miss Jessica. She promised you'd work with us, and she's never let us down before. You wanna keep her safe, don't chu?" He pointed a stiff forefinger at Scott and popped his thumb like a trigger. "Besides, the boss is countin' on it, and nobody disappoints the boss."

Immaculate sprang back in the car and slammed the door shut. The sound of rubber against asphalt reverberated between the brick walls that framed the alley.

Scott ran back to his car and scooped up the dirty tens and twenties. He then leaned across the front seat toward the glove compartment, popped the latch on the door, and tossed the cash inside. He snapped the glove compartment shut and settled into the driver's seat before reaching with his left hand to shut the door.

"Dr. Mack? Those thugs try to hold you up? Need me to call the police?" A woman in her late forties stood in the opened driver's door. Scott recognized her as the office manager of the dental office nearby and felt the color drain from his face. Her skin tanned or sprayed burnt orange, the woman stood about five feet and dressed in snug, flowery Capri pants with white slip-on shoes. She carried a clutch purse. Her muddy green-blonde hair was shoulder length, and she smelled of stale cigarette smoke.

"No, they were lost. Just asking directions." Scott noticed the drug dealers' vehicle slow at the corner from the alley even though no traffic passed ahead on the main street. The brake lights turned red for a couple of seconds, and through the rear window he detected movement.

The woman stayed put.

"Can I help you with something?" he asked her.

The brake lights went dark on the Lincoln. It did not move.

"No, I just came out for a smoke. Dr. Roland left an hour ago," the office manager said. "The last patient, a junior high kid, finally got a ride home. And from my office window, I saw those two guys approach your car. I almost called out but …"

"That wouldn't have been good. I mean, it's okay. Everything's okay," Scott said.

She seemed interested in the closed glove compartment. "I noticed the cash. Your girl doesn't run to the bank for you? Fill out your deposit slips?"

Scott started the engine. "I gotta head on over to the hospital. Need to make rounds."

"I wouldn't leave all that cash in the car," she said, stepping nearer. "You know, Dr. Roland is a great dentist and all, but he's getting near retirement, and I need to work at least fifteen more years. So, if your girl at the front desk isn't working out, let me know. Name's Pam, Pam Bullock."

Bullock extended a weak hand, and Scott ignored it. He pulled gently at the door handle, and she backed away a few inches.

"You know, I spotted that girl who works for you … a blonde, I think … talking to those two guys out here a few days ago. I'd be careful if I were you, Dr. Mack."

Scott put his Camry in gear and watched the drug dealers ease slowly around the corner and disappear. He searched for something to say; he needed to get away from this woman. "Great to see you, but gotta run," Scott said. "And, Ms. Bullock, tell Dr. Roland if he has any dental patients with bum shoulders or bad knees to send 'em my way."

Pam Bullock backed away from the vehicle, far enough to keep her sandaled toes out of the tire path. Before Scott could shut the door, she said, "Don't ignore this situation, and be careful carrying that cash around with you, Dr. Mack." She produced a cigarette lighter and a pack of cigarettes from the compact purse and tapped one loose. "Those two guys out here in the alley ... I know I've seen them around here before. I mean, who could forget those wheels." She lit the cigarette and exhaled. "Those guys are up to no good."

Bullock released a plume of smoke from the corner of her mouth as Scott drove away.

# Chapter 8

Instead of turning north toward Interstate 10 and the grocery store inside Walmart, Jessica Kile continued west on Highway 90. If she knew she could count on Dr. Mack to deal with the Davis brothers and cover her two-week salary, there would be plenty for groceries and toilet paper and cleaning supplies and the flowers she had planned to plant by the back door of her house. Instead, Dr. Mack would probably kick Jamal in the teeth and call the police, then fire her on Monday—or maybe over the weekend.

She hated to lower herself to her mother-in-law's standards, but that beat pity or charity. Her husband and toddler son expected food on the table—so did she.

"A girl has to do what she has to do, but I sure hope Dr. Mack doesn't let me go," she said, pushing the door open to Kile's Minute Mart, which to the public appeared a tight, legitimate family business on Highway 90. "And I hope Momma don't wring my neck over what I've done ... or worse."

A grey-haired woman in her late fifties with a dark cast over her upper lip and several side teeth missing stood behind the cash register. About four or five inches taller than Jessica, her stance along with the broad shoulders fostered a commanding presence inside the establishment. Jessica's mother-in-law slid the money into the cash register from the sale of a pack of Marlboro Reds. "Thank you, sir. Check back with us the next time you come through here. We appreciate your business."

"Momma Kile?" Jessica said. She pushed through the waist high,

60

hinged barrier to the inside of the sales area. "You told me to come to you if I needed to talk or needed anything."

Even at Momma's height, it was a stretch to rearrange and replenish the packs of cigarettes in the wire rack above the counter and cash register. After that last sale, the display ran low. Momma Kile hated things to be in disarray. She held a few left-over packs of cigarettes from the restock carton in her left hand. She stacked them beside the cash register.

"Dr. Mack didn't have enough to pay me this week, and Brandon doesn't get paid until the end of the month," Jessica said in her best downcast tone. "I'll need to pay for BJ's daycare on Monday, and I need to go to the grocery store bad."

"I thought you had a good job with the new doctor," Momma Kile said.

"That big hospital recruited Dr. Mack down here and then hired me and a nurse to work for him. Now …" She added an exaggerated sigh. "They aren't paying his expenses anymore. I hope something's gonna work out for Dr. Mack, but I'm not feeling so good about it now."

"I told you that you could leave Billy Jack here with me at the store during the day," Momma Kile said. "You'd save no telling how much from that ritzy daycare." She stepped a few feet to the right to a heated unit of glass shelves stocked with slices of pizza and ran her eyes up and down at the selection. She grabbed a flat, metal spatula from the lowest shelf and rearranged the pizza to cover the space left by a recent sale. The oil company truck driver who delivered gasoline for her pumps always bought pizza.

"The money they charge at Happy Tots is worth it," Jessica said. "The teachers spend lots of one-on-one time with the kids. They promised that BJ would be reading before he made it to kindergarten. Besides, you're too busy around here to watch a toddler." Jessica turned to the back of the convenience store and the restrooms past the coffee. "I need to use the ladies' room before I go pick him up."

She noticed the only customer in the store was a twelve-year-old boy thumbing through the magazine rack. "Aren't you supposed to keep the smut behind the counter?" Jessica laughed.

Momma Kile grunted and walked back and forth behind the register, stretching her neck to survey the entire store. "Hey, kid," she said. Her thunderous voice easily reached the rear of the space. The boy looked up, startled, but smiling. "Either pay for that magazine or get the hell outta here," Momma said.

The boy threw the magazine to the floor and ran toward the front door exit of the convenience store. It landed open at the centerfold and hard against a short stack of miniature, six-pack carbonated beverages offered at *2 for $5*. The six-pack at the top toppled to the floor, breaking apart as the string of metal bells draped from the door handle clanged against the glass. "It's that kinda stuff that makes me want to retire and sell this place someday," Momma Kile said. "But I'd miss the side business."

"I'll straighten that up on my way back from the restroom." In a few minutes Jessica returned to the register area after tidying up the magazine and soda display. She hesitated for a few seconds. "Just curious, but did that cigarette customer purchase anything else?"

"He kinda hinted at it, like he knew I peddled dope, but I'm low on stock and didn't take the bait. Besides, I ain't never seen him in here before and can't be too careful."

A few seconds of quiet passed. Jessica decided to stay mum about her calling Jamal and Immaculate to approach Dr. Mack. It would have been easy for her to bring the unused pills directly to the store for resale. But she needed a quick trial run to see if Dr. Mack would go for the idea, and who better to explain the business than those two guys. If Dr. Mack came on board, then she could increase the supply for the store from the clinic patients, and her mother-in-law would be happy.

However, it all depended on Dr. Mack … or maybe it didn't.

"Hold onto this place for now," Jessica said. "I'm trying to work out something with my boss."

A tall, heavy-set man in a tailored, navy suit with thin white stripes pushed through the double front doors. His starched white shirt and silk necktie in a Windsor knot coordinated well with the jacket, whose buttons strained at his midsection. The tie was a yellow background design with tiny, light blue spots, and he wore a plain white pocket square. The bells at the front entrance clanked against the swinging doors behind him.

Momma Kile wiped away the pizza crumbs from her fingers using her apron. "Mr. Foshee, nice to see you. The usual?"

He looked over his shoulder at the young white woman standing to the edge of the sales counter. The hair bun she wore matched that of Mrs. Kile, only blonde.

"Never mind Jessica, here. She's family, my daughter-in-law."

"Okay," Coleman said. A bright white smile diverted attention from the more prominent crow's feet at the corner of his deep brown eyes. "A pack of Newport, please."

Momma Kile reached for the pack of cigarettes and tossed them into her left hand, while her right disappeared under the counter. She produced a small brown envelope and slid both packages to him, the cigarettes on top.

Another smile, this time directly at Jessica. "Your momma-in-law hasn't raised the prices again, I hope." He handed Mrs. Kile a thin roll of bills from inside the front pocket of his pants.

"Nope, Mr. Foshee," Momma answered. "Cigarette prices remain the same so far, even if supplies are low." She removed the rubber band and counted. "This works just fine—new bills. You don't make these yourself, do you?" Her smile spread just as wide as his, but the remaining teeth a light shade of gray.

"You kiddin'? Break the law?" he said.

"Maybe I should be going," Jessica said. She checked the time on her iPhone. "If I'm late picking up BJ, they charge extra."

"Mr. Foshee … I mean, Colonel Foshee … is one of my best customers. Comes by on Fridays, late afternoon."

The man scrutinized the empty store. "Do you work here sometimes, Miss? Jessica—is that right?"

"No, sir. I work for Dr. Scott Mack."

Foshee slid the envelope inside his jacket and tore open the pack of cigarettes. "Seems quiet in here. All right if I sample the product, the cigarettes, that is?"

Momma tossed him a book of matches from the counter display. "On the house," she said.

Colonel Foshee lit a Newport and tapped some keys on his cell phone. "I don't think I've heard of Dr. Scott Mack, and my sister is a neurosurgeon. Is Mack new to the Coast?"

"Been practicing over a year. He'll pop up there on your phone, when you Google him," Momma Kile answered. "And Jessica's been his secretary the whole time, tells me she practically runs the place."

Foshee ran his finger over the screen. "Yep, website says he's in orthopedics. Office is located in that strip mall down 90. Not all that far from here," he said.

"Jessica just told me that Biloxi Memorial lured Dr. Mack down here to Mississippi with a big salary and then cut his knees out from under him."

"Momma Kile, you weren't supposed to repeat that!" Jessica said.

"Don't worry. I'm an attorney, retired military," Foshee said, exhaling cigarette smoke from his nostrils and mouth in a dense cloud. "I work for the U.S. government. I don't talk."

Jessica took a few steps toward the door. "I know I don't need a lawyer, Colonel Foshee, but Dr. Mack probably will, sooner or later."

"Let me know if I can be of service. I've got connections and do work on the side. Like I said … everything's confidential with my clients and other people I do business with."

"Likewise," Momma Kile said.

Jessica forced a half-smile. "I've gotta get BJ. You good here, Momma?"

Kile nodded.

"Nice to meet you, sir." Jessica pushed against the door with an extended arm, just enough to ring the short string of bells at the top corner.

"Orthopedic surgeons write a lot of narcotic prescriptions, Jessica," Foshee called out to her. "And I'm sure your Dr. Mack is no exception."

Jessica turned in the direction of the checkout counter and let the door pop closed behind her.

"Problem is, Dr. Mack used to see a whole lot more patients when we ... when he ... first opened the clinic. Maybe I shouldn't tell this, but the hospital decided to quit paying Dr. Mack when his surgical and patient numbers fell off, and the patients that do come to see us don't half-pay their bills."

"And I bet Jessica ain't much at bill collecting," Momma Kile said. "A young, cute blonde, five-two, ain't much of a heavyweight."

"Smarts can make up for a lot of things," Foshee said. He continued to draw heavily on the cigarette and blew dense smoke in the direction of the chips and crackers section. "No doubt, Jessica, your Dr. Mack is an excellent surgeon."

He waited for a nod.

Jessica only stared back at him.

"However, if the medical profession is anything like the legal profession, there's a lot of competition out there. Maybe not a doctor on every corner like the situation with us lawyers, but it's all about the marketing."

Some of the cigarette plume drifted in her direction, and Jessica waved it away.

Momma Kile straightened a few of the display racks. A man and a young girl rushed into the store and headed toward the hotdog rotisserie case along the back wall.

"I'm sorry, Mr. Foshee—Colonel Foshee," Jessica lowered her voice, "but Dr. Mack laughs about all those billboards with the lawyers smiling down at the highway. I don't think I've seen one with you on it."

"And you're not likely to," he said. "No need to advertise when you have, as I mentioned, your own governmental clientele and built-in consultation referrals on the side."

The man and girl approached checkout. Colonel Foshee stepped to the side. The man paid in cash, and Momma made change. Mustard dripped at the corner of the girl's mouth.

"Thanks for shopping with us!" Momma Kile called out as the two left. She snapped closed the cash register drawer. "Jessica, honey. The Colonel knows the situation around here. You said before he came in that you might be able to work out something with the doctor you work for. Dr. Mack could probably help me keep frequent customers like Colonel Foshee happy."

Foshee nodded in agreement and drew the last of his cigarette.

From under the counter, it was an ashtray this time. Momma slid it to him, and Foshee crushed the butt inside. "And along the way, you and I might be able to help Dr. Mack," she said.

"I've got to pick up BJ," Jessica said.

"Ask Dr. Scott Mack to give me a call if he ever needs anything." Colonel Foshee flipped opened his wallet and handed Jessica a business card. "Everybody wins when I work with them."

A narrow, gold-printed border framed the edge of the business card. The photograph in the right upper corner depicted a several-year younger version of Lieutenant Colonel Coleman Foshee, grinning like the other attorneys Jessica mentioned from the billboards and the ones she had seen on TV commercials. She flipped the business card to the back. Foshee's skill in military discharge upgrades, military divorces, correction of military records, and navigating V.A. benefits were listed among others. She flipped back to the front. His name with credentials, a cell phone number, and an email address were centered in thick black ink. Raised, gold lettering in heavier font read from left to right at the bottom: *Call a lawyer who cares.*

"Your Dr. Mack may think that the power of the scalpel will make his career, but I think I can show him that it's the power of the pen. Good day, Mrs. Kile and daughter-in-law, Jessica," Foshee said, pushing past Jessica toward the front door. "You have my number."

The clanging door shut behind him. "You know what he meant by the 'power of the pen', don't you, Jessica?"

66

"Prescriptions," Jessica answered. *Gosh, this guy and Momma Kile are a step ahead of me.*

She and Momma Kile moved to the window near the cash register and watched as a chauffeur in a dark uniform and tie opened the rear door of a black Lincoln. Attorney Foshee stepped inside, and the vehicle disappeared.

"Momma, I need to talk to you about Jamal and Immaculate," Jessica said and lowered her head.

# Chapter 9

Daylight saving time meant another hour before nightfall, another optional hour of extended daycare for BJ. *I shouldn't have wasted all that time at the convenience store with Momma Kile and the attorney in the big car,* Jessica decided. *Anyway, I'll have to cut out daycare after Dr. Mack fires me—no way to pay for it.*

She took the first visitor parking spot in front of the Gulfport Coast Guard Station. The shadow of palm trees draped the concrete parking lot, just missing Jessica's Chevrolet Spark. Located off Bert Jones Yacht Harbor and not geographically within the Port of Gulfport, the property still received a share of the leftover ocean breeze. When Jessica spotted Brandon, she released the clip on her hair and let it fall gently off her shoulders. The air lifted it a bit as she walked toward her husband and balanced BJ on her hip.

"Hey, how's my future soccer player?" Brandon greeted BJ with a leg rub, then pecked Jessica on the cheek.

Jessica never grew tired of her husband in uniform. She liked the military guise, and the Coast Guard look was good enough. "Did you get off early?" she asked.

"Yeah," Brandon said. "We had Chuck's retirement party over at the Yacht Club this afternoon. Can you believe it? Forty years with the Coast Guard."

The light gulf breeze was no match for her husband's thick, wavy dark hair. He stood six feet—ten inches taller than Jessica—but appeared even taller in the uniform. "I wish the Guard would give you a raise instead of having so many parties," she said.

"You know we ain't had nothing since the Christmas party, 'cept at New Year's," Brandon said. "I guess you gotta count the Super Bowl."

Jessica took in the view of the bay and hoisted BJ up for Brandon to hold. "How long do you think you'll stay with the Coast Guard?"

He lifted the child high above his head and smiled up into his face. "Don't have much choice, Jess. Not much out there otherwise—at least, upfront."

"You need a raise. We got to have more cash coming in." Jessica rubbed the little boy's shoe. She thought about Dr. Mack and the earlier exchange at her mother-in-law's convenience store.

"I'm workin' on it," Brandon said. He bounced BJ on his shoulders. "Chuck finished out big this morning … way before daybreak. Great score to end his career. There's room for me now."

Brandon held the child above his head and spun him around with legs extended like rotating helicopter blades. "Chuck's team intercepted a big-ass haul of weed. Some Mexicans in a forty-foot yacht, moving product from Florida to Texas. They had it stuffed all over the boat: inside mattresses in the sleep quarters, some down in the space left in the bilge, and even around the engine. Don't know how the damn vessel didn't catch fire with all that weed."

"Did Chuck get a bonus for that?"

"It don't work that way," Brandon answered. "If it's illegal cargo, we're supposed to shut it down and apprehend the smugglers, Mexicans or whoever. Lots of pot coming through here. Problem is, I might be out of a job soon."

Brandon spotted Jessica's car and headed toward it with BJ on his back.

Jessica stood for a few seconds and watched them. "Whaddya mean, *out of a job?*"

"If those crazies in D.C. get their way and legalize pot and other shit like that, the Guard's screwed—stuck with running gas cans out to every a-hole who ain't got sense enough to fill up the tank on their boat or get out of the way of a storm."

"You and I can't both lose our jobs," Jessica muttered.

"You say something, Babe?" Brandon asked over his shoulder past BJ. "Let me buckle this fullback in his car seat, and I'll meet you back at the house."

Jessica caught up with them at her car. "I was saying ... that I might need to be searching for a new ..."

Brandon finished securing his son in the car seat and lifted his head out of the backseat area. "Will it take long to get supper started?" he asked, opening the driver's door for his wife. "I'm done with Chuck's celebration and ready to celebrate at home with you." He reached down and patted Jessica on the rear.

Several other officers who worked with Brandon spilled out of the front of the building, most laughing, a few stumbling on the pavement. Chuck's name could be heard among the revelry, with profane references to his Christmas escapade on the couch with a secretary at a party ten years ago.

"Just listen to the news," Brandon said as Jessica settled into the car. "Pretty soon weed will be legal everywhere. The price will drop—cheap as a pack of gum. Smuggling pot will go away—no arrests, no confiscations. No money to make on the side selling the stuff."

"You think that'll really happen?"

"It will ... if the liberal commies get their way."

Jessica buckled her seat belt and started the car engine. "But they smuggle other stuff in those boats, don't they?" She lowered her voice. BJ was already asleep. "Pills and ... stuff like that?"

"Yeah, coke and pills ... even women and kids. But that crap is big league stuff, risky. Flipping confiscated pot is a piece of cake. But if they cut our funding, the officers with no seniority like me will be the first to go. I'll lose more than my lousy Coast Guard salary."

"Maybe your mom can help us through this, and you won't have to take so many chances out there on the water. I think I've got another source for her."

Brandon eased the door shut to the backseat and his sleeping son and gently shut Jessica's door. "My momma is right where she belongs—in the minor leagues. All she's done her whole life besides smoking cigs is stand behind a counter and push buttons on a cash register."

"You'd be surprised what Momma Kile can do." Jessica leaned her head through the window and motioned for her husband to bend down for a kiss.

It lasted longer than expected.

"What's that for?" Brandon said. "A teaser for tonight?" He ran his hands down the front of her blouse to the button at the top of her skirt.

Jessica removed his hand, straightened her blouse and skirt, and put the car in gear. She glanced back at BJ, all quiet in the car seat. "Some girls don't like who they got for a mother-in-law, but mine is special."

# Chapter 10

A black cloud hung over the Emergency Department of Biloxi Memorial every week about this time. It was 10:00 PM Friday, five hours and counting into the weekend and its constant stream of traffic through the emergency entrance. The automatic door slid closed behind the most recent delivery from the ambulance service.

"Are you sure you can't come in and work the eleven-p, even for three or four hours? You'll get double-time," the nursing director said into the phone at the check-in desk, her fifth call down the list of nurses who worked other shifts. Her patience already thin, she had earlier phoned the unit secretary after his third, un-excused no-show for work and fired him. His failure to answer his cell was no surprise, so she left a voicemail: "Turn in your employee badge to HR and clean out your personal locker, then you'll get your final paycheck."

"Okay, okay, your I.V. is in. No more needles," Dr. Scott Mack said in the first patient treatment bay located to the left of the entrance to the Emergency Department and about twelve feet from the check-in desk. The nursing director remained busy on the phone and computer.

"You promise, Doc?"

"Yes, I do. At least for now." In the absence of an available nurse or physician assistant, Scott had once again recalled his medical school and surgical intern skills and started the elderly man's intravenous fluids. Demographic information in the computer placed the patient's age at seventy-eight. Scott checked the bag of Lactated Ringer's that seemed to flow smoothly through the tubing connected to the man's forearm. He pushed the controls on the infusion pump and slowed the I.V. rate. Over the last two hours he had started several other I.V. lines, managed clerical work entering additional medical history into computers, taken his own patient vital signs, and pulled his own supplies from the storeroom to dress wounds.

"MVA in Bay 6," erupted over the loudspeaker. The same in text popped up on his iPhone. "Sir, you're gonna be fine," Scott smiled at the man. "X-ray says your ankle is only a sprain, and so far, we see no internal injuries. You're lucky … but I hear your truck didn't come out nearly as good."

"It's okay, Doc," the man said. "My kids told me to stop driving that pick-up over four years ago. Seems like they finally got their damn wish."

Scott looked around the E.D. No family in sight. "You needed these fluids. You've been waiting so long in here, you're dehydrated," he said. "We've got to monitor you for a couple of more hours and wait for a few more blood tests to come back. A nurse will check up on you in a sec, and a nice lady from Social Work will be by. She'll arrange for your discharge."

"I ain't no charity case, Doc."

"No one said you were, sir." Scott again checked outside the patient bay—no one headed his way, no one else seemed interested in helping the man or him. "But we'll need to make arrangements to get you home or to a shelter somewhere before we let you—"

"I'll take over here, Dr. Mack." The triage nurse stepped next to Scott. "If they're paying me double my nursing salary to cover another hospital shift and handle the patient flow around here, then I might as well help out hands-on. And the way things are going for me with my clinic day job, I'm likely to need the money."

"Know what you mean," Scott said and stood from the stool beside the man's bed. Her name tag read: Betty Thibodeaux, RN, BSN. He set the remainder of the roll of adhesive tape on top of the I.V. control box.

"I guess you got the text," the triage nurse said, "about the new admission a few beds over. Some thirty-year-old accountant split his new Acura in two with a light pole somewhere between Gulfport and Biloxi."

"Thanks," Scott said. He patted the elderly man on the shoulder. "This nice lady, Nurse Thibodeaux, will take over from here and get you all fixed up."

"I ain't goin' to no homeless shelter or to the damn looney bin, Doc." The man jerked away from Scott and pulled himself up the best he could toward the opposite side of the bed. He clung to the railing. "And get this damn Florence Nightingale away from me."

Betty Thibodeaux pulled a syringe from her front pocket. "I was anticipating this. We've got a standing order for Vistaril, sir. You need to settle down." She reached for the medication port in the intravenous tubing and began to inject the sedative. "When you settle down a bit, we'll talk about what's next."

Scott took a deep breath and stepped away.

"The MVA is waiting for you in Bay 6, Dr. Mack," Betty said, "but stay out of his face. The guy's breath will knock you to the floor." The triage nurse seemed pleased when the last of the Vistaril diluted in intravenous fluids reached the old man. He released his hold on the bedrail and slowly slid onto the sheet.

"I already ordered your films, Dr. Mack," she said.

It was now almost eleven PM. Scott brushed by the police officer who waited to interview the accident victim in Bay 6 and checked the patient's leg splint put in place by the EMTs for stability. He pulled up the preliminary images from the radiology department using the bedside monitor.

"Doc, I'd say this fella overstayed his welcome at happy hour." The officer continued to scribble on a citation pad as he spoke. "Good thing he didn't hit no other vehicle after he left the yacht club or run over a pedestrian. We got more and more homeless strolling along 90."

Scott shook his head at the computer while studying the male patient's oblique femoral shaft fracture. The EMT notes indicated a skin puncture as a result of the shattered bone, classifying the wound as a compound fracture.

"Yep, sad situation, for everybody," Scott said. "I'll be taking this patient to surgery to fix that leg as soon as an O.R. opens up." He lowered his eyes briefly to the policeman's I.D. badge and further regretted the evening's interaction with the two guys in the alley. He had locked the money in the trunk of his car.

Scott shifted his feet and wondered if he carried the same air of guilt now as earlier with the dental practice administrator.

"The state mandates a toxicology screen in cases like this. It's protocol," the officer said.

"What? Oh, yeah. Sure. That's right," Scott shook off his last sight of the mid-eighties Lincoln Town Car slowing down before it left the alley. He scrolled through the pages of patient information on the computer. "I see it right here. Says: TOXICOLOGY RESULTS PENDING. Officer, I'm sure the judge will get whatever records he or she needs."

"Hey, you the doctor?" the young male accountant jerked the oxygen mask away and struggled to speak. The voice was slurred, and the smell of alcohol permeated the cramped area. "The guysh in the ambulanshus shaid my leg wash broken."

Scott turned away and took a deep breath of fresher air. "Yep, from the looks of your X-rays, it seems the guys in the ambulance know their stuff," Scott said. He scrolled through the additional patient information available on the computer. "You seem to be in pretty good health, but you're going to need surgery. We need to place a metal rod to stabilize the bone so that it will heal properly."

The accountant's eyes widened.

Scott continued. "There's always risks to these procedures. Like if the bone doesn't heal well or if infection develops with the rod in place. You could even get a blood clot in your lung and not make it home." The patient's cardiac monitor beeped faster. "The procedure you need and your recovery are a little more complicated because the bone tore through your muscle and skin."

75

The accountant forced a deep breath. "I'm sure you're aweshome, Doc, but Dr. Cahston'sh been my ortho before."

The patrolman listened in the hall, just outside the patient treatment bay. He stepped back inside and said, "Isn't that the guy they arrested for narcotic—"

"Dr. Caston's not on call. I am," Scott interrupted. "So, do you agree to let me proceed with the surgery, understanding the benefits and risks? If you're okay with the plan, I've got one of the Coast's finest right here to witness for me."

The highway patrolman half-grinned.

"Do whatever you gotta do, Doc. I got good insuranshish, and I understand what you're shaying. I jusht don't want it to hurt. When I broke my arm in college, Dr. Cahston never let me hurt. He gave me plenty of pillsh."

Scott stepped back from the patient and turned to face the officer. The overhead lighting caught the gold tint of the patrolman's badge and the series of recognition buttons that lined his lapel. The reflection nearly blinded Scott. "From what he's had already, you got to think that this poor fella is feeling no pain at the present. Finish up with what you got to do. We need to get this man's leg fixed before sepsis sets in."

The patrolman jerked to attention. "Yes, sir. Whatever you say. I've called everything in, and I've got a copy of his driver's license. He'll get notice of the traffic violation in the mail with a court date and number he can call."

The nurse reappeared. Thibideaux was about five-ten, maybe eleven. Her wide shoulders and thick forearms bettered Scott. The tips of the lapel and the sleeves of her white coat were yellow-tinged. "Some fifty-year-old chick twisted her motorcycle around a street light near Mary Mahoney's," she said. "I think she's a literature teacher at one of the junior colleges. They're putting her in Four. Your cell phone's going to light up in a sec about it."

From where Scott now stood, he could hear the automatic sliding doors at the entrance to the Emergency Department open and snap shut and observe the commotion spanning the area. Although there was a near miss or two, attendants pushed stretchers loaded with human beings of all sizes past one another without collision. Bags of intravenous fluid dangled from the metal poles of the gurneys as they came from all corners. Nurses continued to talk into landline telephones at the manager's station and type information into computers, and lab technicians carried little white trays of syringes and blood samples.

Scott said, "This place needs more than just me. I don't get paid enough to sort all this out."

"Know what you mean, but I need this hospital work to fall back on," Betty winked. "Since both the teacher and that drunk accountant back there subscribe to the hospital's PPO, the facility is gonna get paid, and that's bound to help you and me."

"The ones that come out on top are the suits that run this place. They get the promotions and the bonuses," Scott said. The screen on his cell phone lit up. The text announced the new patient in Bay 4. Scott shook his head at the beehive of commotion in the center of the E.D. The nurse manager at the desk shot him a thumbs up, then texted him a modification of the smiley emoji, the one with the frantic expression and shedding tears.

Scott pushed through the curtain into Bay 4. The literature teacher wore a tight black-and-gold bandanna imprinted with a prominent New Orleans Saints fleur-de-lis symbol. Streaks of blood stained the sides of the head covering. Thin plastic prongs attached to tubing seemed to pinch the woman's nose but were taped in place nonetheless to allow oxygen to flow from a metal plate on the wall. Scott noticed a superficial laceration about three centimeters long on her right hand and left unattended—but she had more pressing issues.

An I.V. ran in the opposite forearm. He touched the injured hand—no movement in response. Normal sinus cardiac rhythm flashed across the monitor adjacent to the patient's bed. A steady beeping sound matched each burst of white light running across the black screen. The woman's normal blood pressure and oxygen saturation numbers supported a stable medical condition. *The EMTs must have loaded her up with Dilaudid on the way here*, Scott thought. *But she'll need a head CT.*

He checked the woman's arm splints. The text message reported a suspected open fracture of the left arm and dislocated shoulder, possibly more. Orthopedic supports were properly in place, and additional notes documented that the shoulder dislocation had been resolved. *One of the EMTs must want to be a hero.*

Scott entered nursing and lab orders into the small computer on the bedside stand. "She'll need arthroscopy when I set this arm," he said.

"Do whatever she needs." Betty stood behind him. "Like I said, at least this chick has some health insurance coverage like that accountant in the other bay. By the way, surgery called and said that they'll be sending for him in about thirty minutes. They told me to let you know."

"Okay, Nurse Betty." Scott continued to type on the keyboard to complete his patient assessment. "The hospital is going to treat these acute patients no matter their ability to pay. It's the law," he said. "Besides, why do you care? You get your check one way or the other."

"My day job with Dr. Caston may playout soon. I guess you keep up with the news … at least the gossip in the medical community," she said and checked the volume of urine in the Foley bag. It was blood tinged. "Caston and I have been a team for quite a while."

Scott clicked SUBMIT and started a page of orders for the Imaging Department. "I heard Caston beat that rap in court, so you're safe, and he will keep his patients and big house and nice cars. But my measly bank account? That's another story," Scott said.

His back remained to the nurse, and he sensed that she had moved away. "But maybe if Biloxi Memorial would send me a better payor mix, I wouldn't need Jamal or his sidekick."

"You say something else, Dr. Mack?" Betty asked. "And who's Jamal?" She had returned with a disinfectant and antiseptic, along with antibiotic ointment, steri-strips, gauze, and surgical tape to dress the minor wound on the woman's hand.

"He's just some kid," Scott answered.

A gurney moved slowly behind them driven by two male attendants headed to the Imaging Department. The patient in transport likely weighed over 300 pounds.

"Hey, Dr. Mack," one of the attendants driving the gurney called to Scott. "Radiologist says the drunk guy from the one-car accident messed up his femur pretty bad. Broke in three places."

"Got it, Lamar," Scott said. "Surgery just called pre-op. I'm pulling up the reports now." Digital images of the accountant's lower extremities populated the screen. Scott noted the knee involvement. "Knee's messed up too. He'll need two procedures."

Scott smiled at Betty. "Nice job dressing that hand wound." The literature teacher remained asleep. She had started to snore.

"Thanks," Betty said, applying the last piece of surgical tape.

"Have you seen any family with that guy Lamar was talking about? I need to go over some things, make sure we've got adequate consent since he's inebriated."

"Good idea. Tonight's E.D. physician coverage is locum tenens, some young kid from up north somewhere, maybe New York," Betty said. "Right off the bat he pulled the trigger and loaded up that rowdy guy with morphine—even before we had a chance to get consents and complete all the paperwork, much less call ortho."

Scott pulled up another file on the computer and scrolled through the thirty-year-old male accountant's past medical history. The Social History section included a stint in rehab for narcotic addiction in Hattiesburg, Mississippi, located just over an hour or so away. "Did the morphine take him down pretty quick?"

"The order was for four milligrams IV, but I only gave him two. His wife got mad when she figured out what I was doing. She didn't want me to give him any pain meds."

"Wife was nowhere around when I talked to him," Scott said.

"She stormed off—said something about going straight to

hospital administration. But the patient didn't seem to care what she did … or said."

"She assumed he'd get hooked again," Scott said. "Problem is, from the smell of things and from the lab reports, he replaced narcotics with alcohol."

The entrance doors to the department again swung open and a couple of other doctors rushed through. Scott recognized them as obstetricians. The sound of an ambulance siren approached through the space, then muffled as the doors closed. The dispatcher at the desk took information over the phone.

"Oh hell," Betty said, checking the text on her phone. "There's a patient in labor coming in. EMT says it's twins, and Baby A is breech. The girl is completely dilated. I knew better than to agree to work during a full moon."

"Tell those two OB docs not to go up to L&D until the ambulance arrives," Scott said. "I haven't delivered a baby since my third year in medical school."

The nurse turned toward the glass-lined front to the Emergency Department. Oscillating red lights draped the entrance. She would soon learn that another ambulance transporting the victim of an acute myocardial infarction was not far behind. "The OB patient is here," she said. "There's a precip pan in the storage bin. I better get it."

She hurried across to the other side of the Emergency Department as the EMTs rushed the screaming pregnant patient to the designated elevator for the labor and delivery unit. When the elevators closed and the screaming ceased, Betty stepped back to Dr. Mack, still at the computer. "Wow, lucky we dodged that bullet," she said.

Scott nodded and rolled his eyes. "I tackled the medical record on the accountant. Judging from the date of that guy's rehab and if he's been clean until now, getting high at the bar would have been easy and quick," he said. "Any drug to bring him down would have hit hard too."

"I tried to explain that to the wife," Betty said. "She was crying—said they couldn't afford another stint in rehab."

Scott felt the phone vibrate in his pocket. The text was from the O.R.

`Ready in 15 with the femur fracture.`

"Any guess where the wife is?" Scott asked.

"Try the waiting room. And then there's always her cell, if she left her number," Betty said.

Scott found a Caucasian woman sitting alone in the far corner of the waiting room assigned to the Emergency Department. The vending machines stood on the other side of the room. She was staring into her smartphone, her fingers tapping wildly on the display. A purse lay turned on its side next to her chair.

"Mrs. Walker?"

"Yes?" she answered, startled. The phone dropped to the linoleum floor and slid against her purse.

"Sorry," Scott said, and retrieved the phone, then handed it back to her.

She examined the screen for damage and pressed it unharmed into her lap. "That's okay. Are you from the emergency room?"

"I'm Dr. Scott Mack. I'm the orthopedic surgeon covering the Emergency Department tonight, and I'm assigned to your husband's case."

"The last time I saw Bob he was out cold," Mrs. Walker said. "He was barely breathing after that rude nurse shoved that shitty medicine into his veins. The beeping from the monitor by his bed was the only way I knew he was still alive." She picked up her phone and resumed tapping her fingers across the screen. "Sorry, Doctor, but I've gotten addicted to this Bubble Witch game." A dull thud erupted from the phone's speaker. "Screw that! I picked wrong." She tossed her phone face down in her lap, disgusted.

Scott raised his eyebrows a bit, paused a second or two, and said, "I need to give you an update on your husband's condition."

She checked the phone again and dropped it in her purse.

"I'm sorry about your husband's car accident, but he does need surgery. You've already signed consents, and Mr. Walker is in the holding area up in O.R.," Scott said. "There's a knee injury plus a fractured femur, and he'll need rehab post-op."

"Rehab? Ha! I know all about rehab—the other kind." She picked up her phone, swiped up on the screen, and resumed play, shaking her head. "I can't go through that again."

"Your husband's overall medical condition is stable. The knee injury dictates the rehab, but I've taken care of these types of injuries many times before. He's young and should do well and is very lucky that are no abdominal or neurological injuries. We'll keep him comfortable," Scott said.

"His condition is stable?" she mocked. "He's lucky? And you're going to keep him comfortable?" She started to cry. "What you're not saying is that you're going to poison my husband with more drugs."

"We … I'm … aware of his addiction history. We'll give him only the anesthesia and post-op narcotics required. There are protocols to manage these situations."

"We can't—*I can't*—take another one of his stints in drug rehab. I'm fed up with family therapy sessions. I'm fed up with being blamed for being a rotten girlfriend and wife. Every time he goes to a therapist or group meeting, he says it's my fault. And the counselors always back him up."

Scott checked his text. The patient was being prepped for surgery. He knew the reassuring thing to say, that alcoholics and addicts often blame someone else. "Once your husband takes responsibility for his own actions and reaches out for help, things should get better."

"Oh, yeah, yeah, yeah. I've heard all that crap before," Mrs. Walker said. She hit a key on her iPhone with her forefinger, and the phone played a few seconds of music. "There you go. Made it to the next level. Go girl!"

Scott checked the time on his phone. He needed to head to surgery. "Your husband has been in a wreck, a very serious one," he said. "It wasn't your fault."

"Of course, it wasn't. However, somehow, he'll blame the wreck on me too. Bob was supposed to come home early from the office. We were going to dinner at White Pillars to celebrate our anniversary, our fourth." She exchanged her phone for a compact mirror from her purse and checked her make-up. "All the family support meetings, all the cups of coffee, the small talk, the hugs in the rehab center. I just can't do it again. And, besides, our insurance quit paying, and we can't afford it."

"I'll get one of the social workers on your case, but physical therapy rehab after the wreck should be a different situation with your insurance."

"Yes!" Mrs. Walker's phone emitted several seconds more of celebratory music. She shook her fist in victory.

"Addiction specialists tell us that medically indicated narcotics for the relief of acute physical pain, like that of surgery or trauma, should not affect sobriety, or chance of sobriety."

"I don't mean to be so difficult, doctor." She looked up from her phone at Scott. "Please do whatever you can to make the situation better, but can you excuse me a second?"

Robert Walker's wife stepped away to the restroom in the corner. She did not close the door, and Scott could hear the water run. She returned with a wet paper towel, blotting her neck and wiping clear her smeared eye make-up. "My friend told me that surgeons use new tools, new things to make patients get through surgery easier—make the surgery hurt less after it's over."

"Your friend was probably talking about robotics or arthroscopy. Unfortunately, your husband's injuries will require open surgery, a larger skin incision, if we want to do the best job."

Mrs. Walker stepped back into the restroom. She returned with another damp towel.

"Dr. Mack, I've heard of you. I think my neighbor came to you a couple of months ago with a twisted ankle. She liked you, said you were nice, said you had a great bedside manner and kept her comfortable. Go ahead and do whatever you need to do to help my husband. I've already signed his life away on those consent forms."

"The hospital has a good team. We'll do our best," Scott said. He walked to the exit from the family waiting room into the hall and turned in her direction. The employee elevators to the Operating Room suite were around the corner to his right. "The O.R. nurse will call you with updates during the case. She'll use that landline near the water cooler. Just stay nearby the waiting room, and I'll find you after we're finished."

Without waiting for a response, Scott walked in the direction of the elevators. He heard heavy footsteps approach from behind. "They called me in the E.D., looking for you. They're screaming for you in O.R.," Betty said.

"I got tied up with the guy's wife. She's a basket case."

"Hang on a sec." Nearly Scott's height, but wider, the nurse leaned into him. "You know, Dr. Caston can't handle the volume much longer. He needs some help, some fresh blood," she whispered. "The cops lost their case and got a lot of bad publicity. Dr. Caston's pretty shook up over the whole thing, but I think they'll leave us alone from now on."

"'Fresh blood?' That's why I'm stuck here in the E.D. and operating at all hours of the night." He extended both forearms, wrist up. "Bleeding that fresh blood for free and almost broke."

"You don't seem to get it, Dr. Mack. There's a way out of this for you and me. I've got a family to support, an expensive one. No way I can keep up on a clinic nurse's salary, even if I pull these night-owl hospital shifts. I need a little extra on the side."

Scott said, "Not sure what you're talking about." He reread the name on her hospital employee badge, issued even to part-time staff. It still read: *Betty Thibodeaux, RN, BSN.* "Gotta go, Betty. Like you said, I'm needed upstairs." He pushed the UP button on the elevator control panel. In seconds the doors parted, and he stepped inside.

Betty blocked the closing of the elevator doors with her right forearm and held them open. "They tried to shut Dr. Caston down, even subpoenaed me to testify." She checked up and down the hall. They were alone—only security cameras, video only, so she tried to appear calm and spoke quickly. "But I vouched for him in court, so did several of his patients, and he got off. Dr. Caston's reputation might be bruised, and I almost lost my nursing license, but he's still in business. We got lots of customers, and the market's wide open. He ... *we* ... need some help."

Scott spotted the security camera inside the elevator and did his best to nudge her away from the opened elevator doors and out into the hall. He hit the **CLOSE** button and pushed 4 for the floor housing the O.R. He heard her repeat, "Market's wide open," as the elevator doors shut.

Soon after relocating to the Mississippi Gulf Coast, Scott understood that Paul Caston, M.D., was a pillar of society in both the social and medical communities and in the top tier of local philanthropy. His orthopedic practice and, Scott supposed, his good name had survived last month's legal troubles. The papers and local TV carried little news of the allegations and court case other than to mention Caston was vindicated of wrongdoing in narcotic trafficking.

Until tonight, Scott had never met the doctor's nurse, Betty Thibodeaux, but her concern about finances and Dr. Caston seemed obvious. Recently someone remarked in the doctors' lounge that Caston looked tired and seemed worried.

A few of the more established orthopedic surgeons on the Coast had referred a patient or two to Scott for hand surgery or other tedious, often horrific cases that many preferred not to manage themselves. Often the procedures involved complicated, physical rehabilitation or low financial reimbursement. However, Scott had never been contacted by Caston—never a referral, not even a cast off. Scott always suspected that the senior specialist in orthopedics had fought his recruitment and hiring at the onset.

So, why would Caston's nurse approach him now?

The elevator ascended to the fourth floor, and Scott's thoughts returned to the conversation with Walker's wife about his narcotic addiction and struggle with sobriety. Now a DUI charge, likely to add to past others, loomed over the difficult physical recovery ahead for the accountant.

Then a vision of himself with the two thugs in the alley behind his office played repeatedly in his head. *Man, what was I thinking? I gotta make that right somehow.*

The elevator opened. Scott ducked into the cramped area outside the O.R. suite reserved for physicians to complete patient charting, dictations, and computer entries. He grabbed the back of one of the cheap office chairs on rollers and spun it seat forward to face one of the computers. With the back of his forearm, he raked the half-eaten banana and empty can of Coke Zero left at the side of the keyboard into the waste receptacle at the desk.

Once logged back into the electronic medical records system, Scott pulled up the information on Robert S. Walker and clicked on the standard template for post-operative orthopedic orders assigned to the patient. A few more clicks and the nursing care and physical therapy instructions appeared next to the medications in a tidy list on the screen. He scrolled down to the narcotics section and decreased the dosage strength of intramuscular Dilaudid and oral Percocet while increasing the time interval between doses.

Next, he highlighted the pharmacy orders for the non-narcotic pain relief options. Scott Mack, M.D., would officially sign the orders once the leg was set with rod and screws, the knee replaced, and the case completed.

A male voice barked from the speaker on the wall. "Dr. Mack. Ready in 7. You comin'?"

Scott exited out of the computer program, pushed away from the desk, and walked quickly into the hall toward the suite of operating rooms. The sensor in the floor noted his movement and the double doors slid open in welcome. He stood motionless in the opened doorway and blocked the two side panels from closing.

He knew that Mr. Walker would come out of anesthesia in pain, a lot of pain. Scott relived his conversation with Walker's wife in the patient waiting area, interrupted by her obsession with her iPhone game, and remembered her concern about more addiction rehab as a result of the accident and surgery. The PACU nurses would question Scott's scaled down orders for post-operative narcotics, and he would confirm that there had been no mistake. The recovery room nurse would desperately want to quiet Walker. The guy would be complaining—maybe even yelling and screaming—about the pain in his leg and knee, not to mention the discomfort of the urinary catheter. Walker would probably try to grab the tubing.

The recovery room nurse would call Scott for additional orders, and he would refuse—so she or he would complain to the anesthesiologist covering the case, who would likely give in and increase the patient dosage in the recovery room.

Scott remembered the one short lecture on narcotic and alcohol addiction from medical school, maybe heard during his rotation through the psychiatry department. Addiction, even when the person is in recovery, is not enabled by treating post-operative pain. He had tried to explain that to Mrs. Walker but actually questioned the concept himself. As the doors slid back and forth to close but halted by Scott's stance between them, he decided to sign back into the computer and reinstate the full-strength dosages of Walker's post-operative narcotics.

Scott quickly stepped away from the entrance to the O.R. to return to the computer records work room and heard the automatic doors snap shut behind him.

# Chapter 11

Exhausted after two consecutive surgeries, Scott leaned his head into the family waiting room, hoping that Mrs. Walker had grown tired of waiting and had left for the comforts of her own home—or at least dosed off. Instead, there she sat, still glued to the screen of her iPhone. Scott knew he had little to add to the staff updates from the operating and recovery rooms, but he was nevertheless obligated to talk with her about her husband's condition.

She sat in the same chair, alone in the waiting room, a soft drink can next to her on top of a short stack of magazines that nearly covered the fake woodgrain side table. Her hairstyle no longer fresh, strands of brunette hair fell into her face and almost camouflaged her smeared eyeliner. Some of the dark make-up ran from the corner of her eyes as though purposefully streaked in a melted, exhausted design—Scott unsure if from sobbing or wiping her eyes in an attempt to stay awake. She tapped her iPhone screen furiously between each upward scroll.

Scott assumed that anyone with the teacher/biker waited in the slightly larger room down the hall.

"Mrs. Walker?"

Her head jerked to attention at the voice, and she dropped the phone into her lap.

"Your husband did great," Scott said, standing in the door. "Bob's fracture reduced nicely, and the rods are in place to stabilize his femur. The knee replacement went smooth. He's a young guy, in great shape otherwise. He'll be playing golf in no time at all."

Mrs. Walker cupped the phone against her chest, jumped from her seat, and ran to Scott with a tight hug.

"Thank God. But forget the golf," she said nearly breathless. "There's no time for that. My husband needs to get caught up at work. Accounting clients don't like to be put off."

"There was no head trauma. Head CT was negative. He should do fine with returning to work," Scott said.

"When will Bob be discharged?"

"Not for a couple of days," Scott answered. "Due to the late hour and the extent of the accident and damage to the vehicle, we're going to keep him in ICU for prolonged observation. No sign of any internal injuries, but we'll get the general surgeons to take another look."

Mrs. Walker hugged him again. "When I first met you, Dr. Mack, I knew Bob was in good hands ... great hands," she said. She tossed her phone onto the seat cushion of the nearest chair and stepped back, breaking a smile. She reached for Scott's arms, grabbed them at the wrist, and pulled them toward her.

Surprised, but he did not resist. "Mrs. Walker, I've got other patients ... I need to go and—"

"Shush." She put a forefinger to his lips. "I know you're busy and have others to see to, but I've got something I want you to do with me."

"Like I said, I need to check on—"

Mrs. Walker flipped Scott's arms over, palms open toward the ceiling. "Spread your fingers, fan them out, like this," she said and demonstrated. Walker ran her long, pink manicured fingers along the contour of each of Scott's fingers, spreading them like a proud peacock or a gobbler in strut. "Yes, strong hands. You have the hands of a healer, a true healer."

Scott checked another time around the room. He knew they were alone but wanted reassurance. When Mrs. Walker next pushed her fingertips into his, he yanked his hands away and dropped his arms to the side.

"I guess you think I'm too much," she said. "Too forward. I just want to keep my husband comfortable as he heals." Tears ran down her cheeks, the mascara finished. "I know he's got his problems with drinking and pills, and I wish it was different, but I've been sitting here alone … thinking. I was wrong before. I don't want him to suffer, never have." She dropped away from Scott, back to her chair.

"Will you help me please, Doctor Mack? I can't bear to see any of my family in pain. Bob gets by most days, and you could help him with that. Do you have a business card or something?" Mrs. Walker grabbed a fresh tissue from her purse and wiped under her eyes.

Scott peered down into the top left pocket of his white medical coat and fished around through scraps of paper notes and a few ink pens. He found a business card leftover from the ones provided by the hospital marketing department when his practice first opened, this particular one dog-eared with worn, thin edges. He straightened the bent corner of the heavy stock paper card and handed it to her. His office phone number was prominently printed on the front in gold letters although much of the surrounding black lettering was smudged. She dropped the card into her purse.

"Maybe his parents will help pay for another stint in rehab," she said, "but if they won't, he'll need you. He told me once about a Dr. Caston, but I'm not familiar with—"

"I'll make sure the nurses follow through with my post-op orders and keep your husband comfortable," Scott interrupted. "They've taken care of many other surgical patients, patients very similar to your husband."

"When can I see him?" Mrs. Walker asked.

Scott checked the time on the wall clock. "If you head up to Surgical ICU right now, they'll let you in for a few minutes. Take that elevator around the corner."

Mrs. Walker gathered her phone and purse and the thin sweater on the chair beside her. "Thank you, doctor," she said under her breath. In her haste to exit into the hall she barely avoided a housekeeping cart and the surprised employee behind it. She called back to Scott: "I'll be in touch."

Scott groaned and turned away. "I hope not … but maybe they'll call Paul Caston. He must be pretty casual with the scripts."

A report to the family of the female teacher and part-time biker followed. Earlier that night there had been no family members around or anyone otherwise interested in her condition. Scott moved quickly down the hall, past the restrooms, to the second family waiting room. The situation had now changed.

Apparently, word of the teacher's motorcycle accident had spread like wildfire in the community. Scott scanned the bustling throng. This second waiting room included a recessed area in one wall complete with its own miniature coffee bar as well as beverage and snack machines. Long vinyl couches lined the other walls, and club chairs were scattered about to fill the space.

A young boy eating potato chips jumped from his seat. "Are you the doctor? How's my teacher doing? Is she gonna live?" he asked.

*I guess the lady is popular,* Scott decided. *Maybe even a good teacher.*

Each of the three wall-mounted flat screens streamed separate video or live TV programs. A group of teenage boys and girls, perhaps other students, sat under one monitor eating pizza and watching a replay of a basketball game. Children somewhere between pre-school and early elementary sat near another, while cartoons played above them. Young women, likely the children's mothers or maybe alumnae, mixed in between them. There were half-eaten bags of chips or cookies and candy wrappers on the floor.

Although muted, *Fox News* occupied the third television. Closed captioning ran across the bottom of the screen. Two men in their mid to late-seventies snored in chairs off to the side.

Except for the young boy who first greeted Scott, no one seemed particularly anxious about the outcome of the teacher/biker's orthopedic procedure.

Scott approached a woman with short, cropped grey hair who looked near the age of his surgical patient. She wore a baggy, cotton-polyester blend dress in a pink-and-red flower pattern and sat in the nearest club chair with her head turned toward the muted television. A tall fountain drink with straw rested on a small table near her.

She swiveled the chair toward Scott and raised her head. "Are you the doctor, the surgeon?" She rubbed her eyes. "You look so young."

"I'm Dr. Mack. Scott Mack."

"Well, how'd she do?"

Another boy, this one about eight years old, appeared behind Scott. "Yeah, did she make it? My dad and I rode by the bike." He took another bite of his candy bar, gooey chocolate mixed with peanut butter. Bits of nuts wedged between his teeth. "Man, that bike was totally messed up."

"Hush, Stuart," the woman said. "And you've had enough junk to eat. Go read one of those children's books over there on that table."

"Those books are for three-year-olds, Gramma. I wanted to watch the game, but Lindsey and her boyfriend over there are hogging the couch and eating face. Lindsey told me to get lost."

"Good-looking Snickers bar you got there," Scott said.

The boy finished the last bite and tossed the wrapper toward a trash can. He missed.

"Yes, your teacher did make it," Scott said.

Without acknowledgement, the boy stepped away toward another part of the room, and the woman wiped crumbs from the front of her dress. Scott noticed a half-eaten hamburger with napkin in the folds of her lap.

"But she's got a long road ahead of her," Scott added. He detected the smell of stale beer mixed with cigarettes, onions, and ketchup. He spotted the empty fast-food bag, but there were no empty cans around. The enormous purse on the floor next to her could easily have contained a small cooler.

"You tell Lindsey to make room for you. It's late," the woman said to the boy who had eaten the Snickers. "We'll be goin' home soon anyway." She rummaged through her purse.

Scott expected her to pull out another beer. In its place, she removed a miniature pack of tissues and used one to blot the corner of an eye. A tear fell from the other, and she missed it. "She's my twin sister, and you say she's got a long road ahead of her?" Alarm filled her face. "She'll be able to go back to work—to teaching, won't she?" she asked.

"It took several pins to set your sister's arm and shoulder," Scott said. "The surgery lasted almost two hours, but everything came together and should heal well."

"She's got to keep working; she can't live with me. My house ain't big enough." The woman crushed the tissue in her hand and tossed it into the nearby trash can. It made it.

"Your sister is going to need a lot of physical therapy. If she'll follow what the therapist says, everything should be okay," Scott said, "and she should be able to go back to work in a couple of months."

"Oh, a couple of months. Maybe I can handle that."

Scott noticed the deep wrinkles at the corner of her mouth and the crow's feet. "But she's a smoker—and that can complicate recovery."

The sister turned her head away, grabbed another tissue, and coughed into it. The deep, raspy sound of her own smoking habit filled the corner of the room. She crushed the tissue in her palm and turned back to Scott. "I'll make sure she keeps her appointments," she said. "My sister's got a good teaching job that comes with state health insurance. She can't lose her job. There's no way she can come live with me for good."

Scott found another business card in his pocket, smoothed the dog-ear, and handed it to the teacher/biker's twin sister. He began to see a faint resemblance. "That is how you can reach me," he said and turned back into the hall as she studied the card.

He believed he heard a weak: "Thank you, Dr. Mack." Then a much louder, "Lindsey, get your face out of that boy's lap," came next.

Scott walked down the hall toward the hospital employee exit and thought more about his earlier discussion with the accountant and his wife. She had sent mixed signals. Despite her apparent anger and frustration over her husband's addiction problems, she wanted to shield him from pain and suffering. An addict with a high drug tolerance for the effects of narcotics but with little tolerance for pain would likely want—and need—larger amounts of opioids. She would be calling him. Scott was sure of it.

He stopped and thought about the economic worries of his surgical practice and what his secretary had said about the unused narcotics, then checked the time on his phone. He assumed that by now Mrs. Walker would have reached the visitor section located outside of SICU. She may have talked her way past the nurses and the established visiting hours to a seat at her husband's bedside in intensive care. He turned away from the direction of the employee exit and headed to the elevator bank reserved for the surgical suites and the SICU.

When he reached the elevator, Scott hesitated and stepped back to lean against the opposite wall. He stared at the bank of elevators. The lighted panel of numbers above the doors descended from number 4 to return to ground floor level.

*What in the hell am I doing?* The elevator opened and Scott stepped quickly inside.

"Mr. Walker?" Scott closed the glass door behind him that separated Robert Walker's room from the adjacent, but deserted, central nursing station. Bob Walker was alone—no Mrs. Walker around—and all the nurses were busy with other patients. Per doctor's orders, Walker's leg remained elevated in traction, and the knee was fully supported. A sling stabilized his arm and injured shoulder.

Walker slept in a narcotic coma.

A toilet flushed in the cramped, adjoining restroom. The accountant's wife emerged, straightening her skirt, and headed for the small chair pushed against the bed. She stroked the side of her husband's face. "Dr. Mack … I guess you came by to check on Bob. That's very kind."

"Yes, I thought I'd—"

"I know my husband has a history of alcohol and drug abuse, but like I said earlier tonight, I can't stand for him to be in pain. When he hurts, I hurt. The nurse stuck a syringe in his I.V. just as I walked in here and heard him screaming. I'm so grateful now that he's knocked out."

The central work area of the Intensive Care Unit was still quiet, everyone otherwise occupied—no nurse or medical therapist headed Scott's way. He waved his hospital identification badge over the sensor in the bezel of the computer next to some ventilation equipment. The template of physician's orders assigned to Robert Walker populated the screen.

Scott quickly scrolled down the page, noting that identical check marks filled most of the tiny boxes to the left of each instruction. Standard provisions were in place for a urinary catheter, lab work to be drawn the morning after surgery, and treatment intervals for respiratory and physical therapy. Medication orders followed for certain antibiotics as did blood thinners to lessen the chance of post-operative vascular blood clots. There was even one checkmark for a daily stool softener.

The section for non-narcotic pain relief medication followed—intravenous and oral NSAIDs, non-steroid anti-inflammatory drugs in the same class as ibuprofen—all designed to prevent or lessen the need for narcotics to control pain. He unchecked those blanks, cancelling the pain relief options for anything but narcotics while leaving the orders for morphine in place and selecting a higher dosage with a more frequent interval of administration.

Besides, some patients suffered GI issues from NSAIDs, and now there would be no chance of that for Robert Walker. He would get more Morphine and more often.

"My husband is so handsome, even with that plastic oxygen thing in his nose. And he looks so peaceful when he's sleeping," Mrs. Walker said, now stroking her husband's arm. "Let's keep him that way—peaceful."

Scott considered altering the medication list for a third time, selecting a stronger milligram oxycodone tablet at an even shorter interval between dosing. Neither Mr. Walker's nurse, nor the pharmacy, were likely to challenge the newest orders. The revised strength and dosage intervals remained within protocol, and Walker's oxygen saturation and vital signs monitors would alert the medical staff of secondary problems if he became too sedated. Scott felt a rush of adrenaline and made the changes.

If Mr. Robert Walker recalled his stay in the SICU at all, he would remember floating on a cloud—and he would want that again and again.

"There we go, Mrs. Walker. I've made sure that your husband remains comfortable," Scott said. He surprised himself with the decision to adjust her husband's narcotic medication upward. He had zigzagged the line between right and wrong—or maybe chosen a grey area. He fought the nervous take on his smile, which was offered as one of reassurance or maybe solicitation, and slid his hands into his jacket pockets. They were starting to shake.

"Thanks again, doctor." She caressed each of her husband's fingers. "And let's be sure my poor Bob doesn't hurt after he goes home." She motioned to her purse on the floor behind the chair. Scott had not noticed it earlier. "I've got your card and your number."

No other patients waited for Scott in the Emergency Department, at least for now. He checked his phone; there were no new texts from the afterhours paging service. Friday night and early Saturday morning had been tough. In thirty minutes or so, he was headed home to sleep until his next shift later that day. Another on Sunday night through early Monday would complete the weekend.

His heart raced; his conscience screamed at him. Sleep would be impossible.

At this late hour, little to no traffic crowded the hospital corridor leading to the physicians' first floor workroom also reserved for completion of patient records and making phone calls. Furnished with two lounge chairs pushed against a wall, the space included a less-than-sturdy, plastic table sandwiched between the chairs that supported a dollar-store lamp. A plain yellow plastic bowl offered a discolored, half-eaten banana and a soft, over-ripe red apple.

In another corner hummed an undercounter refrigerator sometimes stocked with soft drinks and bottled water and the occasional several-day-old sandwich. The surface of the counter matched the same brown laminated material used to construct the lamp table. There was an Out of Order sign taped to the top of the coffee maker over the refrigerator.

Public library-style cubicles constructed of artificial wood laminate, a near match to that of the counter and lamp table, filled most of another wall. A chair on rollers, upholstered in skimpy black fabric, waited at each cubicle. All but one cubicle was fitted with a flat screen computer, the missing monitor reported a month or so ago but as of yet not replaced. The computer screens were blank, on guard for physicians or their assistants to sign in and complete patient medical records.

Scott chose the computer cubicle nearest the refrigerator, reached to open the refrigerator door, and removed one of the two plastic bottles of water inside. He twisted away the top and guzzled the cold water, then sailed the empty container into the waste receptacle along the opposite wall. His fingers trembled across the keyboard as he signed into the computer.

"Shit," he said and lifted his hands from the keyboard when the computer denied him access after he missed a few keystrokes. He shook his head in disgust and stretched and bent the joints of his fingers until they felt steady. He studied the tips of his fingers before correctly entering his username and password on the fifth try.

The monitor hesitated, then flashed to attention. Scott wished for more than bottled water as directive prompts and arduous pathways populated the black screen. A warning flashed that suspension of his hospital privileges remained imminent unless he completed his overdue electronic medical records.

The rest of the on-call weekend of hospital duty was much the same: careless drivers, another of whom was intoxicated and all with fractured bones or joint sprains; a child who fell off the slide of her backyard playset and broke her clavicle; and an elderly woman who slipped in the grocery store with a fractured hip. By the time Scott finished with all direct patient care responsibilities and completed the delinquent computer charting with more trips to the first-floor medical records room, it was 5:00 AM Monday. The waste can next to the computer overflowed with drained plastic bottles of water.

Weekend call was over.

Scott compared the time on the computer screen to that of his phone, amazed over the quiet of the last several hours—no hospital or patient calls and no texts. Bob Walker remained hospitalized as did the teacher, so he expected no demands for out-patient narcotics from those two.

Other than the few hours Scott slept at home Saturday, the walls of Biloxi Memorial had consumed his weekend. He checked the time again on his phone and shook his head. "Office opens in less than four hours."

However, after Friday's exchange with Jessica over the shortage of funds to run the practice followed by the incident in the rear parking lot, Scott wondered if he would be alone in the office that morning—except for the police. "I need a shower and some breakfast—and maybe I can grab a couple of hours of sleep," he said and dropped his phone into the back pocket of his scrub pants. "My last meal and chance to sleep in my own bed before they lock me up."

If Jessica had the nerve to show up for work today, she would likely clock in at the clinic around 8:30 and settle into at her desk, then make coffee. The after-hours answering service would sign off about that time and post another bill for services rendered, not to Biloxi Memorial, but to the business account of Mack and Associates Orthopedics. The clinic phone lines would likely be quiet, no requests to see Scott Mack, M.D. Maybe the mail service would drop off a few pieces later containing payments from patients or insurance companies.

*Not likely,* Scott decided.

A couple of times he had faked a coffee break at the machine to watch Jessica from behind as she slit open the mail. He held his breath, hoping she would extract a few checks and stamp them *For Deposit Only.* Somedays, most days, there were no payments at all—only junk mail.

Scott felt sure the scene at the clinic across town would be different today. Even after the "great" Paul Caston's legal troubles, he would still be churning it with paying orthopedic patients. Scott imagined frazzled appointment clerks, hair on-end, answering one phone call after the other or scrolling through pages of emails from desperate patients begging for appointments.

Then he recalled what Caston's nurse had said earlier in the weekend: "You know, Dr. Caston can't handle the volume much longer ... cops'll leave us alone from now on ... market's wide open."

"The jury let him off," Scott whispered. "He got away with it."

It was now 5:10 AM. Scott picked up the last soft banana and apple from the wicker basket and left the medical records room for the doctors' parking lot.

# Chapter 12

As expected, Scott encountered light traffic during the early hour. He welcomed this short commute between Biloxi Memorial and his house in Gulfport, Mississippi. He turned off Highway 90 along the Gulf of Mexico onto a modest street that ran one block perpendicular to his neighborhood of two and three-bedroom homes built in the fifties and early sixties.

Compliments of the wind and storm surge of Hurricane Katrina in 2005, many of the majestic trees and stately homes built along the coastline were gone, affording Scott an unobstructed view of the ocean from his front porch—if he strained his neck a little to the right. To add to the gaps in the landscape, the scraggly palm trees and other vegetation left in the wake of the devastation had been slow to regrow or were never replaced after the storm, and of the few houses rebuilt between his house and the beach, most were much less grandiose than their predecessors.

Beyond the flow of traffic on Highway 90, the porch entertainment included a glimpse of sunbathers, beachcombers, and an occasional bonfire. When Scott signed the purchase contract for the small house, the lure of the casinos located five or so miles away along Highway 90, the easy seventy-minute drive to New Orleans, and the convenience to golf and fishing offset the skimpy square footage of the residence. Convenience to shopping and the laid-back atmosphere of the area were other attributes touted by the real estate agent, although Scott never imagined he would have the spare time to take advantage of any of the amenities.

Now he had the extra time, could not afford the amenities, and would probably go to jail.

Scott pulled into his single-car garage and unlocked the door to the tight kitchen, only steps away from the living area connected by an archway lined with bookshelves. A shallow foyer led from the front door, through the archway between the living room and kitchen, and morphed into a narrow hallway that extended to the back of the house. Barely wide enough for two people to pass without rubbing shoulders, the hallway split the house in two. A bedroom and bath stood on each side of the corridor.

He tossed the banana and apple from the doctors' lounge onto the kitchen counter and jerked open the refrigerator. He spotted the single cold beer on the second shelf and grabbed it, then popped the top before the door to the refrigerator swung shut. The first sip turned into a guzzle of nearly two-thirds of the bottle. It was not even six o'clock in the morning. He studied the brown bottle in the ceiling light and swirled the last of the beer before downing it.

The weekend was over, so was another contractual, on-call duty obligation for orthopedic emergencies at Biloxi Memorial. Scott knew he remained vulnerable to a text or phone call from the recovery room regarding any post-op problems from the weekend's surgeries. The same went for calls from nurses assigned to his few other hospitalized patients, whether those patients paid him or not.

*They better watch that accounting guy for DTs.*

Scott never had more than one or two beers a night during the week, even if not on call, and usually only after five or six in the afternoon. To partake in the morning was a first. He tossed the empty bottle into the trash and walked from the kitchen past the bookshelves onto the front porch, which ran the length of the house.

Scott settled into one of the three rocking chairs, the sky moonless and starless, the scene around him pitch-black except for the streetlight in front of his neighbor's house. Sunrise was about fifteen minutes away, and the darkness hid any possible view of the ocean. But Scott could hear and smell the sea over the traffic. He took a deep breath and felt a strange sense of tranquility as he rocked back and forth, then thought about another beer and jumped up for the refrigerator. He opened the fridge and muttered, "Damn, drank the only one."

He poured a glass of orange juice instead and found a quarter pint of vodka above the stove. After the burn of a hard swallow of screwdriver, Scott managed, "Oh, God, I sold narcotics to slime balls." He slammed a fist against the porch railing and took another gulp. "And I listened to that crazy-ass nurse." Another strike against the railing—it shook. "Jesus, I was gonna set up the accountant as a customer."

The ocean, the slower pace of life, a promise of financial success—all three had drawn him to this medical practice in the South. Moving to Mississippi had been his only viable option to launch a career, and while the other orthopedic residents had laughed at his plans, he had hoped to prove them wrong ... and failed. Even with a guaranteed start-up income and coverage of overhead expenses, he had screwed everything up.

Scott finished more of the cocktail. He now faced unemployment either from the poor financial condition of his orthopedic practice or, worse, from arrest and the loss of his medical license. *I sold narcotics to thugs in an alley.*

A fresh wave of salty air permeated the porch. *How am I going to make this work? Can I come out of this okay?*

Scott had no other job opportunities, but if the police came for him, he wouldn't need to worry about a job. He could claim that the two guys had tried to rob him, although he had not reported any shakedown in the alley. *There were two of them, and I just played along so they wouldn't cut me up. I was scared. Who could blame me?*

Scott suddenly remembered the manager from the dentist's office. He got up from the rocking chair for something else to drink—maybe just a Coke Zero this time—or maybe some plain orange juice. His cell phone vibrated.

102

"Damn," he said, and stumbled on the wide, uneven wooden planks of the porch while checking the screen of his iPhone. The number displayed was not the E.D., not intensive care, and not the physician on-call answering service. "Too early for a telemarketer," he said and touched the screen to answer.

"Hello. It's Dr. Mack."

"Hey, Doc. It's good to hear your voice."

Scott stumbled again, not because of the uneven flooring or the two early-morning drinks. Before responding, he inspected the porch, the houses to each side, and even turned around to check the area toward Highway 90. Everything remained still. There was no one. "Jamal? What the hell? How'd you get my—?"

"Dat's right, Doc. It's me. Hope you ain't too surprised to hear from me."

Scott was alone but still spoke in whisper. "Yeah, you might say that. Surprised."

"You crazy, man. Get a hold of yourself. You're a doctor—a smart, savvy guy. We got something huge going here."

"What the hell are you talking about?" Scott said. The neighbor's cat jumped onto his porch, and Scott nearly screamed. The sun started to rise.

"I already sold the merchandise you supplied me Friday," Jamal said. "I told you I had a hungry clientele."

Scott almost leaped from the porch through the foyer into the living room and slammed the door behind him for privacy—and to keep the cat out. Even though certain he was alone, he darted his eyes back and forth around the space to check and cupped his hand around his cell phone. Satisfied, Scott asked in a hush, "Why the hell are you calling me? We don't have anything else to talk about. And, anyway, how'd you get my cell?"

"What the shit, man! Miss Jessica gave me your cell," Jamal said. "We got an arrangement."

"I don't know what you're talking about. Don't call me again." Scott pulled the phone from his ear and stared again at the display.

The number stared back. He could hear Jamal talking. He moved to tap **End Call** but stopped himself.

"Dis thing is big, Doc. Over-the-top big. Lots of Benji out there for us, man. If you and I don't cash in, somebody else will. Come on, Doc."

Scott jerked the cell back to his ear. "Don't call me again," he repeated. "I don't want to hear from you. Am I clear?"

"Clear as a bell, Doc. But my prescription for you is that you better clear your own head," Jamal said, "and work with us."

"I'm getting ready to hang up, Jamal, and block your number."

"Better clear your head," Jamal said again. "Problem is, Doc, you already in dis thing deep. I got an order for thirty more Percs. Need 'em in two days, max."

"Knock it out, Jamal. I'm getting ready to hang up and lose you," Scott said. He pulled the phone away, studied the screen, then returned it to his ear.

"You ain't got no choice, Doc. Like I said ... I'll be in touch."

There were a few seconds of silence before Scott grasped that Jamal had not hung up.

"Might sound like something from an old TV show or a bad movie, but Doc, not taking my cell calls won't be a choice for you. I know where you work, and it won't take much to find out where you live."

This time Jamal did end the call.

Scott stared at the background image of the screen, a selfie taken during a fishing trip shortly after he moved to Gulfport. *Is Jessica out of her mind? Why did she give that asshole my cell number?*

He blocked Jamal's number and walked back into the kitchen and the stack of bills on the table. Scott stood at the refrigerator several seconds before adding the last of the vodka to his orange juice and took a long sip. There were no police sirens. He then unblocked Jamal's number and entered the thug as a phone contact.

Through the window above the breakfast table, Scott could see out onto the porch. The neighbor's dog had replaced the cat. He walked back outside and fell into the castoff chair for a glimpse of the ocean. Traffic on Highway 90 had increased. The dog barked at him.

"Pipe down, you mutt," Scott yelled. He threw the half-consumed, refreshed screwdriver at the dog. Liquid splattered onto the porch railing, and the plastic cup from a take-out meal landed in the branches of the neighbor's holly bush.

The neighbor's side window slid open, and an elderly woman's voice squeezed out. "Sorry, Doctor Mack. Come on back inside, Scoodles, sweetie. The nice doctor must have had a long night. I left the back door open for you."

Scott lowered his head and shrugged his shoulders. The window slammed shut. He regretted the anger and frustration directed at the neighbor's dog. The old lady was nice, even brought a homemade chocolate cake when he moved in. He would send her some flowers—maybe a gift certificate—in apology for being mean to her dog.

*Dogs will be dogs. Drug dealers will be drug dealers.*

Maybe he should step over there and apologize right now. No, maybe some other time when he had not been on call and had not been drinking—particularly not consuming alcohol in the morning. For someone other than him, some guy who lived a nine-to-five life with a semblance of normalcy, it was barely time for breakfast much less cocktail hour. But the schedule of an orthopedic surgeon, particularly one who scraped by to make a living, was not a normal life.

Scott checked the lady's house—all quiet, the shade lowered over the side window. He assumed Scoodles had made it inside through the rear door and was safe and sound with his momma. He sank into his king-size wicker chair, then dropped his feet on the cushion of the white wicker ottoman and wished for the wasted remains of the screwdriver. The ottoman served as a focal point for the porch and a nice prop for his tennis shoes, its upholstery missing the chair color by at least two shades and a nearer match to the worn, dull shoes.

The perimeter of Scott's house grew quiet, not even the sound of highway traffic. He could almost hear ocean waves as the sun cast shadows across the porch. When a bird burst out of the overgrown bush at the corner to break the silence and flew across the porch, Scott was drawn to the other meager porch furnishings and the rest of the surrounding landscape. The shrubs also needed attention as did the lawn. If he stayed in Gulfport and did not go to jail, he would buy an electric hedge trimmer—maybe even a gasoline powered one to go along with the little-utilized mower in the backyard shed.

That chatty realtor selected by Biloxi Memorial Hospital to show Scott available properties in his price range described this house as a quaint, cozy cottage with an updated kitchen just right for a bachelor—with room to grow. Scott translated the description of the non-descript cottage a block or so from ocean as this: *No matter what, you can probably afford this simple, wood frame house and the well-worn porch furniture left behind by the previous owners when their U-Haul was already full.* The chatty realtor, a thin woman about five-four with platinum blonde hair and stylish, dark rimmed glasses, failed to mention the fist-sized tear in the upholstery of the wicker chair.

At the time of closing of the sale, she said, "In no time at all some Gulf Coast girl will snap you up and love this house. It's the perfect starter home. And after a couple of kids and maybe another on the way, I'll be happy to find y'all a larger house." When she handed Scott the keys, she mentioned the much more expensive neighborhood occupied by Dr. Paul Caston.

So far, for Scott, there was no family and no hopes for one, and except for the foregone conclusion about a steady girlfriend or fiancée and kids, the realtor had been correct about the property. Even after the hospital cut his stipend, he had managed the monthly mortgage.

Now his savings were nearly depleted. He would need to find a cheaper place ... or leave the area. Scott wondered if the previous owners had moved because money was tight for them too.

He decided that if he had to skip town in the middle of the night to escape his own mortgage and bank officer, he would forget the moving van or the U-Haul. He would leave most of his own cheap furniture behind—except find some way to take this ottoman and wicker chair. He had become attached to the two pieces.

After repairing the wicker chair with greenish brown electrical tape—the color of the tape a lucky, near match to the palm trees in the background of the fabric—Scott had hidden the spot with pillows covered in a print of white seashells scattered thick across a sandy beach. He stumbled across the pillows in a display of marked down, thrift-store merchandise. Seagulls flew over the palm trees, and the blue color of the sky repeated the exterior color of his house.

*Not such a bad decorator after all,* he thought.

He remembered the half-eaten bag of potato chips in the kitchen cabinet and scratched his stomach under his scrub suit top. *Getting a little soft. Need to hit the gym.*

The cost of his monthly gym membership would be something else that would have to go.

A wide yawn and long stretch followed. In between the weekend's successful orthopedic procedures for the drunk accountant and the teacher/biker, Scott had evaluated other patients in the Emergency Department and scheduled two additional surgical cases now posted for the upcoming week—both with good health insurance. In fact, the accountant and teacher could need additional treatment and surgery. He stretched a second time. Maybe there was hope for him financially—and in a legitimate enterprise.

With that sliver of optimism, Scott tried to shake away thoughts of Jamal and his brother or cousin or whoever was with him in the alley. He knew the landlord of the strip mall was too chintzy to provide security surveillance equipment at the rear of his clinic building, but still envisioned himself in black and white stills cut from video footage of his deal with the two guys. He imagined his mug shot after arrest and compared it to the presumed sweet, innocent persona of his receptionist, Jessica. A smile never left her face.

107

Yet, that receptionist's smile had set him up to sell drugs, though the decision to follow through with the deal was all his. Until Jamal surprised him in the back alley, Scott had assumed Jessica's suggestion a joke—or a desperate fantasy—that they recycle unused and discarded patient narcotics for profit.

Jamal's gold-toothed smile Friday evening ricocheted inside Scott's head like rubber bullets. Over the weekend, Scott had fought the dismal truth of his actions. Because of his dire financial straits, Jessica and Jamal had nailed him for desperate. They presumed that a financially drowning Dr. Scott Mack would partner with drug traffickers to supply and move narcotics and other contraband for profit—even pursue avenues to expand the business further.

Scott felt broken, the sliver of hope gone. His self-respect ruined. His true motive in the higher adjustment of the accountant's pain medication tore at his soul. *I wanted to feed the guy's addiction. I'm no better than Jamal and his sidekick.*

He ruefully stared at his neighbor's house. Inside was Scoodles's master, the old lady who used to speak of him as the "nice, young doctor." She didn't say "respectable" or "ethical."

"Sorry to disappoint you, ma'am, but I'm a sleazy opportunist just like those criminals in the alley," Scott said. Disgusted, he considered a run to the convenience store for a six-pack of cheap beer.

*Nope, I can't afford it.*

The conversations with Robert Walker's wife tugged further on his conscience. She drew him in with desperate pleas of total pain relief for her husband, despite his addictions. Scott understood her endgame and pushed back—at first. To avoid the bother of supporting her husband in sobriety and in what she also saw as social embarrassment, she wanted Dr. Scott Mack to keep her convalescing husband supplied with narcotics. She would gladly pay for it.

"What's gotten into me?" Scott said. He needed to reason with his smiling secretary and receptionist—not by text or cell, but face-to-face. "Am I that easy to turn? How could she see this in me?"

From the moment she was hired by the hospital staffing director and introduced to him, Scott considered Jessica Kile down-to-earth, a hard worker, dedicated to doing a good job, and kind. She was cute, attractive enough, and patients would like her—and they did.

*Jessica's dedicated all right, but to whom or what?*

Scott wished for sleep and a clear head. Beer and vodka for breakfast had not helped. However, he *would* permanently block Jamal's number and avoid the accountant's wife.

# Chapter 13

Monday morning Jessica Kile ignored her usual parking spot on the street for a drive through the alley behind the clinic. She moved slowly up and down the asphalt and checked both sides of the passageway, again spotting no security cameras. Satisfied that there could be no video of Jamal and Immaculate's transaction with Dr. Mack, Jessica pulled into the parking space next to Scott's.

A woman with light-colored, medium length hair and wearing sandals stepped from the rear entrance to the dental office next door. She talked on her cell and carried a kitchen-sized, plastic trash bag to the bin. After tossing it inside, she seemed to end her call and acknowledged Jessica with a weak smile and a wave. She walked toward Jessica's vehicle.

Jessica lowered her window. "May I help you with something?"

"Name's Pam. I ran across your boss out here late Friday afternoon. Seems a couple of guys were bothering him." She lit a cigarette. "You know anything about that?"

"No, Dr. Mack hasn't mentioned—"

"I think I recognized one them. He's a dental patient of Dr. Roland's, likes gold fillings and caps, and always pays in cash," Pam said. "After what I saw Friday, I think I know where he gets his funds."

"Sorry, but I'm running a little late. Need to get parked and open up for the day," Jessica said. She stepped from the car and reached into her purse for the keys to the clinic. "I usually park out on the street, but our patients could use the extra parking."

"You sure about that?" Pam raised an eyebrow. "From what I see out my front office window, your patient street traffic seems mighty slim these days. But I know what's going on back here."

"I need to open up. Excuse me." Jessica brushed by Pam and unlocked the rear door. She shut it behind her, disarmed the security system, took a deep breath, and punched in a cell number. The call rang nearly to voicemail as Jessica paced at the door.

A male voice answered. "What's up?"

"What took you so long to answer the freakin' phone?"

"Miss Jessica, I ain't never heard you talk shit like that, or almost shit. We got some problem, or sumthin?"

"Jamal, listen to me. There's this woman in the office next door, the dentist's office. Says that Friday she saw you and Immaculate with Dr. Mack, saw the whole thing."

"You sure 'bout that?"

"She even recognized you. Says you're one of the dentist's patients, and you always pay in cash."

"What's the big deal? So, I like a nice smile, and chicks dig it," Jamal said. "What's wrong with that?"

"Cut the crap, Jamal. The lady saw the cash, saw Dr. Mack take the money from you. She saw the pills too."

"That snooping bitch. What's your doc got to say about what she said?"

"He hasn't made it in yet. Besides, I haven't seen him since Friday—no call, not even a text—and he's probably gonna fire me this morning ... or have the cops pick me up."

"Your doc ain't gonna do any of that crap. We got it all on video. But that woman at the dental office. That's a problem."

"She's your problem, Jamal."

"Don't worry about that dentist chick," he said.

"She saw *you* deal drugs, not me," Jessica said. "And you better hope I don't lose this legit job here with Dr. Mack, because this association could be the ticket to keep Momma Kile's business afloat. That helps my husband too."

Jamal ended the call somewhere before husband.

"And I need the health insurance," she hissed. "You better not screw this up, Jamal."

Jessica dropped her cell into her purse and walked through the shallow foyer to the lobby, past the philodendron in the corner, and raised the front window blinds. It was 8:25 AM. The first available patient appointment slot was eight o' clock, but both she and Dr. Mack knew the schedule was empty until ten. The answering service would reroute the office calls to her desk in five minutes. Her cell phone rang. The caller ID in her contact list announced Dr. Mack.

Jessica froze for a few seconds before answering. She straightened a few scattered magazines and a couple of Bibles left scattered about the waiting room as the phone continued to buzz. She hurriedly felt the surface of the potting soil around the philodendron. The plant needed water. She'd bring a plastic watering can from home, one purchased at Everything's a Dollar. That is, if it wasn't over for her.

Jessica answered just before voicemail.

"What's up, Dr. Mack?" She pressed her phone deep against the side of her face, but it still shook against her ear. "I'm just tidying up the place. These magazines and plants, always a mess. Sorry, but no patients here yet." She held her breath for the: "You're fired, and I've talked to the police."

She spotted a dog-eared magazine dated the week she started at Dr. Mack's clinic, flipped through it with the phone sandwiched between her ear and shoulder, and nearly dropped both to the carpet. Before Dr. Mack could answer, Jessica tossed the magazine into the trash can beside the couch. A line of coffee stains marred the featured photograph on the front. "Some of these magazines are too old and need to be thrown out," she said.

"Go ahead and do whatever, but, hey, I gotta tell you, I totally cancelled the office cleaning service," Scott said. "I'm sorry, but there's no money in the expense account to pay 'em." He dropped his razor into the bathroom drawer and splashed on after shave.

Three cups of coffee and toast with peanut butter and jelly had revived him of the weekend and his liquid breakfast appetizers.

"It's okay, Dr. Mack. I can do more than just tidy up the waiting room. It's not that we get a lot of—"

"A lot of traffic, you mean?" Scott said. "Patient traffic? I know it's bad. I can fill in the blanks."

Jessica continued to throw away magazines. She picked a few dead leaves off the plant and said nothing. The hammer was about to fall. Dr. Mack would chew her out about Jamal, and Jessica Kile would be history.

Instead Scott said, "But I do have a little good news. I did two emergency surgeries and lined up a couple more cases while on hospital call Friday night and Saturday morning. Sunday was nothing but sad no-pays who kept me up almost all night, but the four surgeries seem to be paying customers."

"That's fantastic, Dr. Mack," Jessica said and wiped the sweat from her forehead with the back of her left hand. She spotted an empty coffee cup on her desk, filled it with water from the patient restroom, and took care of the plant. "But it will take sixty to ninety days before we see anything on the books, moneywise, from any of those cases."

"You sure know how to hurt a guy," he sighed, then laughed softly.

*You're playing cat and mouse with me.* Jessica waited for the sledge-hammer or the sharp blade of a guillotine.

"Those four emergency patients had rotten luck this weekend, except for landing a great doctor." Scott laughed again. "Like I said, at least they had insurance."

"Dr. Mack, I've worried all weekend. I guess we need to talk about what happened Friday after work and—"

"You know my password into the hospital patient list. Access it online and create a medical record account for all the patients I saw, particularly those surgical cases."

"Okay," she hesitated. "Will do. I can go ahead and bill the insurance companies for the two completed surgeries."

113

Scott dropped the towel from his waist and tossed it into the bathroom laundry basket. He passed his cell phone back to his right hand. "I pulled up the patient portal before I took a shower." He checked his hair and teeth in the mirror. "Our only morning patient cancelled, so I called the surgery department scheduler. She let me move the afternoon add-on case from the weekend to ten this morning."

Jessica stepped quickly to her desk and pulled up the day's bleak office schedule on the computer. Dr. Mack was correct about the cancelled appointment.

"It's been a long weekend," Scott said as he started dressing in his bedroom. "I'll be leaving for the hospital in about fifteen minutes. You can hold down the fort at the office until I'm through."

The first set of clean scrubs from the drawer was too wrinkled to wear, even disguised under a long white coat. He remembered another pair on hangers, straight from the dryer from last week, and chose them instead. "Jessica, I don't think I'll be finished with the case until 1:00 or 1:30. You can open up the afternoon for add-on patients; that is, if anyone calls for an appointment," Scott said.

"Yes, sir, Dr. Mack. Whatever you want me to do," Jessica said. "I'll try to fill up the afternoon. Yes, sir. I will."

"See you then," Scott said and ended the call.

Jessica ran to the front door and locked it, sure that the police were outside or at least on the way. On the phone, Dr. Mack sounded like he was still home, maybe running the water in a bathroom, but he could be outside too, waiting to lower the hammer. She took a deep breath and tried to calm herself. Maybe things were okay for the moment; maybe she still had an honest job—although getting fired would be better than jailtime and the loss of her child.

She walked with determination to the computer and accessed the online schedule information linked to Dr. Mack's last-minute hospital procedure. The details of the patient's insurance and employment records glared at her on the computer screen.

The $5,000 deductible required by the patient's individual health insurance plan had not been met. Jessica groaned and punched a few other keys. The situation worsened. "The policy terminated yesterday. Lady must have lost her job. No benefits, no way to pay. Another reason for Dr. Mack to go ballistic."

She shook her head and followed Dr. Mack's request. In a few minutes she created the new patient record for the afternoon surgery, now rescheduled for ten o'clock. Maybe he would fire her before the bombshell that he was likely to do that surgery for free.

She found the other three patient cases from Dr. Mack's weekend time on call and created the additional clinic records. While the financial prospects of payment for those seemed a bit more promising, Dr. Mack's financial outlook still looked bleak.

He needed help.

The computer tasks completed, Jessica stared at the silent phone on the reception desk—no blinking digits on the phone display, no in-coming calls, no waiting messages. In the case of most medical practices, even solo practices like Dr. Mack's, the phone on Monday morning would be on fire.

She opened the clinic's patient appointment schedule for the day. Only two names appeared on the computer screen, both in the afternoon and spaced two hours apart. She could almost hear the roots of the wilted philodendron in the corner suck up the water just poured onto the soil.

Jessica pulled up Dr. Mack's completed surgery list from the last four weeks and no surprise—a short list. Near the top was last Friday's post-op patient, the one who left her Percocet behind in the exam room.

Jessica remembered the woman's words shortly before she left the office: "I couldn't take them all. Too many in the bottle for me."

*There's got to be other patients who feel the same.*

"Too many in the bottle," she said, echoing the woman's words. Jessica thought about her encounter with the lawyer at the convenience store. She stared again at the silent, black modular phone set and ran her forefinger along the edge of the unit's plastic base.

A thin layer of dust stained the tip of her finger. She raised a bit off her chair and looked out into the lobby, hoping for someone to walk through the door, then smiled at herself, shaking her head after she remembered the front door was locked.

*Maybe our website is the problem. If we had a better website, more patients would come, and Dr. Mack would do more surgeries. We wouldn't need Jamal or Momma Kile. Everything could be legit.*

Jessica shifted in her chair—actually more of a squirm. She pulled up the clinic website and clicked through the graphics. The website designer had chosen a collection of handsome men and beautiful women as patients, all smiling and all stock images. Dialogue drawn in cartoon-style, oblong shapes floated above the movie star faces: *Dr. Mack is the best surgeon ever ... His staff made me feel right at home ... Fixed me up good as new ... Changed my life!* ... filled the blanks.

"I could come up with something better than this," Jessica said, "and for a lot cheaper." She stepped away from the desk top computer and scooped coffee grounds into the filter, then paced the room while the machine brewed.

A few minutes later, she sipped hot coffee and clicked to the next page on the computer. She pulled up the patient email board and wondered if Dr. Mack ever looked at the website, much less read through the list of messages received. Jessica remembered the man from Pass Christian, the one in his early fifties with the fractured ankle, the fourth email down the list and another unreferred assignment from the Emergency Department not adequately covered by medical insurance. The man with the fractured ankle never made a personal payment to the clinic, and the insurance company paid very little to Dr. Mack.

*Dr. Mack is a godsend!* the same man said in his email. *Fixed me up super good after I fell off that crazy ladder my boss made me climb. Would pick Dr. Mack again as my doctor, for sure!*

The front door area and clinic lobby quiet, no one but Jessica and the dying plant in the corner, she looked up the cell number on the computer of the man who fell off the ladder. She dialed and in a few seconds he answered.

"Mr. Carroll, this is Dr. Mack's assistant, Jessica. Do you remember me from the office?"

"I sure do, young lady," Mr. Carroll answered. "You're that pretty little thing at the front desk. I talked to you when I came in to see Dr. Mack after my surgery."

"Hold on just a sec, Mr. Carroll." Jessica pulled a folder of printed information provided by hospital marketing from a shelf and wiped the dusk off the cover. She flipped through the glossy pages until she found the list of suggested questions used to poll patients about their medical care experience, queries crafted to generate a positive spin on the surgical practice. Jessica removed the sheet and returned the remainder of the folder to the shelf.

Reading aloud from the top of the page, she inserted the applicable name. "Mr. Carroll, I'm calling to make sure you are doing well after your surgery and to see if you have any questions or any problems." Jessica checked the rest of the page and picked another question, even before he answered the first. "Are you still having much discomfort, any pain?"

"Young lady, you are so nice to call. I'm doing fine, perfectly fine. Exactly like Dr. Mack said I would," Mr. Carroll said. "He told me that I probably wouldn't need much of that pain medicine he gave me to take home. Know what?" he chuckled. "Doc was right."

Jessica pulled up Mr. Carroll's medication list. Percocet 7.5/325 – Dispense 30 tablets popped onto the screen under his high blood pressure and cholesterol medications. Dr. Mack had authorized the Percocet prescription, a primary care nurse practitioner the others. "So, your incision is not hurting you anymore? "Jessica asked.

"That's right, little lady. Been back at work at the shipyard for over a week now."

"Back at work? That's fantastic, Mr. Carroll. Totally awesome!" Jessica clicked to the accounting page in the file and studied the patient's significant, unpaid balance. Jessica tapped a few numbers on the desk calculator. What Mr. Carroll owed topped three or four months of her salary. "What a shame, Mr. Carroll," Jessica said. "Unfortunately, your Freedom for All policy did not cover much of Dr. Mack's fee."

"Those insurance agents never shoot straight," Mr. Carroll said. "Young lady, tell the good doctor that I'll get him his money as soon as I can. I'm good on my word."

Jessica hesitated. Dr. Mack was business as usual on the phone this morning and said nothing about Jamal in the alley or their own conversation about patient pain medication left behind in the office. No police had arrived to arrest her.

She swallowed hard.

"So, you didn't have to take all the pain medication Dr. Mack prescribed?" she asked.

"Nope. Most of the bottle is in my bathroom medicine cabinet. You know, yesterday I was thinking about flushing those pills down the toilet. I've got teenage grandchildren who come by from time to time. Don't want none of them to come across that stuff. You hear so much on TV these days about kids hooked on drugs."

*If Dr. Mack has plans to fire me, what's the harm in seeing where this goes? Momma Kile needs the product.*

Jessica hoped she masked her excitement. "Oh, don't do that, Mr. Carroll. Don't flush the pills. We, I mean, Dr. Mack might be able to help you with that."

"I ... I don't understand," he said. "Dr. Mack has already helped me tons, young lady. I'm back at work, pain free. But my break is just about over. I'm gonna have to hang up." Jessica could hear other men's voices in the background. "I'm pulling overtime just to get Dr. Mack and the hospital paid. So, don't you worry that pretty little blonde head of yours."

"Hold on just a sec, Mr. Carroll." Jessica took a deep breath. "Dr. Mack has started a new program to help patients ... patients that can't afford their medication."

"Oh, I don't need any more medication," he said. "And I don't need charity. I work to pay my bills."

"That's not what I mean. If patients have leftover medicine, patients like you who have had surgery, they can give it to other patients in need."

"Hey, you're right," Carroll said. "I've seen that box in the drug store, right next to the pharmacy counter ... sort of like a big, fat mailbox. You can drop leftover meds in the slot. You talkin' about that?"

"No, sir. The pharmacy will destroy the medicines if you drop them in there."

"Oh, but I gotta make a little confession, young lady. Don't tell the doc, but I didn't take the whole ten days of antibiotics either, the pills he prescribed for my lung infection. My cough went away after a couple of days," he said. "Could somebody use the antibiotics I got leftover?"

Jessica could hear more voices in the background, mixed with what sounded like machinery noises. "Sure, Mr. Carroll. Somebody could use those antibiotics—sure they could. But there's need for that leftover pain medication too."

"Okay. That makes sense. I bet there's at least twenty pills left in that pain med bottle," he said. "I can check when I get off this afternoon."

"Dr. Mack must have done a great job for you with so many Percocet left over," Jessica chuckled. "That operation didn't hurt a bit."

Jessica's attempt at levity went unanswered for several seconds, although the delay seemed much, much longer. All she heard was the background noise of a busy factory and feared Mr. Carroll would hang up.

"So, let me get this straight. You're saying I should donate my leftover pain pills and the antibiotics to another patient?"

Jessica double checked Mr. Carroll's balance in accounts payable. The amount he owed Dr. Mack screamed at her from the bottom of the column. "As a thank you for helping his other patients in this program, Dr. Mack is going to give you a discount off what you still owe the clinic."

"How much discount?"

Jessica considered the street value of twenty Percocet tablets, even the generic brand. "How about two hundred dollars off your bill. Make it two-fifty."

Mr. Carroll whispered into the phone. "You tell Dr. Mack that if he'll write off half the amount I owe him and throw in a free office visit for my wife—she's got a bum knee—then it's a deal."

"Well ... that's a good bit more discount than I thought but—"

"Listen a sec, sweet little lady. This afternoon I get off a little early. I can run home quick and bring that oxycodone right over. I'll even throw in the antibiotics at no extra charge. Just write me up a receipt and include that free appointment card for my wife."

Jessica referred to some numbers on her scratch pad. "I'm sure the other patients will be very grateful. I'll be waiting here at the front desk for you."

"Once I leave work in the next hour, it won't take me long to get there," he said.

"And, Mr. Carroll, if you'll bring the two bottles in a small sack, like a little grocery bag, that would be nice."

The call ended and Jessica checked the next phone number on the list.

# Chapter 14

"Mrs. Sawyer, I have you all checked in for your appointment." The smiling face of Yvette Sawyer brightened the upper top left-hand corner of the computer screen, the image scanned from her driver's license. "Dr. Mack will see you in just a few minutes. He's headed back from surgery at the hospital. Now, if you'll fill in this new patient questionnaire, I'll enter everything into the computer, and we'll be all set." Jessica passed the woman several sheets of a patient questionnaire printed on thick yellow paper and attached to a clipboard. A thin plastic ink pen tied with a string dangled from the top of the clipboard.

About fifteen minutes later Mrs. Sawyer left her seat in the lobby next to the philodendron and returned to the reception desk. "Here you go," she said and handed the now completed questionnaire to Jessica, "and thanks for working me in for an appointment this afternoon. I only called this morning."

"Yes, ma'am," Jessica said. "Glad to do it." She slid the sheets of paper off the clipboard and returned it to a storage bin at the side of her desk.

"But I think you should know that when I was a patient at Dr. Caston's office, I could enter all this medical history stuff online ahead of my appointment. They had it set up that way."

Jessica forced a smile. "We so are happy to have you here with us," she said. Jessica began to type the information provided on the patient questionnaire into the computer.

"I work in sales over in the Gulfport Mall," Mrs. Sawyer said, "so I'm used to point and click." She noticed the rack of magazines mounted on the wall to the right of the reception window and selected several. "Have fun typing in all that crap on the computer."

"Thank you," Jessica said. "Dr. Mack will see you in a few minutes."

Instead of returning to her seat, Sawyer remained at the reception window and thumbed through an old *People* magazine. "I would be at Dr. Caston's office right this very second, but I got a text to call your office instead. No reason why—just that Dr. Caston would be out," she said. "Problem is, my knee can't wait. The swelling is more than I can bare." She shifted her stance. "And the pain, it's over the top. A fifteen or sixteen out of ten!"

"You're the first person on Dr. Mack's patient list for the afternoon. He'll be with you in a sec. Now there's just one more thing," Jessica said. She retrieved the clipboard and handed her another nine by eleven size printed form. "We need to get records from your previous doctor. Just sign here authorizing that request." Jessica pointed to the signature blank with her pen.

Mrs. Sawyer stuck the magazines under her left arm and scribbled her name, then dropped the pen on the additional form. As she gave the paperwork back to Jessica, the pen popped loose of the string and rolled off the clipboard onto the carpeted floor. "You can get all the records you want, young lady, but your Dr. Mack better help me. Dr. Caston wrote me a script for sixty Norcos every month."

"You can discuss that with Dr. Mack," Jessica said and forced a smile. "The chair near that plant is the most comfortable, the best place to wait."

"If this Dr. Mack is any doctor at all, he'll see my pain," Mrs. Sawyer said. Her fingers trembled. She groaned, bent slightly at the waist, and reached around to grab the pit of her back.

Jessica took a deep breath. "I thought the problem is with your knee."

"The ... the car wreck. It screwed up my knee *and* my back," Sawyer said. "Dr. Caston's surgery didn't help, so he gives me pills."

"Please take that chair over by the plant ... you'll be more comfortable there." Jessica waved in the direction and tried another smile. She ran her eyes up and down the original patient information intake form and frowned. "Mrs. Sawyer, I'm sorry but you didn't fill in the blank under Insurance Information." Jessica again clipped the form and passed it back through the opening above her desk. She retrieved the pen from the floor.

Mrs. Sawyer dropped her hand from her back, as well as the magazines, and turned toward Jessica. "I don't have insurance anymore. I couldn't work due to my back, and I lost my job ... and that COBRA payment was too high to keep my health insurance active."

"Then you'll need to pay upfront for your visit today ... in cash ... before Dr. Mack sees you. Sorry, but it's policy ... hospital policy. The hospital administrators make the rules."

"I don't give a flip about your shitty rules."

"They're not my rules," Jessica said. "It's the people in the hospital business office and the administrator over in Biloxi who ..."

"Just let me see your doctor. I need meds for my back. Dr. Caston and I had an arrangement."

Jessica's heart raced. She forced a several second pause before asking: "So, tell me about this arrangement."

The door from the hall leading from the back of the clinic opened into the reception area. Jessica sat with her back to the door. "Hey, Jessica, I'm back from surgery. Case went well. You gotta a patient ready?" Scott noticed the haggard woman in the pass-through window above Jessica's desk.

Jessica turned in the swivel chair and shot an awkward smile at Scott. "Just a minute, Dr. Mack. I've almost got Mrs. Sawyer checked in."

Scott smiled at the patient and nodded. Jessica thought his facial expression strained, his muscles tense.

"Jessica, you got a sec?" Scott motioned for her to step into the hall and she followed.

"Dr. Mack, let me explain," Jessica whispered. "Those two guys out back in the alley ... I was just trying to—"

Scott waved her aside. "Let's save that for later. On the way to the hospital this morning, I found an older doctor shot dead in his car. Name is Paul Caston."

"And you think Jamal and Immaculate did it?" Jessica asked.

"No, I expect those two thugs are guilty of a lot of other things, but not that. The guy shot himself. At least, that's what it looked like to me."

"Caston … then that explains this Mrs. Sawyer out front to see you."

"Let's just concentrate on getting through the rest of the day," Scott said. "I'll be in my office when you need me."

Jessica stood for a few seconds and watched Scott walk down the short hall to his private office and ease the door shut behind him. She then returned to her desk, took a deep breath, and began to enter the rest of Mrs. Sawyer's information into the computer.

"Is that my new doctor?" Sawyer asked. "He's a lot younger than Dr. Caston—cuter too."

Jessica finished with the computer. "Never mind that," she said. "Now, quick, tell me about the arrangement you had with Dr. Caston."

"It was simple," Mrs. Sawyer lowered her voice. "Dr. Caston knew that I needed treatment and couldn't afford it. Maybe he was sorry that the surgery didn't completely fix me, but his nurse told me he would write a script for pain meds whenever I asked for it. I'd get the prescription filled and then give him, or the nurse, half the pills back in exchange for credit on my bill. If I didn't owe anything, I'd get cash back."

Jessica thought about Jamal and smiled up from the keyboard. "You're by yourself today, aren't you?"

"Well, yeah." Mrs. Sawyer glanced behind her into the lobby and scanned the cramped, vacant space. "You see anybody else come in with me?"

"No, ma'am," Jessica said. "After you finish with Dr. Mack, stop by my desk to sign out."

"Don't expect much, because I don't have any cash on me, my credit cards are maxed out, and I'm overdrawn at the bank."

"No problem. Just stop by my desk and show me your prescription," Jessica said.

# Chapter 15

Immaculate Davis leaned against a street sign outside the Moon-dust Casino on Beach Boulevard in Biloxi, Mississippi, and faked a call on his cell. He wore blue jeans torn above the right knee to expose the flesh underneath and a baseball cap with the bill turned to the back. The bright, blinking lights on the casino marquis above him advertised the entertainer inside and the one scheduled for next week. He had never heard of either performer but assumed his mother would do anything to be in the audience. Maybe if business picked up, he could buy her a ticket.

Immaculate scrutinized each person from head to toe as they strolled by. The white woman in a red wig with long fake eyelashes and too much make-up returned his sly smirk after she checked him out, then darted her eyes to the tall muscular man walking next to her. She wrapped her right arm inside the guy's left elbow. Immaculate decided that the redhead's high heels could serve as stilts for a midget clown in the circus.

A more promising customer couple approached from behind, both dressed in tight black leather with a floppy, opened-collared silk shirt for him and a sequined blouse with plunging neckline for her. They each wore lots of cheap, gold jewelry. A huge gold cross dangled from a thick chain around the man's neck and bounced against his hairy chest. She wore so many gold bracelets on her arms that Immaculate wondered how she stood upright, much less moved. A red heart was tattooed above her right breast; a name encircled it—*Ricky*, or something like that.

Ricky and the woman continued past Immaculate, too fast. They didn't need him.

The next guy in the parade wore a white cotton, button-down shirt with khaki trousers, wrinkled to match. His eyes were blood-shot, and he struggled to walk a straight line. Immaculate figured the guy was already high and, like the couple dressed in black leather and gold, did not need his services. A long wallet peeked out from the white guy's rear pocket as he weaved by, but too great a reach for Immaculate.

The age of white guys was sometimes hard to judge. This one with the wallet about twenty-two, maybe twenty-five—somewhere just beyond legal drinking age—the kind that graduates from college and lands a job that falls well short of his parents' expectations; the kind that barely makes enough to cover apartment rent, much less attend concerts or have extra cash to risk at the blackjack table; the kind that provides a steady customer stream for Immaculate Davis.

The wrinkled guy's girlfriend, or maybe wife, walked alongside him. Her pale blue dress that fell below the knees and stringy, brown hair didn't do much for her—neither did no make-up. Maybe she did wear a little lipstick. Her eyes caught Immaculate's stare, and she glanced away quickly. She appeared sober and embarrassed.

The girl jerked the boyfriend, or husband, away from the entrance to the casino and pointed toward the parking lot. Immaculate watched them disappear into a group of people exiting the casino.

Someone about his size and height stepped next to him and asked, "Business a bummer tonight, bro?"

"Get your ass outta here. I don't need no competition," Immaculate said. "These jokers tonight? All of them freakin' losers."

"Losers? Who's the loser? I hope you still got the touch," Jamal said. "Maybe they think they can't score off you, that you ain't got enough product. I already moved the twenty Percs we got off Miss Jessica's doctor friend."

"Without me, you had no way to strike that deal," Immaculate said. "You can pay me my cut later."

Jamal sized up the area and shook his head. "Come clean, bro. You ain't any good going solo," he said.

"Deez jokers might act like they ain't interested in scoring dope, but from what I seen standing out here, most of these junkies are already high. Besides, they paid a shit load to see that crappy show inside. They ain't gonna miss a second of the entertainment, so they ain't gonna stop and give me no freakin' business." Immaculate spat tobacco on the sidewalk. "Besides, Jamal, cut the shit. You distracting me. I got bills to pay."

Immaculate stepped closer to the line of people entering the casino. An older couple hurried to catch up, the woman moved a little faster.

"Come on, Graham. Hurry up. I don't wanna miss a second. We paid a lot for these theater tickets," the woman said. She frowned at Immaculate and Jamal. Two young black men hanging around the outside of the casino, both wearing jeans that sagged several inches below the waist. Grey underwear showed on one, orange on the other.

"You're pissin' in the wind here, 'Maculate," Jamal said. He looked around and lowered his voice. "I don't know what personal shit you got to sell, but I'm onto something new with Jessica and this doctor she works for … a fresh supply of product and maybe fresh meat to unload it."

"You just want my regular territory," Immaculate said. "I move out and you move in … every damn time."

"Don't be so freakin' paranoid, my friend." Jamal slid the small Ziploc bag of white pills from the inside of his jacket and flashed a glimpse for Immaculate. "This is more shit."

"From Miss Jessica?"

"Yes," Jamal answered. "She got it from some lady with a bad back and knee. The lady turned it in to her."

"You got berries to sell? I don't care where you got 'em," Immaculate said, raising his voice a bit. "Go somewhere else to unload that shit. This is my space."

An African American couple moved a few steps through the line to the entrance and seemed to take notice of the argument, then lowered their heads and stepped up their pace in the line.

"My clients know they can count on me for quality product, and they know I ain't lookin' to screw no pigeons," Jamal said. "The only people I ever cheat is those asses that annoy me or treat me like shit, like I'm not a real person with a real life." He returned the bag to his jacket pocket. "This new stuff came straight from the pharmacy, one from around here. Not that crap that comes in on the boats."

"I ain't into holding up no drug store," Immaculate said. He resumed his study of the crowd. "I should have scored with that guy who just walked by. You're wasting my time, Jamal."

Jamal slapped Immaculate's chest with the back of his hand. "So much for tryin' to do you a favor, bro. You clueless to the situation, man. See you around, loser." Jamal disappeared into the alley behind them.

The line of concert goers thinned as the start of the performance neared. A Caucasian man in his early thirties with sunglasses—*Maui Jims,* Immaculate guessed, and a baseball cap worked his way through the line toward the casino. Unlike Immaculate's, the baseball cap was turned brim forward. The man held his concert ticket in his right hand, pulled a bill from his wallet, pressed the cash against the ticket, and approached Immaculate.

Immaculate checked right and left, then over his shoulder—no cops, no one paying any attention to him other than the guy with the ticket and the sunglasses and what looked like a twenty-dollar bill. He slowly removed a clear plastic envelope from his jacket. Cupping the packet of two oxycodone tablets in his palm, Immaculate flashed it in the direction of the new customer.

The man nodded.

Immaculate stepped forward. He needed the twenty bucks. The handoff would be simple—just step a bit to the side, align his right hand with the customer's, and make the transfer. In a fraction of a second the $20 would be slipped to him in exchange for the packet of two generic Percocet, and no one would notice.

A short line of people remained outside the casino and waited for admission as sidewalk pedestrians pushed through them non-stop—all uninterested in Immaculate Davis and the customer. The street was bumper to bumper with cars—lots of diversion. A taxi blew its horn at a couple who jaywalked, and a city bus accelerated in a cloud of exhaust from the stop across the street.

*This gonna be easy.*

Once Immaculate had his cash and the user his meds, he planned to call it a day. He was tired from the tense exchange with Jamal a few minutes ago. He kept his eyes on the concrete and moved to complete the transaction. Immaculate felt the man's money brush against his fingers, and he reached for it, the packet between his fingertips and ready for the hand off. Immaculate could smell the scent of money and taste it.

"Immaculate Davis, you're under arrest for drug trafficking," the man in the Maui Jims blurted. He jumped behind Immaculate and pinned his arms behind his back. The handcuffs snapped on quickly. The plastic envelope containing the pills fell to the pavement.

The people around them scattered. The woman nearest them screamed, clutched her purse, and ran. A black sedan pulled to the curb and a young man in a dark suit jumped from the front passenger seat. He retrieved the envelope.

Immaculate shook his head at the man from the car. He winced at the pull against his shoulders due to the cuffs and tried to twist his wrists free of the metal. "Detective Spearman," he said, "I can 'splain."

"Explain it to yourself, Immaculate. You screwed yourself on this one," Reed Spearman said with a shove to Immaculate's shoulder. "I vouched for you with the judge, told her you were on the right track." Reed held up the package of pills and studied it. "You're very predictable, Immaculate. We've had our eyes on you since that day in court. Now, you're going to jail and rot."

The undercover detective with the sunglasses took Immaculate by the elbow and pushed him toward the rear seat of the unmarked patrol car. "Spearman, there was another guy, darker skin and pumped up. He and this one were hush-hush over there." He motioned toward the front of the casino and the marquis. "The other guy disappeared into that alley."

"Detective Spearman, I want a deal," Immaculate managed between the growing throb in both shoulder joints and the pressure against his wrists from the tight handcuffs. He winced and slid across the back seat.

Reed buckled himself into the front passenger seat and tilted his head toward Immaculate. The undercover detective drove. "We already tried *a deal* with you," Reed said, "and that didn't work so well. Did it, Immaculate?"

"Detective," Immaculate said, "both of you, detectives, I'm just small potatoes. The guy, the one that took off through the alley before you busted me, he's the gold prize. Name's Jamal."

"Never heard of him," Reed said. "Besides, I need more than a first name."

"Got no idea about a last name. He calls me his brother, but that ain't so. Anyway, I 'spect he's always changing his name," Immaculate said.

"Any idea where he lives? Or maybe if he holds a legit job for cover?"

"Guys in my line of work don't ask personal stuff."

"Your gonna do some time for this, Immaculate," Reed said. "No way around it."

"Jamal's always workin' it, finding new product, new customers. Let me help you take this guy down," Immaculate said. "Just don't lock me up."

"The judge won't go for it," Reed said. "She's already gone out on a limb for you, Immaculate, just like I have."

"You wanna do another stake out? You want me to set Jamal up? Judge ought to like that. Huh, Detective Spearman?"

"We've got a lot more to deal with than you, Immaculate. Our plate's full." Reed glanced at this watch, darted his eyes back at Immaculate, then toward the other detective, who seemed to nod in agreement. "Like just this morning on the way into the precinct, I pulled over a DUI," Reed said.

"Oh, man. You swear? Already loaded before lunch?" Immaculate said.

"The Toyota weaved in and out of lanes, almost hit a school bus. I expected to smell and even see booze when the woman rolled down the window. But there was no booze, only empty pill bottles on the seat beside her and several more on the passenger side of the floorboard."

"Geez, I need to be careful on the road out there," Immaculate said. "Drive defensive."

"There're a lot of drivers high on pills or a mixture of pills and alcohol," Reed said. He glanced toward the other detective, who shrugged. "We're gonna give you a pass today, 'Maculate."

The other detective added a nod of approval.

Immaculate sat up the best he could pinned in the rear seat of a patrol car. "You screwin' with me. For real?"

"Come by the precinct tomorrow at ten, no later. And don't show me up. We'll figure out something to do with you," Reed said.

The officer with the Maui Jims pulled to the curb, stopping just short of another alley off to the right. Immaculate looked out the rear and through the side windows of the car. No one seemed to notice their vehicle nor its occupants. Reed opened the rear door and unlocked the cuffs.

"Okay, man," Immaculate said and stepped onto the sidewalk. "See you tomorrow."

"Hope so, 'cause it's your last chance," Reed said as he shut the door behind Immaculate and returned to the front passenger seat. Officer Maui Jim drove them away hurriedly.

Immaculate walked along the street and felt his phone vibrate. Caller I.D. said *Jamal*, and he answered.

Jamal's voice filled his ear. "Open your eyes, bro. Over here at the alley." The grill of the jacked-up Town Car appeared at the entrance to the passageway between a pastry shop and a liquor store. "Get your skinny ass in here. We got business to take care of."

The Lincoln turned into the street in the direction of Dr. Scott Mack's office. Immaculate hopped into the front passenger seat.

# Chapter 16

The Mississippi Forensics Laboratory, or state crime lab, consisted of a main facility in Pearl, just outside of Jackson, and three regional laboratories, including one located on the Gulf Coast. The Gulf Coast Regional Laboratory was a sleek, modern, red-brick structure with a collage of square-shaped windows at the entrance and rows of similarly designed, single glass panes interspersed along the front façade. Overshadowed by the expanse of brick, these windows resembled portholes of an ocean liner, although square.

Inside the building's lobby, the receptionist swiveled her chair to attention and smiled at the young man who stood at her desk. She took his business card, then straightened her posture, pulled at the neck of her blouse, and tugged at the hem of her dress. She ran the tip of her forefinger across the edge of her lips. The pink lipstick applied after lunch an hour ago still felt moist and smooth as she admired her reflection in the computer screen.

She referred to the card. "May I help you, Detective Spearman?"

Spearman resembled her sister's boy, the oldest one, the one she would have a fling with if things were different—tall with broad shoulders and sharp, confident facial features—thick, dark hair cropped tight on the sides but fuller on top and combed back off the forehead to stand up straight, like it grew that way.

"Is the medical examiner free?" the detective asked. "Or is he tied up on a case?"

"Let me check." The receptionist tapped on the keyboard and a series of six digital video panels populated the monitor. Dr. Carlos

Ramirez appeared in the lower right. "I just love these security cameras. Lets me keep an eye on things." She hesitated and winked.

Reed shot a weak grin back at her. "Can I speak with Dr. Ramirez for a few minutes?"

The receptionist took another study of the images. "Looks like he's starting the next autopsy," she said. She clicked a few more keys, ran the pad of her finger down the casing of the computer monitor, and pointed a slender, pink fingernail at the screen. It matched her lipstick.

"I was right. It's that case you've been working on." She lowered her voice to a whisper. "I still read the paper. I have to. It keeps me in the loop 'cause nobody around here tells me anything." She grabbed the stack of papers beside her and waved him down the hall. "Dr. Ramirez uses the first room on the left for his autopsies." The desktop phone rang, and she answered it, then placed her hand over the mouthpiece. "Come back anytime, Detective Reed Spearman," she said and repeated the wink before announcing Reed's visit into the speaker phone linked to Ramirez's lab.

Reed managed not to grimace and forced a nod and smile, along with a thank you. He felt her gaze on him as walked to the door that led down the hall to the autopsy rooms. Reed peered through the narrow window in the first door and spotted Ramirez.

"I didn't sign up for this, detective," Dr. Ramirez said without interrupting his work. "I'm getting too many of these." Biloxi, Mississippi's chief forensic pathologist and medical examiner held the scalpel firmly and sliced through the chest to reach the pulmonary cavity.

Reed turned his head away then stole a glance. White foam oozed from the incision over the lungs and onto the autopsy table.

"This white foam is typical of acute opioid intoxication," Dr. Ramirez said. "The patient's neighbor underwent a robotic hysterectomy a few months ago and had almost a full bottle of Percocet left over. She only needed a few of the pills prescribed by her gynecologist, at least that's what the neighbor told someone in your department." He waved the knife at the body as though a laser pointer.

"It seems that this lady slipped into the neighbor's bathroom during a break from a weekly Bunko party and pocketed the narcotics in the medicine cabinet. Her husband found her face down in bed next to a spilled wine glass and empty bottle of Chardonnay. A prescription bottle was on the bedside table with the neighbor's name on it. It was empty too."

"So the toxicology report read opioid overdose. Likely listed alcohol too," Reed added.

"Let's consider another organ." Ramirez pointed the knife at the specimen pan. Swollen, pink and tan tissue rose above the lip of the metal rim. "This brain is edematous, quite edematous, something typically associated with opioid intoxication. Of course, we had to rule out other causes of death associated with the brain such as a blow to the head or an aneurysm."

Reed stepped back a few inches, swallowed hard, and managed, "But ... you've got a toxicology report."

"We do—except running that analysis is not quite as much fun as an autopsy."

Reed swallowed even harder.

"The procedure itself usually takes about two hours," Ramirez said. He adjusted the microphone suspended from the ceiling and dictated a few sentences of his medical findings. "We get the occasional homicide in here or fatal car accident—sometimes the result of a DUI. I assign myself either the victim or the drunk driver or both." Ramirez continued to work with the scalpel. "But this opioid epidemic ... it's overloaded my little morgue with examinations. I can imagine what it must be like in the inner cities up North."

Ramirez walked across the room to a large metal sink mounted on the wall and shifted a lever under it with his right knee. A heavy stream of water burst from the faucet and splashed among the surgical utensils left in the sink basin. He tossed the used surgical gloves in a trash can labeled with the word BIOHAZARD in bright orange tape, then streaked bactericidal liquid soap from a foot-activated dispenser across his hands to wash them. As though an afterthought, he removed his surgical cap and grabbed a brown paper towel from the adjacent wall dispenser to dry his hands.

The surgical light overhead accentuated the pathologist's thinning grey hair and pale, parchment complexion. "I moved here from Jackson over twenty years ago, planning to retire after a few years. But that didn't happen. I just turned seventy-five, Detective Spearman."

He pulled a pen from inside a desk drawer and begin to sign several sheets of paper mounted on a plastic clipboard. Until now, Reed had not noticed the slight tremor in the doctor's finger movements. "The state medical board should have put me out to pasture ten years ago," Ramirez said. "In fact, a couple of years ago I tried to retire for good. However, we were short on manpower, and nothing's changed. Those administrative hot shots in Jackson told me just to take it day-to-day. And here I am."

Reed stepped past the autopsy tables arranged parallel in the center of the morgue to the wall opposite the sink and work desk. Set into the wall were three rows of stainless-steel body coolers, most with a tag suspended from the handle. A string of numerals and capital letters were printed across each tag label in bold, black font. Reed assumed this information to represent individual medical cases. In much smaller print were surnames followed by a comma and a single initial.

"Looks like you've been busy, Dr. Ramirez," Reed said. "Most of these cold lockers are occupied."

"As you just saw, we get more than deadly car wrecks, gunshot victims, and terminal heart attacks in here. The Mississippi Gulf Coast is not immune to the ballooning national trend of deaths by overdose," the pathologist responded. "Some statistics report drug overdose as the leading cause of death among Americans under fifty."

Reed continued along the bank of cold lockers and the printed labels. He stopped at the name: Caston, P.

"Unfortunately, business is good in this department. This

workload is too much for someone half my age," Dr. Ramirez said. "Also, overdose deaths from synthetic opioids is skyrocketing."

"Yeah, like fentanyl," Reed said.

"I have a colleague up North. He has to rent additional cold-storage trailers and keep them in the parking lot to handle the overflow. And there's another chief medical examiner over in Florida who utilizes a private transport company to store corpses in other facilities until her office can get to them. Our own autopsy volume is up ten percent in the last six months."

"Ten percent? Wow." His back still to Ramirez, Reed reached the end of the row and turned around to retrace his steps.

"I can't keep enough assistants. They reach burnout quickly and quit," Ramirez said. "If we lose accreditation at our next inspection, the court can challenge our forensic findings."

Reed thought about Immaculate Davis and his other narcotic cases. The court-appointed defense attorneys did their best to vindicate the dope-pushing scum arrested in his undercover stings. Those lawyers worked just as hard as the more highly paid ones hired by the ritzy, dope-buying clientele his department also busted.

Ramirez yanked open the top drawer of a brown, metal file cabinet and stuffed his papers inside. "I've signed off on the major autopsy findings. That dolled up receptionist out front is supposed to help me with the clerical stuff, but she won't come near the morgue," he said. "Too busy putting on make-up and nail polish."

"Seems like a nice lady," Reed shrugged. "Shows up and does her job."

"You got a point there," Ramirez said.

"We're definitely seeing more drugs out on the streets," Reed said, "along with underage drinking and adult alcohol abuse. I suspect you see a high alcohol content on a lot of the toxicology screens. The addicts toss a hand full of pills in their mouth, sometimes without knowing the strength, and down 'em with booze."

"And if it stays down and the combination is more than they can handle, then they wind up here with me." Ramirez said and waved a hand around the morgue. He tapped a few keys on his computer keyboard. The patient schedule for the next day appeared on the screen.

"The DEA says that 850 million pills … opioids … made their way into Mississippi between 2006 and 2012. Hundreds have died from opioid overdose in the last few years, and the problem is not just with the Coast," Ramirez said. He referred to another file, this one in the top drawer of a desk. "Up in Alcorn County enough opioids were dispensed to provide every resident eighty-seven pills a year, and not far from here in Marion County it was ninety-five."

Reed raised his eyebrows and nodded. Those numbers would have kept Immaculate Davis and his buddy Jamal very busy.

"And, hell, you won't believe this, but some fool pharmacy over in Meridian dispensed an average of 5,300 painkillers every single day during that same six-year period," Ramirez said. He tossed the file back inside the drawer and slid it shut, hard. "Detective Spearman, you guys gotta do something about this. The media calls it *the opioid crisis*. But even though this situation is the worst-case scenario of substance abuse that anyone could imagine, it plays second fiddle to every other crisis in the news."

Reed pulled out his smartphone and entered opioid prescription rates in Mississippi. "Says here the number of opioid painkiller prescriptions has dropped." He again referred to the screen. "But Mississippi still ranks pretty high—enough to cover every single resident in the state with a narcotic prescription between 2014 and 2017."

"And that's legal prescriptions. Plenty of docs are listed in the phonebook or on the internet for patients to shop around," Ramirez said. "And that doesn't count the drugs smuggled in over the border."

Reed cleared his throat to squelch a chuckle at Ramirez's phonebook reference. "If an addict's doc won't prescribe enough, then they take to the streets," Reed said and thought again about Immaculate. "When the price of popping pills gets too high, the dealers see an uptick in consumer demand for heroin—at least that's what the dealers tell me. And the precinct likewise sees an increase in meth use."

"I know you guys are working the streets for pushers and dealers and smugglers, but what about my comrades out there who overprescribe?"

"Anyone in particular?" Reed asked.

"A family practice doc in North Mississippi prescribed over 1,200 Lortabs over a seven-month period. Some patients never even got an examination. Who does that?" Ramirez said. "The state licensure board seized his patient records. That doctor's deeds put one woman on life support and another on my autopsy table."

Reed checked the time on his phone. He was due back at the office.

Ramirez continued. "Surgeons and physicians complain about the hassle, but in Mississippi they're supposed to review a patient's prescription history online before writing a script for a controlled substance. It's called the Prescription Monitoring Program."

"Surgeons write most of those narcotics, I guess. I wonder what they tell their patients to do with the leftovers," Reed mused, half to himself.

"Ought to tell them to flush the pills down the toilet," Ramirez said. The postmortem examination completed, an assistant entered to return the body to the bank of cold storage lockers. Both Reed and Ramirez watched in silence as the man snapped shut the stainless-steel door.

"Unfortunately for that lady, her bunko partner did not flush the leftover Percs," Ramirez added.

Reed motioned to the end of the bottom row of lockers to the door tagged CASTON, P. "You do the doctor's case, the one who shot himself yesterday?" Reed asked.

"Missed that one. Dr. Caston came in during one of my rare days off. The state finally hired two additional pathologists to work under me—the young lady, a pretty young lady, was on duty. Name is Leslie Charles."

Reed made a note of the female pathologist's name.

140

"I reviewed Dr. Charles's report. The cause of death was a penetrating gunshot wound to the head. The majority of men who commit suicide use a firearm, and Paul Caston knew what he was doing. Shoot to kill, you might say."

"To the first officer on the scene, it was a cut-and-dried suicide," Reed said. "No sign of forced entry into the doctor's vehicle, no sign of struggle."

"Other types of projectile head injuries may not always be fatal but result in horrific disabilities if the person survives. In this case, however, the bullet from the victim's handgun passed through vital brain tissue and disrupted important vascular structures. There was no exit wound and no chance of survival."

Ramirez opened Caston's cold storage and slid the corpse out. Using a pencil, the pathologist pointed to a reddish brown, somewhat circular abrasion on the skin. "This area marks the entrance wound of the bullet, the tattoo some call it."

Reed referred again to his phone and scrolled through his notes. "The weapon was found near his right hand," he said. That hand tested positive for GSR, and the barrel had evidence of blood, skin, and brain tissue—all Caston's DNA. And I talked with his office nurse, a Betty Thibodeaux. She confirmed that Dr. Paul Caston was right-handed."

Ramirez took another look. "Yes, the circumference of the fingers of the right hand seems a bit more than the left and the forearm more muscular, typical of the dominant upper extremity."

"Any toxicology reports?" Reed asked.

Ramirez raised an eyebrow. "Positive for traces of opioids and alcohol."

# Chapter 17

Reed Spearman stepped from his unmarked police vehicle parked directly in front of the office of the late Paul Caston, M.D. He glanced across and down the street to the location of the van used during the Immaculate Davis/Paul Caston sting that failed to convict the good doctor. A Christian-style cross memorial fashioned of dark green leaves overlain with white roses hung across the glass entrance door and covered the name of the clinic emblazoned across the glass. A simple cardboard sign in bold black letters on a white background hung below the cross and read:

CLINIC CLOSED. EMERGENCY? CALL 911

Reed held the warrant to search the premises in the inside pocket of his jacket. Even though Caston was recently acquitted on the charge of trafficking narcotics, the judge quickly granted the search warrant based on the surveillance information and Caston's subsequent shooting death. Reed failed to disclose to the judge that from his visit with Dr. Ramirez, the M.E. was to rule the Caston death a suicide.

Officer Owen Smith pulled up beside him and stood next to Reed on the sidewalk. His polyester blue uniform pulled at the waist, and his standard issue law enforcement service cap hid the disappearing hairline. "Seems that Dr. Caston's nurse was also the office manager," he said and checked his note pad. "A Betty Thibodeaux. I talked to her. She moonlights over at the hospital but plans to change to full time."

"Guess so, since Caston's dead," Reed said.

"I asked her to meet us here, but her supervisor at the hospital wouldn't let her off her double shift. At least that's what Thibodeaux told me."

"Too bad she didn't show up with the key," Reed said. His kick to the metal frame of the single door slammed it against an interior wall, wildly swinging the memorial wreath suspended from a tiny hook by thin fishing line. On the door's impact with the wall, the wreath broke away to fly across the medical office lobby. White rose petals littered the carpet.

The only recently closed office already smelled musty. Reed and Owen donned gloves and entered. Minimal light streamed around the edges of the closed blinds that covered the front window facing the street. Reed flipped a light switch just inside the door and illuminated the waiting area. He and Officer Smith entered the room.

"I questioned Ms. Thibodeaux the day after we found Dr. Caston in his vehicle," Owen said. "She said that none of the clinic employees had discussed Caston's trial or acquittal, at least not around her, and the day before he died was business as usual around this place. Caston kept to himself and didn't seem troubled or depressed."

"Caston should've felt lucky. His name was cleared, and he got to keep his medical license," Reed said. "Jury sure blew that one."

He and Owen walked through the lobby of the Paul P. Caston Center for Orthopedic Surgery. Original artwork covered the walls and hung above plush, richly upholstered furniture. Neat, thin stacks of current magazines waited under the lamps on the end tables. The tiny trash receptacles spaced around the room had been emptied. Several matching pillows were neatly arranged on the two sofas. A sturdy, thick-leaved plant grew tall in a corner, and several smaller just as healthy plants decorated some of the furniture.

"On the other hand, if the nurse is shooting straight, and Caston's last day here was business as usual, then the clinic ought to be just as they left it at the end of the day," Owen said. "Guess they got a good cleaning service."

"Let's get our hands on any security footage—see if either Caston or his nurse came back here after closing time the day before Caston shot himself or if she's been here since."

"Will do," Owen said.

Reed found another electrical panel and lit the entire front office space. "Dr. Caston must have had a personal, private office around here somewhere, and from the furniture and wall hangings around this place, it's a nice one," he said. He motioned for Owen to follow. "Let's check out what's down this hall."

"I know I'm not a patient, but being in a doctor's office is pretty creepy for me," Owen said. "And poking around this place, all stuffy and gloomy with the doctor stone cold in the morgue, kinda tests a guy's nerves even more."

Reed found the light switch to the hall. Large windows with drawn shades covered the front exterior wall of the corridor, and both men stopped outside the door to a room at the end.

Paul P. Caston M.D. in raised, gold letters filled a plaque mounted on the door. The wood looked expensive. *Mahogany,* Reed decided. "Maybe you should enter first," Reed said. "Not sure I want to walk ahead of you and your gun."

Medical degrees and other certificates of recognition matted in gold-leaf, hand-carved wooden frames filled the wall behind an executive desk, also mahogany. With strong lines and dark wood, the piece dominated the room. Reed envisioned Dr. Caston sitting in the high-back, brown leather chair behind the desk writing one narcotic prescription after the other. A matching leather couch with pillows was against the adjacent wall, and tall glass reading lamps on end tables framed the area.

Owen's flashlight cast eerie shadows at odd angles off the lamps and the gilded wooden frames around the certificates.

"Put that flashlight away. Now you're giving me the creeps," Reed said. He located the control in Caston's office and turned on the overhead light, then studied the materials on the physician's desk.

Next to a short stack of patient charts was a notepad personalized at the top with Caston's name and the address and phone number of the orthopedic practice. A sleek, shiny black ballpoint pen lay between the charts and the notepad. A laptop sat near the center of the desk with a modular phone off to the side. A paperweight in the likeness of the Moondust Casino building rested under the desk lamp. Reed read the inscription along the base of the paperweight:

A HEAVY WEIGHT FOR A HEAVY WEIGHT.
THANKS FOR YOUR PATRONAGE.

"Reed, there's a safe in this cabinet opposite the window." A six-foot high, black metal safe with digital keypad, three-spoke chrome handle, and eagle insignia with spread wings above the handle stood inside the tall cabinet opposite the couch. It was typical of that used to store hunting rifles and other guns. The door to the safe was ajar. Owen opened it and ran his flashlight across the shelving. "That doctor left behind quite a pharmacy," he said.

Reed returned the miniature casino to the top of the desk and joined Owen at the safe. Trays filled with plastic prescription pill bottles lined the shelves, and Reed read aloud the label on many of them. "Oxycodone, hydrocodone, acetaminophen with codeine, alprazolam ..." He stumbled over a few of the other generic brand names. "These all belong to different patients—and not all the bottles have Caston as the prescriber. There're names of other doctors too."

Owen also riffled through the safe. "Here's a big bottle of cough syrup, the good stuff," he said. "Says cherry-flavored on the label, and I don't think the seal has been broken." He held the bottle of dense, red liquid to the recessed lights in the ceiling. "What I wouldn't have given for some of this stuff last month when I had the flu and that bad cough. I didn't know you could get a bottle this big."

"I guess you gotta have connections," Reed said. He slid a tray off another shelf and shifted the contents from side to side. Syringes of fentanyl rolled clumsily over and under each other. The tray beside it was filled with injectable morphine. Reed picked up several of the syringes and studied the labels. "Even if the expiration dates have passed, there's enough stuff in here to take down a herd of elephants."

A thumping sound worked its way from the front lobby down the corridor to Dr. Caston's office. "It sounds like somebody's banging on the front door," Reed said. "You shut the front when we came in?"

"Got it secured, despite the number you did on the lock," Owen answered. The sound grew louder, frantic.

"Let's check that out." Reed reached inside his jacket for the .40 caliber Smith & Wesson semi-automatic concealed in his left shoulder holster. He stepped quickly into the hall.

The noise at the door swelled and then stopped, the area now quiet. Reed moved away from the door and peered through the blinds of the lobby window onto the street and sidewalk. A woman's face surprised him. She had stringy, dark hair and pressed her face deep into the glass, her lips flattened into suction and her eyes frantic in an attempt to see into the room. Reed stepped back, his gun still raised.

At the sight of Reed and the weapon, she jerked away from the window and paced between the parking meters. She checked up and down the street, then jumped back to the entrance of the clinic and resumed her pounding against the door. Reed wondered if her fists and knuckles would bleed.

"Dr. Caston?" the woman yelled. "Nurse Betty? Dr. Caston? Anybody? Somebody open this freakin' door. I got to have my meds."

Still at the window, Reed glanced back at Officer Smith.

"Go ahead and let her in," Owen said, his weapon also drawn. "If you and I can't take her down, we got problems. I'll cover you."

"Dr. Caston, why does that guy in the window have a gun?" she screamed. "I ain't no criminal!" The woman ran her fingers down the side of her face and twisted the ends of her hair in her fingertips. She attacked the door again.

146

"The office is closed, ma'am." Reed returned his gun to the holster and popped open the door to the lobby. He ducked his head to the right to miss her fists, then presented his badge with his left hand, still dodging her movements.

"Hey, lady. Slow down. This is a crime scene investigation. What's your problem?" Officer Smith said. He moved behind her in the doorway. "You want me to cuff her, Detective Spearman?"

The woman shook her head away from Reed's police credentials to brush past both men into the room, crushing some of the white petals under her feet. "Hey, is Dr. Caston not here ... and where's Betty? Where'd they go? I need them bad."

Reed recognized the Moondust Casino insignia embroidered on the collar of her polo shirt. The purple fabric hung loosely untucked at the rear, and the same insignia peeked out from the back pocket of her black stretch pants.

Owen followed her into the center of the patient waiting room. She seemed to admire his navy-blue polyester uniform, complete with gleaming metal badge pinned on the front alongside the shiny pins and patches—a sharp contrast to Reed's slim-cut, dark suit and tie. The woman stood in the middle of the lobby, shaking her head. Her eyes darted back and forth between the two men.

"The doctor and the nurse aren't here," Owen said. "Nobody's seeing patients today. You'll need to go somewhere else."

"There're other doctors who can help you. Biloxi's a big town," Reed said. "Here's my card. Call the station. We can get you lined up with a social worker."

"You guys don't get it," the woman said. "I wasn't seeing Dr. Caston as a patient—not in that way. He used to come down to the casino a lot. I trusted him." The woman's fingers were trembling.

"You trusted him? About what?" Reed asked.

The woman began to stumble in circles about the room. She grabbed her abdomen with her right hand. "Listen, you guys. I'm really nauseated," she said. Her hands trembled and she breathed rapidly. "I'm about to lose it."

"Detective, she don't look so good," Owen said.

"You guys gotta leave me alone. I need the restroom." She ran down the hall and slammed the door. Reed and Owen could still hear her throw-up.

"She oughta feel better now," Reed said. "Maybe you should go check on her."

More retching followed, then the sound of a flushing toilet.

"Me? I ain't goin' into no women's room. Get yourself a female partner if you want that stuff."

"There's no need for you guys to trouble yourself." The pale woman tottered back into the front lobby, her arms covered with goose-bumps. She held them crossed over her breasts and ran her hands up and down the exposed skin. "If Dr. Caston isn't around, then I'm out of here."

Reed again flashed his badge from inside his jacket and read her name off her casino employee badge. "Before you take off ... Miss ... Selena, you need to tell us about your relationship with Dr. Caston and his nurse."

"No way." She pushed past Reed toward the door. Officer Smith stopped her.

"Hey, Detective Spearman just wants to ask you a few questions," he said. "Besides this office is not open for business, and we might have caught you breaking and entering, or something like that."

"Whatever." Selena shook her head and sank into one of the lobby chairs. "Could one of you gentlemen get me some water?" She gestured to the water dispenser in the corner. Owen filled a paper cup and brought it to her.

"Dr. Caston is one of our big-time players at the casino," she said. "I was his blackjack dealer on Friday nights. Then he started showing up on Saturdays, and I saw him every night I worked. All the dealers got to know him ... the cocktail servers, the casino managers ...even the security guard."

Reed and Owen looked at each other. "Then Dr. Caston racked up player points, bigtime," Reed said.

"If I let you know the whole story, you're not gonna arrest me. Are you?" Selena finished the water, rubbed her stomach again, and held up the cup. "I need a little more of this," she said. "Please?"

Owen complied with another cup, this one filled to the brim, and she sloshed a bit on her blouse.

"Dr. Caston shot himself," Reed said.

Selena sat forward in her chair. "What? You're freakin' kidding me!" She jumped from the chair, spilled the rest of the water, and paced the room. "I trusted Dr. Caston that he would be there for me." She stood at the opposite side of the room and lowered her eyes. "I considered Doc a friend; I needed him."

"A friend?" Owen said.

"Yeah, a friend. He wrote me prescriptions."

"Narcotics, I assume." Reed said.

Selena nodded. "Mostly OCs, oxy, Percs, and vics—a few xannies." She straightened her posture and became silent, as though questioning her decision to talk about her relationship with Dr. Caston.

"It's okay," Reed said. "Just tell us what was going on."

She hesitated a few seconds and continued. "I filled the 'scripts at pharmacies all along the Coast and toward New Orleans, mostly the big chains, but sometimes it seemed easier at the mom-and-pops. I figured pharmacists were supposed to monitor what they dispensed, so I usually hit them at the busy times with lots of customers and less time for paperwork—or right before closing. When I could get back home to where I grew up, there were even fewer questions from my old drugstore."

"So, you filled the prescriptions for pain meds and downers at various pharmacies, and then what?" Reed asked.

"Now, hold on a minute. Since I'm comin' clean on this crap, you guys still promise you ain't gonna arrest me?"

Reed shook his head at Owen. "We didn't come here to arrest anyone. Just tell us what else you know."

"I liked Dr. Caston. He was so sweet. The first 'script he ever wrote me was after I tripped in the rain outside my apartment.

149

I came to work with my wrist wrapped in a bandage. He was a player at my table that night, and he said that he felt sorry for me."

"Felt sorry for you?" Owen asked.

Selena's brow dripped sweat. She ran the back of her hand across her forehead to wipe it. "Dr. Caston examined my arm and told me I had a sprained wrist. He offered to give me something to help with the pain but told me I wouldn't have to see him in the office or anything like that. He wrote a prescription on a pad he had inside his jacket, said it was a tip for good service and good cards at the casino, a party favor."

"Guess we know what happened to those party favors," Reed said.

"I've got bills to pay, detective. The casino owners don't payout to the employees like they do the players." Selena sat back down and ran her hands back and forth along the arms of the chair. The upholstery matted under her sweat. "Now with Dr. Caston gone, not sure what I'm gonna do."

She shook her head and jumped from the chair in panic. "I've said too much. You cops can't be trusted. You're gonna take me in. I know you are."

The entrance to the medical clinic rattled as someone else tried the door. Owen stepped back to the window and peeked through the window blinds. A pale Caucasian man in a casino uniform similar to Selena's stood outside. His actions mimicked hers. His head and hands trembled, and beads of sweat peppered his forehead.

"Must be another one of the doc's patients who wants to see him," Owen said. "Some guy who works at Moondust." The male casino employee paced back and forth on the sidewalk, stopping only to yank the door handles and pound his fists on the door itself.

"Let me see." Selena nudged Officer Smith away and checked for herself. "Gee, that's Mark. He works the roulette tables. I didn't know he did business with Doc Caston." She took another look. "Wow, his shirt tail is hanging out, and his hair is all greasy—like he hasn't taken a shower in a week."

The pounding on the door grew and screams followed, the sound

150

barely muffled by the exterior walls of the building. "Dr. Caston, Betty. Somebody, please … open up. Come on, you gotta help me!"

Selena checked again through the blinds. "I've never seen Mark in this shape before. He's always neat as a pin and all business at work, but it looks like he's in withdrawal," Selena mumbled to the two policemen. "I wonder who else at the casino was in with Dr. Caston?"

# Chapter 18

Reed pulled into his reserved parking space in front of the Biloxi Police Department. Transplanted palm trees anchored the landscaping and framed the structure. The Municipal Court chambers were an extension of the building.

"How long were you with the department before you landed this spot?" Owen asked. He counted the palm trees surrounding Reed's parking space. "Four damn trees, right here, right by your vehicle. Hell, you've practically got shade, man."

Reed turned off the ignition and popped open the driver's door. "Come on. Palm trees aren't that great for shade."

"My cousin works in landscaping. Wanna guess how much the taxpayers forked over for these babies?" Owen said and motioned to the palm trees. "Not to mention installation. They had to air lift those babies in by helicopter." He followed Reed toward the entrance to the police department.

"I got no idea what those trees cost," Reed said, "and don't care."

Owen was quiet for a few seconds. "Where I park across the street, the space left after the discount furniture store burned—" he tossed his head toward the empty lot, "—it's first come, first serve."

"All you gotta do to move up the ladder is show up for work and do your best job … like you've done for the last three years. It's been two or three years on the force, right?"

Owen nodded.

"You'll get there," Reed said.

Owen shook his head. "Doesn't look like it. No change in where I park and no change in my rank."

"Could be all luck," Reed said. "There was this guy in his sixties— about to retire when I joined the force. He was goin' out as lead detective in investigations and took me under his wing. I actually admired the guy. A couple of days before his big send-off party, he had a heart attack. The secretary in the front office gave me his parking spot—like he willed it to me or something."

Owen followed Reed to his office and sank into one of the chairs opposite Reed's desk. "Besides luck, maybe I should have been sexy too," he said and checked the reverse image on the screen of his phone. "At least a little taller and all white. Yeah, a lot taller and with better hair."

"Right place at the right time, you know," Reed said. "I was polite to the lady in charge; that's all. Next time I take a vacation, I'll tell her to let you use my space."

"Might take you up on that," Owen said. He slid a note pad from his shirt pocket and flipped through a few pages. "This connection between the casino employees and Caston—at least two of them. You surprised about that?"

"The fact that Dr. Caston gambled? I guess not," Reed said. "Some doctors play golf, some gamble, but most don't trade narcotic prescriptions for favors. If Selena's shooting straight with us, the Gaming Commission will get involved. The Bureau of Narcotics is already on it."

Owen referred to another page in his notes. "Wonder why the doc shot himself? He beat the rap in court. Maybe guilt over that oath those guys swear to?" he said. Owen stood and reached for the foot-tall waste receptacle in the corner of the room and began to clip his fingernails with the tool attached to his key chain.

Reed shuffled some paper files on his desk. "Some doctors get a god complex, that a physician can do anything, even illegal stuff, as long as they're helping patients," he said. "Then they get used to that little extra cash on the side, like from winning at the table or selling leftover pills, especially when it turns into good money."

Owen continued with the self-manicure. "Besides those two who showed up at Caston's office a couple of days ago, I wonder how many more junkies he supplied."

"Dealing drugs to junkies is a better way to put it," Reed said. He flipped through another file. "But the jury said no."

Owen grinned. "If he was acquitted, then why off himself?"

"Even after the trial, the Mississippi Bureau of Narcotics was not going to call off the tail on Caston, and the doctor understood that, I expect. Maybe he felt guilty about the Hippocratic oath you mentioned … or thought that if he got busted again, he might not be able to face the music."

Momma Kile knelt to pull the last few cans of Pringles Crisps from the shipping carton and slapped a price sticker on each with a handheld machine. The Memphis Barbeque and Pizza varieties sold even better than Cheese, but the supplier's stock was low on those flavors. So Original and Honey Mustard would have to do, at least for this week. As she straightened the row of cans along the shelf and turned the marked price to the rear, the string of bells on the front door rattled. Momma kicked the empty box away and pushed against the concrete floor with her right hand to stand up in the aisle.

"May I help you?" she asked, stretching her neck and head around the corner for a glimpse of the new customer.

The front entrance to the store swung shut behind a Hispanic woman in her late thirties or early forties. She was about five-three with dark hair just off the shoulders. Her clothing stretched at the seams, and Momma thought she recognized the type of uniform as one of the wholesale vending suppliers. The woman appeared nervous, almost agitated, and rubbed her stomach in rapid, circular movements.

Momma Kile retrieved the empty Pringles carton and moved nearer to the woman. "I only accept vendor sales calls on Tuesdays," she said before noticing the casino employee insignia on the front of the woman's blouse. The name tag on the uniform read: Selena Garcia.

"Can I help you with something?" Momma asked.

Selena checked the aisles around her, her hands trembling. She noticed no other shoppers in the store except for some teenage boys who fingered their way through the soft drink cooler toward the beer section. Stacks of merchandise filled the aisles topped with promotional sales signage. *Buy two bags, get a third free. Free beach towel with one of these coolers.*

"I ... uhhh ... need to buy some stuff." Selena's voice trembled.

"Stuff?" Momma Kile made her way to behind the sales counter. She straightened the already tidy packs of cigarettes in the racks above the cash register and slid the packets of Slim Jims back and forth without ultimately changing their location. "Not sure what you want," Momma said. "What stuff?"

The three boys brushed ahead of Selena to the checkout counter, each with a twelve ounce can of Red Bull. Momma Kile took the can from the first one and passed the barcode over the sensor connected to the sales register. "That'll be $2.77 each with tax. Y'all paying together or separate?"

The same boy passed her a ten. Momma Kile handed him the change, and the boys disappeared.

Selena watched them leave and stepped close to the counter. She looked behind to verify she was the lone customer and whispered, "I need some OCs. My source is gone."

Momma Kile strained her neck through the pass-through above the sales counter to hear better.

"This doctor ... name was Caston," Selena said. "He got me what I needed, then helped me to supply my own users. But now he's gone. He ... he died."

Momma Kile checked the security monitors and leaned forward a bit more for a better look down the store aisles, even stepped to the end of the counter to eye the area far right toward the back exit. In addition to the security camera inside the front entrance, she had other inexpensive units positioned behind her, at the end of each aisle, and outside the restrooms—not to mention the exterior cameras behind and in front of the building. All the cameras fed into the multi-panel monitor to the left of her register. Mirrors in the corners of the building's interior, at the front window by the register, and at the entrance served as back-up to the grainy images. From her perch behind the counter, she felt in total control—even though the cameras were secondhand. God could not see any better.

Reassured that the interior of the store was empty of other customers, Momma Kile responded to the woman in the Moondust Casino uniform. "I run a simple business here, a convenience store," she said and leaned back, more relaxed. "I don't know nothing about some doctor who died, but how'd you find out about me and this place?"

At the moment, only one of the three gasoline pumps was occupied. The female customer had paid at the pump with a debit card and filled her Tahoe with twenty gallons of mid-grade gasoline. She leaned against the far side of the vehicle and started jabbering on her cell phone.

"The more the servers show up with free drinks for tips, the more my table patrons talk. Some of my regulars have bought from you, but they prefer to deal with me—and not just in cards. I slip merchandise to them in small packets during play or meet up later in the parking lot or in the restroom when I'm on break."

"What about casino security?" Momma glanced at one of her own ceiling-mounted cameras directed at the sales counter. She flipped a switch under the lip of the counter to disable it.

"Moondust is a big place. I'm tight with security personnel and know where the cameras are. I can stay under the radar when I need to."

Momma Kile continued to keep an eye on the woman outside at the pump and checked the gasoline read out at the counter.

The gasoline customer had not returned the fuel dispenser to the cradle and had opted out of a receipt. Suddenly, the woman's head and phone snapped up and down and from side to side in unison as though the conversation had turned heated. She slammed the palm of her other hand against the hood of the SUV.

Momma reread the name on the uniform. "So, Selena, you wanna buy product for resale or for yourself?"

The woman at the pump abruptly finished her call and returned the dispenser to its cradle. She got into her Tahoe and drove off.

Selena answered, "Why does it matter to you what I do with the goods as long as you get paid? Twenty Percs—that's all I need. That'll get me through the weekend." Selena dropped a roll of bills near the register.

Momma Kile spread her fingers and covered the money with both hands. The cash disappeared. "I can give you fifteen," she said. The faint sound of rustling paper rose from underneath the counter. Her hands reappeared with three tiny plastic bags, all sealed at the top. She slid them to Selena. "I package my Percs in multiples of five."

Selena dropped the oxycodone acetaminophen mixture into a jacket pocket. "Then I need change. Give me my change."

Momma Kile turned away and bent down for the boxes of Taylor's Pride and Cannon Ball chewing tobacco packets on the floor behind her, pushed tight against the wall. The display rack of solid tobacco plugs was almost bare. Momma answered Selena over her shoulder.

"You got what you came for, lady. My prices just went up. And if you're lucky, I won't charge you double the next time you need me." Momma slid a few plug packets into the empty slots. "And don't let the door hit your butt on the way out."

Selena jumped forward and groaned as her ribs hit the edge of the counter. She reached for Momma's arm, but missed, toppling a box of Slim Jims and the credit card processor to the concrete floor.

Momma dropped the rest of the box of Taylor's Pride and swung around to face Selena. Her posture stiffened. Several packets had popped out of the carton to scatter at Momma's feet, and she kicked them away. Momma Kile's several-inch height advantage over Selena grew to a foot.

Selena jumped back from the counter when Momma kicked the rest of the box of tobacco with her heel, this second time with purpose—smashing it against the wall. The floor behind the counter became littered with more dry plugs of chewing tobacco. She pounded the surface of the counter with her a fist.

"Are you dense? I said you need to leave now," Momma growled. "The first wave of the shipyard lunch crowd from up the road will be coming in soon. They ain't looking for no OCs, at least not at lunch, but I need their cash for the legal stuff too."

Selena's voice and hands trembled. "You owe me five more pills," she managed.

"See those hot dogs and the sausage and cheese pizza in the rotisserie over there? By 1:30, it'll be a sellout. Now, get your ass out of here. I don't want no junkie trashing up the place and scaring off the food and drink customers."

Selena tore open one of the new packages from her jacket, popped two of the pills, and swallowed them dry. A warm haze passed over her.

"You might be good at dealing cards, but you laid all yours on the table when you first came in here today," Momma Kile said. "It's all about supply and demand."

"Excuse me?"

"You lost your sugar daddy, sweetie." Momma straightened up the mess on the counter. "Your Doctor Caston is out of the picture, and you're here, begging. Like I said, supply and demand. And I got the new supply."

The oxycodone began to slow Selena's breathing and steady her fingers. "I'm getting screwed here," Selena said. She darted her eyes about the store. "But I need this crap, and my clients at the casino want to buy from me. I was supposed to meet one of 'em outside the restrooms this morning. I couldn't deliver, so I stood him up."

"There'll be others like you crawling in here begging for quality stuff. They got nowhere else to go—except deal with slime out on the street. I'm all there is."

A group of boisterous men in oil and grease-stained overalls pushed through the front doors and headed for the hot food island. Each man grabbed an individual white cardboard serving container from the stack provided and snapped open the door to the rotisserie cabinet. The roasting, ballpark-style hotdogs disappeared from the unit within seconds. Mustard and ketchup dispensers flew among the men.

"Hey, Momma Kile, we're running out of hotdog buns over here!" One of them yelled in the direction of the checkout counter. "And where's the relish?"

Another said, "You got some more dogs we can load into this thing?"

"Wouldn't need no more if you hadn't took three, you asshole," another man said.

"I got more in the cooler. Won't take long to heat up," Momma said, glaring at Selena. "I'll take care of it in a sec. I've rung this lady up, and she's gotta go."

One of the men lumbered toward the register with a six-pack of soft drinks. One can broke away from the plastic ring packaging and hit the concrete. Yellow-green fluid spewed from the punctured can, spraying the rack of Doritos.

More business spilled through the front door—first, a young black woman with a screaming infant in a baby wrap carrier. She rubbed the baby's back to quiet him. "Hey, lady," she called to Mamma Kile. "Y'all sell diapers and wipes?" She walked to the side of the store opposite the drink coolers. "They back here somewhere?" she shouted over her shoulder.

"This place is a freaking zoo." Selena crammed what was left of the tiny package of pills back into her pocket. "Too many people around to push or buy product, even for a clever cheat like you." Selena pushed past the next group of potential customers, a family of four dressed in swimwear. The older of the two children pulled a blue inflatable raft from the front sales bin and carried it toward the register. His sister and parents gathered snacks from the displays.

Selena lowered her voice and turned toward Momma Kile. "Look, Kile, you better watch your back. You'll never rip me off again." The end of the boy's blue raft popped Selena in the face. She shoved it out of her way and left. The string of bells on the glass front doors swung behind her as the doors slammed shut, barely missing her.

Momma Kile grabbed the cordless phone on the counter beside the cash register. She punched in a number and balanced the phone between her shoulder and her ear. The rest of the shipyard workers brought their food and drinks to the front and paid in cash. The little boy clung to the raft and managed to stay clear. Momma made change quickly for the men.

"Sorry about the mess, Miz Kile," the guy who dropped the Mountain Dew said. "And what's with that chick in the casino uniform? I think she dealt me some rotten hands last weekend."

"Oh, she's just having a bad day—knows she's out of her league," Momma said. "Way out."

"Here's a twenty for my hot dogs and drinks. The change ought to cover the bags of chips that got wet."

Momma Kile ignored him. She held the twenty-dollar bill to the light and slipped it into the cash register without putting down the phone. "Hang on a minute. Got payin' customers," she said into the receiver and held the phone in place.

"See ya tomorrow at lunch, Momma," the last of the shipyard workers said and took a large bite of that third hot dog. She waved the guy off as the door shut. Still holding the phone against her ear, Momma Kile stepped from behind the counter to retrieve the credit card processor Selena knocked from the counter. It hung by an electric cord, inches from the floor. "What an ass," she said and grabbed the device to return it to the counter.

"Say what?" came through from the other side of the call.

Momma tightened the connection between the power cord

and the machine, and a tiny green light reappeared in the upper right-hand corner of the unit. The credit card processor was back online. She cut her eyes at the boy cowering with his raft at the side of the counter. "Son, if you ain't gonna pay for that thing, then put it back in the rack."

"He's my son, ma'am, not yours. Ring up that raft with this other stuff," the father said. The mother and the little girl stood behind him. All three piled purchases of canned soft drinks, chips, and candy on the counter. The father reached over his son and handed Momma Kile a credit card.

"You kidding me?" she said. "Your card has a chip. Slide it into that slot on the machine. It's right there in front of you."

The father frowned and shook his head. "We could've gone somewhere else, you know." He pushed the credit card into the reader. A series of nagging, flat beeps erupted from the processor joined by a series of blinking red lights.

Momma grunted and jerked the jammed card free, then reinserted it chip first. The transaction went through swiftly, and the father scribbled his name on the screen with the attached plastic marker. "Don't suppose this place gives fuel points for buying stuff," he said.

Momma grunted again. Except for the boy's inflated blue swim raft, she packed the family's purchases into several plastic bags and handed them off across the counter. "No points, only top-quality stuff. Now, you folks run along and have a lovely afternoon on the beach."

The family headed toward the exit. The bells clung behind them, the store now empty and quiet.

Momma moved away from the register toward the opposite end of the counter with the phone. "I just heard from a dealer at Moondust that the Biloxi doctor is dead," she whispered. "The chick used to buy from him. She came by the store a few minutes ago looking for OCs."

"You take care of her?" the young male voice asked. "You fix her up?"

"The girl was out of options, so I charged her a premium—plus extra for getting under my skin," Momma said. She checked the parking lot through the window. The family wedged the fully inflated raft into the back of a mid-sized SUV. The man carried two bags of ice that he had not paid for. Momma chose to let it go.

"This means the pill business is gonna pick up around here, and our supply is already stretched. It's gonna get worse, son."

"With Chuck retired and out of the way," Brandon Kile said, "I might be able to work some things out with the contraband when we arrest and seize a vessel."

"I've always been so proud of my smart boy," Momma said. "I've built a steady clientele around this place and got clients in high places. I sure don't want to let them down."

"That ain't gonna happen, Momma. You can count on your Number One," Brandon said and ended the call.

Momma Kile heard the bells again at the door. The father of four was back at the register. "I couldn't say anything before with my wife and kids around. But I heard something about your place at the motel up the highway." He glanced nervously around the store and toward the parking lot before lowering his voice. His fingers began to tremble. "I told my wife I was going back inside to pay for the two bags of ice, but I need to buy something ... something else—even if you can only give me a few."

"I can take care of that."

"Need some Xanax."

"Let's start with paying for that bagged ice," Momma said.

# Chapter 19

Selena found the only empty slot near the rear entrance to the Moondust Casino and squeezed her Ford Focus between a Ford F-250 and a Chevy Suburban. She had decided to ignore the inscription, *Wash Me*, fingered in the dust covering her back window, a souvenir from yesterday's trip to the convenience store. The chief suspect was one of the noisy men who came in for hot dogs or maybe even that little boy with the blue raft.

Selena freshened her lipstick in the rearview mirror and stopped to straighten her narrow black bowtie. Tonight, she wore one of her newest white shirts, medium starch for a casual, friendlier tone. *More welcoming to the clientele*, she thought.

The casino management had adopted new uniforms and required both male and female dealers to wear long-sleeved, white shirts and identical black bowties with tight, black pressed trousers or shorts for gentlemen and mini-skirts for ladies—all provided by employees at their own expense. Selena stepped from the car and pulled at the hem of her skirt, an unsuccessful attempt to cover the lower part of her cheeks.

"Oh, my hair," she remembered and stooped to check her reflection in the driver's outside mirror. She felt a large hand grab her buttocks.

"You want me to warm this up? I know it won't take much," the man said. "Or I should I reach around to the front."

Selena's jaws clenched. Her body stiffened and pulse quickened. "Get lost, Clive," Selena said and stepped away from the car.

"Besides, you wouldn't know what to do with it. You're better off tossing your balls at the roulette table."

Clive Jones pushed up against her from behind, touching the fabric of her skirt with the front of his pants. He leaned into her right ear. Selena could feel the thick mustache. "I'm ready when you are."

"Get lost, perv," Selena said and shook free. "I'm running a little late for my shift." She tossed her hair in her wake and pranced toward the entrance.

The casino pit manager paced in front of the cards table assigned early to Selena after the dayshift dealer called in sick with the flu. There was no other relief apart from Selena, and he was anxious for her to get to work and make up for lost revenue.

"You're five minutes late, Selena," he said, dropping her cards onto the felt surface of the table. The manager checked his watch again. "No, you're seven minutes late, although that's better than the no-account, no-show before you. Third case of the flu she's had this month, plus her grandmother died again."

Selena decided against placing blame for her tardiness on the nuisance interaction with Clive Jones in the parking lot. Instead, she forced a quick smile and made the cards ready for players. She planned to have a big night tonight—legitimate play that would impress both the floormen and the pit manager and boost her side business.

She started with an unsuccessful appeal to the gamblers headed for the slot machines in the next aisle that featured the *Star Trek* and *Game of Thrones* franchises. Despite a solicitous smile and posture that accentuated her cleavage, the men passed her table by.

"Guess I'm no match for Captain Kirk and Jon Snow," Selena muttered. She again checked the cards at her table, glanced up at the ceiling, and imagined someone with security watching her every move.

No one had ever informed her of the cameras in the ceilings—or anywhere else in the casino for that matter. *But all casinos have security cameras—everyone knows that.* In old movies like *Ocean's Eleven* or *Casino* there was always this big room at the top of the building or hidden somewhere important where scary men dressed in suits watched the action through monitors or two-way mirrors. They knew everything that went down on casino property—or thought they did.

An enormous cupola, easily visible from the street, topped the roof of the Moondust Casino. *That's where they sit and watch us,* Selena determined.

She removed a compact from her purse, puckered, and rubbed her lips together in the mirror, pretending to check her makeup while she glanced again at the ceiling. A slight tip upward of the mirror with a turn of the head side to side provided a better view of the hidden camera as she applied more purple lipstick. Selena caught her eyes drift upward, but quickly redirected her attention to the mirror inside the compact.

A few hundred feet over were the more dimly lit areas of the building that allowed cigarette smoking. Nonetheless, the visual effect of the ceiling overhead was to mimic a bright summer sky. Scattered within the mural of white clouds that floated against a light blue background were tiny black circles, from Selena's distance no larger than a dime and each representing a security camera.

She imagined a dangerous, but unnamed, broad-shouldered, muscular man—probably with a shaved head and likely not dressed in a business suit, who commanded a swivel-type captain's chair positioned in the center of a series of monitors fed by the cameras. He chewed on a straw and studied the live action throughout the casino, paying particular attention to all the female employees, like her. His black T-shirt and tight leather pants fit as though poured over him. A handgun packed inside a holster hung around his chest under a short jacket.

That bald man watched her every move, just waiting for Selena Garcia to screw up.

"You gonna primp all day, or you gonna deal blackjack?" A squatty man with a comb-over took one of the empty stools at Selena's table. He wore a blue shirt inscribed with the name of an automobile tire dealership and dropped a tall stack of multicolored, plastic chips on the green felt.

Selena snapped the compact shut and dropped it into her purse.

A woman whose build matched that of the man from the tire store, but with enough hair for a haircut, plopped onto the stool at the opposite end of the table. She wore a white and pink sundress, which plunged at the neckline and billowed at the waist. The fabric pulled and stretched at every curve. She deposited her chips in a neat pile in front of her. "Like the gentleman next to me said—Deal."

"Hey, wait for me." A slim male in his late twenties or early thirties dressed in jeans with a starched, white cotton shirt took the middle stool. His blond hair was cut short at the sides but left thick at the top and combed back off the forehead. Despite the hair gel, a few strands fell in his eyes. He fanned his chips across the surface of the table. "Deal me in," he said and winked at Selena. "I need some hot ones."

Selena studied the man's large hands, neatly manicured and absent a wedding ring. She smiled. With long fingers, masculine despite the manicure, he grabbed his Bud Light and downed it. Returning the smile, he ran his fingers up his forehead and through his hair to freshen the style.

The overweight man from the tire store let out a soft groan in Selena's direction. "Hey, no favoritism. My chips are as hard as his," he said. He lowered his right hand below the table as though to grab himself, then laughed.

"You're disgusting, Marvin," the woman said. She seemed to take notice of the embroidery on Selena's shirt. "Selena, please make the fatty perv keep both hands on the table," she laughed. "But I've known potbelly since high school. He's harmless."

Selena shuffled the cards using the riffle and overhand technique, then asked the young guy to slide her red cut card anywhere in the middle of the deck. He smiled again at her, added a wink, and set his empty beer bottle down to oblige. "Cut 'em thin to win," he said.

Selena split the deck and finished the shuffle. "Place your bets please," she said and waited for each to place chips in the tight circle in front of them, her eyes not leaving the table.

From left to right, Selena dealt one card to each blackjack player, sliding each from the top of the shoe and flipping the card face-up during the slide across the felt. In one slick motion, she centered each card in the yellow-outlined box in front of the player. She slid the next card from the top of the deck face-down in front of her and kept her eyes on the players.

Again from the left, she dealt each another card face-up and on top of the first so that both numbers could be read. She then set the next card face-up in front of her. While her visible card was an ace, it was a three and a six for the heavy-set woman in the sundress, a ten and also an ace for the attractive young man with the great-looking hair, and an eight and a nine for Marvin.

Just as Selena announced: "Insurance anyone?" another woman walked up behind them, this one with wavy, shoulder length red hair and bangs. Her sequined, blue dress dropped to the ankles and dazzled in the reflection of the mirror ball light hanging in front of Selena's table. Miniature mirror-ball shaped earrings dangled from her lobes.

The woman lit a cigarette and tried to appear disinterested. Selena decided to let security bust her for smoking in the non-smoking area.

A thick, seductive smoke ring parted from the woman's lips as she waved down the cocktail waitress. "A martini," she said, "and please take this empty for the trash, sugga. Maybe an actual cocktail glass next time and not plastic? I'm playing my best blackjack tonight."

"We'll get you in on the next hand, ma'am," Selena said. She dropped her eyes to the table.

"That's okay. I'll squeeze in here, next to my friend and wait." Miss

Martini sat between the young guy and the overweight one. She placed her hand on the young guy's forearm and leaned into him.

Selena's ace covered all but the edge of the face down hole card. "I've got an ace but so does my cutter boy over here, so please place your bets." She gestured to her left at the woman in the sundress.

All three players placed additional bets.

"Now, deal," the woman in the sundress said.

An hour later, she and Marvin walked away shaking their heads and cursing—the heavy-set woman in the sundress down over fifty bucks and Marvin two hundred. Selena smiled at the remaining two players: Miss Martini and the attractive young man with the styled hair. Except for the hand skipped waiting for drink service and the next deal, Miss Martini had missed none of the action since she joined the table.

In hopes that her table would fill back up, Selena paused a few seconds before the next hand and noticed that Miss Martini played with her hair while watching the casino action like a hawk.

"Y'all still in?" Selena reshuffled the hand and smiled her best. A busy table impressed the manager and floormen. She pulled at her skirt.

Beyond the video scrutiny in the security room, the pit manager and floormen or supervisors watched casino business in person. Equipped with microphone headsets, the managers reported the gambling traffic to the people upstairs and considered some black-jack dealers more popular than others—popularity defined by the number of high rollers as well as regular customers at tables. Dealers scored a plus if busy even on weeknights. Selena knew this from breakroom scuttlebutt.

Up until the fat lady and her friend Marvin left, this night for Selena had been more impressive than usual. She was moving up the ladder.

"Are you gonna deal, sugga?" Miss Martini asked. "Or are ya

gonna goggle at the hottie behind me?" A server, this time a muscular man in tight black shorts and white tuxedo shirt with black bow tie, presented her with a fresh drink. He balanced the dry martini on a round, dinner plate-sized tray with gold rim. Two plump green olives drowned at the bottom of the glass.

"Ready for a fresh one, sweetie?" he said and grinned—his smooth, bright teeth a sharp contrast to the dark complexion. He cut his eyes to a vacant spot on the tray. "Just set the empty right there and take the new treat," he said. "Special delivery, especially for you, beautiful. Enjoy!"

Miss Martini lifted the glass by the stem and balanced the bowl between her right forefinger and middle finger. She sipped slowly before lowering the cocktail to her space on the table. "Perfect," she said and blew a kiss over her shoulder to the server. "Check back by in a few. I'll be ready for another."

The male server straightened his bow tie and disappeared into the crowd. Selena noticed the two remaining players exchange whispers. She dealt each their cards, then hers.

"Hold a sec, sugga," Miss Martini said.

"Why?" Selena asked. "You two don't wanna play? They want us to keep things moving around here."

The blond guy admired his cards and produced a wad of bills from his pocket. He immediately palmed the cash. Selena noticed the money and eyed his winning stack. "If you want more chips or need to cash out, you gotta check with the cashier on the other side of the fountains. I can't take care of that here."

The fountains were a synchronized myriad of blue, green, and pink colored water jets that blew from deep within a shallow pool. Statues of Greek gods and goddesses, each illuminated by underwater uplighting, bordered the pool's perimeter. Choreographed, recorded voices of Cher and Celine Dion knockoffs rose from speakers concealed in the statuary and warbled in the rhythm of the fountain jets.

"Name's Brandon, and I'm not wanting more chips," the guy said. Miss Martini smiled and seemed to nod in agreement.

Selena shifted on her feet. The snug, polyester mini-skirt of her casino uniform confined her to casino business, but the three small baggies inside her bra burned her flesh and screamed, *Make a play.* "What's your play?" she said first to Miss Martini and then shook her head clear. "I mean … with the cards."

Martini shoved five ten-dollar chips to the center. "Do it for me, sugga. Deal me a winner." She tilted her head in Brandon's direction. "If not for me, do it for this guy. Me and him are here for the same thing."

Brandon dropped a $100 bet. "Hit me too," he said and ran his fingers up his forehead and through his hair again.

Selena hesitated a second before dealing. She thought again about the cameras and the security walking the floor. Martini shifted her eyes to the outside of the table and back toward the guy named Brandon. "My friend and I are just getting to know each other. But funny thing, we both buy and sell product, and we know you do too," Martini said. "Me and him want to talk a little business with you."

"I heard that your source dried up," Brandon followed quickly. "I shared that with the pretty lady here, and I think we can help."

Selena kept her eyes low and finished her deal, then the players bet. Martini had eighteen and Brandon twenty. Selena stole an upward glance at the ceiling. "Keep your face down when you talk and your voice low. They can read lips through the cameras," she said, "and floormen are everywhere."

Selena had a ten showing, flipped her hold card to a six, took another hit, and busted. "You take this one," she said with a tense smile at Brandon. His broad shoulders stretched an open-collared print shirt. A miniature gold cross inscribed with USCG across the face hung by a gold chain from his tanned neck. Whenever he moved, the emblem shifted like a pendulum across the top of his chest.

"It's the insignia for Chief Petty Officer," Brandon said, "and I know how to play the game—and I'm not talking about cards."

Selena matched Brandon's chips, and he scooped them toward him, the money still cupped in his hand.

A man with a beard and mustache, dressed in Hawaiian-styled shirt and white linen slacks, stumbled up to Selena's table. He sipped beer from a glass decorated with the Moondust Casino logo. His slacks pulled at the waist and hips, and the shirt was unbuttoned to below his naval to expose a plain white T-shirt. Beads of oily sweat peppered his balding, milk-chocolate scalp between the strands of his light brown comb-over. "Can I join the party?" he asked.

He clumsily pulled a stool underneath him and sloshed some of the beer onto the surface of the blackjack table—barely missing the deck of cards. "Seems things are mighty steamy over here," he said in a deep voice.

"Glad to have you, sir." Selena kept her head low and started the next hand.

The new player checked his right ear with a gentle rub. The earpiece was in place and unseen to those around him. "Take it easy, Owen. Don't push too hard at first," a voice oozed from the earpiece. "Remember how frazzled the chick was at Dr. Caston's office."

Police Officer Owen Smith fought a grin and wanted to whisper, "I got this, asshole," into the miniature microphone hidden under his shirt collar or better yet throw the finger at the security cameras overhead. Reed would get a kick out of either.

# Chapter 20

From his hidden perch in the video surveillance center of the Moondust Casino, Detective Reed Spearman watched the somewhat blurry image on the screens. He stood with the head of security detail, a medium-height, stern-faced African American woman dressed in a navy suit with the casino insignia on the lapel.

"So far, so good," Reed commented.

"I hope you guys can make this go down smooth," she said. "As quiet as possible."

When Owen resumed speaking, Reed motioned for them to focus attention on their own earpieces.

"Name's Hal," Owen said, glancing at the other two players as he settled firmly on the stool beside them. Without the blue polyester policeman garb and hat and with the added fake facial hair he looked unrecognizable to Selena. At least that's what he and Reed hoped.

Owen had practiced his new voice and dialect—deeper pitch and slower cadence—compliments of a YouTube video and more to the style of a Mississippi Delta southern drawl. In the past, he had tried the same on an old girlfriend or two. One of them told him it sounded sexy. The other never returned his calls. He wondered if the accent would have the same sexy effect on Selena.

"Glad to be here," Owen said in his disguise as Hal. "Drove down from Indianola after lunch and ready for some action—some hot, over-the-top action."

"Sugga, you came to the right place," Martini said. She straightened her posture a bit and leaned in a little toward Hal.

He turned his head to her and smiled. "Lady, I'm talkin' about gamblin'," he said. "But you stay right here … snuggle up as much as you want."

Selena dealt the cards. Each player slid $20 in chips to the center.

Hal studied his hand and stiffened his neck. He overcame the reflex to flinch when Reed Spearman's voice erupted deep inside his ear canal. "Try to draw this out, Owen," Reed said. "Make Selena Garcia feel at ease. Build up some trust. Besides, you're working this Brandon fella too."

Owen's ear throbbed. He wished the electronics would fail. Anyway, he knew how to handle himself on these undercover jobs—like when Reed got him to dress as an overweight hooker in Spanx with long, multi-colored braids and thick, fake eyelashes. He agreed at the time to the two-inch nails in bright purple but balked at the gold nose ring.

He busted three johns that evening.

"Remember, man. We got to break this outfit," Reed said again too loudly.

Owen shuttered. He should have adjusted the volume control after he dressed. He shook his head clear.

"Sir, you okay? You ready to play?" Selena asked. She turned the cards.

Owen nodded. "Yeah, sure." He knew he needed to play the part of a serious gambler, one who would drive over three hours to play—and he could do it. "This damn sinus infection." He squeezed the nasal bridge of his nose between his right forefinger and thumb. "It's about to take me down."

Selena smiled. "Well, mister, I hope I deal some cards that make you feel better, much better."

Owen returned the smile. He may not have been with the Biloxi Police Department as long as Reed Spearman, nor have as great a parking space, but he knew how to handle himself in a situation.

"Hey, you two lovebirds," Brandon said. "What about me and

this nice lady I met here tonight?" He gestured to Martini. "Can we join the party? We like to play cards too."

"Don't stall on this, Owen." Reed's voice was more direct. "Move in tight. This may just be the tip of the iceberg."

Hal won the hand. Martini stared at his nice stack of chips. "Hey, this Delta boy does know how to do it," she said. She downed the rest of her drink. The same male server passed near her, and she waved her empty glass at him. "A hot player, maybe, but not as steamy as that fine piece coming up behind me with the tray."

"Be right back, ma'am," the server said. He leaned into her slightly and brushed his bicep against her shoulder, then winked and set her empty glass on his gold-rimmed tray. "Another 'tini comin' right up—very dry."

"While Teddy is getting me that drink, I'm gonna sit the next one out and slip away to the little girls' room," Martini said. "You fellas save my place. Brandon here's got things nicely warmed up." She patted Brandon on the shoulder and smiled at Hal, leaving a space between them. "Good luck on this next hand. Keep it steamy," she said.

Selena completed the shuffle and nodded good-bye to the female player. Owen thought he caught Selena glance toward the ceiling and the cameras before she watched the woman walk away. Selena dealt the cards.

"Okay. Here we go." Hal dropped his bet at the center of the table. He looked to Brandon for the next move. The Biloxi Police Department had been tailing Brandon as a person of interest in the illegal narcotics trade, identifying him as a Chief Petty Officer with the Mississippi Coast Guard. "Hit us with your best while the fancy lady is powdering her nose," Hal said.

Soon out of sight of Selena's table, Martini strolled through the aisles toward the ladies' room. She stayed in character and swayed her hips gently from side to side. Near the aisle in the adjacent smoking section, a deeply wrinkled, elderly woman sat in a motorized wheelchair at one of the slot machines. Instead of using the electronic pushbutton option, she yanked the lever hard with her right hand, a lit cigarette held tight in the other. She inhaled deeply and blew smoke away from the machines in Martini's direction just as the ringing of bells erupted from a machine several units over. The *Star Wars* theme played in the background.

"Damn, it ain't fair. I almost picked that freaking machine!" the woman yelled, bouncing in her wheelchair.

Martini sauntered to the far left of the walkway, away from the woman and the commotion and the smoke. She brushed against a short bald man dressed in a snug, deep brown leather jacket and pants and returned his grin with a grimace of apology. The bald man cupped himself with his right hand and motioned with his left toward a spot at the roulette table crowded with several high stacks of chips. He grinned again and tightened the grip on himself. Martini moved away and turned the corner to the bank of restrooms. She glanced over her shoulder. The man had not followed.

Miss Martini checked under the doors, finding all the stalls empty. She ducked into the one farthest from the entrance and locked the door. The martinis were a watered-down, clear sugar syrup and her full bladder ached. Once the toilet flush settled, Officer Kendall Brisdell reactivated the tiny microphone concealed in her wig and spoke in hushed tones. "Reed, you there?"

"I got you," Reed answered, his headset in place at the top of the Moondust Casino.

"I left Owen at the table by himself for the ladies' room, but I guess you saw that already. I actually did need to pee."

"Thanks for muting," Reed said.

"Ha, ha," Kendall said. "Maybe this Brandon guy will make a faster move with fewer people around. Right before Owen showed up, it was obvious he wanted to connect with Garcia and make a buy, so I played along."

"How's Owen handling himself?"

"Like he's God's gift to womankind, if you know what I mean. But he's running second to that a-hole I just bumped into on the

175

way to the restroom," Kendall said. "Thank god he didn't follow me. And tell Todd he's smokin' hot in that server's outfit."

Reed's loud chuckle rang through Kendall's earpiece. She shook her head and pushed her right forefinger under the auburn locks to adjust the volume.

"Todd always likes to dress up," Reed said. "He's a much better hooker than Owen—goes both ways." Kendall joined the laugh but hushed to attention when someone else entered the ladies' room. Water ran in one of the sinks.

"Remember that prostitution sting at the motel last month? Todd probably wanted overtime," Reed said and laughed even harder. Kendall bit her lip.

The restroom visitor left leaving Kendall alone, yet she continued to whisper. "You did good with this thing tonight, Reed," she said. "You guessed right that our friend Brandon would show up. So how far should I push this Selena Garcia chick?"

Kendall needed to go again and touched the MUTE control on her headpiece.

"We've been tailing Garcia since she showed up at Caston's office and went to pieces over his death. A genuine entrepreneur, that woman—some return trade, but always on the make to build her clientele," Reed said. "But with Caston gone, her supply's dried up."

Several seconds of silence passed. "Kendall, you there?"

Kendall flushed the toilet, waited a few more seconds, and turned off MUTE. "I'm here." Another person had entered the woman's room and taken the stall one over from hers. She lowered her voice some more. "Hold a sec." Kendall dressed and stepped out of the stall toward the bank of empty sinks, pumped fragrant hand soap into her palms, and rinsed in warm water. "Can you get me anything else on this Brandon guy?" she asked. "I connected with him in no time."

"The guy's wife is a secretary or a receptionist at a doctor's office, works for the same guy who came up on Caston after he offed himself. Strange thing, but the guy she works for is also a bone doctor."

"It's orthopedist. They like to be called an orthopedist or ortho-pedic surgeon," Kendall said.

"Yeah, the fancier the name, the more they can charge," Reed said.

Kendall turned off the water and dried her hands in the touch-less air blower.

"Just found out that Brandon's mother owns a rundown conve-nience store on Highway 90. I'm gonna check that out tomorrow. Maybe take Owen with me if I can get him to skip that outfit."

"Best of luck," Kendall said and checked her wig in the mirror. The earpiece remained well concealed. She grabbed her purse and resumed her Miss Martini persona on the walk back to Selena Garcia's blackjack table.

Owen—AKA *Hal*—remained a player as did Brandon. A man in a black and old gold New Orleans Saints T-shirt sat in her place. His buttocks spilled over the edges of the stool, his weight straining the legs. When he bent his torso over the table to study his cards, the T-shirt rode up his waist to expose sickly pale skin. Kendall grimaced slightly and stood to the side to observe the hand.

"Come on, Baby Doll, slap a seven on me," the Saints fan said. He moved back and forth on the stool, further straining the sup-port. His shirt moved up and down with the movement. "Keep it hot. Daddy wants you."

Selena seemed to fight the desire to roll her eyes in disgust of the man and flipped a queen on his Jack and four of spades. With a total of twenty-four, he was out. Selena looked relieved, almost happy and satisfied.

"I'm history," the man said. "Selena, honey, you might be hot at dealing candy, but you suck at cards. Catch you later." He grabbed his tall glass of beer and staggered away from the table into the throng of passersby.

Kendall retook her seat as Selena pushed the winning chips in Brandon's direction. "Gee, what's his problem? Did I miss some-thing on my trip to the ladies' room?" Miss Martini asked.

Todd appeared and set a fresh drink in front of her. Two plump

177

olives jostled in the syrupy water. Settled into her old spot, Martini stirred the drink with her right forefinger and sucked the tip dry. At least this time the concoction was chilled.

Selena wasted no time and began a new hand.

Hal lowered his head to read his cards before raising his eyes slowly as though to verify the dealer's name. "Yo, Selena, what was that guy in the T-shirt talkin' about? Said something about dealing candy?"

Martini sipped her drink and fingered a few locks of her wig. "Yeah, I might want some candy too," she said.

Brandon studied his hand in silence.

Selena did not miss a beat. "You want a hit or pass?"

Hal tapped his finger on the top card.

Selena placed the next card face up for the guy in the Hawaiian shirt, who now had twenty-three. "Sorry, fella, you bust," Selena said and scooped away Hal's chips and cards.

Hal lowered his voice to a near hush. "I want some candy too," he said, "but can't afford no sweets if my night keeps going on like this."

Selena checked her surroundings and found no pit manager or other supervisor. She fought a glance at the ceiling cameras and shot her eyes across all three faces at her table. "I get off at eleven. I park in Lot 2. Grey Ford Focus. Meet me," she uttered.

"I'll be there," Hal said. Martini nodded, *Me too.*

Brandon's fingers rested on his cards. Kendall noted a slight twitch in his fingertips and maybe a drop of perspiration on the guy's forehead.

"Let's finish this game before somebody notices the conversation." Selena dropped her eyes to the felt surface and dealt cards to Brandon and Miss Martini. Both joined Hal and busted.

A man in his mid-forties with a crop top haircut and sharp facial features took the fourth stool at the table. He wore a tailored navy blazer and dress khakis with a starched white shirt and striped blue and yellow silk tie. A brimming vodka and soda garnished with a lime wedge waited in his right hand.

The man ran a finger behind his collar. "My wife's getting a late-night spa massage with her bridge club friends, something about a twenty-percent off group deal," he said, slurring the ends of his sentences. "I got us a room upstairs for a night away from our teenagers and took tomorrow off from the bank."

The banker looked to the right and left. The other three players smiled at him. "Happy to have you, fella," Hal said.

"I've only got a few minutes till the wife's massage is over. I need a fast table, one with extras."

"This dealer knows how to take care of her clients," Miss Martini said.

The new guy remained silent. He slipped a closed hand into his pocket.

"I'll be here until eleven," Selena said and finished the shuffle after Miss Martini slid the cut card. All four players at the table studied her fingers. "Now, let's play some more blackjack," she said.

# Chapter 21

Scott checked the display at the bottom right of the computer screen. The time read only 2:05 PM. He entered the medical information for the final patient of the day and hit SAVE, then pounded his fist against his desk, loud enough for Jessica to hear up the hall. The act of frustration was meant for himself. Any respectable medical clinic—whether primary care, medical specialist, or any type of surgical specialty—should be busy with patients well beyond two o'clock in the afternoon.

He switched programs, and the next day's surgical schedule populated the screen. He scrolled up and down the page: no surprises, no posted patients for Dr. Scott Mack—no miracles. The two surgical patients scheduled from the recent all-nighter hospital call later cancelled. The initial one preferred another orthopedist in the same hospital system who had been in practice longer and the other patient lost her health insurance when she was fired from her job.

Scott picked up the coffee cup from his desk and stared into the empty bottom. He walked up the hall to Jessica's desk. "Any calls from patients wanting appointments or surgery in the last hour or so? Any calls I need to return to referring physicians?"

"No, sir, Dr. Mack," Jessica said. She darted her eyes away. "Nothing."

"Any add-ons to the office schedule for later this afternoon?"

"No, Dr. Mack. And ... uhhh ... I'm sorry, but the first two add-on patients for in the morning called back and cancelled. Said they didn't have the money for their insurance copay," Jessica explained. "And your first appointment tomorrow is after lunch."

Scott filled the coffee cup and tried desperately to exude confidence, but failed. "Then it's too bad there's no surgery scheduled for in the morning. Would have been an easy day to work at the hospital."

Jessica opened a drawer as though to appear busy. "There's one more thing, Dr. Mack. The knee replacement for day after tomorrow? She just called … and cancelled. Said she had a cold, might be pneumonia or the flu." Jessica pulled a tangle of rubber bands from the drawer and dropped them into another. She moved to the second drawer and did the same for a group of ink pens. "The lady said she would call back when her primary care provider said it was safe to have surgery, but she would have to work around her husband's work schedule—and he's always very busy at his job."

Jessica grabbed a fistful of paperclips and let them drop like rain onto the counter.

Scott fell into the spare chair near Jessica. He wished he had something other than coffee to drink. "Not sure what's gonna happen around here, Jessica," he said. "With no patients to see and operate on, I'll understand if you decide to start looking around for a new—"

"I don't want to go anywhere else, Dr. Mack." She slid a white, letter-sized envelope from one of the other drawers. The contents strained under a tight, thick rubber band.

"Whatchu got there?"

She dropped her eyes and returned the envelope to the drawer. "Maybe I'm wrong about all this—never mind. Please just forget what you just saw, Dr. Mack."

"You got me curious, Jessica," Scott said. "Come on. What's in the envelope?"

Jessica opened the drawer and handed Dr. Mack the envelope. "It's cash, two hundred," she quivered.

"You always make the deposits, though I'll be glad to take care of it on the way home. I don't have anything else to do, no rounds to make," Scott said. "You got the deposit slip ready?" He gently flipped the envelope back and forth in his hands. He remembered seeing Jessica use an official bank bag on other days, a requirement for an after-hours depository.

"How much did you say is in here? Two-hundred? Even with the light schedule, I would have thought higher for today's take."

Jessica slid a key from her pocket and unlocked a cabinet door below the counter and to the right of her workspace. She lifted a light, but thick cloth bag from the cabinet. Sea Breeze Bank & Trust was stamped across the outside. "The patient receipts from today are in here," she said. "The money in that envelope is not from patient copays."

"Then where'd this come from?" Scott pried free the flap of the fat envelope and ran his thumb across the top of the currency.

"Mr. Wells, from this morning, the post-op hip replacement? When he checked out after his appointment, he told me he barely had any pain once he got home, only took a few Advil. He only took two of the pain meds you prescribed."

"Yeah, he was looking good today. I had lots of time to spend with him. The surgery was minimally invasive, where I approach the hip from the anterior, the front of the hip. The hip implant is put in place through three very small incisions. There's very little bleeding and—"

Jessica interrupted, the color drained from her face. "Not so sure I'm good with that kind of detailed medical stuff, Dr. Mack."

"Sorry about that," Scott chuckled. "So, what's with the extra money in the envelope."

"I checked Mr. Wells's medication record and asked him what he did with the leftover narcotic prescription. He said the rest of the Percocet was in his medicine cabinet. He planned to flush it down the toilet when he got home."

Scott studied the envelope of cash. He relived the interaction with the drug dealers in the alley and their reference to Jessica. He shook his head; he never did have that talk with her. He relived his discussion with Walker's wife in the waiting room.

Scott removed the cash from the envelope and flipped through the short stack of bills, mostly fives with a ten and twenty here and there. "Good idea," he said. He took another flip through the money. "That is, it was a good plan to flush the leftover Percs."

"But Mr. Wells brought the pills back to me. Said maybe somebody else could use them."

"Why'd he do that? Why would he bring the pills to the office?"

"Don't be angry, Dr. Mack. I suggested it."

Scott slid the money back into the envelope and dropped it on the counter. The only thing in his refrigerator at home was a bottle of beer and the other half of a Subway turkey sandwich on wheat bread from last week. "Jessica, so where did this money come from?"

"My mother-in-law knew someone who could use them, and I thought you could use the cash. I dropped the bottle of Percocet by her store during my lunch break," Jessica said. "I counted. There were 28 pills in that bottle."

Scott looked around the reception area. Even though he knew he and Jessica were alone, he checked the lobby and the hall. He stared at the envelope of money, grabbed it from the counter, and again thumbed through it. He needed the cash. He needed much more than this. "Jessica, this is crazy. We can't … I can't do this." Scott thought about the hundreds of narcotic prescriptions he had written for patients since he earned a medical license, completed his orthopedics residency, and started a surgical practice.

He counted the cash himself—his tally $220.

"What kind of store did you say your mother-in-law runs?"

"A convenience store off Highway 90 with a few gas pumps out front, lots of traffic comes and goes through there. People headed to the beach or going back and forth to the casinos. Sometimes moms and kids stop by after school or after soccer or swim practice."

Scott felt sweat trickle down from his neck to his back. His underarms were sticky. His scrub suit stuck to his shoulders and upper back. He pushed up from the chair and began to pace the cramped office space.

"First, there was that thing in the parking lot last week. I was just gonna let that situation pass. You made a mistake, and I made things worse by going along with it. I let those thugs and their threats get to me. But you do good work around here, and you're all I can afford." Scott stood at the window that faced the street. The blinds were half-opened. He pulled at his shirt. "I'm sorry. I didn't mean anything bad by that *all I can afford* thing."

"Doctor Mack, every time I see you with a patient, you seem so kind and caring. The patients do seem to like you. I was only trying to figure out a way to help you out of this slump," Jessica said.

Scott tossed the envelope to her desk. Jessica grabbed it before it slid off the edge to the floor.

"You gotta take that money back to your mother-in-law and get that Percocet back from her, get the pills back so we can destroy them … and tell that old man, Mr. Wells, that we got rid of the whole bottle for him."

"I can't do that, Dr. Mack," Jessica said. "I mean, I can tell the patient that we flushed the pills for him or dropped 'em in the disposal bin at the pharmacy, but Momma Kile already sold them. She had a buyer waiting."

"Go ahead and call her right now!"

Jessica flinched, the frustration and panic in Scott's voice obvious.

"Tell her, no more!" This second outburst jolted Jessica from her desk chair, but she said nothing.

"I'm sorry, Jessica. I didn't mean to yell. I'm not mad at you for trying to help. I'm mad at myself for letting things get so bad financially that I was tempted to let this happen." Scott turned from the window, and Jessica looked away. He forced calm and control in his voice. This was not his secretary's fault, but his. He could have stopped the transaction in the alley. However, out of weakness, out of desperation, he let temptation take control. He had seen an opportunity to get out of his financial mess and had not only broken the law but compromised his integrity as a physician.

184

"Please, Jessica," he said. "Somehow you've got to stop your mother-in-law from reselling any more of our patients' pills. I assume there have been other transactions—just keep 'em to yourself."

"I'm sorry, Dr. Mack, I was only trying to help." She made herself busy with something on the computer and fought tears. "I'll see what I can do."

Scott started to pace again. "I gotta ... gotta ... think of something to tell Mr. Wells. Maybe that it was some sort of research study about pain medication. There's been a lot about narcotic abuse and addiction in the news. Maybe he'll believe the story and not tell anybody that we kept his pills."

"Dr. Mack, I ... I ... just ..."

"I gotta think this through. I'll be in my office," Scott said.

Jessica punched a few more idle keys on the computer. She held back from pounding the keyboard.

The front door to the building opened. "I'm sorry, but the clinic is closed for the day," Jessica muttered, then raised her voice to be heard through the reception window. "But I can make you an appointment for another day."

"I don't need an appointment." Several shades of medium-length blonde hair stood at the window. "Name's Pam. Pam Bullock. I manage the dental office next door, and I'm not here for an appointment. I'm here for your job."

"Does it look like I'm going anywhere?" Jessica's back stiffened. Somehow, she had not been fired. "Sorry. There's no opening for my job."

Bullock ran her hand over her scalp from front to back flattening her hair, but it sprang back into place just as frizzy. She seemed to study Jessica's appearance and the interior office space that surrounded her. "That situation could change 'cause I've seen you with those two characters out back."

"What characters?" Jessica found a clip board on her desk and fumbled with it.

"I recognized one of them. He's a patient of Dr. Roland's—the skinny, little guy. He likes gold caps. We take his cash for dental work and don't ask questions."

Jessica slid the clip board inside a drawer and found a note pad to flip through next.

"I saw him and another guy approach your doctor at his car, and I don't think he liked it ... but I saw cash exchange between them. And Dr. Mack kept it."

"I don't know anything about that," Jessica lied. She pushed away from the reception desk. "I need to finish up the day."

"Your Dr. Mack know anything about your connection with those guys?" Bullock asked. "If not, maybe he should."

Jessica forced a smile. "Not sure what you're talking about." She managed an index card from a drawer and a cheap plastic pen. "Jot down your name, cell, and an email address. Dr. Mack will let you know if he's interested."

"Uh-huh." Pam Bullock took the pen, scribbled the information on the card, and tossed it to Jessica. It floated to her desk. "We'll see how this turns out."

The door shut hard behind Bullock. Jessica punched a number into her phone.

"Yeah. Whatchu want? You got some more product?"

"Nope, that latest I picked up ... I slipped it straight to Momma. That stuff you got from Dr. Mack in the alley might be your last."

"Whatchu mean *your last*? We got an arrangement."

"I already told you—that lady next door at the dental office. She made you in the alley. It's over, Jamal."

A woman balanced an infant carrier in the crook of her left arm and against her hip as she left Kile's Minute Mart. She gripped a pack of Marlboro Lights in the left hand and dangled a flimsy plastic bag from her right forearm. The bag contained a 16-ounce Coke from the cooler and a bag of Ruffles potato chips, along with several other packs of cigarettes and the credit card receipt for her purchase.

Attorney Coleman Foshee held the front door open for the woman to exit. Foshee scanned the interior of the store. It seemed quiet, so he stepped inside, past the checkout counter to the display of Little Debbie products. He picked up a pack of powdered mini-donuts from a shelf and a twenty-ounce Mountain Dew from the cold beverage cabinets along the rear wall. Signs taped to the glass fronts touted special prices for combo purchases.

He returned to the checkout area with his selections and found Momma Kile busy behind the counter. She slid fresh packs of Marlboro Lights from a carton into the empty cigarette rack slots above the register.

"You were the first one I called," Momma said and tapped the ends of the cigarette packs flush with the metal edge of the display rack. "It's good stuff, fresh. Pharmacy grade."

Foshee put his doughnuts and drink on the counter and pulled a brochure advertising deep-sea fishing trips from another display on the counter. He pretended to peruse it. "How many Percs you got on hand?"

"How many you want?" she answered. Momma Kile walked to a different wall cooler at the rear of the building and removed a package of jumbo franks, then unlatched the rear of the rotisserie nearer the front. The miniature Ferris wheel of hot dogs halted, and she replaced the missing pieces of meat. When she snapped the back of the unit closed, the glass-paneled box on the Formica surface came back to life. From the cabinet underneath, she grabbed enough napkins to refill the dispenser next to the packages of hotdog buns. Most of the bread was several days old.

"I'll take all you got, and I don't mean wieners." Foshee slid his wallet from inside his sport coat. "I gambled this trip would be worth my while."

"I ain't gonna let you down," Momma Kile said. She finished the maintenance chores at the foodservice counter and stepped back behind the register to her stool. Without even a thought, she again disabled that security camera. Her throne-like image froze on the monitor that displayed the camera coverage. Momma slid the tiny envelope from under the counter and glanced out the window toward the pumps for other customers.

A white van pulled up to the fuel pump nearest the highway. Momma checked the exterior security camera feed for a better look at the van. It was marked on the side in blue with the name of a local plumbing company. The driver paid with a credit card and the payment display board lit up: CREDIT PAY ACCEPTED. Other than Foshee's vehicle, there were no others parked outside, and no one approached the building.

Momma Kile waited until the plumber got out of the van and stood at the adjacent fuel pump.

"These pills came from a new supplier that's gonna be good for business. I know I can trust you, but I didn't want to give out too much info over the phone," Momma said. "A girl can't be too careful."

Foshee peered through the glass front doors and cocked his neck toward the plumber's van. "That van out there at the pumps—one of your regulars?" he asked.

Momma looked deeper into the display of security camera video then again peered through the window. "Seen him around every few weeks or so. Uses his card at the pump. Never comes inside, not even for a pack of gum or to use the john. Always drives off after a fill up."

Foshee removed the iPhone from his pocket and entered the name printed on the side of the van. GULFSIDE PLUMBING SERVICE popped up in a Facebook listing. Foshee texted his driver.

Still shopping. Check out the van

Momma Kile and Foshee both watched him get out of the limo and lean against the back fender. The driver flipped open the fuel door, twisted off the gas cap, and stuck the dispenser nozzle into the gas tank receptacle. He stepped a few feet away out of site of the plumber and snapped a photo of the van's license plate number with his cell phone.

"Wouldn't have been so damn obvious, him snatchin' a pic of the license plate," Momma said, "if your guy had at least pretended to run a credit card at the pump and pick a grade of fuel."

The plumber returned the fuel dispenser to its cradle and waited for the receipt to print from the pump. He seemed to consider a trip inside the convenience store, but returned to the van and drove away instead.

Foshee's driver returned to his own vehicle.

"That guy in the van, harmless—just needed gas," Momma said.

"Probably so, but I'm going to run the plate anyway." Foshee texted the instructions to his driver. "So … how many you got?" he asked. "I hope this trip was worthwhile."

"I got twenty, at fifteen a piece," Momma Kile said.

Foshee pulled at his collar. "Hold on," he said. "You jacked up your price. What happened to ten bucks a Perc?"

Momma sighed and rubbed her nose. "I can't keep flipping product if there ain't no profit."

"I get it." Foshee smirked. "Capitalism—but don't price yourself out of the local market."

"I don't handle anything but quality product, and I don't have time to haggle about price. Take it or leave it for the next buyer." Momma rang up his doughnuts and bottle drink. "I got to make a living like everybody else. Your total with the junk food is $308.28."

Foshee leaned forward on the counter just as his driver walked through the door. "Everything slick in here, boss? I'm working on those plates, but you got that meeting with the Port Authority in less than a half hour."

Momma Kile ignored the limo driver and tilted forward on her elbows. From her vantage point atop her stool on the elevated platform of the checkout area, she and Foshee were now eye-to-eye. "These Percs came from a local Walgreens. Pure FDA-approved stuff—not crap that was taped under the seat cushion of a smelly shrimp boat or stored with illegals hiding in the cargo bay," she said. "Take it or leave it."

189

Foshee looked to the driver, who shrugged his shoulders.

"You can put the $8.28 on your business expense card, but I guess you'll wanna pay the rest in cash." She handed Foshee a plastic shopping bag containing the Little Debbie doughnuts and the Mountain Dew.

He tossed the package of doughnuts to his driver and unscrewed the top to the light green soda. The empty bag drifted to the floor.

"Let me see the cash, and I'll let you have the rest of your order," Momma Kile said. She checked the front. A red sedan with a banged-up front fender and in need of a wash job turned into the parking lot. "Make it quick. Take it or leave it."

Foshee peeled $300 in twenty-dollar bills from a roll inside his pants pocket, retrieved the empty bag, and dropped the cash inside. He choked the neck of the bag and held it in Momma's face.

"Smart boy." She grabbed the bag and exchanged it for a sealed, small brown envelope. Foshee covered the envelope with his right hand, quickly slid it toward him, and dropped it into the inside left pocket of his jacket. "You'll like what you find inside, and check with me next week when you're ready for more," Momma Kile said. "I think my new source is a good one."

A man in his late thirties, one of Momma Kile's regular cigarette and beer patrons, pushed through the front door. He grabbed a large bag of Zapp's Voodoo Potato Chips and approached the register. Momma smiled at him and waved Foshee away as she tucked the bag with Foshee's cash into her apron pocket and reactivated the security camera.

"We'll see," Foshee said. He and his driver left the store for the car.

"It's Marlboro, right? Two cartons?" Momma said. "And don't you want your six pack of Michelob to go with those chips?"

The man set the potato chips on the counter next to the cigarettes and headed for the wall of beverage coolers.

Outside the convenience store, Foshee's driver opened the rear passenger door for him and waited for his boss to be seated. "Forget it, Ralph," Foshee said. "Get behind the wheel and drive me over to Martha's quick." He put his hand to his jacket pocket and shook his head. "She'll be glad to see this."

# Chapter 22

"Mom? Mom!" Hailey Hazard yelled down the stairs. "Where's my cheerleader outfit? You were supposed to wash it after the game. We've got yearbook group pictures tomorrow." A few seconds later she ran down the steps and into the laundry room.

"Mom! Oh, my god. I just found it." She ran to her mother in the kitchen, clenching the cheerleader outfit. "It was still in the dirty laundry—all tangled up in Hunter's sweaty football jerseys. I need to wear this!"

"I'm so sorry, honey." Hailey's mother tapped a Percocet from the tiny, brown envelope inside her bathrobe and swallowed it with the dregs of a glass of chardonnay leftover from last night. She slipped the envelope and her one remaining Percocet into a thin pouch adhered to the back of her cell phone case—a tight fit alongside her driver's license, Platinum American Express card, and a folded twenty with a couple of ones.

Once dressed for the day, she would drop the phone into a nylon bag suspended at her waist by a strap around her left shoulder. This functioned better than storing the cell in the back pocket of her surgical scrubs. The phone's weight pulled at the waist and tended to expose the top of her panties.

Martha Foshee Hazard felt the phone vibrate a message and remembered she was still on call for her neurosurgery practice. "Come on, Hailey. Why don't you just chill? Save the yelling and screaming for the pep rally."

The rebuttal came swift and sharp. "Mom? You're impossible!"

"Your spare uniform is hanging in the laundry room—all pressed and smelling fresh. I guess you didn't see it with all the screeching."

Hailey forced a smile. "Sorry, Mom."

"Justeen took care of it last week. She hasn't been back to work yet to take it upstairs and hang it in your closet." Martha checked the roast in the Crock-Pot and adjusted the temperature a bit. The meat would be tender and cooked by the time she returned home after clinic. She expected her brother Coleman to come by tonight. Hailey could rattle her so. "I'll get your uniform for you."

Martha walked into the laundry room and returned with the clean cheerleader outfit from the rack. She handed it on the hanger to Hailey. "Justeen's out till Monday with her back, so we've all got to pitch in around here. And I don't have time to do the rest of the laundry. My patient's surgery case is scheduled for second today."

"I'm sorry, Mom, that I yelled and got so upset. Thank you." Hailey blew a short kiss, grabbed the garment off the hanger, and ran back upstairs to her room.

Martha stood with the empty hanger. *Martha, you're getting careless. You forgot the Tic Tacs around Hailey. You left them in the car.* She thought about taking that last Percocet.

Hailey called again from the top of the stairs. "And don't forget. My competition squad won state title, and regionals are in two weeks in New Orleans. Need everything clean. Gotta look good with that trophy."

"My daughter," Martha sighed. "Cheering on the school squad isn't enough. She has to do the extra competition stuff too." Martha's cell phone vibrated again, and she tapped the number in the message. The pouch on the back of the phone case popped off and landed near the refrigerator. Her credit cards and cash scattered along with the tiny envelope.

"This is Dr. Hazard," she said. "What? My patient's already in holding? Then go ahead and stick him with an I.V. and give the pre-op meds. I'll be there in less than thirty minutes."

Martha decided against the other Percocet.

193

She gathered her phone pouch and the credit cards, cash, and envelope from the floor. She felt through the envelope with her fingertips for the pill. By the time she reached the master bedroom at the other end of the house, she had changed her mind and broke off a third of the tablet to swallow it dry.

Her feet felt warm, and her breathing slowed a bit. Calm washed through her body, and the piece of the second Percocet had not even hit her yet.

Martha's cell phone rang. Coleman appeared in the caller I.D. "Cole, my God. I've been waiting for you. The kids are out for fall break next week, and we're supposed to fly out to Phoenix."

"Sounds awesome," Coleman Foshee said.

"Jeff's got a meeting out there. He and Hunter are supposed to play golf, and Hailey and I are going to hit the spas and the shops and—"

"Relax, Sis. I gotchu covered. I dropped by late yesterday. No one was home. Package is in the usual place."

"I should have known you wouldn't let me down. I should have checked, but I was on call yesterday and got home late. Jeff ordered out Chinese, and he and the kids left the mess for me to clean up. The maid's out sick, then there's supper tonight for everybody and the laundry—"

"I don't know how much longer I can keep this up for you, Martha."

"Don't give me that crap, Coleman, not now. I'm gonna stop using. I promise. I just need to get these kids through high school and—"

"I'm not talking about NA and your going into treatment. I've given up on that for you. You'll never go."

"Come on, I'm not an addict. I can stop. This is the only thing I do. I don't smoke. I don't fool around. I go to church. I—"

"It's getting harder to get this stuff for you, Martha. My current supplier ... your supplier ... this woman who runs a convenience store, says she's got a new source ... but I'm not so sure we ... *you* ... can depend on her."

"I can get stuff at the hospital like I used to, but I don't want to risk my license. I've got to work, full steam," Martha said. "Jeff's law practice is hit or miss. They've pushed him into the real estate division, and that's so up and down." Martha held the phone between her right ear and shoulder and fanned her fingers. "My hands are steady as a rock. Besides, I know lots of doctors who take something—antidepressants, Valium, Xanax. Some smoke pot. What's so different with what I'm doing?"

"As long as you keep those kids of yours safe, I'm going to prop you up till you can take some time off and get help. But Jeff has got to step up to the plate."

Martha took a deep breath and gritted her teeth. "Thanks for helping me out, brother, but leave Jeff out of this and stay out of my marriage," she said. Martha ended the call and tossed her phone and the contents of the Velcro pouch atop the unmade bed, then dropped her robe to the carpet. She peeled off her nightgown as she headed to the shower.

Today would be no make-up with her hair pulled-back in a clip. *And I gotta get out of driving them to that cheerleading thing in two weeks. I don't have time for that.*

The family trip to Phoenix did little to squelch Martha's stress. Despite one of the Percocet tablets her brother dropped off, her mind raced on the plane to Arizona. Another pill taken later, three or so hours after the family boarded, did nothing more to steady her nerves. As Martha flipped through a magazine, she worried over the long-term patient outcome of a recent, difficult craniotomy case and then there was her fear of inadequacy as a mother to two young teenagers. Of course, that unrelenting sense of impending doom over her husband's dwindling legal practice haunted her. The vodka and soda with lime an hour before they landed in Phoenix helped squelch that worry.

Martha had hoped that joining Jeff on the golf course a couple of times and the visits to the desert resort spa would help her relax without the oxycodone or alcohol. However, her brother Coleman's words weighed heavily. Even though a lawyer, maybe her brother was smarter than she thought, maybe even wiser.

Maybe she did need to put into place what she heard at that one Narcotics Anonymous meeting: change your ways—find strength in self-confidence and not pills, take a personal inventory, rely on a greater power. The family trip had been over for a few days, and now was the time. Today was the day. She could do it, just as the NA group leader said: "Choose more than a physical makeover. Totally change your lifestyle and create a healthier you."

*I do need that makeover,* Martha told herself. The prospect of a healthy reboot seemed thrilling, today's start scheduled at the club with a personal exercise trainer and a masseuse, the appointment now less than two hours away. A hair salon makeover and new cosmetics treatment would follow.

Healthy for Dr. Martha Hazard meant that instead of a Percocet or two that morning, she would drink a Bloody Mary—a tall one garnished with a fat green olive and a stalk of celery but no hot sauce. Her two objectives were to celebrate a carefree day away from her neurosurgery practice responsibilities and to clear her head after Jeff's protracted birthday celebration last night.

She still had a bit of a buzz and the start of a headache.

Behind the Bloody Mary mix in the refrigerator and above the vegetable bin stood a bottle of champagne, a survivor of last New Year's Eve all-nighter. Martha popped the cork, sat on the daybed in the keeping room off the kitchen, and drank more than half the bottle before passing out, her face buried in a down pillow.

When the phone rang, she raised her head, confused, and answered. A morning talk show blared from the television near her; the male and female co-hosts giggled along with the audience. Yes, she was at home, but this was not her bedroom. She was in the keeping room, and this was her day off. Her eyes were dry, but they stung and felt hot. Martha twisted her neck and jerked her head back and forth, dissecting the room's contents.

A young, panicky female voice was on the other line. Martha wiped the drool from the corner of her mouth. "Yes, yes. This is Dr. Hazard," she successfully fought the slurred speech.

"Dr. Hazard, this is Mandy Reeves, Hailey's cheerleader coach. You know, for the competitive team?"

Martha rubbed her eyes and shook her head to try to clear her thinking. She wanted to splash cold water on her face. "Oh, God. Is something wrong? Has anything happened to Hailey?"

"No. No, ma'am. It's nothing like that. But the squad could absolutely use your help. The other mother is sick."

The coach described the other mom's abrupt gastrointestinal illness in great detail until Martha nearly felt the same and interrupted. "How awful. I'm … I'm so sorry for her."

"Me too. But Hailey mentioned that you had the day free from the hospital." Several seconds passed. "Hailey … sort of volunteered you to fill in and drive the other van to the competition in New Orleans."

Martha tried to stand but her swimming head knocked her back to the daybed. She referred to the time on her phone. Her appointment with the personal trainer was in ten minutes.

"I already ran it by Mr. Armstrong, the principal, to see if he could drive them, but he has parent conferences scheduled all day plus a board meeting at lunch with the private school association. I'm at my wits end. I hope you can help us, please."

Martha rubbed her eyes again. She had showered and dressed for the gym before she planned the Bloody Mary, even applied a little makeup and mascara, the mascara now smeared onto her fingertips. She considered her new workout clothes: an Adidas sports bra and high-waisted leggings. She had even bought new tennis shoes for her new, healthier start.

"Mrs. Hazard … I mean, Dr. Hazard. The other mom is just so sick. Can you please drive the van?" She repeated the dreadful details of the other mom's acute illness.

"Yes, yes. I get the picture," Martha said.

"Was that a Yes? Oh, thank you, thank you, thank you! We leave from the school at ten o'clock. We have a four p.m. tryout. That will give us a couple of hours to—"

"No ... I meant that ..." Martha again tried to shake her head clear and felt even more nauseated. "I meant that ... well, I guess that I ..." Martha stared across the room to inside the kitchen. The empty coffee maker was visible next to the refrigerator. Jeff would have made coffee if he had not flown out so early for his last out-of-town liability case. It would be real estate closings from then on. "Are you sure ... sure that there isn't anyone else, another parent or maybe a teacher?"

"I checked with Tomeka's mom and even Chasidy's mom. Sometimes they can fill in, but they were at work already—crazy, hectic mornings at the office today—and their bosses are pretty strict about last minute requests off work." The cheerleader sponsor pleaded, "We're in a desperate situation, Mrs. Hazard."

Martha sat up as straight as she could on the daybed. She tried another eye rub and attempted to straighten her hair. She wished for a mirror. "Thank God I already showered," she muttered and swallowed hard. The nausea passed. She massaged her scalp and temples.

"Did you say something?" Mandy Reeves asked. "I was so hoping that you could help us out. Hailey seemed so excited that her mom didn't have to work at the hospital and might could save the day for us. We have a shot at first place this year, and I would hate to forfeit the competition."

Martha breathed deeply. Like so many times before an early morning case in the operating room, she fought off what she called brain fog. A cup of coffee and a donut from the doctors' lounge usually cleared her head. She wished for a chocolate-covered one. Maybe Hello Donuts Gulfport would deliver if she tipped.

"Mrs. Hazard? Dr. Hazard? You there?"

Another deep breath. Martha shook her head, set the phone down, and fanned out her fingers to study the mascara-stained

198

tips. Her hands did not shake. "I was looking forward to that manicure today."

"Excuse me?" The panicky voice of the cheerleader coach could be heard from Martha's cell phone on the cushion beside her.

"I'll splash some cool water on my face, gargle with Listerine, redo my make-up, pull my hair back like Hailey does, and change clothes in a hurry," Martha mumbled. She grabbed the phone and cleared her throat. "I can't let my sister keep substituting for me. Yes, I can do this. I can do this for Hailey."

"So, ma'am? Did I hear an official, *Yes?*"

Martha again stared at the empty coffee pot. "I can grab some at McDonald's on the way. Maybe they have sweet rolls."

"Ma'am?"

"Miss Reeves, I'll be there in twenty minutes, thirty at the most," Martha said.

"Oh, thank you! You are so sweet. This is totally awesome," Reeves almost squealed. "Hailey and all the other girls will be so excited. They are actually going to make it to the competition! See you outside the gym in a few." The cheerleader sponsor clicked off.

Martha stared at the cell phone for a few seconds then dropped it. It struck the cushion and bounced to the floor. *What have I done?* She raised her hand to her mouth. Her breath smelled beyond sour and her stomach boiled. Martha swallowed hard, grabbed her phone to run to the master bedroom and bath, and tossed the phone next to her purse on the bed.

Inside the bathroom, Martha jerked the brass water fixture toward her, ashamed of her disheveled reflection in the mirror. A strong stream of cold water hit the bottom of the sink and she felt relief, then splashed some of it in her face. The water dripped down the sides of her cheeks and finished off what remained of the makeup, the sides of the white porcelain sink now streaked in black.

Martha ignored the mess and studied her complexion, disappointed that she would miss today's facial and added appointment with the makeup artist for a redo. Once more, her crow's feet sank much deeper today, despite the every-four-month cosmetic injections into her facial muscles. She ran her fingers along the corners of her eyes and under the puffy lower lid. "I've got to get something done about these dark circles."

Not only when she and Jeff went out to dinner or to a party, but on any morning, even before a long day of office patients or surgical cases, Martha Hazard, M.D., strove toward perfection in her appearance—not the flawlessness of her mother's dreams, but good enough for a girl who managed medical school and completed a neurosurgery residency.

Martha knew she had wasted valuable time in the mirror and grabbed her toothbrush and the toothpaste. The smell of the sweet, minty toothpaste made her gag, and her gums bled a bit when she brushed. She tossed the toothbrush in the sink, took a swig of mouthwash, and spat. Light blood-stained expectorant mixed with toothpaste and mouthwash spattered the sides of the sink to compete with the runny mascara. Her mouth felt sore.

She pulled a hand towel from the brass bar on the wall and knocked the other towels to her feet. Martha kicked them away and dried her face before rummaging through the makeup drawer for her favorite tube of lipstick. She hurriedly reapplied the beige color. She decided she could finish-up with the makeup travel kit in her purse while the cheerleaders loaded their equipment and piled into her SUV.

Suddenly, she felt queasy and a scalding, bitter liquid shot up her throat. Even though she had not drunk the Bloody Mary, she could almost taste it mixed with this morning's champagne and last night's crab cakes from the heavy birthday dinner. *I should have eaten breakfast, at least some toast, and gone to bed earlier last night,* she decided and swallowed a medication sample from the cabinet designed to manage reflux.

Last night's celebration of Jeff's fortieth birthday kicked off at Mary Mahoney's restaurant with appetizers and dinner. A local trio of jazz musicians provided the entertainment. The cocktail and dinner crowd at the restaurant was dense, lively, just the right fuel to spur someone to party uninhibited—especially a user, an addict, an alcoholic.

The revelry continued for the birthday boy through wine and liqueurs after dinner with shots of tequila until closing. Jeff sometimes tried to temper Martha's drinking, but not on his birthday and not when leaving town the next day with no concern for the aftermath. He did put his forefinger to her lips just before dessert when she slurred her words and blanked out on a few.

Martha's last memory at the restaurant was of a clumsy, blurry signature on the credit card slip and a whisper to the head waiter to add the tip. *I hope I only told her 20 percent.*

Jeff had propped her up on the walk to their car in the restaurant's parking lot and let her doze on the drive home, slumped against the passenger front door. He pulled the car into the garage and lowered the door so no one would see and helped her inside the house. A can of Red Bull in the back of the refrigerator next to the champagne perked her up. Jeff waited in the kitchen for her to finish the remaining dessert from her to-go box and then practically carried her down the hall to the bedroom. His birthday celebration continued after he peeled away her clothes.

She remembered him saying, "Come on, Martha. Tomorrow's your day off. You can sleep late. I'll take an Uber to the airport." He turned her over in bed and knelt into her. "Let's do it again, but this way. Make it good. Those out-of-town depositions will keep me gone for a week."

Her new cocktail dress and panties were on the floor when she woke up this morning, but she never found her bra.

She lay naked in the bed under a thin sheet when Jeff asked, "You want me to get you some Advil or a couple of Tylenol before I leave for the airport?" Jeff straightened his tie in the bedroom mirror. "I keep some in my briefcase if there's none in the cabinet."

"No, I'm good," she had managed. "There's stuff in the medicine cabinet."

"How 'bout some orange juice or a bottle of water?"

"I'll get something in a few minutes. You know, I could have driven you to the airport, Jeff."

"As much as you had to drink last night? No way you're getting behind the wheel this morning," Jeff said. He tightened the tie in place. "You'd still register above the limit if you got pulled over."

"I'm fine. I feel just fine," Martha remembered saying.

"And I'm not sure what we would've done if Sheila hadn't offered to pick up the kids for school today. Something about a cheerleader competition out of town that Hailey couldn't miss. Great sister you got there."

Martha had pulled the sheet around her and gotten out of bed. She held the sheet to her chest in front of the bedroom mirror and rubbed her temples. "A shower and a little makeup, that's all I need."

"You don't need to be driving this morning, maybe even for the whole day. Go ahead and cancel the massage and the personal trainer." Jeff tilted his head down to kiss her lightly on the cheek. "You gotta be dehydrated, and your head must be killin' you."

He picked up his briefcase from beside the antique chest and grabbed his keys from the nightstand, then popped her right buttock gently with the hand holding the keys. "Take that shower. Get dressed. Drink some coffee. Put on that face that I fell in love with in college," he said and walked to the bedroom door. "Oh, and you were great in bed last night. Happy Birthday to me."

Martha pushed the button to raise the garage door and stumbled into the suburban, frowning at her face in the rearview mirror and the bloodshot eyes immune to eyedrops. There was a bottle of Visine in her purse, and she would give it another try at the first red light.

Martha jerked her BMW X7 into reverse to back from the garage into the driveway and ignored the beeping tone that screamed, *Buckle your seatbelt!* She relied on the rearview display on the dashboard monitor to squeeze the steering wheel clear of clumps of pampas grass that marked the bends in the long driveway.

The digital video image of the mailbox grew larger and larger in the center of the monitor until she reeled the vehicle clear of the mailbox toward the street.

Only about thirty or so feet away, the driver of a package delivery truck snatched the bar code scanner from its dashboard mount and leaned away from the windshield to scan the parcel on the floor. It lay on the other side of the truck, against the passenger door. The same address flashed across the top of the scanner, but still no match for any street marker that he could spot. He had already studied each house on the street. He lifted his cap and ran his fingers through his hair, then wiped the sweaty gel on the front of his shirt.

"I need this job, really bad," the driver groaned. "I gotta get these deliveries right." He thought about his girlfriend and their new baby in the one bedroom across town and the overtime hours he pulled, this morning's included. Except for the last two numbers on the tiny metal sign at the curb of this next residence, the package was a match. The numbers were reversed. "I guess this house address is good enough."

He eased his foot off the brake and stretched again for the small parcel on the floor, the one marked *Fragile* with the name *Hazard* on the shipping label. He wrapped his hand and fingers around the package and pulled it toward him, but it somehow tumbled away. "Damn!" the driver blurted, reaching and groping to grab the box as it bounced inside the front of the truck, unaware that he had turned the steering wheel to the left.

Still focused on the dashboard monitor's rear view of the end of her driveway, Martha checked the time display just before she reached the curb. "If I skip McDonald's, I can make the school on time."

Martha quickly backed into the street, pleased with herself.

"Another damaged delivery, and I'll lose my freakin' job." The package bounced one more time between the floor, seat, and dashboard before the delivery truck driver secured it in the crook of his arm and pulled it into his chest. "Got it! Thank ya, Jesus!"

In the commotion, his foot slipped onto the accelerator and the large truck lurched forward, crushing Martha's side of the SUV and propelling it airborne. Despite the full size of her vehicle, it spun and landed in the street on its side. Martha's head snapped back and forth before striking the side window just as the airbags deployed.

A retired English professor of the University of Southern Mississippi at Long Beach who lived several doors down witnessed the accident while walking his dog. He called 911 from his cell phone.

# Chapter 23

Sheila Foshee Evans huddled with her husband and three kids in the cold rain and stared at the shallow puddles in the uneven artificial turf. Coleman Foshee stood next to his younger sister with an oversized umbrella to shield the three adults while the kids had their own. On cue from the funeral director, Jeff Hazard and his two children took their seats front and center at graveside under the tent. The other family members and friends filled in around them.

When Coleman called his ex-wife about his sister's accident, she passed on attending the service. Coleman never thought his ex-wife liked Martha, that there was a streak of jealously somewhere.

The minister of the Gulfport Church of the Everlasting God eulogized Dr. Martha Foshee Hazard as a strong woman of integrity, a healer in the truest sense of the word, an instrument of the Father. He lauded Dr. Hazard for excellent, compassionate treatment of several members of his own family—that a few years ago she must have prayed to the heavens for guidance and performed a procedure that rescued his nephew from life in a wheelchair.

There was not a dry eye in the house—except for Coleman Foshee. He had killed his sister.

Maybe not by himself, maybe he was not the only culprit in her death—but he could have stopped the narcotics abuse or at least not contributed to it. He could have handled the situation better. He could have walked away.

Coleman took a deep breath and observed Jeff and the beautiful girl and boy Martha left him. Before the funeral, Jeff assured Coleman that the children remained oblivious to Martha's addiction issues, the secret secured since the media did not publish the results of her toxicology screen nor the 0.12 blood alcohol level. Coleman had made sure of that.

While the amount of alcohol in her system surprised Coleman, the presence of opioids did not. The fact that he would have to find some way to help Martha's kids financially was also no surprise.

Last month Martha called in tears when the senior partners at Jeff's law firm ended his tract to make partner. They judged him inadequate, too weak to handle major financial deals or the legal work required to defend important clients. The out-of-town trip to take client depositions scheduled the day after his birthday would be the last. He would be reassigned to work side-by-side with the paralegals and legal secretaries in the firm's satellite office in the cozy, nearby community of Ocean Springs.

The minister concluded his eulogy, and as the casket lowered, Jeff Hazard stood to toss a handful of loose soil spared from the rain into the grave.

"My sister was your meal ticket," Coleman mumbled.

Sheila wiped her eyes with a handkerchief and whispered, "What did you say, Cole? Something about a ticket?"

Hailey and her brother followed their father's lead. Muffled sobs drifted throughout the crowd. A man known as one of Martha's patients cried loudly, "What will we do without her?"

A woman in the back of the crowd also wailed. Another began to sing a hymn.

"I was just thinking out loud," Coleman said to Sheila. "Martha needed a ticket for a true vacation."

The rain dissipated into a light drizzle, and the crowd slowly dispersed. Sheila moved quickly away with her husband and children for their car, taking the umbrellas. The visitation after the service was scheduled for her house, most of the prepared food and liquor already set out for the grieving guests. All she had to do was fill the large chafing dish with hot spinach dip and refresh the ice supply at the bar.

Coleman did not leave. Without concern for his suit and tie and without the umbrella, he waited in the drizzle until everyone was gone except the cemetery personnel. He watched as they filled the grave with more dry soil shielded from the rain and covered the site with casket sprays of red and white roses, yellow and purple lilies, green ferns, and other plants with names unfamiliar to him. He felt drawn to kneel at his talented sister's grave, a wasted life for which he felt responsible.

The sound of tires rolling across the narrow gravel road that wound through the cemetery broke Coleman from his trance. A tall Caucasian man in his late thirties got out of a navy-blue sedan and walked toward him. He was attractive and dressed in a dark grey suit, appropriate for a funeral. His thick hair was brushed upward off his face.

"I'm sorry, sir, but you're a little late. There's a visitation at our sister's house on Bayou View Road, Number 23, if you want to pay your respects," Coleman said. "I'm the only family left here."

Detective Reed Spearman presented his badge. "I'm sorry about your loss. I hear Dr. Hazard was a great doctor. We had our eyes on her."

Coleman Foshee stepped back a bit, then checked the man's credentials. "Eyes on her. What are you talking about?"

"The hospital administrator at Biloxi Memorial came to us. He didn't want to go to the medical association until he was sure. Some of the nurses in the operating room had noticed what they called *strange behavior* on the part of Dr. Hazard. One even thought he saw her steal medication off a patient's tray."

"That's … not true. Must be hearsay," Coleman said. "My sister was a gifted surgeon, a fine person."

"I'm sure she was, but police departments don't usually get calls like that. Seems that Biloxi Memorial wanted to give Dr. Hazard the benefit of the doubt, or at least that's what they told me."

"If you had been here for the service and seen all the people who loved her ..." Coleman's voice broke.

"I got the feeling from that hospital administrator that Dr. Hazard was important to his bottom line. He needed her surgery cases and didn't want to damage her reputation in anyway—unless there was reason to."

"So, Officer ... Spearman, why are you here? What do you want from me?" Coleman took a more studied view of Reed Spearman. The face and the mannerisms seemed familiar.

"It's *Detective*," Reed corrected him. "My department put a car outside your sister's house, but we missed the day of the accident. In fact, I was in that car most of the time. On more than one occasion, I spotted your limousine and driver drop off small packages or envelopes at the Hazard residence—even when she was not at home, most recently about two weeks ago."

"Martha was my sister. Why wouldn't I visit her? And I find it highly inappropriate that you would come here at this time of family loss and intense grief to defame my sister and—"

"I also spotted your vehicle and driver outside a convenience store off Highway 90 and matched your plates to those in front of your sister's house. I doubt your driver had much luck with my plates that afternoon since police department surveillance vans have unregistered numbers."

Coleman remembered. He recognized Spearman as the plumber outside Kile's convenience store. "Not sure about the incident you're referencing, detective. My driver and I stop for gas wherever we happen to be at the moment. Now, if you'll excuse me, I need to join my family at the visitation." Coleman unbuttoned his jacket, turned, and walked toward his car. It was parked off the road about thirty yards in front of Reed.

"If you'll hold up a moment, Mr. Foshee," Reed said and stepped after him. "How does an attorney who works for the state afford that Lincoln and the driver. You running some kind of side business?"

"That's all I have for you, Spearman." The same driver emerged and opened the rear passenger door.

"We've got eyes on that convenience store too and that Kile woman," Reed said.

Coleman slid onto the back seat and, without waiting for the driver, reached to pull his door shut.

Reed stepped in the way and motioned to Coleman's driver. "You and this fellow stop frequently at Kile's place and seldom buy gas. Sometimes you leave the store with no visible packages."

"Back away from my vehicle, Detective Spearman," Coleman said and reached again for the door handle. "I think you're on some kind of wild goose chase."

"I'm not backing away from anything, Mr. Foshee. A court order is on the way for the interior security footage of that convenience store. I suspect you're a star in several scenes," Reed said.

Coleman dropped his grip on the door handle.

"And when we raid the place, we're going to find more than packs of chewing tobacco behind that Kile woman's checkout counter."

Coleman did not respond, only looked the other way through the car windows, back toward the gravesite. The gravediggers were nearly finished.

"Mr. Foshee, I hear you're a good attorney and near retirement. You want to work with me or face the consequences? What would a smart man like you advise a client to do under these circumstances?"

Coleman snapped his head back to Reed. "Detective, I would advise my client that we have legal ways to stop police harassment. Please step back from the door of my vehicle. I need to be with my family."

Reed smiled with a soft chuckle and backed away.

Coleman slammed the car door shut. His driver was already behind the wheel. "Ralph, get us the hell out of here."

Reed watched the Lincoln pull away and scatter gravel in its wake. His cell phone buzzed.

"Yeah, Owen, what's up?"

"A dentist just called in a 911, somebody named Dr. Roland. Said he came back to his office and found his office manager slumped over her desk. Throat was cut."

The patient exam rooms of the Mack and Associates Orthopedic Clinic seldom required restocking of supplies; however, today was one of them. Jessica double-checked her phone for the correct time and dropped it into a front pocket of her dress. The first patient for the afternoon was due in less than fifteen minutes, barely enough time to replenish the cabinets and drawers of the exam rooms.

This appointment, any appointment, was important to the clinic's bottom line, and Jessica needed to be up front to greet her. That is, if the patient showed up. She also expected another text from Dr. Mack any minute with an update about the progress of his morning surgical case, delayed when the hospital anesthesiologist showed up late.

Despite the surprise of a modest uptick in cash flow to cover the past two weeks' practice expenses and despite their previous conversations, Dr. Mack made no mention of replacing the clinic nurse, nor did he probe Jessica about the origin of the increased practice income. Jessica remained as the lone clinic employee, responsible for replacing supplies, light janitorial work, secretarial duties, and watering the plants.

Dr. Mack seemed to have a few minutes to spare here and there, and her hints that he tackle some of the chores went either unrecognized or ignored. He did find time to teach Jessica a few basic nursing skills such as bandage changes or suture removal—tasks she easily handled without a medical license or increase in salary.

She never informed Scott about the visit from the manager of the dental office and the woman's interest in a new job.

Jessica glanced at her phone. She now had only thirteen minutes. "That patient better show up. I need her Xanax," she said. "I promised Momma Kile."

The woman expected in thirteen minutes or less was the anxious type—overly nervous about the long-term outcome of her surgery. Dr. Mack took Jessica's suggestion to prescribe the patient thirty Xanax with a refill. Fortunately, when Jessica contacted her after the surgery, the patient needed only a few of the tablets and promised to donate the rest to one of Dr. Mack's needy patients.

*Benzos move fast in Momma's store,* Jessica said to herself after she hung up the phone.

Jessica retrieved the cart from the compact storage area at the far end of the hall. She loaded boxes of gloves, paper supplies, and sutures on the silver-colored handcart constructed of metal alloy on four spindly wheels and guided it hurriedly toward the patient treatment area. Only her left hand loosely placed on the top handle controlled the direction. Her phone was in the right.

When the supply cart wobbled a bit to veer from the center of the corridor toward the far wall, a box of surgical exam gloves fell from the top of the pile. With her left hand still on the handle of the moving cart, Jessica stretched for the box in midair with her right, her grasp hindered by the cell phone still in hand. She missed her mark, and the box of gloves struck the floor to slide down the hall before twirling to a stop. One of the cart's wheels popped over the box, further tilting it off balance to its side. The metal side rail dug a furrow into the adjacent wall, cutting the inexpensive wallpaper and the sheetrock underneath.

Jessica jerked the cart in the opposite direction in a failed attempt to right it, and the cart overturned to skid across the floor. The short corridor became littered with rolls of gauze dressings, more boxes of exam gloves, packets of surgical sutures, toppled stacks of patient dressing gowns, rolls of surgical tape, and paper drapes for the exam tables. Some of the unpackaged paper products tore in the calamity, and Jessica gasped when packets of expensive surgical suture spun across the linoleum. They disappeared between the slats of a floor air conditioning register.

"Dammit," Jessica cursed, the outburst a surprise to her. Even though certain she was alone, Jessica nervously smoothed her clothes and looked up and down the hall and into the nearest exam room to verify. Except for the lost suture packets and torn paper products, the spilt supplies were otherwise salvageable. The damaged wallpaper was another story. She ran her fingers over the torn wallpaper and the deep crevices in the sheetrock underneath. "Double Dammit."

Jessica gathered the supplies from the floor and returned them to the cart. "The cost to fix this screw-up is on me. But my share of the Xannies sales should cover it." Dr. Mack would never miss the lost packets of suture, and she would find some way to use the torn paper exam drapes.

She checked the time again—only four minutes to go. "That Mrs. Pitts better show after all the time I took up with her," she said and entered the first exam room to restock with a box of surgical exam gloves.

When the middle-aged Mrs. Pitts called a few days ago to confirm the date and time of the afternoon appointment, Scott stood behind Jessica and poured coffee. She stalled while he filled his cup, added the sweetener, and stirred for a few seconds. "Mrs. Pitts, I need to verify some of the information in your chart," she said into the phone. "You know, everything is electronic now and the information has to be complete. Now, what is your date of birth? And I'll need your home address and emergency contact information."

"But I just had surgery. Shouldn't you know that already?" Pitts had said, nearly loud enough for Scott to hear.

Jessica stalled for time and deleted, then re-entered the patient's demographic data including date and place of birth until Scott left with his coffee for his own office. Mrs. Pitts even divulged her mother's maiden name. With her boss out of the way, Jessica continued with Mrs. Pitts—but changed the subject. She needed to know about her unused pain medication.

"Okay, Mrs. Pitts, I've got all the information updated for you." She scooted her roller chair to the edge of the exit into the hall, stretched the phone cord to the limit, and hesitated a few more seconds while she observed the rear corridor—complete silence at the end of the hall with no sign of Dr. Mack. The door to his personal office was shut. He was well out of earshot.

Jessica scooted back to her desk and computer. "Dr. Mack likes me to go ahead and get a little more information, even some additional medical information, from his patients in advance to … to save a little time for them at their appointments."

"That's a wonderful idea. How nice of Dr. Mack," Mrs. Pitts said and laughed. "I hate wasting time in a doctor's office, no matter how polite or handsome they are."

"One question: how did your pain medication work for you, the pills that Dr. Mack prescribed for you after your surgery?" Jessica asked, almost under her breath. "Did you have enough of them to last?"

"Oh, my, yes, and thank you for asking, young lady. My cute surgeon did such a wonderful job. I had so very little pain after I got home that I could complete all those exercises he prescribed and felt just fine. And I wasn't as anxious as I thought I'd be. I took only a few of the Xanax—bottle's almost full."

Jessica had hesitated slightly. She referred to the notepad kept hidden behind the computer monitor, spotting the words *leftover* and *better for you and your family* in the list of suggested responses in case she came up blank. "I'm so glad that you're doing great. It's definitely better for your health that you did not need all of your prescription. I see that Dr. Mack prescribed thirty Percocet tablets in addition to the Xanax. How many of those are leftover?"

"Well … let me think. I'm not taking any more of that pain prescription, only plain Tylenol," Mrs. Pitts said. "I was just getting out of the shower when you called, and the bathroom medicine cabinet is right here. Let me check."

"I would appreciate that, if you could. Dr. Mack likes the records complete."

Jessica heard what sounded like a click and a cabinet door swing open.

"I'm shaking the bottle. I know it's about full. Now, if I can just get that *childproof* cap off the top to count the pills. Oops, I dropped my towel."

"I sure do appreciate this … I mean … Dr. Mack appreciates it … for his other patients," Jessica managed.

"Whew, got the cap off the bottle. Let's see," Mrs. Pitts said. "About twenty or maybe twenty-five left? That should be about right. Same for the nerve pills."

Jessica heard the cabinet shut.

"Now, young lady, why is it that you need this information?"

As in previous similar conversations, Jessica strained to listen for Dr. Mack approach while she worked up the best answer. In her most sincere, yet convincing, tone she crossed her fingers and said, "It's a good idea to destroy unused narcotics and other controlled substances like Xanax, but there are patients who need medicine and can't afford it. Even generic prescriptions can sometimes be expensive." Jessica swallowed hard. "We take donations for them."

"Those poor folks," Mrs. Pitts said. "Of course, I'll donate my medication to the less fortunate, and thank you and Dr. Mack for safeguarding my family. You're right. If I leave these pills lying around my house, my grandchildren might swallow them and need to have their stomachs pumped out—or worse. Or my noisy bridge partners might sneak the medication out of my cabinet."

Jessica referred to the time again. Mrs. Pitts was almost ten minutes late. Momma Kile counted on those Percs, and the Xannies were to have been a surprise.

Jessica continued to rewind and play that patient conversation in her head, questioning every rehearsed statement or comment to Mrs. Pitts. *This just can't be a strike out. I've got to get better at this,* she decided.

Another five minutes went by. Jessica felt sick. Mrs. Pitts was going to be a no-show.

Jessica envisioned the woman's awkward situation—forced to juggle her cell phone, bath towel, and the plastic prescription bottle while naked in her bathroom—and regretted the call and bother to her. As she stocked the last room and emptied the cart, Jessica realized that she should have called Mrs. Pitts back and apologized. Maybe she would have kept the appointment and brought the drugs.

While Jessica shoved the supply cart into the storage closet outside the reception area, the buzzer at the front door sounded. Someone had entered the lobby. She turned the corner to smile at Mrs. Pitts and breathed a long sigh of relief.

"Here they are, young lady. I hope these things help someone," Mrs. Pitts called out. She placed the two plastic containers of medication on the reception counter over Jessica's desk.

*They'll sure help me*, Jessica wanted to say. No, she wanted to scream it. Momma Kile needed the product, and she and Dr. Mack needed the money. Furthermore, Momma Kile was not pleasant when angry or disappointed.

"Hey, Mrs. Pitts. Let me check you in for your appointment." Jessica took another quick listen for Dr. Mack, broke another large smile at the silence, and took the bottles. She verified the prescription labels, withdrew two little brown envelopes from a drawer, and slowly emptied the contents of each container into a separate envelope—counting. The white pills matched other generic Percocet she had seen. The Xanax were yellow.

Jessica did a mental tally of their street value. "That's almost a thousand bucks," she mumbled.

"You say something?" Mrs. Pitts asked. "You need me to fill out some more paperwork? Oh, and I brought my newspaper in case Dr. Mack was running late, and I had to wait." She pulled a folded copy of the *Sun Herald* from her purse.

Jessica shook her head. "No, ma'am. I have what I need. I'll label these and put them in a safe place for a deserving patient." She reopened the same drawer. "Please just go ahead and sign the patient register on the clipboard in front of you, and Dr. Mack will be here in just a sec."

"Will do, my dear. I've got an ink pen inside here somewhere." When Mrs. Pitts began to rummage again through her purse, Jessica dropped the empty pill bottles into the trashcan near her feet and slid the envelopes with pills into her own purse.

"I certainly don't mind if I have to wait to see the doctor," Mrs. Pitts said. "I haven't had a chance to finish the paper. That's why I was a little late for my appointment."

"He shouldn't be long," Jessica repeated. "Please take a seat out there, wherever you like."

"I was having my coffee and reading through the obituaries before I left home. The older you get, the more you pay attention to them. And my, my … there were so many in there today."

Jessica wanted to count the pills again but resisted and instead worked on Mrs. Pitts's medical record in the computer.

"A very nice, long write-up about that lady neurosurgeon who died in the car wreck," Pitts continued. "Such a tragedy and such a waste—left a husband and two children and all those patients who are sure to need her. No telling how long she went to school."

Jessica remained busy at the keyboard.

"And the other article in here about the poor woman who managed a medical office not far from here. I think maybe even next door to you? Named Pam Something-or-other."

By now Mrs. Pitts had taken a seat in the lobby near the ficus tree but spoke loudly enough for Jessica to hear clearly. Jessica stood from her chair and looked through the reception window at Mrs. Pitts.

"Yes, she ran the dentist office," Jessica said.

Mrs. Pitts flipped through the pages of the newspaper. "You're right. The obit didn't give all the gory details, but I guess you know the woman died at work." She walked back to Jessica's window with the newspaper and whispered, "I heard she was murdered— her throat cut. And the dentist she worked for is the one who found her."

"Are you sure?" Jessica asked and stopped typing. "Her throat was

216

cut?" No details had been formally released by the media except that the manner of death was under investigation.

"You never can be too careful, young lady," Mrs. Pitts answered.

Jessica managed a weak smile as the woman returned to her seat. She grabbed her phone and fought to slow her breathing as her heart raced. Jessica needed to call Jamal and headed to the one of the empty patient rooms for privacy.

# Chapter 24

Selena pulled into her parking spot behind the Moondust Casino. She opened the door to her vehicle, stepped out onto the asphalt, and checked her hair and make-up in the driver's review mirror. The rain shower and puddles between her apartment and the casino left the glass in the mirror streaked and splattered. She found a tissue in her bag and rubbed the glass surface clean.

The late-night shifts at the casino with little sleep had taken their toll with bags under her eyes and deeper crow's feet. Worry about living expenses after the child support dried up did not help. Selena tossed and turned with worry over rent and utilities and money for her daughter's school clothes and the extras demanded by a thirteen-year-old.

Selena reached into her purse for her employee badge and felt a firm hand on her shoulder.

"Brandon is handling the store tonight, so I left early. Thought I would see for myself how my product is moving."

"Who's Brandon?" Selena asked.

"My son. He's in the Coast Guard, and he works for me on the side."

Selena remembered the attractive guy at her table with the Coast Guard insignia. "I've never seen him in the store, but I wanna do business with you," Selena said. "I need to keep this simple."

"Simple? I'll tell you what's simple." Momma Kile grabbed Selena's forearm. "You need me as a supplier, and I don't sell to careless idiots. You understand?" Momma squeezed Selena's arm even tighter.

Selena shot a glance at the rear exterior of the casino and tried to pull away. "The security cameras … they'll see us."

"There's no way those eyes reach this far," Momma said. "Listen to me. I wanted to test you. I sent Brandon to try you out."

"What are you talking about?"

"When I choose a dealer to move product through wholesale, I want to keep the circle tight, keep the spokes within the wheel. Less mistakes that way."

"Move out of my way," Selena said. Even outdoors, she felt uneasy standing near this woman. She much preferred contact inside the convenience store where at least a counter separated them. "I'm going to be late to my table."

Momma Kile followed her to the employee entrance, almost encircling her every step. "I know from Brandon that your tables stay full. You work a lot of cards, and you got lots of potential users for my product. But you can go a little overboard with pushing under the table."

"I have to. I need to turn the stuff quick. I'm a single mother and—"

Momma Kile's broad shoulders, thick arms, and wide hips blocked the single rear entrance reserved for employees. Selena attempted to reach around to slide her employee badge through the electric scanner and open the solid metal door. A security camera mounted in plain sight above and to the right of the door frame captured every movement.

"Honey, after my husband left me for a French Quarter whore, I've been carrying my own weight for almost twenty-five years. He was out with that woman when he lost control of his car on the bridge over Lake Pontchartrain and drowned. Bastard left me no insurance, only that crappy store, and the whore floated to the top."

The opaque lens of the exterior security camera stared down at Selena and Momma Kile. Gone was the tiny red light at the base of the metal casing. The unit was dead.

"This business is a two-way street. You help me; I help you," Momma Kile grunted. "Get it?"

219

"I guess so." Selena shot another look at the dead camera. Maybe it was better if the camera did not work. Security could raise questions if she was spotted with a non-employee at the back entrance. Selena turned at a slight angle to Kile and stepped nearer the door. She grabbed the handle to pull it toward her. If she had to, maybe she could bring the woman down with a foot to the knees.

At the sudden movement, Momma Kile planted her hand on the door, tight against Selena's. "I'm selective with my wholesale dealers. I size 'em up and decide who to sell to and who to get rid of," she said. "The more pills you push, the more I sell to you at discount. In your line of work with your type of people, you can turn product fast, very fast if you're careful. That benefits both of us."

"How'd you know where I work?" Selena asked, then remembered the embroidery on her shirt with her first name and the casino's logo. She was dressed for work that first day in the convenience store.

"I followed you here before, and, like I told you, my son Brandon checked you out inside. I know you have potential to move pills good, or at least try to," Momma Kile said. "I spotted you making a deal out at your car one day." She tilted her head back toward Selena's vehicle and then shifted her eyes upward toward the dead camera. "I do hope those things don't reach out that far, when they work, that is," she grinned.

"Don't come back around here," Selena said. "When I need something, I'll contact you. I'll come by your store."

Momma Kile released the door handle and stepped back a bit. "Counting on it. See you soon," she said and backed away quickly. She stumbled a bit on an uneven section of asphalt but corrected her stance.

Inside the rear of the building in the electronics mechanical room about 150 feet down the hall, technician Jerome Parrish replaced the burned-out component in the security system control panel. This panel rerouted camera input from throughout the casino to the top floor observation room. The circuit to the exterior units went live just as Mamma Kile began to step away from Selena, her face and full body image captured on recorded video.

"The casino employee is Selena Garcia, the one you've been interested in." The head of security tapped a few keys, and the video sped through a series of frames. "There was a failure of the exterior cameras yesterday, lasted about a half-hour or so. When we got the system back up, Garcia was spotted with this woman."

She hit PAUSE. Momma Kile's image froze just before she stumbled on the parking lot asphalt. A few more clicks enlarged the image. Kile's determined face filled the screen. "You ever seen this old lady before, Detective Spearman?"

Reed took the seat next to the head of security. "Can you play the rest?"

The video continued a second or two and Momma Kile vanished deeper into the parking area as Selena Garcia entered the casino building. She appeared rattled. Another click and a different camera followed Selena until she disappeared into the female employee lounge, to emerge several minutes later, tugging at her skirt and heading to the dealers' tables.

"I do recognize the woman with Garcia, last name is Kile—owns a local convenience store, Kile's Minute Mart, or something like that. Any more footage of her? Has Kile approached any of the other employees … or any of the gamblers?"

"I ran her through our customer and employee facial recognition software, and nothing came up."

Reed did not recall Garcia during his surveillance of Kile's store. He slid his cell phone from the inside pocket of his jacket and called Owen Smith.

"Any luck on the subpoena for that security camera footage?" Reed asked Owen.

Reed noticed the perplexed look on the face of the head of casino security. She shrugged her shoulders and held her hands out to her own video as though to say, *So, I've shown you all I've got. What more do you want?*

"The footage at that convenience store, Kile's Minute Mart," Reed said to Owen, waving off the head of security's concern before he ended the call. He returned his phone to his pocket and added, "That was nothing to do with you here, but what we find if the judge grants that convenience store subpoena may help bring down Selena Garcia."

"Casino management is getting a little uneasy about the police busting an employee on the property. Cops and blue lights around a casino are not good for business, shakes up the patrons," security said.

"The department will keep that it mind, but it won't be long before we shut Garcia down," Reed said.

# Chapter 25

"Garcia's shift starts in fifteen. Camera first picked her up tonight in the parking lot at the employee entrance."

"The entire security system must finally be up," Officer Kendall Brisdell said into the hidden microphone.

"Even without the cameras, we know she's here. She punched the clock outside the employee breakroom. No wild goose chase tonight, Kendall."

"All dolled up and nowhere to go is no fun for a girl." She tugged at the cap of her wig. A few strands of her own hair fell against the back of her neck, and she pushed the strays into place. "Did I wear the blonde or red the last time I approached Garcia to buy?" She smoothed the back of the wig with her fingertips. "Hope I was right with tonight's choice of blonde."

Reed studied Kendall's movements on the security monitor. Her high cheek bones, sculptured nose, and naturally pink lips were no handicap when she pulled over speeders or responded to domestic abuse calls. A gun and a uniform always demand attention. Nevertheless, he admired the get-up for this special assignment. Tonight's light hair and heavy make-up were a pleasant contrast to her typical pulled back, dark hair and only a little blush or powder on the cheeks.

Kendall had gone all out for this sting—maybe a little over the top with the fake eyelashes and long fingernails and the bright red lipstick. The shoulder length, layered blonde wig created somewhat of a Dolly Parton persona, absent the chest.

223

"No disrespect meant to you or anyone else," Reed said into the microphone. He noticed Kendall touch her ear and the tiny hidden speaker. "But when Garcia was a no-show last night, I could have sent you over to the other gig. Owen could have used some help at the motel."

Kendall slipped into the nearest restroom and adjusted the wig a bit more in the mirror. She blotted her lips with a sheet of toilet paper and smiled at the refection. "No offense taken, but busting prostitution rings is Officer Smith's baby."

Reed again laughed too loudly into her ear, and she winced—then shook her head clear. "Glad you're enjoying your job," Kendall said.

"We need to see cash change hands this time, catch Garcia in the act, not just a tease. I know from Caston's office, she's desperate. I think she'll turn CI in a heartbeat and do anything to stay out of jail," Reed said.

Kendall left the restroom and pulled a cell phone from her purse. She faked a call to cover her continued conversation with Reed. "From what I heard the other night, Garcia will want to make the deal after her shift, out in the parking lot and out of range of the cameras," she said softly.

"You gotta push her to do it at the table, tell her you gotta get home to your kids or nerdy husband."

"Ha, ha," Kendall said. She passed by a hall mirror and caught another reflection of herself. "This good-looking chick wouldn't put up with nerdy."

"Or maybe tell Garcia you need to get your stuff quick and hurry off to turn a few tricks before calling it a night."

"Still want me to help Owen, don't you?" Kendall said with a smile into the next mirror. She applied extra lipstick.

"If Garcia needs to push product bad enough—and I think she does—she'll give in," Reed said. "If you tell her it's now or never, she won't want to miss the sale. She's a sly chick. I think she believes she can make the exchange under the table and avoid the overheads."

"And then you'll move in. That's the plan, right?"

"The casino security manager will be with me. She wants to downplay the scene on site. Hopefully, Garcia will go quiet. We'll take her in and make the deal."

Kendall spotted a security camera and snuck a thumbs up. She purchased chips at the casino bank, stopped at the bar for a virgin appletini, and walked in the direction of Selena Garcia's blackjack table. There was no sign of the short, fat man who propositioned her during the earlier stakeout.

At the moment, evening action at Moondust Casino was light. Only one player sat at Garcia's table, and Kendall took the seat at the opposite end. Selena greeted her with a cautious smile. "Glad to have you back. You changed your hair."

*Smart cookie. I guess I did go red last time*, Kendall decided. As a redhead, she decided she was a dead ringer for Ann-Margret. Kendall placed her evening bag on the table directly in front of her. "Yes, I like to keep it interesting. Is it okay to put my purse here on the table?"

"Come on, ladies." The other player looked up from his chips to check Selena's name on her uniform. "Selena, I only got time for one more hand. Let's get down to business. Cut the chitchat." The slightly built white man, in his mid to late-seventies or early eighties, sat with stooped shoulders and wiry hands, his voice much more authoritarian than his looks.

Selena dropped the smile and dealt the two hands. The bossy old man busted, and Kendall as Miss Martini scored $200 in chips.

"This is the last night for me at this crappy joint. I've had it with the Coast. Action's much better in Philadelphia," the man said. He scooped up his remaining chips and slid off the stool. A chip fell to the floor, and he bent with a wobble to retrieve it.

Kendall almost stretched to help him but remembered her wig and communication equipment. She stayed put and fingered her chips.

"Maybe I'll stop by the Beau, just one more time, before I leave town," he said under his breath and walked away to cash out.

Selena shuffled the deck. "I usually don't talk about the players, but I'm glad to see that hateful old crab go," she said.

Kendall tilted her head slightly to the left and right. No one else approached the table. She and Selena remained alone. She reached below the table to her right knee and rubbed it. "Man, these heels scream, "screw me," but are a real bitch on the knees and ankles."

"Know what you mean," Selena said. "But for me, they make us wear 'em."

"Doctor's already operated twice on the right knee. Said he couldn't do anything else for me," Miss Martini said. "Doesn't matter, 'cause the dude is dead."

Selena stumbled with the deal. The dealer's down cards flipped up as the tips of her fingers trembled. "Oh, crap. I'm gonna have to call the pit boss over. This has never happened to me—the last thing I need tonight."

Kendall took a sip of her drink. "Pit boss? Now … who is that?" she asked.

"Pit manager. He supervises all the floormen, the dealers, and even the players. Corrects mistakes, like that fuck-up," Selena answered. "Four on two," she called out.

A tall, slender man with thinning grey hair appeared. "What's up, Garcia. Never seen you look pale before," he said. Her pit boss noticed the overturned dealer cards and the tremor. "Calm down, calm down. We'll let it go this time. If okay with your player, just play the hand out."

Kendall nodded and stirred her drink with a fingernail. "All right with me," she said and took another sip. Things needed to move along between her and Garcia. Another player could show up any minute, even with a slow night at the casino, and spoil the sting.

Selena hesitated a few seconds until the pit boss walked away. She resumed play. "I guess with your knee you were talking about Dr. Caston, Dr. Paul Caston?"

"Yeah, that's him. He said I was out of options, so he gave me pills. Now that he's gone, I have to live with the pain, and it's a bitch."

226

"Sounding good, Dolly," came through her earpiece. "Don't see any other players to cramp your style. No one near, but keep pressing."

Kendall watched Selena deal the cards.

Reed said, "I pulled a plainclothes officer in from another job. He's at the table, three over. Check him out: green shirt, untucked, and white pants—average build."

"Damn, this knee hurts tonight, throbs so bad. I just might have to call it an evening." Kendall faked a massage of a sore knee. Exaggerating the hand movement, she lowered her right shoulder to steal a glance at Reed's new officer.

"Yeah, Dr. Caston offed himself, at least that's what I heard," Selena said quietly. She kept her head down. "But … I can help you since he's not around."

"You know another doctor? But those guys take so long to give you an appointment."

Selena continued the deal.

"A new doctor won't be the same," Kendall said. "They'll tell me to take Advil or want to shoot up my joints with steroids. That steroid crap makes you swell-up and gain weight. That's not for me."

A couple walked arm-in-arm behind Kendall. They laughed while studying their drinks. The man reached and pinched the woman in the rear. Both Selena and Kendall were relieved when the couple moved away.

Selena whispered, "That's not what I mean. I'm not talking about another doctor. I can help you with your pain." She seemed to check the overhead camera and changed the pitch and tone of her voice to straight casino dealer. "Okay, place your first bet."

Kendall remained the only player at the table. She slid a twenty-dollar chip to the center. "Help me how?" She caught the undercover officer dressed in green and white take a glimpse in her direction.

Selena kept her eyes down and resumed the whisper. She spoke hurriedly. "I can get you some Percs, enough to tide you over until you get in with another doctor." She dealt the other cards, and

Kendall won with twenty to the dealer's nineteen. Selena turned the cards to start another quick hand. Kendall upped the game and bet forty.

Selena said, "I can meet you out back when I go on break in a couple of hours or later after my shift. I can let you have ten Percs." She looked up from the cards at Miss Martini.

Kendall reached for her drink and sipped. "Sorry, but I won't be able to wait around for the end of your shift. We got to do it now. Need to be at the salon early tomorrow for work."

"I'll need a hundred bucks," Selena lowered her eyes. "No, for a first-time customer, I'll give you a deal. Make it eighty."

Another couple walked behind Kendall, two men. Selena's face fell when they stopped briefly as though to join the table. The men viewed the area, admired the fountain, but moved on toward the roulette table.

"We need to make this happen before anyone else comes up," Selena said. "If you got the money, we can do it. Under the table so the overhead cameras won't pick it up."

Kendall moved her purse to her lap and pretended to check the contents. "I've got the cash. Now what?"

"Keep the money where it is and place another bet."

Miss Martini complied.

Selena dealt with her right hand, placed the rest of the deck on the table, then slipped her left hand into a side pocket of her blouse. She cupped a tiny white envelope inside her palm, then eased the left hand under the table. "Let's keep the game going," she said. "Hand the money to me under the table, and I'll slip the pills to you."

An attractive black woman in tight blue jeans and pink, open-collared silk blouse materialized to occupy one of the empty stools at Selena's table. Sky-blue topaz and sterling silver earrings dangled from her earlobes. As she arranged her chips, the undercover cop from three tables over rushed Selena and unintentionally knocked the woman in jeans to the floor. The woman screamed.

Another woman dressed in a grey suit rushed forward out of nowhere, Kendall assumed the manager of casino security.

The few players at the other tables scattered after first scooping up their chips. A few more high-pitched screams added to the drama.

"So much for the quiet takedown," Reed said into Kendall's ear. "But still a nice job."

Miss Martini as Kendall lifted the middle finger of her right hand toward the security cameras in the ceiling.

# Chapter 26

Jessica dropped her purse deep into the bottom drawer of her desk, turned on the morning coffee pot behind her, and watered the potted plants in the clinic lobby. The indoor garden had expanded in the last few weeks, and Dr. Mack seemed to accept that the blooming and green leafy plants were all gifts from grateful patients.

Her hand shook, and she spilled a little water on the carpet. There had been no sign of Jamal or Immaculate since Mrs. Pitts dropped the gossipy details of Pam Bullock's murder. Neither had answered any of her calls. Jessica had never thought of Jamal, much less Immaculate, as a killer. However, she understood that the two could have felt threatened by the dental office manager's curiosity and possible intrusion into their business.

Jessica felt guilty about discussing Pam with them and, for that matter, realized that Jamal could be angry with her for shifting the supply of drugs to Momma Kile instead of to him and Immaculate. She remembered once spotting Jamal with a knife calf holster when he pulled at the lower leg of his baggy jeans to lace a shoe. With that, she spilled more water on the carpet.

"You and I never discussed that crazy thing over at the dentist's office," Dr. Mack had said yesterday after the patients left. "Poor woman. I heard at the hospital that the police think a patient killed her. So, we better keep our eyes open."

"Yes, sir. We need to," Jessica said.

"You feel safe enough around here?" he asked and noticed the waiting area crowded with houseplants. He scanned a few of the thank you cards attached to the plant containers. "We've seen a nice uptick in surgery cases and in numbers of office appointments, but I'm not sure I can afford a full-time security guard … or even one part-time. Of course, we've got those new cameras outback, but it took someone's death for the landlord to see the need."

Jessica assumed Jamal and Immaculate would lie low for a good while. "I think we'll be all right. I've never heard of anything like that around here before."

"Wonder if they've arrested anybody," Scott said. He read a another thank you note, this one attached to a broadleaf plant with red-tinged foliage.

"Don't think so, Dr. Mack."

"From the looks of all these healthy plants and notes from pleased patients, I guess things are perking up around here, Jessica," Dr. Mack said. "Lots of happy folks. Need some good news after our slump and that murder next door."

Finished with the watering chores, Jessica logged into the computer. It came to life slowly, and she forced a smile at her boss's comment from the day before. Some of those happy out-patient surgical and office appointment folks might send plants, cards, and small gifts, yet not pay their bills. "Yes, sir. Lots of grateful folks," she mumbled. "This place would sink if I weren't around."

Jessica continued as the sole clinic employee and ran her recycled pharmaceutical business with her mother-in-law. She kept the books and paid the clinic bills, along with watering the plants and restocking the exam rooms with supplies. Now and then, she emptied a garbage can or two and brushed out the toilets.

The clinic's cut of the brisk sales of unused narcotics and anti-anxiety medications kept the checking account in the black and covered the delinquent patient payments and the low reimbursement from insurance companies. What's more, Jessica's salary was paid, the lights stayed on, and her mother-in-law remained happy with continuous product to fuel her under-the-counter drug business.

Jessica even squeezed enough cash from those profits to purchase additional patient appreciation plants from the sales rack at the local garden center. She found that the plants tied with big bows seemed to ease Dr. Mack's worry over the finances of the practice and avoided questions. Consequently, as the flow of recycled narcotics through the clinic increased, so did the number of plants.

The computer downloaded the day's office and surgical schedule and the overnight patient emails. Jessica began to read the first email just as the desk phone rang. The email was from a female patient in her late sixties in recovery from a recent pelvic fracture.

```
I'll be by first thing in the morning.
Please meet me out front. I've got some-
thing for Dr. Mack.
```

The same patient had taken Jessica's earlier suggestion and brought one bottle of unused Percocet to her follow-up appointment the week before, surprised and grateful that instead of surgery her pelvic fracture required only bedrest and physical therapy to heal.

Jessica finished reading the email and answered the phone.

"Honey, did you get my email?" the same lady asked. "I'm right out front, against the curb. I've got a happy for you and that cute Dr. Mack. Oh, and don't you worry. I've been a good girl. My nephew Tommy is driving. Oh, and bring one of those carts on rollers. The happy is heavy!"

Jessie put down the telephone receiver and grabbed the supply cart from the hall storage. She headed through the lobby to the front door and out to the street.

The woman's opened car trunk greeted Jessica outside the clinic. A three-gallon rhododendron rested near the center and rose from a ropey, tightly-woven wicker container. A floppy, baby blue silk bow decorated the base of the plant.

Jessie called out toward the front of the woman's vehicle. "Thank you, so much. Dr. Mack is over at the hospital, but I know he'll love the plant." She strained to lift the plant from the trunk and place it on the cart. "He's all about baby blue."

232

The weight of the rhododendron and container almost upset the thin metal supply cart as she shoved the bow out of her face. Somehow, Jessica managed to steady it and push the cart to the passenger window where the woman waited. The woman lowered the window.

"Like I said, Dr. Mack appreciates this," Jessica said, "same as what you did for his other patients at your post-op."

A teenager about sixteen sat behind the wheel, mesmerized with the screen of a cell phone. Wireless earbuds sprouted from the sides of his head.

"It's great you've got a driver," Jessica said and tilted her head toward the teenager. "You're following Dr. Mack's orders and not driving yourself for six weeks."

The woman rolled her eyes. The boy remained fixed on his phone. "That's my nephew. Tommy is always on that thing. He plays games or something like that. But the boy's a decent driver."

Jessica smiled. "That's good to know," she said.

"But the plant is not the only thing I wanted to drop off." The pelvic fracture patient reached into her purse and handed Jessica a small, plastic grocery sack tied at the neck. "I'm glad you asked me about my leftover prescriptions when we scheduled my last appointment. This is such a kind thing you're doing for the unfortunate folks who can't afford their medicine."

Jessica darted her eyes up and down the street. With no one else around, she balanced the cart against the parking meter with her foot, untied the bag, and rummaged through the contents. "There's two more bottles in here," Jessica said. "But the other day when you gave me that first bottle of pain killers, you said that was it."

Tommy seemed to mouth the words to a song and nod in rhythm while rocking his head sideways.

"I know, but I got to thinking," the woman said. "The emergency room doc wrote me a prescription when I tripped over that concrete barrier in the parking lot outside the grocery store. Then Dr. Mack gave me another script—so that made two bottles—and I only took a few, no more than three or four in all."

Jessica took another look in the bag. "But this makes three bottles you've brought me."

"I remembered some pain pills from about two years ago, when I had my gallbladder taken out. I guess they're still good. The lid to the bottle's been screwed on tight."

Jessica crushed the top of the bag closed in her hand. "Oh, they're good, totally good."

The woman reached into the right front pocket of her sweater. "I've been thinking about these things too." She handed Jessica another plastic bottle nearly filled with tiny pills, off-white in color. It carried the label of a local pharmacy. "I don't need this Valium anymore either. My primary care physician gave 'em to me last year when my sister passed away. He said they would help me sleep. But I'm okay now. Sis is in a better place."

Jessica shook the bottle gently and did the math in her head. She fought a smile. The wholesale deal with her mother-in-law from just this patient alone would pay the clinic building utilities for about three months. She dropped the bottle into the plastic bag with the others.

"I am so sorry about your sister," she said. Jessica laid her other hand on the woman's shoulder, gripping the precious bag against her chest. The cart remained secure with her foot wedged under a wheel.

"Come on, Aunt Miranda. You said this would only take a few minutes. I'm already late for school," Tommy said, without dropping the phone. "I might as well not even go to class at all today. And you gotta write me an excuse—and it better be a good one."

As the shiny white Cadillac pulled away, the woman returned a weak smile and raised the car window. Jessica waved good-bye and held the plastic bag even tighter. She pushed the top-heavy cart with the large plant and wicker basket to the front door of the clinic building without losing control. With the side of her foot and a forearm, she managed to prop the door open and roll the cart and its contents inside.

"Hey, Jessica. We get another plant? Wow! We're going to have to add on to the lobby."

Dr. Mack's voice startled her. Jessica dropped the bag. The cart almost toppled.

Scott lurched forward and steadied the cart, then bent down toward the carpet for the bag. "And what's in the bag?"

"I've got it." Jessica beat him to the sack of pills and pressed it deep into her chest. "This bag? It's just some ... some trash I picked up on the sidewalk. And, Dr. Mack, you're ... you're here early."

"Yeah, my last case cancelled. The guy's potassium was outta whack."

A tall, fit man in a lightweight, dark seersucker suit stepped from the hall into the lobby. "That sounds like the right thing to do, young lady—picking up that trash," he said. "Gotta keep the place clean. After all, it's a doctor's office."

The man's suit looked expensive—the blazer cut slim and short at the hips and the pant legs tapered to fit snuggly at the top of his shiny, black leather shoes.

"Jessica, this is Mr. Trey Buckley. He's the administrator at Biloxi Memorial."

Buckley extended a hand. "Please call me Trey."

Jessica shifted the precious bag of narcotics and sedatives to her left hand without releasing it from her breast and shook Mr. Buckley's hand with the right. "A nice lady from last week, a patient, she brought Dr. Mack this plant. He's been doing a great job lately. See all the plants?"

"Yes, and seems healthy and clean around here," Buckley said, looking around. "Sure does."

"Excuse me, but I need to throw this trash away." She left Dr. Mack and Mr. Buckley alone in the lobby to stuff the bag of narcotics and Valium deep into her purse stored in the office drawer.

Trey Buckley asked, "Cute girl. Been with you long?"

"Your personnel director hired Jessica for me. Good choice. She's been with me since the first day."

"I remember at least three employees on the books when our hospital board last funded your practice," Buckley said.

"Jessica Kile wears a lot of hats around here," Scott said. "She has to. I had to let the other two employees go. Couldn't afford them."

As they walked to his office, Scott studied the young hospital administrator's suit and tie and the haircut. His dark hair was cut severely short on the sides, then much thicker on the top—tapered or wedged upward from the side to side and front to back in the shape of an overturned ax blade. Scott assumed that a bottle of Buckley's hair gel cost more than two Scott Mack haircuts.

Scott kept his own hairstyle longer and thicker on the sides, well below the ears but not to the shoulders. That last girl he dated seemed to like this casual look, and since there was less styling involved, he owed less to his barber every six weeks. Regarding the hospital administrator's silk tie, Scott owned a couple of those himself, although seldom-worn and not such a rich design or tight weave.

Buckley took the wood frame chair in front of Scott's desk, purchased at a local flea market with its original, somewhat dingy upholstery of seagulls flying against a blue background. Despite his slight build, the flimsy construction strained under Buckley's weight. He grasped the arms of the chair to support himself and ran his hands up and down over the cotton fabric. Once satisfied that the chair was sturdy enough, he rested his hands in his lap.

Scott remained midway between the door to the hall and his desk, able to see Trey Buckley's face. "Cut to the chase, Buckley. You saw me in the doctors' lounge after that morning case cancelled and wanted to talk in my office. So, here we are. You getting ready to shut this place down and fire me, or what?"

Buckley leaned forward slightly and straightened the tie, adjusting it even tighter. "The Board of Directors of Biloxi Memorial has monitored your practice from the day you started," he said.

236

Scott interrupted and briefly took the seat behind his desk. "I'm sure you have, probably have the place bugged … hidden cameras too."

"We know things have been tough since your expense and salary guarantee expired per our contract with you. We have budgetary constraints ourselves. But the fact that you're still in business and seem to be building a patient base has got to mean something."

"What it means is that I have worked my butt off for you people and taken care of the patients nobody else wanted. The *dregs of society* is what you and the assholes on your board would call them." Scott stood and started for the door. "Jessica may have a patient ready for me. Thanks for coming by, Buckley. I hope your fancy duds didn't get dirty on that old chair."

"Please, Dr. Mack … Scott. Hear me out."

Scott stopped and turned back toward the hospital administrator.

Buckley said, "You know about Dr. Caston."

"Of course, I do. I found him dead in the front seat of his car. You guys ought to be saving a bundle now on advertising since he's not around anymore."

"The Biloxi Memorial family is devastated over the loss of Paul Caston. Like you, I'm sure, we considered him not only an active, productive member of the staff, but a friend and colleague. While Dr. Caston's practice had begun to slow a bit as he got older, he still left behind a sizeable patient base."

Curious, Scott took a few steps toward his desk. His posture relaxed.

"The other orthopedic physicians and the physician assistants on staff tell me they have little room on their schedules to accommodate Paul Caston's patients."

"Must be nice to be so busy," Scott said. "What exactly are you proposing, Buckley?"

"The operating budget for physician salaries and hospital sponsored clinics is already in the red for this year, but our marketing people can assist you financially in other ways."

"And how is that?"

"We can direct many of the Caston patients to you. It's our understanding that the estate's efforts to sell his practice to other providers have reached a dead end, and Biloxi Memorial did not want to get involved because we don't want to sink any more money into …"

"I get it. You mean that you don't want to gamble on bringing in another new doctor to replace Caston. You want me to take on Caston's load and keep his patients loyal to Biloxi Memorial, but not pay me."

Buckley stood and walked the few steps to face Scott. "You're correct. We don't want to put a new orthopedic physician in the Caston clinic building." The seriousness in Buckley's face morphed into a grin, and the smile brightened. "But the exclusive transfer or referral of Caston's former patients to your practice could be a true shot in the arm for your caseload … and your bottom line."

*Jessica could definitely handle a heavier workload and would probably enjoy being more productive,* Scott thought.

"We believe that Caston's patients will take the Marketing Department's advice that Scott Mack, M.D., is the new doctor they should see. You'll have to replace most of those big plants in your lobby waiting room with chairs to accommodate the influx of patients."

Scott again considered Jessica. She always appeared hardworking even when there was nothing worthwhile to do in the office, and her dedication seemed relentless. He was certain of her loyalty. Plus, he had never caught her talking on her cell and could overlook the few times he had noticed her texting over the last several weeks. She had even dropped those crazy ideas about patients' leftover meds.

With more patient revenue, he could afford to rehire the janitorial staff and a nurse to relieve Jessica of the extra duties. He could give her a raise.

Buckley dropped his smile. "Scott, this is a tremendous opportunity for you, but the Board needs your answer very soon. We will shift some, if not all, the marketing budget from Caston's column

238

to yours. We don't want our competition to get Caston's patients and drain our hospital revenue."

As Buckley spoke, Scott's mind raced through his rationalization for moving to Mississippi in the first place: life near a beach, the mild winters, presumably friendly southern people, the near proximity to New Orleans, the less expensive real estate versus that back home—all trumped by no other reasonable job offer or opportunity.

He had no ties to the area and still did not—no family, no steady girlfriend, and few friends other than some acquaintances at the hospital—nothing to keep him in Mississippi. His modestly priced house should sell quickly if he left, and perhaps with a little surgical practice experience under his belt he could land another job, maybe in an area underserved by orthopedists.

Over the last few weeks, calling it quits had looked better and better. But now any decision to abandon the Gulf Coast did not seem so easy. Buckley's unexpected visit and offer had altered that. If he would possibly assume some good, healthy patients from the late Paul Caston, patients who needed surgery and would pay their bills, he could stick it out financially on the Gulf Coast. With increased patient volume and a better patient payor mix, he might even be able to afford to take a few days off and enjoy what the area had to offer.

"Scott ... Dr. Mack? Do you have any questions?"

Scott's mind drifted further to that late afternoon encounter with the thugs in the alley and his conversation with the accountant's wife about her husband's need for narcotics and how Scott could supply them. His thoughts again turned to Jessica and the temptation to resell unused narcotics and anxiolytics donated by patients.

Crazy.

Scott shook all of that away.

Trey Buckley sighed, "I have another meeting and need to get back to Biloxi Memorial. Thank you for your time. I'm sorry this proposal did not work for you." He picked up the gold trimmed, leather folder laid earlier on Scott's desk and walked past him toward the door. "At the meeting tomorrow morning I'll tell the hospital board of directors that you're not interested in the opportunity."

"No, wait," Scott said. He knew that the patient clinic appointment schedule was skimpy for the afternoon and that tomorrow morning's was completely empty. "I think that …" Scott liked the warm breeze on his front porch, the smell of the ocean a block away, and the friendly southern people. Scott liked living on the Coast. Besides, moving would be a hassle.

"I'll take it," Scott said.

Buckley stopped and turned around.

"I'll see Caston's patients." Scott dropped his scowl. "Thank you for the opportunity. I'm on board."

"I can see this is not an easy decision for you," Buckley said with the smile of a used-car salesman. "Are you sure?"

"Just give me the specifics, the fine print. Tell me what your people are going to do to make this happen and grow my orthopedic practice."

"Smart man. I thought you'd come around." Buckley shifted the leather folder to under his left arm and extended his right hand. Scott shook it. "The marketing department will issue formal notice that all patient records have been transferred to your practice," Buckley said. "Of course, patients have the right to choose another doctor; however, in these situations most won't go to the trouble. We'll get Caston's patients under your roof in no time."

"They certainly won't have to wait for an appointment," Scott admitted. "I've already seen a few of Caston's patients."

"I'll call the chairman of the board as soon as I get back to my office and let her know of your decision. She'll appreciate the good news."

"Is there any paperwork to go along with this little arrangement?" Scott asked.

"No paperwork needed. You have the word of Biloxi Memorial

Hospital," Buckley said with another smile, then lowered his voice, almost to a hush. "Nonetheless, we do have an understanding: You'll admit Caston's former patients, as well as your other patients, to our hospital when they need surgical services, and you'll continue to use our out-patient lab facilities."

Scott nodded slowly.

"Of course, when needed, you'll continue to refer to other specialists within our hospital network." Buckley reached into his coat pocket and removed a business card. "I'll leave one of these with your secretary out front too. My assistant will notify our Information Technology people to contact her."

He laid the engraved card on Scott's desk and walked to the hall.

"Oh, and I noticed the name of your practice posted out front," Buckley stopped and said. "This could be a fresh start for you. Why don't you consider a new name for your practice—something simple and to the point, like Mack Orthopedic Specialists. BMH will spring for the cost of the new sign."

# Chapter 27

Four days later a technician with the Biloxi Memorial Hospital Information Technology Department arrived at Dr. Scott Mack's office with a HIPPA compliance officer in tow. Jessica stood at her desk at the check-in window to greet the two individuals. "May I help you?"

Dressed in faded jeans, white T-shirt, and red baseball cap turned bill forward, the man in front stiffened his posture to match Jessica's height of five four. Despite his best effort, Jessica bested him by an inch, maybe two. "We're IT from Biloxi Memorial," he said. "Here to update your EMR software and upload the patient data from the Caston medical practice."

Jessica nodded. "Dr. Mack told me about that, that we're getting all of Dr. Caston's patient files and data. Do you need my desk?"

"No, ma'am. Just the main server."

"All that computer stuff is behind the first door down the hall, just past this office. Not the supply closet but the door before it." She looked expectantly at the person behind him. Dressed in a simple dark suit with light brown hair pulled severely back in a clip, the woman punched the keypad area of her phone, then made scrolling motions with her finger.

"I'm Johnson, HIPPA Compliance Officer. Just along for the ride to keep an eye on this joker," the woman said. She tilted her head to the side in the direction of the IT technician.

"I'll need about thirty minutes, maybe forty-five, to upload the files," the technician said. "Could've done it online but more secure this way. That keeps Johnson happy."

The compliance officer did not look up from her phone at the mention of her name.

"I've already checked out your software. Seems that Memorial set up this practice, and we updated Dr. Caston's practice one or two years ago, so the file format should be compatible," the technician said. He regarded the empty lobby behind him and shrugged as he stepped away from the check-in desk. "Like I said, your system will be down for a while. Is that a problem?"

Jessica referred to her computer screen, jotted a phone number on the notepad to the right of her keyboard, and clicked out of the patient chart in front of her. She stuck the note in the front pocket of her skirt and planned to make the call later from her cell.

"Not a problem at all," Jessica answered. As the two hospital employees stepped around the corner into the hall, she pulled up the patient schedule for the next hour. It was blank, just as expected.

"Hey, you mind keeping an eye on the place?" Jessica found the technician already snuggled up to the computer equipment and tapping furiously on a laptop. She assumed he had already logged into the clinic's electronic files. Johnson occupied a short stool in the corner and continued to scroll through her phone. Neither looked up. "I need to run a couple of errands for Dr. Mack. He's over at the hospital," Jessica said.

"Sure," both answered nearly in unison.

"We'll hold down the fort," Johnson added.

"Thanks," Jessica said. "I'll be back before you finish up." She grabbed her phone from the top of the desk and her purse from the drawer and left through the front door. The convenience store was less than fifteen minutes away, plenty of time to call the post-op patient for tomorrow and suggest that he bring any unused medicine with him to his appointment. She punched in his number before she started her car and plugged her phone into the dashboard charger.

"Another score," Jessica said at the first red light. The sixty-eight-year-old man with the successful wrist surgery told her that sixteen of the eighteen prescribed pills were unneeded and that he would be glad to help another patient. Jessica felt dizzy over the sales profit of sixteen tablets of hydrocodone. She pulled up behind the convenience store, locked her car, and pushed the call button at the rear door. The sign above the door read:

**EMPLOYEES AND DELIVERIES ONLY.**

Jessica shot a thumbs up at the security camera mounted to the right and aimed at the concrete stoop. Cobwebs covered the base of the antiquated camera, much larger and more conspicuous than the new ones outside Dr. Mack's clinic building. A loud buzzer sounded, and the lock mechanism clicked. Jessica depressed the lever on the door and entered the cramped stockroom.

"Don't have much time. I wanted to share some good news."

The sound of bells clanging at the front door ricocheted into the storeroom. "Grab another one of those cases of drinks. Get one of the diets, the ones with caffeine," Momma Kile said. "Somebody's come in the store. I need to get back up front."

Jessica picked up the case of soda and followed her mother-in-law into the retail area of the convenience store. A well-dressed woman in short jacket and slacks with a skinny strand of pearls poured a cup of coffee and reached for the packets of artificial sweetener. She noticed Momma Kile. "Oh, hello there. Is this coffee fresh?"

"Made it about an hour ago. Take a sip and decide for yourself," Momma answered, then muttered to Jessica, "Those types. What does she think this place is? A five-star restaurant?"

She and Jessica each set their case of soft drinks at the sales display and walked toward the register. The female customer paid for the coffee and left.

"So, what's the good news, and aren't you playing hooky? You can't screw up that job at the doctor's office."

"That's just it. The supply at the clinic is gonna pick up." She

244

checked the time on her phone. The IT guy should be about half-way through. She still had time. "Remember that older doctor who used to sell to you, the one who died?"

"Yeah, but Caston was getting cold feet. Not sure how much longer he was good for."

"That doesn't matter anymore. The hospital is giving Dr. Mack all of Dr. Caston's patient charts. Dr. Mack thinks that most of the patients, probably all of them, will come to us. And a lot of them will need surgery ... and post-op meds."

"You have to carry a bunch of heavy boxes of medical records over from Caston's old office?"

"No, Momma, it's all transferred electronic from Dr. Caston's computer to Dr. Mack's. These two people from the hospital are over at our clinic right now moving everything over." Jessica checked the time again. She needed to leave soon. "I thought the info about all the new patients coming into Dr. Mack's practice was exciting ... gonna be good for business."

"I'd like to see what's in some of those computer files. Once or twice, Caston emailed me about our business agreement. It was during a weekday, so it had to be from his office. I told him that it was better to talk in person, that even over the phone was safer than email."

Jessica reached into her purse. The manila envelope inside contained 120 Percocet. "I was going to drop this by after work today, but I decided that the sooner you get the product, the sooner you can move it. And I made another deal on the way over here." She handed the envelope to her mother-in-law and looked at her phone. "Time to go," Jessica said.

The IT technician and Johnson exited through the clinic front door as Jessica pulled into her parking spot. She grabbed her purse and stepped out of her car.

"Hey, you're back," the technician said. He pointed his key fob at a mud-splattered, light beige van and Johnson followed. The Biloxi Memorial Hospital logo, a strong black outline of the façade of the medical building complex, extended the entire length of the vehicle. The moniker of the hospital rose like a cloud or a floating roof above the design. The same insignia marked the opposite side of the van.

"We finished up in there. Some lady walked in a few minutes ago, maybe five or ten, could have been fifteen. She said if somebody didn't check her in pretty quick, the place was history."

"Yes, that's what she said," Johnson added. She glanced up from her cell phone, barely making the step down at the curb. "The woman seemed aggravated for sure."

"Got everything downloaded from the Caston server into your program," the technician said. He opened the rear of the van and set his bag and laptop inside, then shut the door. "I left a list on your desk of the passwords to open the Caston files," he said. "Just jotted them on a notepad. I guess you know you ought to change them."

"Yeah, new passwords. That's a good idea," the HIPPA compliance officer said. Johnson took her seat inside the passenger side of the van and shut the door, window raised.

The technician opened the driver's door and hesitated while Johnson remained in her seat, glued to her phone. She appeared in no hurry to leave. He stepped back toward Jessica. "I came across a file of Dr. Caston's emails on the hospital server," he said under his breath. "I downloaded those for you, I mean, for Dr. Mack. I know that doctors and nurses don't only talk on the phone to patients but send a lot of emails back and forth."

"Okay, thanks. I'll let Dr. Mack know," Jessica said.

He stepped even closer and peered over his shoulder at the hospital van. Jessica strained to hear. "I ... didn't read through any of the emails, but you've got 'em all, just in case you need to check them out. I didn't delete a single one."

"Got it. Thanks again."

He shot Jessica a thumbs up, hopped in the van, and drove off. Johnson tossed her right hand up in a weak good-bye wave.

# Chapter 28

Coleman Foshee gave his driver the day off. He drove by the police department building four times before he reasoned that whoever monitored the security cameras would note the repeated passes. He opted out of the visitors' parking spots available in the lot across the street and pulled into the one of those directly in front of the main building. He had conducted business in the nearby courthouse, but never had the occasion to venture into police headquarters—until now.

He had not been arrested. No search warrant had been issued. And as far as he knew, Detective Reed Spearman had not delved into any of his personal or business affairs—only that he had been spotted several times at Kile's Minute Mart.

A compromise, the arrangement to meet at police headquarters, sounded more appealing than an interrogation at his own office or a corny meeting elsewhere, like at a coffee shop. The objective of the meeting: an informal, non-threatening interchange, at least that was Coleman Foshee's understanding.

As planned, Reed met him inside the entrance to the building.

"Can we avoid one of those rooms with the two-way glass, Detective Spearman?" Coleman requested, almost in jest.

"First of all, it's Reed. And yes, we can meet in my office."

"Thank you, and Coleman will work for me." Reed escorted him to his office and avoided the main thoroughfares within the building. Coleman took the seat opposite Reed's desk.

Reed flipped open the laptop on his desk, tapped a few keys, then swung it around so that both men could see the image. A still frame of Attorney Coleman Foshee standing at the checkout counter of Kile's Minute Mart flooded the screen. He held a bag of chips.

"Ready for me to hit PLAY?" Reed asked.

"Other than offending my Primary Care Provider with that choice of snack, what's so fascinating about buying some junk food?" Coleman asked.

"We got that court order for the security footage. No matter what the merchandise, Kile's place seems like a simple mom-and-pop outfit. Its video surveillance system might be dated, but it's still pretty sophisticated. The owner can turn access on and off. We got to the video through Kile's subscription to a regional security system monitoring service. No way she's aware that we got this."

Reed tapped another key and the video played. "There are some jumps in the frame sequence. Kile likely stopped the recording during deals," he said. "But she got careless, I guess, and missed one."

A few other keys and Reed froze the images of Momma Kile and Attorney Coleman Foshee at the checkout counter. He magnified the view of the hand and arm movements between the two and resumed play. The resolution of the black and white depiction of the money exchange was not the best, but above average.

"Coleman, you slipped her enough cash to buy out the chip aisle," Reed said. Momma Kile dropped her hand under the counter and slid a light-colored envelope to Coleman. He cupped it in his right hand, and it disappeared inside a jacket pocket.

"What was in the envelope?"

"What is it that you want from me, Detective Spearman?"

"Sounds corny, Attorney Foshee, but the truth."

"I can be just as *corny*," Coleman said. "I want to talk to a lawyer— or is that necessary?"

"It depends. I doubt if an arrest for buying illegal narcotics will set well with the court, much less the bar. So why don't we try to work this out, no need for any other lawyers."

Reed punched more keys and played several more videos. In

each, the attorney purchased junk food including a couple of hot dogs and a frozen drink from a dispenser, always the same flavor. Most sequences of video had holes, but Momma Kile's carelessness showed another time. Coleman Foshee paid for his food with too much cash and received another small envelope. Reed looked away from the screen at Coleman.

"You sure do buy lots of crappy food or pretend to," Reed said. "You must spend a lot of time in the gym."

"I don't think you called me down here to discuss the attributes of my personal trainer," Coleman said.

Another image appeared on the screen followed by a short run video. Reed paused it.

"Ever seen this woman? Ever run into her when buying your snacks?" Reed pointed to Selena Garcia, the casino insignia visible on her uniform. He resumed the play, and the video jumped to another shopper, a junior high-aged female buying a Coke. Reed touched the reverse control and stopped again at the short footage of Selena Garcia.

Coleman said, "Appears that the woman works at one of the casinos, but I don't go to the casinos. Never seen her before."

"We busted her single operation," Reed said, "buying product from Kile, not for personal use—not that we know of—and turning it over at the casino for profit."

"Again, the purpose of my being here?" Coleman said. "These videos of envelopes and junk food don't prove anything."

Reed smiled, although his eyes burned seriousness. "Your sister was an addict, and you supplied her."

Coleman took a deep breath and exhaled, then shifted in his seat. He squeezed the right arm of the chair and then the left. "It's not like that. I was just trying to … bridge the gap for her … until she could take the time from her family and medical practice to go into treatment."

"Did you ever consider the fact your sister was operating on the human brain during that time?"

Coleman jolted from his seat. "That's it. I'm out of here. Detective, you don't have anything on me."

"This is a chance to make this right, to ease your conscience about your sister," Reed said.

"I don't get this." Coleman paced in front of Reed's desk and continued around the office.

"You're obviously a smart guy, Coleman. Don't you see it? You can help us save lives and stop these scumbag narcotics dealers."

Coleman returned to Reed's desk and sank into the same chair with a deep breath. He gazed into space for a few seconds and said, "What is it that you want me to do?"

Scott studied his high school and medical degree diplomas on the wall across from his desk. He envisioned the wire behind each, straining on a nail, and hoped he had driven the nails deep enough into the sheetrock. As soon as Biloxi Memorial had signed the lease for this place and he moved in his personal stuff, Scott hung all of the framed work himself. No need for a ruler or tape measure or a level, he eyeballed it. Maybe the group photograph of his senior residency class did need a little adjustment. It tilted somewhat to the right.

The guy who got the most sought-after position to practice orthopedics in California stood at the far left in the residency picture, top row. The sag of the heavy, framed photograph to the right placed him further at the top of the group of five. Scott pushed his chair back and stepped to the wall. He straightened the frame and admired his decorating skills, scrutinizing the rest of his personal office before realizing it was just decent.

Installed to dress up the space, although Scott had napped there a few times, a brown leather couch stood pushed against the wall opposite the collection of framed photographs and certificates. A cheap brown blanket waited folded on a shelf in the cabinet beside it. Any patient who visited his office typically skipped the couch and sat in the same office chair used by the hospital administrator, Trey Buckley.

Scott plopped onto the couch and crossed his legs at the ankles. He stared into the flat screen TV also mounted across from the couch.

He knew his practice was painted deep red, this afternoon a prime example. First, Medicare would pay zero for the redo of the elderly patient's hip replacement, the surgery that chewed up the early afternoon and kept him from doing anything else productive—patient revenue wise. Then, the two new patients on the clinic schedule cancelled, and no add-ons popped up to replace them. The phones didn't ring all afternoon for last-minute appointments, and nothing came in by email.

"From the looks of today, I did right on that deal with Buckley," Scott said and grabbed his phone. Rather than walk up the short hall to speak to Jessica, he texted her:

We got room. Let's make a go for Caston's patients.

She responded with a Smiling Face emoji.

He sent another text.

Head on home. See ya tomorrow. Thx.

Jessica texted back:

U 2.

Too early to go home. Empty house.

So, get a dog?

Jessica ended her text, adding the 😗 emoji.

"Maybe she's right. I should get a dog," Scott said and tagged 👍. Scott googled *animal shelter* and several local listings populated the screen. "Next weekend. Yeah, project for next weekend." He dropped his phone screen-down on his chest. "But if I'm gonna dump this place? Maybe not."

Scott studied the bookshelves, the wall hangings, and the furniture in his office. Wouldn't take much to box all this stuff up and load it in a van, he figured. Wouldn't take up much room in the landfill.

He ran his hands along the back and cushions of the seldom-used office couch as though to assess it for the first time. He had chosen leather over the plump, off-white cushions and fabric pushed by the sales lady at the discount furniture store. Scott pulled the blanket out of the cabinet, grabbed the TV remote, and stretched out. He flipped past the late afternoon talk show and the female host's dance moves, a kid's cartoon program on another channel, an old western on the next, and settled with a replay of a football game on a sports channel. He just missed a touchdown. A commercial for Biloxi Memorial Hospital popped onto the screen.

The commercial featured attractive, smiling doctors and nurses as they conversed with patients and colleagues in the halls of a beautifully decorated medical facility. One physician patted an elderly man on the back before he pushed him through the lobby in a wheelchair. A nurse handed stuffed animals to sick, but appreciative, children. Scott did not recognize any of the medical personnel, likely actors. An authoritative, though compassionate, male voiceover enumerated the multiple services provided by Biloxi Memorial Hospital, a state-of-the art hospital facility that always cares.

Just as the minute-long commercial neared the end, two actors dressed in blue scrubs and white physician coats pointed to x-ray images while two other actors or maybe even authentic patient volunteers gazed on in wonder. Unexpectedly, a professional, close-up photograph of Scott Mack, M.D., borrowed from the hospital staff membership directory popped up mid-screen before drifting to fill the right half of the space. Scott's office address and phone number appeared to the left and imprinted across a distant shot of Biloxi Memorial Hospital.

The same voiceover artist introduced Dr. Scott Mack as the physician selected to carry on the work of the beloved Paul Caston, M.D. "How fortunate we are here on the Mississippi Gulf Coast and beyond to have Dr. Scott Mack. Dr. Mack is ready to provide the same dedicated and skilled orthopedic surgical services to all patients in Dr. Caston's practice—and to others as well. Call the number on your screen now for an appointment with Scott Mack, M.D., board certified in orthopedic surgery."

The commercial faded to another spot, this one advertising dog food. A trio of dogs fought over a full bowl of moist food.

Scott lay on the couch with the remote and stared at the television screen—the announcer's emphatic, though compensated, endorsement of Dr. Scott Mack still rang in his ears. By now, Jessica would have left for the day and transferred any phone calls to his office rather than pay for an early turnover to the answering service. For a few seconds, he listened for the phone to ring and laughed at the silence. *Guess BM got stiffed on those high-dollar commercial actors and announcer.*

Then the phone rang.

Scott tossed the remote to a cushion, grabbed his phone, and sat up on the couch. He answered on the second ring without noting the caller I.D. "Dr. Mack—may I help you?" he asked.

Jessica laughed. "Dr. Mack, you do a great job with that. Maybe you can do my job too."

Scott took a deep breath. He shook off the twinge of disappointment. "Oh, hi, Jessica. No, I'm better off doing something else. We all are. What's up?"

"I tried your cell but no answer, but I thought you might be at the office."

Scott checked and noted the missed call. "I was watching TV. Guess I didn't hear it. The hospital ran an ad about Caston's patients coming to our clinic."

"That's why I called. I'm kinda thankful that I got to leave early … you know … since we weren't busy …'cause I needed to pick up my child from daycare. But I need to talk with you about those two people from the hospital."

"What two people?" Scott asked.

"It was a man and a woman. They came to transfer all the files from the other doctor's office into our computer. They needed to do it onsite. But I think they were curious, wanted to look the place over. Anyway, they said we have all the information now, the names and information of all of Dr. Caston's patients—the demographics, they called it."

"Good, let's just hope those patients call us." Scott shook his head, embarrassed at waiting for the phone to ring after the commercial ended.

"And there are a bunch of emails too—even the doctor's old emails back-and-forth with patients. The IT guy and that lady with hospital marketing thought all of it might be important."

"Emails?" Scott said. "Not sure I want to get into exchanging emails with patients."

"Whatever you want to do, but the emails are in a separate file. They asked me for a password. I gave 'em your birthday and the first two letters of your last name. You can change it if you want."

"Okay, I'll check it out," Scott said.

"See you tomorrow. Bye," Jessica said and ended the call.

Scott signed into the desktop computer next to the phone. The background picture covered the screen with Scott in white shorts, tan deck shoes, and a blue T-shirt standing on a sailboat. He pulled on ropes to adjust the sail and smiled at the cell phone photographer—a tall, blonde ICU nurse he met at a bar shortly after he moved to Gulfport and dated for a few months. When she took a better job in Dallas, Scott flew over to see her on a rare weekend off, but the long-distance relationship ended soon thereafter.

This background photo replaced the earlier version that included the ICU nurse. Both stood on the deck of the same rental boat, moored in its slip at the dock. The manager did the honors with the nurse's phone, and she shared it with Scott. When the relationship ended, he deleted that photograph for the current one. Except for a single Friday night date made on line with a young lawyer from New Orleans that ended before ten and the no-show blind date arranged by a hospital secretary, there had been no opportunity for other photographs.

*This sort of looks like I'm stuck on myself,* he thought, studying the picture on the screen. He could no longer squeeze into the shorts, and the T-shirt was in the rag drawer. *Maybe take a new shot of the beach at sunset or at sunrise on the way to work.*

Scott shook his head and moved the cursor to the sign-in icon for his clinic's electronic medical records system. He referred to Jessica's password information, pulled up the list of transferred patient files, and scrolled through the pages. There were thousands of new names.

"Maybe I need to talk to that IT technician myself. Make sure I know how to navigate through all this stuff," Scott said. He noticed an icon for a program labeled Appointment Scheduler. He clicked on the symbol and a template of appointment times and assigned patient names spanning the previous and upcoming 180 days populated the screen. The schedule designated patients once seen by Dr. Paul Caston either as new patients, recheck follow-ups, or post-op evaluations. Also documented was the time each patient checked in and out of Caston's clinic. An occasional No-Show appeared by a name. "I guess this is what a day in the life of a busy orthopedic doc is supposed to look like."

Scott glanced up at the television and continued to scroll through the electronic calendar. He stopped at the date he discovered Paul Caston in his car with a gunshot wound to the head. Early that morning and despite Caston's absence, a few patients checked into the clinic. Post-op, Dressing Change, and Recheck were reasons listed for appointments—tasks easily handled by an experienced clinic nurse, physician assistant, or nurse practitioner if the physician was not available. *That would have been ER Nurse Betty,* Scott thought. *Confident enough to do any procedure herself.*

Scott looked at the time on the computer. There was nobody waiting for him at home; he had nothing else to do.

He continued to scroll through the rest of Caston's schedule. During the early afternoon of the day he died, Caston was to have performed a knee replacement and had seen the male patient in his office for pre-op the day before.

*Wonder who wound up with that guy. Could be nobody. Maybe fella still needs a new knee.* Scott jotted down the name of the patient and his phone number on a desk pad. "No telling how many surgical cases this could lead to," he muttered and kept scrolling, even going back a few more days through the late Paul Caston's appointment list.

His eyes drifted back up to the television before dropping to the computer screen and the bottom of the page. The name KILE in all caps appeared at the end of the schedule the day before Paul Caston was found dead in his car—no given name, no patient identification number, no date of birth.

"If Jessica had some ortho issues, she would have checked with me." Scott frowned and changed screens to pull up the large file listing the patients available to transfer from Caston's practice. He typed KILE into the search bar and chose a time period that spanned the previous and upcoming 180 days. Four names populated the screen—but no Jessica. The first two names were males, the birthdates indicated early twenties and late forties, the last name a young female. The third name listed was a woman in her early fifties: Wanda Jones Kile.

He stared a minute at the screen and clicked the name. The file belonging to Wanda Jones Kile filled the space. Scott scrolled through the list of appointments scheduled at nearly the same time every two to three weeks and paired with an indication such as Follow-up, Recheck, New Problem. Scott clicked on the patient medication list and slid his forefinger down the screen.

"What the …?"

Each office visit generated a new prescription, a patient service not unexpected for a doctor's visit, but every medication was a narcotic. Most were for at least thirty pills, some sixty, one called for a hundred oxycodone. There was one prescription for Xanax, thirty of them with three refills.

"Wow, how was that chick still standing?" Scott returned to the page of Paul Caston's calendar of the day before he died and

256

searched the name KILE under the appointments—no Wanda Jones Kile. The KILE notation on the calendar must have been for something other than an appointment. Scott grabbed his cell phone and checked his contacts for Jessica's number.

*No, I think I can check this out myself.* He tried to recall the in-service computer training from the hospital medical records department provided when his practice was first set-up. "How did that girl say to do it?"

Scott clicked back through the dates, to one of the scheduled appointments and highlighted Wanda Jones Kile, then right clicked. A digital photograph of a Mississippi driver's license topped the left-hand corner of the page. The Caucasian woman pictured did not smile. Her cell phone number, place of employment, email, mailing address, type of medical insurance, and preferred pharmacy filled the rest of the screen along with emergency contact information. Two names were listed.

"Brandon Kile," Scott read, "Jessica Kile."

Scott scrolled back up and noted the place of employment: "Kile's Minute Mart." He stared blankly at the TV screen away from the computer monitor then typed the business name into the GPS app on his phone. The driving directions from his office populated the page.

# Chapter 29

Selena Garcia sat in the interrogation room of the Biloxi Police Department. She fidgeted in the heavy metal chair bolted to the floor and pulled at the collar of her pullover shirt, the same type of Moondust Casino-issue polo she wore at Dr. Caston's office, her first encounter with Reed and Officer Owen Smith. "I told you already. I don't know what that woman was doing in the casino employee lot. I think maybe she told me she was lost, trying to find the bus station or something like that."

"Think through that again. We need straight answers," Reed said.

"Get me out of this room. This place is too cramped. I'm claustrophobic." She tilted her head past Detective Spearman and Officer Smith to study the dark grey, concrete block walls behind them. What appeared to be a tiny, domed-shaped camera mounted about six feet high was pointed directly at her.

Selena twisted her neck to examine the rest of the space, estimating the room's dimensions at about eight by ten feet. The cinder block walls extended from the concrete floor past the ceiling. She assumed the windowless door to be solid metal, at least it sounded that way when another police officer slammed it behind her—like the heavy metal door at the rear entrance to the Moondust.

"This place is like a tomb or a meat locker, except you guys are too cheap to run the AC." Selena yanked a couple of tissues from the box on the table in front of her and blotted her forehead and neck. She came up empty after a quick look around for a waste receptacle, so she wadded the used tissue inside her fist.

"The thermostat's set to standard seventy-two degrees in here, Miss Garcia," Reed said. "But for you, we'll turn it down two more." Reed slid his hand under the table, a buzzing noise followed, and the same uniformed policeman unlocked and opened the door.

"Cool it down a bit in here, Jake. Our guest is a little hot under the collar."

"Will do, Detective Spearman." The door snapped shut—again the thunderous, hard sound.

"Give it a few minutes. The AC system's not top-of-the-line," Owen Smith said.

"And where's the mirror on the wall," Selena said. "I know there's people somewhere watching and listening to me."

"You've watched too many old detective series on TV," Owen said. "We got rid of the mirrors and replaced them with hi-def cameras, like the one you just spotted behind us, and the one at the end of the room, more eye level." He pointed to both. "We got supersensitive microphones in here too. I guess you missed the whole redo on the second episode of Police Station Makeover."

Reed lowered his head and shook it slowly. He suppressed the smile.

Selena wanted to spit.

"Let's move on," Reed said. "We informed you that your statement would be recorded. We know you offered to sell narcotics to an undercover Biloxi police officer."

"It's just their word against mine. I don't sell no drugs. You're just profiling and judging me. Just because I'm Latino and work at a casino."

Owen flipped open the laptop in front of him and turned the screen so the three could see. He tapped a few keys and the security footage from inside the Moondust Casino played along with the audio recorded from the undercover police officers. In the video Selena slips her hand under the table, presumably to transfer an envelope to the officer. Owen followed with a video of another encounter.

"Miss Garcia … Selena, nobody's profiling anybody here. We're trying to save lives and stop the illegal narcotic and drug business on the Coast. Even the small-time operators like you." Reed hesitated a few seconds, but there was no response—not even an *I want a lawyer.*

Reed continued, "We know you're a struggling, single mom. You have a legitimate job at the casino. I've talked to your bosses. You show up on time to your shifts and rarely if ever call in sick. You pay your taxes."

"I want a …"

"Hold on a sec," Owen interrupted. He again brought up the short video of Selena and Momma Kile at the rear door of the casino.

"The judge will appreciate it if you help us bring down this woman." Reed pointed to the screen just as Selena was shown in the video to enter the casino. Wanda Jones Kile stood in the doorway a few seconds before leaving and Owen froze the image.

Selena said, "I want a lawyer. Not saying nothing till I talk to a lawyer."

"Shouldn't go there, Selena. You lawyer-up, and Officer Smith and I can't do much to help you with the judge," Reed said.

Scott pressed the open button on the fob of his keychain. The driver's door clicked. He tossed his bag onto the front passenger seat and dropped behind the steering wheel. The hospital surgery calendar on his cell phone showed wide open for the day, the same as it did last night. "Hope the clinic schedule makes it worth leaving the house today."

He plugged the phone into the charger and tapped a few more times on the screen to access the day's office schedule—busy enough to show up for work but plenty of time to work a crossword puzzle. He backed down the short driveway to the street and remembered the television commercial from his office the night before. "How long is it gonna take for Caston's patients to make a difference?" he said and stopped at the curb. Traffic was light.

Scott knew he could be inside his clinic in fifteen minutes to see the first patient—if the patient showed up. Instead, he googled the address for the Kile convenience store, changed gears, and pressed the accelerator.

A diesel truck branded with the name of a wholesale food supply chain blocked both fuel dispensers. Scott pulled up to the far-right side of the property near the air dispenser and stepped from his car. Ahead of him was a light blue car with a partially deflated back tire. An attractive young woman with long, slender legs squeezed into tight, chocolate-colored slacks and matching leather jacket stood with the car. She pumped quarters into the air machine and held the air hose in the opposite hand. She studied the end of it, hesitated, then squatted to screw the attachment onto the tire valve.

Scott wondered if her slacks would pop open or slide below the waist.

One of the glass double doors to the entrance of the convenience store swung open, and he shifted his attention to an older woman holding a broom. She began to sweep cigarette butts and other bits of trash from the doorway. "You get it figured out, hon?" she yelled to the young woman at the air pump.

Scott recalled the driver's license photo in the medical record; the woman with the broom was a match to Wanda Jones Kile.

"Yes, ma'am, Momma Kile. My boyfriend usually takes care of this stuff, but he's working offshore this week."

"That's a good-looking hunk you got, hon. Fillin' out nice. Tell him to come see me when he's back in town. I got a good supplier now, and I might even be able to help him if he needs some extra testosterone." Kile laughed and continued to sweep.

Her multiple appointments with Paul Caston ran through Scott's mind—all resulting in a controlled narcotic or anxiolytic prescription. He did not recall any prescriptions for hormone therapy.

The tire now inflated, the young woman jumped up, apparently

261

surprised that someone stood near enough to hear Momma Kile call out to her. She smiled nervously at Scott and glanced back at Kile. "Sure. Will do. But I gotta go."

She dropped the end of the air hose to the concrete and left quickly in her car.

Kile continued to sweep along the concrete walk that lined the front of the store to the right and left of the double doors. Another vehicle—a small, familiar blue Ford—hurriedly pulled into one of the parking spaces along the front and separate from the fuel pumps. Jessica Kile stepped out of the car and headed toward the entrance.

Against the backdrop of multiple appointments and prescriptions for Wanda Jones Kile, Scott tried to shake away the obvious association between Jessica and this woman. Jessica's push that he recycle controlled prescriptions for profit became clear.

"Jessica," Scott called out, "we need to talk."

Jessica froze at the door and turned around. "Dr. Mack? What are you doing here?"

Scott moved nearer to Jessica and the woman the girl in the tight slacks referred to as Momma Kile. Kile now swept at the far side of a large metal sales bin filled with bagged ice. Scott noticed the nearby exterior security camera and gestured to Jessica. "Are you related to that lady?"

Momma Kile stepped out in front of the sign that read:

Honor System. Pay Inside.

"Jessica sure is," she said. "My daughter-in-law, and what's it to ya?"

"Momma, this is Dr. Mack. I work for him," Jessica said.

"Nice to know. Now, what can we do for you, Doc? You need gas?" Kile pointed to the bin. "Some ice? Or what about something inside."

"No thanks. I'm good," Scott said and turned away from both women. He had made the connection. "I'm on the way to the hospital to make rounds before heading to the clinic. I'll grab some breakfast somewhere else." He stepped to his car, slammed the door, and drove away.

An hour later Jessica busied herself with tidying the lobby and her desk before she opened her computer. Thanks to the hospital IT guru and the upgraded computer software, the new sign-in steps to access all patient files and notes would take a few extra seconds. She took a deep breath.

Was it a coincidence that Dr. Mack showed up this morning at the store? He didn't act too mad, but maybe a little curious—a little surprised? She wiggled the mouse next to her keypad and the computer screen lit up, then remembered his car door slammed shut before he drove off. He *was* mad.

"I must not have signed out of the system before I left last night. Dr. Mack was still here when I left. He must have been reading through the new files before I had a chance to—"

Jessica heard the rear door open and shut, the sound louder than usual, not quite a slam like earlier this morning—but definitely much louder. The sound echoed up the hall, followed by Dr. Mack's steps coming toward her. "He's going to fire me. I just know it," she said under her breath.

She listened even more intently, certain that only one person approached. *The police wouldn't use the back door. They would bust in through the front*, Jessica reasoned and took a deep breath. She reached for her purse, keys, and cell phone. She could be out the front door and to her car in seconds.

The door from the wall to the front office swung open.

There were no blue uniforms, no raised guns—only Dr. Mack.

"Dr. Mack, I can explain." She flashed a tense smile.

He pulled the other office chair up beside her. "That was your mother-in-law, I guess, at the convenience store."

"Yes, that's Brandon's mom."

"You left the computer turned on last night."

"Yes, sir, I—"

"So, I was able to get into Caston's files. I came across your mother-in-law's appointment history and medication list. That girl at the air pump called her *Momma Kile*."

"I didn't know Momma Kile was one of Dr. Caston's patients. She never mentioned any orthopedic problems."

"Pull up her clinic record again for me—please."

Jessica noted sarcasm in the *please*. She changed computer screens and in seconds Wanda Jones Kile's information displayed for Scott: one appointment after another accompanied by a lengthy list of prescriptions for controlled medications.

Scott ran his finger down the list of medications, all generic brands, but most names easy to recognize as narcotics, anti-anxiety drugs, or sedatives—even by someone not in the healthcare field. There were no prescriptions for testosterone. "Did you know anything about this?"

"No, Dr. Mack, I didn't know she was a patient at the Caston clinic. I swear," the answer honest. Jessica skipped any confession of her supplying Percocet and Xanax for Momma Kile's inventory, measly numbers in comparison to what stared at her.

"We've discussed these kinda things before," Scott said. "You're not involved in any of this, I hope."

Jessica remained fixed on the computer image, her fingers near the keyboard.

"Are you involved, Jessica?"

Only a moment passed, but to both Jessica and Scott it seemed much longer.

"No, sir. I'm not. I didn't know anything about Dr. Caston." Jessica's fingers trembled, and she clenched her fists to hide them. The lying was off to a great start or as Jessica would later describe it—the *half-truths*.

# Chapter 30

The front door to the clinic opened, interrupting the tense moment between Jessica and Scott. A man dressed in navy slacks and open-collared, white dress shirt with jacket thrown over the shoulder walked into the lobby. He appeared a bit confused. The shiny blue patterned fabric of the jacket coordinated with the solid slacks. Jessica guessed expensive and figured Dr. Mack would agree.

"We've got a patient. I think it's the one on the schedule from the Dr. Caston file," Jessica whispered, mustering enough courage to lift her head. Her eyes met Dr. Mack's stare. She pointed at the name on the screen.

"Go ahead and check the guy in. I'll be in my office."

"Yes, sir."

"I'll eyeball his medical record," Scott said. "As you know, I can pull up Caston's files." He slipped away through the door into the hall. His steps down the hall were quick, angry.

Jessica stood at her desk and spoke through the window into the lobby. "May I help you? Are you Mr. Dandridge?"

George Dandridge paced near the plant in the far corner and thumbed through a magazine. He tossed it onto a chair, put on his jacket, and in a few steps leaned into Jessica's reception window. The sleeves of the jacket slid back to expose the cuffs of his starched shirt. Heavy, square-shaped, gold cufflinks bordered in miniature and closely set diamonds caught Jessica's eye. The initial "D" in bold script filled the center of each piece. Jessica stared and jerked her eyes away from the jewelry, red-faced.

"I have an appointment with a Dr. Scott Mack. You need to see some I.D.?" He slid a hand into the left inside pocket of his jacket, hesitated, then checked the opposite side and produced a small wallet. "Here you go."

Jessica noted the photo and name on the driver's license, the likeness a match for the one previously scanned into Dr. Paul Caston's files. "Thank you, Mr. Dandridge. Yes, I have you at 9:30 to see Dr. Mack," Jessica said. She placed the license on top of the two routine pages of paper forms attached to a clip board and handed everything to Dandridge. "If you'll please complete these patient update forms and bring them back to me."

Dandridge removed his driver's license from the papers without taking the clipboard. "Young lady?" He then seemed to notice the name placard on the narrow counter of the reception window. "I see… it's Jessica." He flashed the plastic card at her. "I need to get you an updated pic." He brushed the lower half of his face and neck and the skin around both eyes with a few fingers of his right hand to draw Jessie's attention.

"I guess your Dr. Mack knows Dr. Jamarcus Odell. Dr. Jam is the best plastic surgeon on the Coast. Even guys from New Orleans drive over. Painless surgery, every time."

"The forms on the clipboard? I'm sorry, Mr. Dandridge, but it's our policy." She returned the paperwork to the patient.

"No need for all that, young lady. My visits with Dr. Caston were always brief. Should be the same with your doc."

"But I need the info to update …"

"Word around town is that Dr. Mack needs the business, and my knee's shot. Either get me into one of the exam rooms ASAP, or I'll head on to the next clinic."

Jessica put the clipboard down. She motioned for Dandridge to enter the hallway to the exam rooms. "Right this way, Mr. Dandridge."

She ushered him into the first exam room down the hall. "I'm sorry, but without the update forms, I'm not sure what you're here for, so please just take a seat over there."

266

Dandridge ignored her and studied the patient information display on the wall. An anatomical diagram of a knee joint hung near the corner. Arrows pointed to sites of common orthopedic injuries and led to boxed insets of explanatory information. Several lines of black print were bulleted and highlighted in bold.

"Let's see." He ran a finger down the anatomical rendering of a knee and stopped midway. "The guy who drew this picture—so much detail. Every ligament, all the bones. He … I guess it's a he … he's even got the common knee injuries listed for me down in this corner and how they happen."

"Dr. Mack will be with you in just a minute," Jessica said and reached for the wall cabinet and the patient gowns.

"Dr. Caston had something like this poster in one of his rooms, but about the elbow. This makes it so easy."

"Easy?"

"With Dr. Caston, all I had to do was read the poster and play the part. But I wasn't sure about Mack's clinic."

"Sure about what?"

"Before this first appointment, I checked InternetMD, so I would know the right symptoms and answers to the questions—enough to get a prescription." He motioned to the other detailed patient information posted and displayed on a counter. "Boy, with all this stuff you've got around here, that time online was a waste."

His eyes watered a bit and he snorted. A box of tissues waited on the counter, and Dandridge grabbed a handful. He blew his nose and tossed the used tissues into the corner waste receptacle.

"If Dr. Mack needs for you to undress, you'll need this." Jessica removed a cloth gown from the cabinet, placed it on the exam table, and stepped toward the door back into the hall. "I'll give you a few minutes, then let the doctor know you're ready," she said. "And I'm sorry about your cold."

"Mack won't need to do an examination. Caston never touched me again once he did the third procedure."

Jessica left the exam room and pulled the door closed from the hall. Scott stood behind her.

"So, what's going on with the guy with the overdone facelift?" he whispered, startling her. "I got a good look at him from my office. The door was open."

"Not sure. He didn't fill out the intake forms."

"I think I recognize him from his TV commercials," Scott said. "He owns almost all the car dealerships on the Coast. I checked the computer. That's him."

"Seems sort of pompous, if you ask me." Jessica handed Scott the uncompleted paperwork and stepped away for the reception area. "Good luck."

The form led with the patient name at the top, date of birth, and clinic medical record number. The lower half included fill-in-the-blank and circle-the-correct-answer prompts for the patient to complete. Information regarding the orthopedic exam and physician assessment followed on the next page. When completed, Jessica would transfer the information into the computer.

"Mr. Dandridge, I'm Dr. Mack." At six-two and muscular, Scott stood about four inches above the male patient's medium-built frame.

"No need for introductions, Doc. Didn't have much choice but to come and see you."

"Yes, Biloxi Memorial transferred all of Dr. Caston's files over to my clinic, but you're free to go anywhere you want."

"Cut the formalities, Dr. Mack. I've been without almost a week, so just write me a script." Dandridge reached into the front pocket of his jacket and handed Scott an unsealed envelope.

"What's this?" The letter-sized envelope popped open to a thick stack of green bills.

"Doc, if you want, you can jot down on that clipboard that my left knee's been hurting, that the pain's been excruciating." He raised his pant leg. "Kinda swollen, don't you think?"

"The receptionist will check you out when we're finished. Her name's Jessica." Scott placed the envelope on the exam room counter under the storage cabinets and beside the sink. "You need to pay her, not me. She'll collect whatever your insurance is not going to cover when you leave."

"Whatever." Dandridge dropped the pant leg and stood. "Just write me the script, and I'll be on my way."

"Let's see what's going on with you first, Mr. Dandridge. Sometimes PT is the way to go, not meds or surgery."

Dandridge's face reddened. He took a deep breath. His fingers tremored slightly.

"I noticed in your file that Dr. Caston fixed a meniscus tear in that left knee two years ago and about three years ago did the same for the right knee before you needed a knee replacement—old high school football injury, I think."

George Dandridge's complexion deepened to burgundy. Beads of sweat erupted on his forehead. He jumped from the end of the patient examination table and grabbed the envelope as Scott stepped back.

Dandridge pulled the cash from inside and lunged forward, waving it in Scott's face. "You can see there ain't nothing wrong with these knees anymore, asshole. I paid Caston dearly for those surgeries, and he's kept me supplied with pills since."

Scott backed away toward the door of the minor exam room.

"Now, all I need you to do is write the same script for me." Dandridge forced self-control in his voice. "Here's three hundred—cash. That's what I pay. That's the deal."

Dandridge tossed the stack of twenty-dollar bills at Scott, some hit him in the chest before the money floated to the floor. When he next lunged at Scott, he missed and instead toppled the metal stool on rollers near the examination table.

Jessica heard the commotion from her desk and ran to exam room one. She listened at the door for a second. A heavy thud landed on the wall inside. She jerked the door open to Scott's successful dodge of Dandridge's second try at him as the man rammed his fist into the sheetrock.

Bleeding and cursing, Dandridge massaged his knuckles with the opposite hand.

"Dr. Mack? You okay? What's going on in—"

A now paled Dandridge grabbed his stomach, smearing blood on his shirt, and pushed past them to the sink. He began to vomit.

"Go ahead and call 911. I think this guy's in the middle of opioid withdrawal," Scott said. He lowered his voice and spoke out of the corner of his mouth. "And tell them to send the police too."

Jessica's complexion matched the white of Dandridge's shirt minus the blood stains. "Yes, sir. I'm on it," she said as the patient slid from the sink to the floor.

Scott put a finger to Dandridge's neck. The man's face twitched and his eyes were shut. "There's a carotid pulse, and he's still breathing," Scott said.

# Chapter 31

Scott stayed in the exam room with George Dandridge to monitor his status until the ambulance arrived fifteen minutes later. The man's respirations remained steady, his complexion pale. The vomiting had stopped, and there was no repeat outburst. Scott cleared the way for the paramedics.

"We haven't notified any family, and please let the E.D. know the guy's likely a narcotic abuser—very likely," Scott quietly told the emergency medical team as they stabilized Dandridge on a gurney and began to roll him out toward the lobby and front exit. An elderly couple, she with a walker and he with a cane, sat wide-eyed in the loveseat against the far wall. Scott walked to them and said, "The gentleman wasn't feeling well when he came for his appointment. I believe the hospital will be able to help him."

"Well, I sure hope they're takin' him to Biloxi Memorial," the man said. "That's where Dr. Caston fixed my hip, and he was supposed to operate on Gladys here, too, until her ticker started to act up. They had to give her a pacemaker."

Gladys looked at Scott and spread her fingers over her upper chest. "But my heart doctor told me I'm good to go for surgery," she said. "Too bad Dr. Caston died, but the commercials on TV say you're just as good. Ain't that right, Leonard?"

"Dr. Caston never let me hurt a darn bit through my surgery or afterwards either," he answered.

Scott shot his eyes back to Jessica, who stayed clear of the commotion in the reception area. She stood with a couple of clip-boards and pens and walked into the lobby.

"I'm with my wife to help get her hip fixed, get her surgery scheduled," Leonard said when Jessica handed him his clipboard. "But I'll need some more of the pills Dr. Caston gave me every month … and a stronger dose. The world's gone half-crazy and my nerves are shot."

A police siren exploded outside, and Leonard jumped in his seat. The cane fell to the floor. "See, what did I tell ya?"

Scott glanced down at the names on her clipboard. "Jessica, go ahead and please take the Rankins back to the exam area. Use the one at the end of the hall."

"Is everything all right with that man in the ambulance?" Gladys Rankin asked.

"Yes, ma'am," Jessica interrupted. As she helped the woman to her feet and retrieved Mr. Rankin's cane for him, Gladys used her walker as support. The siren had hushed, but blue lights revolved through the front windows. The paramedics had left.

Jessica glanced away nervously when the clinic door reopened to the police, and she ushered the elderly couple down the hall. Soon she would be unable to hear what was to be said in the lobby and was not sure she wanted to.

Scott greeted the two men just inside the front entrance area. Reed Spearman presented his credentials as did Officer Owen Smith. "We passed the ambulance leaving, got here as soon as we could," Reed said.

"Not exactly sure why I called you guys. I just didn't like what was going down with a patient."

Reed referenced the rear of the elderly couple, escorted away by the doctor's female assistant. "You couldn't handle those two?"

Owen and Scott laughed.

"No, it was the man in the ambulance, George Dandridge. He got pretty violent when I wouldn't write him a prescription for pain killers. But Dandridge had no more orthopedic problems, no pain. He waved cash at me and said his former physician was always happy to keep him supplied."

"You're the bone doctor that took over Dr. Caston's practice," Owen said. "I've seen the commercials."

"Apparently everybody has," Scott said.

"We were the second car at the scene of Paul Caston's shooting," Reed said. "Saw you there."

"Yeah, there was nothing I could do, so I left. Caston knew his anatomy. Mission accomplished."

Owen raised his eyebrows and glanced at Reed. "Maybe you should give the doc an update," he said.

"We've been reviewing that case," Reed said. "I'm not so sure that's how it went down." Reed checked the surroundings of the compact lobby and empty reception area. The three men were alone, the assistant nowhere in sight. "We'd like to talk to you, if you've got a few minutes to spare."

"Sure, those two patients can chill for a second," Scott said. "They're elderly. My receptionist will be tied up with them for a while."

"How 'bout your office?"

"Let's talk here. No need for my private office." Scott stared at Reed. "Are you saying that Paul Caston didn't commit suicide? That's crazy." He lowered his voice. "I saw it myself. Caston dropped the gun on the floorboard, not far from his hand."

"Were you surprised that Dr. Caston killed himself?" Reed asked.

"I was a nobody to Paul Caston, just another new doctor the hospital hired to compete against him. But I heard the scuttlebutt about his trial. Who didn't?" Scott answered. "And after dealing with that guy who got carted away by the EMTs, I think the jury got it wrong." He shot his eyes to the other officer and then back to Reed. "After Caston wasn't convicted, I figured the professional and personal embarrassment of the accusations were too much for him. So, he killed himself."

"Seemed he planned it well," Owen said. "Yep, perfect timing: early in the day … light neighborhood traffic. Strange to think, though, that it would be easy to stop at a stop sign with a gun to your head and nobody notice."

"A gun is first choice for most male suicide victims. Dr. Caston could have thought about it for a while and then snapped," Reed said. "However, after taking another run through the evidence, we don't think that's what happened."

"I spoke to one of the women parked behind Caston, the one with little kids, the one who ran up to my car in a panic," Scott said. He turned for a second to check for Jessica and look out the window—no sign of her and no other patients.

"You talked to the lady parked directly behind Caston?" Reed asked.

"No, I noticed she was on her cell. I ran past her to Caston's vehicle and thought she was calling you guys."

"You assumed right, Doc," Owen said.

"You didn't have any connection to Dr. Caston at the time, Dr. Mack. Is that right?" Reed asked. "That taking over his patients later was just a coincidence?"

"Hey, what is this all about?" Scott focused his attention on Reed. "Biloxi Memorial made a deal with his estate and needed somewhere to dump his patients, and they picked me. I seldom if ever crossed paths with Paul Caston until he was dead."

"And you didn't see anyone else approach his vehicle or depart the vehicle that morning?" Reed asked.

"As I drove up, I only noticed the two vehicles behind him, the two women and the kids."

"The lady in the car directly behind Caston, the one who called in the shooting, told us later that a woman was walking away from the intersection when she pulled up," Owen said.

"I only saw the two women drivers, and it was obvious to me that Caston committed suicide. I don't have anything else for you fellas."

"Dr. Mack?" Jessica called from the door that led from the lobby to the hall, then backed away. "I've got Mr. and Mrs. Rankin all set up for you to see them. You ready?"

"Be right there. These two gentlemen were just—"

"One more thing, Doctor." Reed removed his cell phone from an inside a jacket pocket, tapped the screen, and turned it to face Scott. In the upper left corner of the image, a sign hung above a gasoline fuel pump. The picture was slightly blurred but the black print on the sign still readable.

Pay Before You Pump

Thank You

The Kile Family

Scott studied the image on Reed's cell phone. "What's this?"

"It's a still from a convenience store's exterior security camera. You stop by Kile's place often?"

Scott hesitated a few seconds, wondering if Jessica sat at her reception desk and could have overheard the detective. "Sure, I … gas up there."

"How often?" Owen asked.

"Well, I …" Scott stumbled.

"I ran the video back several weeks, at least eight. I never spotted you near the fuel pumps or anywhere else on the site except for this one time," Reed said.

The detective's firm, tight shake of the cell phone still in his face was not lost on Scott.

The front door to the clinic popped open again. A perplexed-appearing woman in her mid to late twenties guided a small boy through the entranceway. He supported his limp right arm with the left hand.

"Is this where Dr. Caston's patients are supposed to go?" the mother asked. She first directed her question to the three men standing in the lobby and then toward the empty reception window and then back to the men. "Daniel fell off the climbing tower at preschool during morning playtime, and his teachers told me to bring him here. Said the school's insurance would pay for it. I hope so 'cause my husband might get laid off."

"Yes, ma'am, come right over this way." Jessica's voice filled the area. Her hand motioned through the reception window.

"Hey guys," Scott hushed, "not sure what you're after here, but I gotta get to work. This isn't the place or time to—"

Reed lowered his voice to match. "I know you're a good guy, spent lots of years in school to help people. Now we need some of that time too, Dr. Mack."

"But I don't see what you think I can do?"

"There's more to this Kile's Minute Mart thing, a probable connection to Dr. Caston."

Scott swallowed hard and gazed past the two policemen to the lobby wall behind them. An unsigned oil painting of a beach scene hung centered above the upholstered chairs. *Had the police subpoenaed Caston's medical notes and appointment calendar and already been through them? Wouldn't Biloxi Memorial have informed him of any subpoena?*

He felt his fingers tremble and slid both hands inside his lab coat pockets. Jessica must have heard most of this conversation. The two of them needed to talk—and in a hurry.

"Doctor, you still with us?" Owen asked.

Scott shot his eyes at the policemen. "I've got patients to see. You'll have to excuse me."

Reed smiled and handed Scott a business card with his cell number jotted across the top. "Seems like you're going to be busy with Dr. Caston not around. Why don't you give me a call when you're through for the day? No matter what time. But let's make it today, okay?" He motioned for Owen to follow him to the door.

"We're not totally sure what went down in Caston's car that morning before you and those two ladies found him dead," Owen said. "Sure, you got no idea, Doc?"

Scott stepped forward as though to urge them out the door. "I agree with the news reports that Caston shot himself. That's what I saw through the car window," Scott said. "Why would I know anything more than that?"

"For your sake, Dr. Mack," Reed said. "If you want to keep fixing bones for sweet, old couples or cute little preschoolers, I hope you don't."

276

For a few seconds, Scott glared at the closed door behind the two policemen.

Jessica's voice startled him from the trance. "Dr. Mack, I put that little boy's arm in a splint until you can get to him. You probably ought to go ahead and see the Rankins first. You know how elderly people are. Mr. Rankin is fussing about the wait."

"Jessica, I believe your mother-in-law was either buying narcotics or narcotic prescriptions from Dr. Paul Caston or was selling pills for him. I think the police are on to her. Why else would they have surveillance photos taken outside her store?"

"I ... I ... don't know, Dr. Mack. I got no idea," Jessica lied.

Scott lowered his voice again. "A while back, you said something about us recycling patients' leftover pills, helping others save money on their prescriptions. You know what a bad idea that was, don't you?"

Jessica backed away slightly, and Scott pushed closer.

"Jessica?"

"Yes ... yes, sir. I remember that we talked about it."

"Most of our patients have some kind of insurance, and even the ones with poor prescription coverage should be able to get the generics without breaking the bank. So, I never saw the need to trade spare pain pills between patients—and still don't." Scott studied the exit from the lobby. The two policemen had been gone only minutes.

Scott bent down to her and spoke at a near whisper. "Besides, that's illegal."

Jessica swallowed hard, took a deep breath, and tossed her head over her shoulder. "Dr. Mack, we need to take care of those patients back there."

"We will, in just a minute," Scott said. "I saw a female patient with the name Kile all over Dr. Caston's appointment calendar, his patient schedule and even his personal calendar. I pulled up the patient information. The woman listed her next of kin as Brandon Kile. I've never met your husband, but I've heard you mention the name more than once."

277

"Then that's why you came to the convenience store. You checked my mother-in-law's address. She lives in the two-room apartment in the back."

"I remembered the accusations filed against Dr. Caston, even though he beat them in court. When I saw those multiple meetings with the woman I now know as your mother-in-law, I thought about your interest in the leftover narcotics."

"Dr. Mack, I—"

"I had hoped there was no connection with you and that woman. But when I saw you at the store, I knew different." Scott shook his head. "And then the police show up today in my office because they saw me on security footage at the same store? What am I supposed to think?"

"I'll get my things and leave, Dr. Mack. You don't have to say out loud I'm fired. I'll just go." Jessica disappeared into the front office. Scott could hear desk drawers open and shut.

He followed her.

"No, Jessica, no. I don't want you to go." He chuckled nervously. "If you leave now, what am I going to do with those patients back there?"

The sound of the front door opening interrupted Scott. A college-aged male appeared at the check-in window. "Hey, guys. I saw on TV that Dr. Caston's patients are supposed to come here," he said. "Doc did surgery on my knee after I injured it at basketball a year ago. I played with some of my buddies this past weekend in my parents' driveway—pretty tough competition. Now my knee's all swole up, and I can barely walk." He winced and redirected his attention to Scott. "You the Dr. Mack they talk about on the commercial?"

"Yes, I'm Scott Mack. My assistant Jessica here will get you checked in. Please give us a sec and have a seat back there in the lobby."

Scott waited for the young man with the swollen knee to get settled and whispered to Jessica, "Let's put this discussion on hold for now. I need your help to get through this day."

Jessica set her purse on the counter. "There's something you need to understand, Dr. Mack." Gone was the gentle, welcoming smile and tone cultivated the day the hospital staffing department interviewed and hired Jessica Kile. "You asked me to pay the bills around here and I did. And when we had nothing coming in, how do you think I covered those expenses?"

She pulled the notebook hidden in her purse and grabbed earlier from the deep desk drawer when she was about to leave. She held it up to Scott and flipped through the pages. "All cash, Dr. Mack. Money I collected from my mother-in-law for the unused meds she could resale at a profit. I've kept a record of the patients' names who contributed their Xanax, Percocet, Norco, even some generic Flexeril. Momma Kile even has a market for Flexeril." She dropped the notebook back into her purse. "So, you still want me around?" A tear ran down her face.

The young male called out, "Come on, when's the doc gonna see me? My knee feels like crap. He might have to amputate."

The woman with the small boy and the broken arm stuck her head into the reception window. "I hope you haven't forgotten us. I need to get my son's arm taken care of and get back home to my other kids. I left their dad with them. He works nights and needs to sleep."

"Yes, ma'am won't be long." Scott managed a pleasant, reassuring smile. "Please wait back in the exam room for me."

"That brace your wonderful helper fixed up for my son does make his arm feel better, and it's not crooked anymore. So maybe we can just put extra tape around it and leave? Maybe come back later?"

Scott raised his hands palms forward in a hold but managed to smile. "Hang on for just a minute or two more. We'll get him fixed up for good."

The mother considered the comment, appeared uncertain, then nodded and disappeared back into the hall. Scott's pained facial expression returned.

"Let's both take a deep breath and finish out the day," he said. "I sure can't agree with the method, but I appreciate your trying to keep this place afloat. No doubt I needed help—still do." Scott noticed the box of tissues on the counter and handed her a sheet. "Go ahead and put your purse and that notebook away—way down deep in that drawer. And shut the drawer tight. Maybe … maybe we should install a lock on it."

Scott wrung his hands. "It's gonna be okay. Yeah, it's gonna be okay. We'll figure something out."

Reed sat at his desk and returned to the security footage from the convenience store. He scanned through the video file of the several weeks leading up to Paul Caston's death and a few days after. He paused the playback with the initial image of the new orthopedic physician, Dr. Scott Mack. Mack had played it cool when he and Owen dropped by his office unannounced. Reed enlarged the image. Scott Mack appeared to be talking to someone at the convenience store out of camera range.

"If I could change the angle of that outside camera." Reed unfroze the image and the doctor turned slightly away as though redirecting his attention to something or someone to the left of the store entrance. Several frames passed before Mack turned his head back to the right.

Reed skipped ahead several minutes of video and clicked over into the interior of the store. A young, white female with light hair tied in a bun entered and approached the counter. Reed felt a vague familiarity and froze the image. The hair color was uncertain in the black and white resolution, but Reed guessed blonde. He had caught a brief glimpse of a young woman behind the reception window of Mack's office but remembered no name signage or identification plaque, at least nothing that he could have seen from the distance.

He studied the grainy image on his computer. "That's the same chick," he said. "I'm sure of it. Both Dr. Scott Mack and his receptionist were at that convenience store. I'll get her name from Biloxi Memorial HR."

Reed pulled out his cell and googled the phone number for Biloxi Memorial. The director of the Human Resources Department was quick to answer and provide the information.

"Jessica Kile," Reed said, scribbling the name on a desk pad. "Kile, yes, that's it. No, no, I don't need the middle name or any contact information, but thank you for your help."

"Is there a problem? Something hospital administration should be concerned about?"

"No, I … was recently a patient at the clinic, and the receptionist was very kind. I just wanted to send her a note."

"Then you will need her address. I'm so glad the employees we place in our doctors' offices do such a great job." The woman's assumption and sly grin could be felt through the landline. "I know Mrs. Jessica Kile would love to hear from you."

"Mrs. Kile?" Reed said. "What's her husband do? Do you keep that kind of information?"

Long seconds of silence followed. Reed feared that the Human Resources director had hung up, annoyed with his pushing for personal information. He stared at the display on his desk phone.

"I had to scroll back a bit, but Jessica Kile lists her husband's employment as the United States Coast Guard. Date of employment about three years ago. His name is Brandon, Brandon Kile."

Coast Guard? Reed was aware of suspected increased drug trafficking along the Gulf Coast and several attempted arrests of marijuana smugglers by the Coast Guard, even one unsuccessful narcotics sting.

"Detective? You still there?"

"Yes, I'm here," Reed said. "Maybe I'll send her a gift certificate to a local restaurant, for her and her husband."

Reed sensed another smile. "You do that, detective. Anything else?"

"No thanks. That's all I needed. I appreciate the information," Reed answered. "Oh, and there's no need to let Mrs. Jessica Kile know that I called. I'd like to surprise her … surprise them."

"No problem." A soft chuckle followed. "Again, I'm glad there isn't any problem with Mrs. Kile's job performance or any suspected legal issues. Bye-bye, now."

The call ended.

"If that lady only knew," Reed said. He returned the phone receiver to its cradle in the desk set, folded his hands together, leaned forward on his elbows, and rested his chin atop his hands. *The husband serves in the Coast Guard,* he ruminated. "Interesting. He's the same guy we've been tailing, the same guy at the casino. BPD is going to cleanup on this case."

# Chapter 32

Reed returned to his office after lunch at Shaggy's. Despite the packed crowd at the restaurant on Beach Boulevard, his smiling female server managed plenty of time with him while he consumed a cheeseburger, fries, and unsweetened iced tea. He declined her offer to make the fries a double order and even turned down the mayonnaise and ketchup. During the last few weeks, the fatigue and long hours of a ballooning workload in the criminal investigation unit had been his excuse for skipping the gym.

However, as he loosened his belt another notch, he regretted the cheeseburger and even the single order of fries. The blackened amberjack special with grilled squash and zucchini—minus the side of mashed potatoes—would have been a healthier choice.

The gym stayed opened 24/7. There was no excuse.

Reed's laptop remained in the center of his desk, surrounded by the clutter of paper files, sticky notes, several junk pens, a few paper clips, and a stapler. He considered the metal casing of his laptop for a moment before popping it open again to the video file of Kile's Minute Mart. Even though most judges on the Gulf Coast were hard on suspected narcotic traffickers and would have granted that subpoena, Reed went a different route to gain access to the security footage of Kile's business. Not wanting to alert Wanda Jones Kile to the investigation, Owen came up with a solution and wrote the script that acquired the security video that day:

"Excuse us, ma'am, but there's been an armed robbery at the souvenir shop a few miles up the highway," Reed had said.

Wanda Jones Kile looked up from the soft drink cooler at his and Owen's credentials. A tall, athletic-looking young man with similar hair color and complexion stood next to her and worked to open cases of canned soft drinks. He held a box cutter in his right hand and had a distrustful look on his face. "What? Fred's place?" he asked.

Mrs. Kile reached for her cell phone on the counter. "I gotta call Fred. Hope he's okay. And his wife? She's in a wheelchair."

"No need. Mr. Fred's fine … and so is … Mrs. Fred. Neither were hurt," Owen interrupted. "What you can do is help us catch the guy."

Much taller than both Reed and Owen suspected, Mrs. Kile seemed to study both men and frowned. "All right, but what is it that you want me to do? Go chase the guy down?"

"A witness spotted the suspect drive away and followed him to your store," Owen said. "Saw the guy run inside."

"This place has been pretty busy lately. Lots of traffic through here," the young man with her said. Reed now knew him as Jessica Kile's husband, Brandon.

"That's just it," Reed improvised. "We hoped to get a look at your security cameras, get a sharper image of the suspect, something the witness can identify. We can search the database with facial recognition."

"We gotta catch this guy, before he robs somebody else," Owen said.

"I don't know," Mrs. Kile said. "I like Fred and his wife and all that. But I have to respect my customers' privacy."

A woman with two children entered the store. "I want some pizza," the older of the two said.

"I want some Cheetos," the other whined.

"Quiet, both of you," the mother snapped. "I'm here for a six pack, and that's all."

"Just let us checkout your security camera footage, and we'll be out of here," Reed said.

"I don't need to help you," Mrs. Kile said. "You guys, take a hike."

Reed remembered his glance at Owen. *Now, what. Any ideas?*

284

Owen followed with, "The judge frowns on thugs who hurt local businesses down here, especially nice folks trying to make a living. She'll give us a subpoena for that video—in a heartbeat, no questions asked."

Kile seem to consider the comment. "I ain't got nothing to hide," she said. She gazed past Reed and Owen to the family of three in the corner and the argument over who was getting what. The mother was losing the battle.

"The monitor is in the back. Through the door to the right of the ladies' restroom. Be quick about it. You're just gonna look at today's stuff, right?" Kile had asked.

"Yes, ma'am," Owen answered. Reed nodded a soft salute and followed. Owen was already nearly past the door to the ladies' restroom and only a few feet from the storeroom. In seconds Owen stood in front of the video equipment and popped a flash drive into a USB port.

"Hey, man. Didn't know you were so tech-savvy," Reed said. "This stuff may not hold up in court, but some research won't hurt."

Owen tapped several keys on a dusty keyboard. "Tell the chief to give me a raise … and that better parking place."

A tiny light on the end of the flash drive blinked in a stutter. "There, got it. At least eight weeks back. That should do it."

"You guys finished?" Kile stood in the doorway to the cramped space. Her light green flipflops were a sharp contrast to the dark stains on the cracked concrete floor. Reed stood between her and Owen to block her view of the flash drive. Owen jerked it from the console and slid it into a pocket of his uniform.

"We got what we need. The perp that ripped off your friend Fred's place is toast," Reed said. "You guys and your businesses along the Coast are safe."

Mrs. Kile followed them to the door, then joined Brandon Kile behind the sales counter.

"Did you hear what that woman mumbled to the young guy sitting behind the counter with her?" Owen said as they got into Reed's vehicle.

"Yeah," Reed answered. "She called him Brandon. Told Brandon to pick his battles, that we only wanted today's video."

Owen buckled his seat belt and said, "That guy, Brandon, probably spends lots of time helping his mom with the business. I recognized him from Garcia's table, that first night of blackjack."

Reed smiled and tapped a few more keys on his laptop. Officer Owen Smith was really a big help to him.

An image of the current driver's license assigned to Brandon Kile filled the screen of the computer. He studied the guy's face, the blond hair cropped tight at the sides, the cocky military smile, the Coast Guard uniform—except for the frowning, distrustful demeanor the day he and Owen pirated the convenience store video, a certain match to the white male at the convenience store with Wanda Jones Kile and at the casino with Garcia.

Reed flipped screens again, enlarging a still shot from the security footage of the much younger woman in the store, whom he now knew as Jessica Kile. "The daughter-in-law."

He dragged the image to the top right-hand corner of the screen and brought up another file: more grainy, black and white video, this time of Coleman Foshee at the same location—head lowered and face turned away from the camera. Foshee also appeared briefly in a few frames of other video, altered as though the camera had been switched on and off to delete certain scenes. Video of other customers seemed to skip frames too. "I guess the director forgot to cut the camera this time," Reed chuckled.

As the video played, Foshee looked up quickly and tilted his head to the rear as though hearing a sound behind him. The next person in line would soon come into view.

For Foshee's transaction, Kile's hand motions were slick. The camera documented an exchange of cash, but the product purchased was hidden under her hand—positioned palm down as it slid across the surface of the checkout counter, fingers cupped. Foshee's hand covered hers, and he pocketed the contents. He then placed a bottled soft drink on the counter and a bag of chips.

Without any effort to conceal this second transaction, Kile placed the two items in a bag and accepted a cash payment.

Foshee exited the front of the store, and Momma Kile helped the next customer, a man who appeared to be in his late thirties or early forties and who stood back several feet from Foshee in line. He seemed to smile in recognition of the owner and placed a six pack of beer and a pack of gum next to the register. When Kile reached under the counter seemingly to repeat the same service as done for Foshee, he smiled and nodded yes. He paid in cash and stepped to the door—then said something briefly to her before exiting the building.

Reed dialed Coleman Foshee's number on his cell, and Foshee answered on the first ring. "Colonel Foshee, I need you to come by the precinct. Got something to show you."

From his office window Reed could see the approaching traffic. Coleman Foshee arrived in less than an hour and without his driver. Reed waited for him at the entrance to the police station, bypassed the receptionist, and escorted Coleman to the same seat in front of his desk. Beads of sweat lined Coleman's forehead and unlike the previous meeting in Reed's office his tie hung loose at the collar.

Reed swiveled the laptop screen to face Coleman and stood over him while the video from Kile's Minute Mart played. "Why so secretive with that first purchase, Colonel?" Reed asked, after he hit REVERSE and froze the frame. "You weren't so shy with the soda and the chips."

"What is it that you want from me, Detective Spearman?"

"I want you to wear a wire and repeat this performance," Reed answered.

"You're kidding me. Do you guy's still do that? Besides, Momma Kile knows my sister passed away, and I don't use."

"You're an attorney, Coleman. You know how to put on a good show, and I expect you're a pretty good liar too."

287

Coleman Foshee pushed the laptop away. "I don't want any part in this. Anything you've got on me is circumstantial."

Reed enlarged an image of Momma Kile. "I'm going to bust this woman, one way or another, with or without your help. Of course, if you help me, my job could be a little easier, more straightforward, and I would appreciate that. So will the judge."

Coleman pulled at his collar and wiped his forehead with a handkerchief from a back pocket of his trousers.

Reed continued, "And I suspect you'd appreciate avoiding court martial and keeping your pension—and that fancy car and driver." Reed glanced out the window into the parking area. "By the way, where is your sidekick?"

"When you called, I told him to take the rest of the day off."

"You know, I might need to talk to your chauffeur. I might not even need your help."

Coleman fumbled some more with his tie. Sweat stained the armpits of his tailored, light blue dress shirt. A jacket was nowhere in sight. "All right, I'll do it. I'll think of some reason to go back to the convenience store for more than just gas and junk food."

"You're a smart guy, and you'll figure it out. But we'll still rehearse," Reed said. "And you'll need to wear a jacket."

Coleman stood and turned for the door.

"Remember, man, you owe it to your sister."

"What?" Coleman turned back toward Reed. "What are you talking about?"

"You supplied her habit, her disease. Maybe you can help shut these scumbags down and save some lives."

Coleman's eyes watered a bit. He almost dabbed the corner of an eye with a knuckled finger but seemed to think better of it and used the same handkerchief. "I never understood why she was that way, an addict. I thought I was helping her keep her life together until she decided to get help. I told her that I'd do it for her just that one last time."

Reed hit PLAY again, and Coleman was shown pushing

through the glass door to the outside of the convenience store. "Oh, but there's one more thing." Reed skipped ahead a few frames to the male customer who approached the checkout counter a few seconds after Coleman left the store. He carried a six-pack of beer and wore a baggy T-shirt and shorts and either flip flops or sandals.

When he reached for the pack of gum, the man tilted his head up and back enough for the camera to capture his face under the bill of the baseball hat.

Reed then tapped PAUSE and enlarged the image, now even more grainy. He encircled the man's blurred face with the tip of his forefinger and realized he might have seen him pull away from Dr. Hazard's house on a stakeout. "Ever see this guy before?"

With reluctance, Coleman stepped back to Reed's desk and the laptop. "What now? Can't you lighten up for a second?" He wiped his eyes again and studied the image. "Impossible," he said. "Let me see the rest of him."

Reed complied and adjusted the size of the image on the screen.

"Now, the face again," Coleman said. He grabbed the sides of the laptop and pulled the screen to him. His hands shook.

"Steady man," Reed said. "That's city property. You trash that thing, and it comes out of my pay."

Coleman steadied his hands and gently lowered the laptop to Reed's desk. He took a deep breath. "How could I have missed him in the store that day, and that convenience store's nowhere near their house."

"Who's the guy?"

Bent over the laptop for a closer study, Coleman said, "That's my late sister's husband, and he looks stoned if you ask me."

Reed unfroze the video. Momma Kile slid her hand palm down across the counter, much in the same way as before with Coleman Foshee. Dr. Hazard's husband put something in the front pocket of his shorts with the gum, paid in cash from the wallet in his back pocket, and exited the store.

"Maybe your brother-in-law also supplied your late sister, and maybe he uses too," Reed said.

Coleman dropped back into the chair behind him, nearly missing the seat. The chair slid an inch or two across the floor at impact. "I know my sister had a problem, and I made a big mistake. But my brother-in-law?"

"Your nephew and niece might lose another parent—maybe not for good, if you help me put this all together," Reed said.

Coleman Foshee gave a quick, firm nod. "Let me know exactly what I need to do."

# Chapter 33

The remainder of the afterschool business milled out of Momma Kile's store. The last kid, somewhere around thirteen or fourteen, hesitated a few seconds too long at the register, long enough for her to count the pimples on his face. She remembered him from a few weeks before when he seemed to tag along with a couple of college-aged boys, or at least post-high school.

*Maybe one of those guys was an older brother to this pimply one.* She knew the older ones were at least twenty-one, because she carded them, and their I.D.s passed for legit. Momma Kile carded anyone under the age of thirty who purchased beer and much to the surprise of her under-the-counter clients asked the same of them.

"Run on along, now," she said to the acne-faced boy when he glanced down and nodded slightly forward to the inside area of the counter. "You head on home to your own momma and get your homework done. Come back and see me when you're sure you got your head on straight."

Momma Kile secured the stool with her right hand and scooted back onto the tall prop behind the register. She glanced at the security monitor and then up at the small TV mounted above her, to the right of the cigarette rack. She recalled the day when the two policemen investigating the robbery up the highway showed up in her store.

"I need to get Brandon to get his technician friend to add a camera in that storage room," she said. "I wonder if those cops ever caught those asses who ripped off Fred. I ain't heard nothing else about that."

Momma Kile unmuted the television with the remote and flipped channels to watch *Jeopardy*. The local TV station went to commercial. An image of Biloxi Memorial Hospital filled the screen, and she picked up the remote to choose another channel. "Hospitals give me the creeps. I ain't never going into that place." She studied the series of faded color snapshots taped to a metal bar that framed the passthrough over the checkout counter. Her late husband, Steve, and son Brandon posed with wide smiles next to their deep-sea catch. She rubbed her finger over Steve's image.

"I've been hard on that fool since he died, but the sonnavabitch did leave me in pretty good shape with this place." She ran her fingernail across his face. "I sure could use his advice on what to do now. Maybe I need a séance."

Before she could press the CHANNEL UP button, the image of an attractive, male doctor filled the screen. He wore the typical monogrammed, white doctor jacket. "That's the fine-ass doctor Jessica works for," she said, "the fella who showed up outside the store—like he was tracking her down. Brandon might need to up his game."

She increased the television volume as a voiceover announced that Scott Mack, M.D., was now caring for the patients of the late Dr. Paul Caston.

"Dr. Mack ... pretty hot. Sure could give Brandon a run for his money," Momma Kile said as she stretched her neck for a better look. The Mack Orthopedic Specialists phone number and address scrolled across the lower half of the screen.

"Jessica said that money's been tight over there." Momma Kile grabbed a pen, jotted down the information, and entered the address into the GPS of her iPhone. Short driving directions populated the screen. "That's not too far from Dr. Caston's old office." She held the phone against her chest. "I guess sexy Dr. Mack has got a back door, too, and might need a little encouragement to play the game."

The inside of the store remained empty of customers. Momma

never trusted the scope of her outside cameras, so she opened the front door to scan the fuel pump and front parking area for any possibilities. There were none—everything all quiet, even the highway seemed calm as the sun began to set. She flipped the sign hanging in the window CLOSED, lowered the blinds, and locked the front doors. In less than a half hour, she pulled her car in front of the orthopedic clinic where Jessica worked and parked across the street.

Despite the dim lighting, the curtainless windows and the opened blinds afforded Momma Kile a full view of the empty lobby that fronted the street. Nevertheless, her eyes were drawn to the compact, brightly lit office to the right side of the clinic lobby. The figure of a young woman walked back and forth carrying papers and files. "There's my Jessica, always busy. Even after quitting time."

She surveyed the area and spotted Jessica's vehicle parked parallel outside the building, then eased around the corner to the alley behind the strip mall. The alley was windowless. Only rear doors marked each business with the name designated at the top in uneven lettering. The monotony was broken by a large trash receptacle located just beyond the exit labeled MACK ORTHO-PEDIC SPECIALISTS.

Suddenly, a woman bounded out the door of a business on the other side of the alley, her purse swinging from her shoulder as she pointed a key fob at a small SUV in her path. The interior lights popped to life, and she jumped inside. In seconds the SUV sped beside Momma Kile to exit the alley, barely missing her.

"Must be the little twit's quitting time," Momma Kile grumbled. "That girl can't wait to get home. She ain't got the same drive as my Jessica." One vehicle remained in the alley, a dusty, faded Camry parked near the rear door to the orthopedic clinic. "*Humph!* Maybe business ain't so good if that cheap car belongs to the hot Dr. Mack. He must be working late too. Wonder how many scripts he wrote today."

She imagined the doctor's private desk inside, maybe located down a hall and clear of the hustle and bustle of a busy medical clinic. She envisioned a stack of prescription pads, maybe not situated on the surface of the desk but locked away in a drawer. Maybe the drawer was left unlocked.

Momma Kile eased her car into the alley.

An attractive male in his early to mid-thirties burst from the rear door of the Mack Clinic. He wore a wrinkled, white medical coat opened to the front over blue surgical scrubs. Momma Kile recognized Scott Mack, M.D., from the television commercial and from when he showed up outside her convenience store. She eased out of the alley to drive around the corner to the front of the building. Her headlights streaked across the front.

"Dr. Mack gets hotter and hotter the more I see him," she said and pulled into the space next to Jessica's car to wait. She extinguished the interior and exterior lights of her vehicle and tilted her head back against the seat rest, enough to avoid the street lighting that penetrated the windshield. "That TV commercial don't give that fellow justice, and he didn't even notice me—in too much of a hurry for his car."

She stared at Jessica inside the office, darting back and forth and checking a computer screen as she worked, an even bigger stack of files held against her chest. "What's that girl up to?"

Momma Kile stiffened against the back of her seat when a sports car jerked into a parking space a few feet over to the right. The dim light of a streetlamp a few yards away cast shadows on the automobile. Its bright red paint job radiated even at night. "Everybody sure is in a hurry around here," Momma said.

The engine of the red Jaguar roared to a stop, and the headlights extinguished before the door swung open and a man popped from the driver's seat onto the pavement. He headed, almost ran, for the front door of the orthopedic clinic. In the effort he tilted his head in Momma's direction, the streetlamp catching his facial features for a few seconds. He had light hair, cut short and gently receding at the temples. His jacket and slacks were tailored.

294

"I know that dude. He's bought from me at the store." Momma Kile remembered that he returned a few days later for more after word was out about Caston's death, but her inventory was already scarce by that time. "What's he doing over here at this time of night? Don't see no limp or broken arm."

The man grabbed the door handle and tried to jerk it open. Unsuccessful, he pounded his fists against the glass. Jessica dropped her stack of files on the counter at the sound and looked toward the front, startled. A few seconds later she appeared at the door, shaking her head without letting him enter. Momma thought she read, "We're closed," on her lips. "You've missed your appointment. Come back later."

The man lifted his middle finger at Jessica and kicked the metal base of the door. He stepped halfway back to his vehicle in exaggerated movements, then ran back toward the clinic, ramming his shoulder into the door. Jessica backed away from the thick glass panel, which withstood the blow. The man paced back and forth between the clinic and his car, arms raised high, his hands shaking. "My last hit was over eight hours ago. You know me; I'm a Caston patient. You've got my files, and I need some hydro," he yelled.

Momma Kile checked for the Glock 19 in her shoulder bag and swung open the driver's door. She stepped from her vehicle, her right hand inside the bag. The area was clear of traffic. There were no pedestrians. "Hey, you. Leave that chick inside alone. She ain't got the money to replace that glass door."

"Get lost, bitch." The man prepared for another run at the door, then stopped. He noticed the concrete planter positioned against the exterior brick wall and filled with miniature boxwoods and landscape stones. He struggled to pick up one of the larger rocks and prepared to hurl it at the door. His hands shook as he slowly raised his arms. "Girl, I know you got some stuff in there for me. Caston promised."

Momma Kile spotted Jessica jump back from the door and pull her cell phone from the front pocket of her dress.

"Step back from that door, buddy, and put that rock down—right where you found it," Momma said from only a few feet behind him. "The only thing worse than a bitchy, old lady is a bitchy, old lady with a gun."

The man jerked around still holding the stone and stared at the weapon. "What?" He tossed the rock back into the planter as the rage in his face began to fade and beads of sweat popped onto his brow. The man rubbed his lower back with his right hand. "Shit, my back hurts. What's this? Some kind of shakedown?"

Momma Kile stiffened her arm and her stance, the gun directed at the man's forehead. She darted her eyes to the left and right, and except for this little show, the area remained quiet. She wanted to cross her legs, worried that her weak bladder would leak. "You want some help, or can you go cold turkey?" she asked.

"Hey, I know you—from that crappy convenience store on the highway," the man growled, then yawned and wiped his runny nose on his sleeve. "It's my back, I mean my knee. I've got to get my meds."

Momma watched a repeat performance of the nose wipe. "Your back must be in terrible shape. You need a pill lady," she said with a smirk.

The man replied with another yawn and turned away to face the entrance to the clinic. He put his right hand to his lower back and mumbled, "Caston, that ass. He told me he kept tons of Percs. I believed him because I saw that safe in the corner of his office the first time I was in there."

"This ain't Caston's office. You know that," Momma barked and gestured to his vehicle with her gun. "I've got what you need. Get back in your car and follow me back to my store."

The man reached again for the rock, swirled around, and hurled it at her. The stone hit Momma in the right shoulder, knocking the Glock to the ground. He lurched forward and grabbed the gun to point it in her face. His hand trembled.

"We aren't going nowhere except inside this building. My guess is that you know the pretty little thing inside. Your daughter maybe?"

"Daughter-in-law." Momma rubbed her shoulder and stared at him. She now hoped for a cop car to drive by or diversion from any traffic for that matter. But then she would have to explain the situation and never liked to draw police attention.

"You get her to unlock this door." The man steadied his hand. "If this new doc, the one who took over Caston's practice is any good, then my guess is that he's got a safe somewhere too—a nice stash of Percs and maybe some benzos."

# Chapter 34

Just as Officer Kendall Brisdell entered Reed's office, he pulled the file on Paul Caston and spread the printed photographs of the suicide scene across his desk.

"Kinda late to be drinking coffee, don't you think?" he said to her.

"How do you know this is coffee in my cup?" she answered and took a sip. "But for the record, it is coffee, and caffeine never keeps me up. I made some fresh in the breakroom if you're interested."

She walked around to his side of the desk. "Medical Examiner puts everything online, you know. Those prints are likely just a sample," Kendall said.

"Could be her best work?" Still seated, Reed held up an angle shot of the front seat of Caston's Mercedes and tilted it in the light. "The old timer down at the morgue said the new pathologist was on call and did Dr. Caston's autopsy."

Kendall stood beside Reed and said, "Let's take a look." He slid the laptop to her, and she accessed the complete digital file of the Caston case, marked suicide by the coroner. Included were other digital photographs of the interior of Caston's vehicle and his corpse. "Here ya go. More to the story perhaps."

Caston's body remained behind the wheel in the driver's seat, his head against the rear headrest. An image of the orthopedic surgeon's gun on the floor of his vehicle followed. A wide-angle view of the entire interior of the front of the vehicle was next.

"I agree with the coroner. Looks like suicide to me," she said.

Reed enlarged the last image. What appeared to be a leather

satchel lay in the floorboard of the passenger side of the Mercedes, open to paper files strewn on the carpeted floor mat. Reed leaned in tighter to the screen and highlighted the image of the clutter. A series of numbers in bold black font topped each file preceding a surname, comma, and initial in somewhat smaller print. Reed moved the cursor back and forth over the picture, systematically magnifying each section and tilting his head slightly to the right and left. None of the names on the scattered files seemed familiar.

"What a mess. Dr. Caston must have tossed his bag across the seat, and it slid to the floor. Must've left it unlatched," Kendall said.

"Check this out," Reed said and pointed to the rumpled exterior of one of the last files he studied, the name smeared. Reed could make out the letter G toward the end of the name.

"Interesting," Kendall said. "The name at the top of that file is illegible."

"This is the only one that's crumpled, and there's a faint black smudge across the front." Reed removed his right shoe and held it to the side of the screen, then tried the left instead. "No, it's the right."

"What? I don't get it."

Reed minimized the shot of the scattered files and leather satchel and accessed the forensics. He scrolled through the information and settled on the blowback analysis.

Kendall read through the findings. "Sure, there's no blowback where Dr. Caston sat. Maybe a little on his headrest," she said. She studied the analysis for the passenger side. "In an enclosed space like a personal vehicle, the blood and tissue blowback from a discharged firearm would cover most of the surrounding surface," she said.

"That's the problem. Forensics found no spatter from the center portion of the passenger seat," Reed said. Again, he held up his shoe. "What would block the blood spatter from Caston's discharged weapon."

"Someone else was in the car with him," Kendall said.

299

"Exactly. We need to checkout those files on the floorboard," Reed said. "See if they've been dusted for prints."

The neighbor's cat jumped into his headlights as Scott pulled into his driveway. "Crazy damn cat," he said and hit the brakes. The cat started licking his paws.

His cell rang and caller I.D. read, JESSICA. "Hey, boss," Scott said to her. "You're not still at the office, I hope."

"Yes, sir. I am."

# Chapter 35

Fresh beads of sweat popped onto the man's brow. He held the gun to Momma Kile's head and noted Jessica's name tag to refresh his memory.

"Remember, Jessica, make it short and sweet," he said while she punched Scott's number into her phone. "And no code words. I don't have any problem with shooting either of you."

The three remained in the lobby, out of view from the front of the street.

"Dr. Mack, this schedule ... our schedule ... for tomorrow," Jessica continued. Scott had never referred to her as boss. "There's bunches of new patients ... new to you, that is. I think you need to go over their charts tonight."

The man motioned with his other hand for her to speed up the conversation.

"I sorted through all the paper charts they brought over from the Caston office. Most of the patient treatment information is in those physical files. It's not electronic."

The neighbor's cat moved away, and Scott was able to pull completely up the driveway and into the carport. He left the engine running for the AC.

"Won't take me long to go through that stuff. Good ol' fashioned print ... sometimes a lot easier than trying to pull up what's in the computer."

Another roll of the gunman's fingers to move things along.

"Well ... that's the problem. See ... not much is typed. Dr. Caston

… wrote up all of his notes himself. Wrote in longhand—I think that's what they used to call it. And his handwriting stinks."

"That's odd. Now that I think about it, I did notice him on rounds one day using a pocket-sized digital recorder. I would think he did the same at the office and got some secretary to transcribe his notes."

The man pushed the barrel of the gun deeper into Momma Kile's scalp. She winced.

"Anyway, I'm too tired to come back down to the office, and you should head on home. It's late; go ahead and call it a …"

"Okay, great," Jessica interrupted. "See you here in a few minutes." She ended the call.

Scott stared into the face of his cell.

"Good job," the man said. His nose ran again but there was no effort to wipe it. He moved his gun to the pit of Momma Kile's back and pushed her forward a few inches toward the hall. "Show me your safe—where you keep Caston's stuff."

"I don't know what you mean," Jessica said.

"Come on. Come on. You recognize me from the other day." George Dandridge's right hand was wrapped in a light bandage so that he had full use of the hand and fingers. "I woke up in the emergency room. They pumped me with I.V.s and Methadone for a couple of days, took care of my hand, and let me go. I was supposed to follow-up with a private therapist, but I'm too busy for that crap."

"Jessica, just give the man what he wants," Momma Kile said.

"I bet we don't need Dr. Mack anyhow," Dandridge said. "That young joker wasn't any help the other day." He waved the gun around the room for a few seconds. "I bet they sent more than just patient charts over here from Caston's place. You're bound to have some of his leftover equipment and furnishings and that could include his safe—and what's in it."

He pushed Momma Kile away and pointed his pistol at Jessica. "And you, little girl, can open that safe for me."

Jessica stopped before turning her head in reflex in the direction of her desk. The locked bottom drawer was filled with envelopes of unused prescribed narcotics and sedatives. She had never considered using a safe, but that was a good idea. "The hospital didn't send over any furniture or surgical equipment. We wouldn't have had room for it anyway, and I don't know anything about a safe."

"No problem, then. We'll see what the new doctor has to say," Dandridge said. "But I'm not willing to wait very long. You two better produce." Both his hands shook. He jumped back behind Momma Kile and jammed the gun into the small of her back.

Momma Kile bristled but kept quiet.

"How long is it gonna take for that Dr. Mack to get here. Where's he live anyway? Perhaps he keeps drugs at his house. We can go there."

"No. Dr. Mack doesn't live far away. He'll be here in about ten minutes."

George Dandridge began to breathe more rapidly. His white shirt, nearly wet with perspiration, stuck to his skin, much the same way as his first visit to the clinic, the one with the appointment. His whole body trembled. Momma Kile tried to straighten her back and step forward a bit away from the barrel of the gun.

Dandridge referred again to Jessica's name badge. "Miss Kile, you're bound to have some cotton and downers around here or even Addys, and I bet you know where they are." He pointed the gun again at Jessica and waved it around for several seconds. His hand shook so violently, both women feared the weapon would discharge.

"Can't wait any longer for that doctor. You give me what you got right now, and I'm out of here. If it's not what I need, I can trade out." He returned the gun to Momma Kile's back and pressed even deeper.

"Jessica, go ahead and let him have what he wants before he shoots us, even if he doesn't mean to. You're bound to have pills around here that you haven't brought to me yet."

"What are you talking about?" Jessica glared at her in disbelief. "I just said we don't keep anything like that around here."

303

"You told me you keep 'em in your desk, locked-up, until you bring the stuff to me to sell," Momma said. She squirmed at the trembling and increased pressure of the gun barrel. "Can't you see? He's gonna shoot if he doesn't get what he wants."

From the hall a male figure lunged at Dandridge and knocked the weapon to the floor. The gun discharged in the commotion, striking the ficus in the corner and exploding the tree's ceramic container. Both women screamed.

Scott wrestled with George Dandridge in a rematch, but quickly subdued him with arms pinned behind his back. Several lobby chairs were toppled in the process, the wooden feet broken off a couple of them. A shard of the broken ceramic plant container lacerated Dandridge's forehead, and blood trickled down his face.

To Jessica, the brawl seemed like it lasted forever.

"Let me go. I'm gonna throw up," Dandridge said and lost consciousness.

Scott confirmed a carotid pulse and gave the others a nod.

"Jessica, will you please pull that trash can over here, call 911, and get this guy a bandage for his head," Scott said. He stared at Wanda Jones Kile. "But before the police get here, we need to have a little talk."

# Chapter 36

"Reed … Detective Spearman … will be here in just a sec," Detective Kendall Brisdell said and introduced herself. "He's finishing up with Mrs. Kile, the Mrs. Kile who owns the convenience store."

"Finishing up?" Scott said. The female detective wore her thick, dark hair off her face. Scott liked women with longer hair, worn more relaxed, but nevertheless found her simple style attractive—probably a necessity for a woman in law enforcement. About five eight, she was thin—not the malnourished-looking type of thin, but physically-fit thin—and wore the right amount of make-up for his tastes. Her pale red lipstick, modest layer of blush, and the lightly applied mascara and eyebrow pencil complemented her pretty facial features.

The detective's navy business suit and blouse accentuated her figure, especially at the top. The skirt ended an inch or so above the knee and could pass for expensive. *Doubt that, not on a police salary.*

"Yes, finishing up with her statement," Detective Brisdell said. "Reed asked me to meet you and take you to his office. I'm sure he'll fill you in."

*Reed, and not Detective Spearman? Maybe they all call each other by their first names,* Scott hoped.

Scott followed Detective Brisdell through a series of short halls to Spearman's office. "You been on the force long?" he asked. "The last time I was down here, I was picking up a driver's license. I had just moved here to go into practice."

"I recently relocated from Mobile as a detective," Kendall said.

305

She took the seat to the right of Reed's desk and crossed her legs. The hem of her skirt raised an inch or so. "It was a lateral transfer to Biloxi, and the chief of police here liked me." She removed a cell phone from her suit pocket and studied it. "Reed won't be long."

*I gotta ask her out,* Scott decided, *even if she and this guy Spearman are an item.*

Officer Owen Smith entered the office, re-introduced himself to Scott, and sat next to Kendall. She ignored him at first and stayed buried in her phone.

"We got a lead on that murder at the dentist's office," Owen said. "Immaculate Davis squealed on his cohort Jamal before we could pin the office manager's death on him."

"Probably should not discuss other cases around the good doctor here," Kendall said with a weak smile thrown at Scott. A few seconds passed, and Reed Spearman strolled into the room. Kendall's smile turned wide. Her face beamed, and the iPhone was no longer important.

"Dr. Mack, Dr. Scott Mack." Reed extended his hand. "It's good to see you again. Thanks for coming down."

Scott swallowed hard as they shook hands. Although Scott thought it impossible, Kendall Brisdell's smile grew even wider. Her eyes brightened. His chances with her sank by the minute.

"You did a sweet job taking down George Dandridge for us in your office," Reed said. He produced the mug shots from the night of Dandridge's arrest. "Since you didn't press charges the first time he dropped by your office, we didn't have any reason to hold him until now. So, this is his first photo shoot, and the guy's a real talker."

"Calling the police on your patients on a regular basis doesn't do much for building up a surgical practice," Scott said.

Everyone chuckled softly.

"We also want to talk to you about finding Dr. Caston shot in his car that morning," Reed said.

"Yes, Paul Caston committed suicide," Scott said. "I saw the body and his gun. It was beside him in the car."

306

Owen pulled another photo from a file. "That's what the coroner initially determined, but now we know that Dr. Caston was not alone in the vehicle. Forensics found no blowback in the passenger seat," he said.

"Blowback?" Scott asked to no immediate answer.

"For over two years, the department investigated Dr. Paul Caston for trafficking narcotics. We had informants and suspected that his nurse, Betty Thibideaux, collaborated with him."

"And we still got an eye on her," Owen interrupted. "She's running the Emergency Department over at Biloxi Memorial. But sooner or later she'll screw up, and we'll bring her down for pushing drugs."

Reed nodded in agreement. "We finally went to trial with what we thought was a strong case against Caston himself. The guy had already beat sanctions from the medical association for over-prescribing. They dinged him for the number of opioid prescriptions he wrote and for the number of pills on each script. Then Caston went to some kind of mandatory weekend educational seminar and got a free pass—got the green light to keep writing prescriptions for controlled substances."

Scott looked across to Kendall Brisdell. She uncrossed her legs and smiled, this time at him. Her lips seemed a deeper shade of red than before and from this distance her skin flawless.

"Until Caston's trial and acquittal," Scott said, "nobody at the hospital, at least in my circles, knew anything about his problems with the DEA or any other investigation."

Scott hesitated a few seconds and asked, "Am I here to be questioned or accused of anything? Do I need a lawyer? And that dental office manager who worked for Dr. Roland, that clinic was next door to mine."

"Relax, Doc," Reed said. "When I called you this morning, I asked you to come down and meet my team. That's all. This has nothing to do with what happened to the lady who ran the dental office. That was a terrible thing, and we got the guy. We just wanted to fill you in on this drug investigation and clear a few things up."

"What things?"

"Reed ... Detective Spearman and Officer Smith have identified the assailant at your office as a former surgical patient of Dr. Caston," Kendall said.

"I already knew that," Scott said.

"That's right. I saw the commercial. Biloxi Memorial Hospital transferred Dr. Caston's patient files to you." She smiled again. "You stood to get quite a few new patients as the result of Caston's death."

"Yeah, right," Scott shot back. "Those files. A definite asset so far. I guess you believe that Caston didn't commit suicide and suspect that I shot him to get his patients? Are you serious?"

Kendall straightened in her chair. The smile faded.

Reed scribbled on a legal pad and said, "Dandridge told us that his last appointment with Caston was the afternoon before he died. Maybe since you have the files, you can research that for us."

Kendall tilted her head in affirmation: *Sure you can.*

Reed continued, "Caston was cutting him off and turning over a new leaf, or something like that. Told Dandridge he wouldn't supply him anymore."

"This Dandridge fella tracked down Dr. Caston's home address," Owen said. "The night before you found Caston, he watched the doctor through a window—an honest-to-goodness Peeping Tom, that guy. Dandridge slept outside the doc's garage and surprised Caston when he backed out of the driveway the next morning on the way to the hospital."

"But George Dandridge wasn't in Caston's car when I found him. No one was. I didn't see anyone around but the two women in the cars in front of me, and one of them had small kids." Scott said.

"That's what we were explaining about the blowback," Owen added. "When a gun discharges into a victim at close range, one who is sitting inside a tight space such as a car, blood and tissue should be found on the seat next to the victim. Since it was clean, we reasoned that someone that morning sat to the right of Caston in the passenger seat."

Scott felt sweat trickle down his back. "Still clueless why you people are telling me all this," he said.

"Dr. Mack, you aren't under suspicion for the murder of Dr. Caston," Kendall responded.

Scott hoped for another smile but was disappointed.

"Dandridge's arrest in your office produced a set of fingerprints, and one matched an outlier we recovered from the weapon in Caston's vehicle. All the rest of the prints on the gun were the doctor's," Reed said. "Dandridge has admitted that the unregistered gun was his. He bought it off the internet from some dealer in New Mexico."

"So, it's Dandridge who shot Caston? Come on guys," Scott said. "What is it that you want from me?"

Reed ignored the question. "Dandridge wore gloves when he forced himself into Caston's car that morning. He said that at first Caston didn't put up a fight, seemed depressed. Almost like he had been crying."

"Caston beat the legal charges against him. He should have been elated," Scott said.

"Dandridge told the doctor to stop, pull back into the garage, and get him whatever meds were in the house," Owen said. "But Dr. Caston kept driving, just babbled on and on about how much guilt he felt over breaking his medical oath, like he was fed up with himself."

"I wish I had taken a different route to work that day," Scott said under his breath.

"Dandridge tried to convince Caston that he needed only one more fix, a few pills to tide him over until he established another supplier. When he mentioned the Kile woman and the convenience store as a new source, Caston only laughed at him," Reed said. "Caston told him that he supplied Kile."

Scott shifted uncomfortably in his chair. He expected somehow to come out short on this discussion. "Since this Dandridge wasn't getting what he wanted, he went ahead and shot Paul Caston?"

"Dandridge said he demanded that Dr. Caston give him the meds he needed, and the argument at the intersection got heated," Owen answered. "Dandridge claims that Caston grabbed his gun and shot himself. That explains the gunshot residue on Caston's hands and the validity of the bullet trajectory findings. And like we said, Dandridge claims he was wearing gloves and thought he had completely wiped down the weapon. The print we found on his gun was an old one."

"We recently recovered Dandridge's gloves exactly as described and tossed in shrubbery near the scene," Reed added. "No evidence of gunshot residue on the gloves, but they contained his DNA.

"Guys, I'm glad you're checking off the boxes, but I got to get back to my patients. My practice has started to pick up, and this is a waste of—"

"Your time?" Kendall said and reversed crossed her legs. A wry smile followed. "I think you'll want to keep your free time, so listen to what else Reed has to say."

# Chapter 37

"I've lost a free babysitter," Jessica said, "and I was already having trouble paying for daycare."

"At least your little boy won't be visiting both his mother and grandmother in jail," Scott said.

Jessica took a deep breath and lifted her fingers off the keyboard. When, "I'm sorry, you're fired," did not follow from Dr. Mack, she exhaled slowly and continued her work on the computer.

"Those detectives were all over your mother-in-law," Scott said. "They even suspected that she may have been the woman seen walking near the intersection where I found Caston, but decided she wasn't. We're lucky there was no mention of you."

"I can thank Momma Kile for that. So far she has left me out of this."

"And that Dandridge guy. No involvement with you. Right?"

"None, except for the first time he came to the clinic and left in an ambulance and the second time when you rescued me and Momma in the lobby and he left in a squad car," Jessica said with a weak laugh. She considered the desk drawer to her lower left, still empty after she flushed the contents shortly after the police left with George Dandridge in handcuffs. "I've never even bought a car from him, not even a used one."

Scott stared over her shoulder to the office computer screen and the clinic calendar for the next day. "Schedule is packed. Don't see a blank spot anywhere, and that's after the two cases I've got posted to do at Memorial."

"Yes sir, a busy day. And the hospital upgraded our software again. Now I can text appointment reminders to everyone on the list."

Scott pulled the spare chair in the reception area under him and sat next to Jessica. "I should have paid more attention to the day-to-day operations around here. Since the lights stayed on and you showed up for work every day, I didn't ask any questions about cash flow—and that was wrong. I guess I was in denial."

"I was the person doing wrong. I shouldn't have gone behind your back."

"Have you had any patients ask you about turning in their unused meds? That could be a problem."

"A lady called yesterday. You fixed her hip about six months ago. She told me she found another codeine prescription in her medicine cabinet and asked if I also wanted that bottle for another patient. I told her that I found out we couldn't do that, and I had destroyed the old prescription for her—never gave it to anybody."

"Did she buy that?"

"Seems so. I told her to flush the leftover pills or take them to her pharmacy for disposal," Jessica said, her voice a bit weak. "Gosh, Dr. Mack, I've told so many lies. I'm getting really good at it."

Scott laughed. "I might need your skills at the end of the year when I have to make our books make sense to the accountant."

Jessica's cell phone rang. "I'm sorry, Dr. Mack. It's my husband. I've told him no personal calls at work, but he's probably worried about his mom."

"No problem," Scott said. "You need to answer that. I'll be back in my office. Let me know when the last few patients check in for today."

Jessica smiled and watched Scott leave down the hall. She hesitated for a couple of more rings before answering. "What's going on?" she whispered into her cell. "Is BJ okay?"

"Dropped him off at daycare this morning like I was supposed to. You don't give me enough credit," Brandon Kile said.

"Why did you call, Brandon? I have to be careful around here."

312

"With Mom out of the picture, I need you to quit that damn doctor and come work for me. I need you at the convenience store. Spearman and the other police on Mom's case bought her story that she acted alone, and they don't have me on tape making any sales at the store."

Jessica lowered her voice further. "I told you. We shouldn't be discussing this on the phone."

"You're good at the small stuff, Jessica. You've proved it. You're ready to step up as a first-class drug mule."

Jessica Kile stood from the desk and peered around the corner—no Dr. Mack. His office door was cracked open, and she thought she could hear him on the phone. "I'm not going to do that for you anymore. I've carried out weed from the Coast Guard Station for you in the baby's changing bag for the last time."

"This ain't weed, Baby. We're getting more boats up from Mexico, good stuff … coke and pills. You know we need the money, what with BJ and all, so we'll do it for only a little while longer. Get the building paid off and then sell the convenience store."

"Brandon, I need to get back to work." She pulled the phone away from her ear, but then decided against hanging up.

"Come on, Jessica. Listen to me. We can't push product through Kile's Minute Mart no more, and the profit from straight retail in that spot is crap. New place down the highway is sucking us dry. Let's do this new thing. Move out of our crappy apartment and maybe buy a nice house with more space and a big yard. You can plant more flowers."

Jessica peeked down the hall again. "I … I … just don't know about all this."

"And you said the other night in bed that you wanted to have another baby. There's no way that can happen on my Coast Guard salary, and you don't make much more than minimum wage working for that doctor. Plus, Momma can't help us locked up, and she's got legal bills. I owe it to her, need to help her out financially."

Jessica's eyes drifted up to the sound of soft footsteps in the hall. "Transport coke and pills from Mexico?" she said a little too loudly. Detective Reed Spearman and Dr. Mack surprised her at the opening into the front office.

"Brandon, I gotta go." Jessica fought the sudden tremor in her voice and felt the color drain from her face. "I'm busy. There's a patient here." She ended the call and dropped her cell into her purse.

"Mrs. Kile, was that your husband?" Reed asked.

Jessica's complexion was ashen.

"We've had Brandon Kile under surveillance for months, suspected of running a Coast Guard smuggling ring. Then we connected him to your mother-in-law at the convenience store."

Scott offered Jessica a weak smile of reassurance. "Talk to Detective Spearman, Jessica. After the news reports, a couple of our patients contacted the police and told them about turning their pills into you," Scott said. "You need ... *we* need ... to help the detective put an end to this drug trafficking—at least put a big dent in it."

Jessica remained silent. She clutched her purse against her chest.

"Dr. Mack is cooperating with us, so there's no need for him to worry about losing his medical license or hospital privileges ... or even worse," Reed said. "I think you may want to help us out too. I heard you mention a child over the phone. You wouldn't want to lose him. Would you?"

"Are you gonna call child services on me? You're trying to force me to—"

"Jessica, the detective is not threatening you," Scott interrupted. "You can deny everything, but I've had to tell them the truth. I heard what you said that second time with Dandridge about the pills for resale in your desk drawer. I want the best for you, but I think you've created a potentially dangerous situation for yourself—and for me."

Jessica swallowed hard. She wanted to run, but Dr. Mack and the detective stood in the exit. "I didn't want this to happen. Seems like I'm always trying to protect someone," she said to stifled tears.

"I was trying to protect you, Dr. Mack, from going under and having to close this practice."

"I understand that, Jessica, and love you like a sister for it. You helped me stay afloat … maybe helped me the wrong way, but—"

All three laughed nervously.

"But we've done some good work for our patients, and overall your intentions were good. I've explained all of that to Detective Spearman."

"And I wanted to save Brandon, to keep him out of trouble, more for the sake of our baby than even him or me." She reconsidered the cell call of just a few minutes ago. "But I know now it's too late. He's in too deep."

"You're correct, Mrs. Kile, and I don't think you know the full extent of your husband's involvement in the drug trade. I can give you immunity if you'll help the BPD shut this Mexican drug ring down."

"I don't understand. What is it you want me to do? I thought women couldn't testify against their husbands."

"Sure, there's spousal or marital privilege at trial," Reed said. "But you can still work with us to further expose your husband's dealings in the narcotic trade, and maybe we can turn him too. If he's smart, he'll come around to our side."

"I don't know. Brandon can be hot-headed. Sometimes he scares me," Jessica said. She grabbed a tissue from the box on her desk and blotted her eyes.

"The detective and his guys will keep you safe," Scott said. "Spearman, here, has promised."

"For now, it's business as usual," Reed said with a nod. "Soon we'll put in more wire taps and expand our undercover surveillance of Brandon's associates in the Coast Guard. You can get them on tape for us."

"I guess I can do that," Jessica said. She relaxed a bit in her chair. "A few of 'em come over and play cards with Brandon on the weekends. Our dumpy place is so tiny, and the walls are so thin. Yeah,

I've heard stuff about smuggling illegals and finding weed and bags of dope in boats. But they just usually laugh it off."

"Like Dr. Mack just said, we will fully protect you and your son … as well as Dr. Mack," Reed added. "I don't want you to go to jail, Mrs. Kile … Jessica."

"I don't want either of us to go to jail," Scott added. He and Jessica laughed again, as though in relief.

Jessica grabbed another tissue from her desk and thought about Billy Jack playing with the other children at the expensive daycare. She thought about her modest but neat apartment and all her hard work to put it together—but the place was still a dump. Jessica thought about her deceased parents and how they had done their best to raise her right.

She shook her head in worry about what was in store for Brandon. Or was it in disgust? Maybe she could help him out of this mess somehow.

"Okay, I'll do it," Jessica said and popped her purse into the desk drawer. "Where do we start?"

# Acknowledgements

M any thanks to Editor Janet Taylor-Perry for her advice and attention to detail as well as to my editing and advance reader team for their diligence and invaluable input: Karen Cole, Lottie Boggan, Betty Stevens Bailey, and Johnna Bickerstaff. Special thanks to the real Jessica Kile, one of the brightest, sweetest, and hardest working persons I know and to Jill and Bruner Bosio for their help in making my description of Mississippi Gulf Coast locales work.

Additional appreciation goes to Billy Brown, Vicksburg Police Department, Lieutenant. (Ret.), for sharing his expertise in criminal procedure as I researched for this story and to Chris Kimmel whose knowledge goes far beyond annihilating mosquitoes.

As always, I owe much to my family, friends, and other readers for their support and to my co-workers at Jackson Healthcare for Women.

# Resources

*Clarion Ledger* Tuesday, August 6, 2019 Page 1 and 4A "How deadly pain pills flowed into Mississippi" by Luke Ramseth and Glacomo Bologna

*nytimes.com,* October 7, 2017, "As Overdose Deaths Pile Up, a Medical Examiner Quits the Morgue" by Katharine Q. Steele

# About the Author

Darden North's mystery and thriller novels have been awarded nationally, most notably an IPPY in Southern Fiction for *Points of Origin*. His other novels include *The 5 Manners of Death*, *Wiggle Room*, *Fresh Frozen*, and *House Call*. The screen adaptation of *Points of Origin* is in post-production.

North has been featured at writing conferences including the 29th Natchez Literary and Cinema Celebration, Killer Nashville, Murder on the Menu, SIBA Thriller Panel, and Murder in the Magic City. He served as Chairman of the Board of the Mississippi Public Broadcasting Foundation and is a member of the Editorial Board of the *Journal of the Mississippi State Medical Association*.

A native of the Mississippi Delta, North is a gynecologist and lives in Jackson with his wife Sally.

Learn more at:

www.dardennorth.com

CPSIA information can be obtained
at www.ICGtesting.com
Printed in the USA
LVHW101003230623
750606LV00038B/935/J

9 781957 344492